THE

HOLLOW

KEY

ESSENCE OF OHR
Book 4

PARRIS SHEETS

THE HOLLOW KEY
Essence of Ohr – Book 4
Copyright © 2023 by Parris Sheets

FIRST EDITION SOFTCOVER
ISBN: 1622536592
ISBN-13: 978-1-62253-659-7

Editor: Darren Todd
Cover Artist: Richard Tran
Interior Designer: Lane Diamond

EVOLVED PUBLISHING™

www.EvolvedPub.com
Evolved Publishing LLC
Butler, Wisconsin, USA

Printed in Book Antiqua font.

BOOKS BY PARRIS SHEETS

ESSENCE OF OHR
Book 1: *Warden's Reign*
Book 2: *Children of the Volcano*
Book 3: *Beyond the Flame*
Book 4: *The Hollow Key*

DEDICATION

*To the readers. Without you, this story would
never have gone further than the page.*

THE
HOLLOW
KEY

ESSENCE OF OHR
Book 4

PARRIS SHEETS

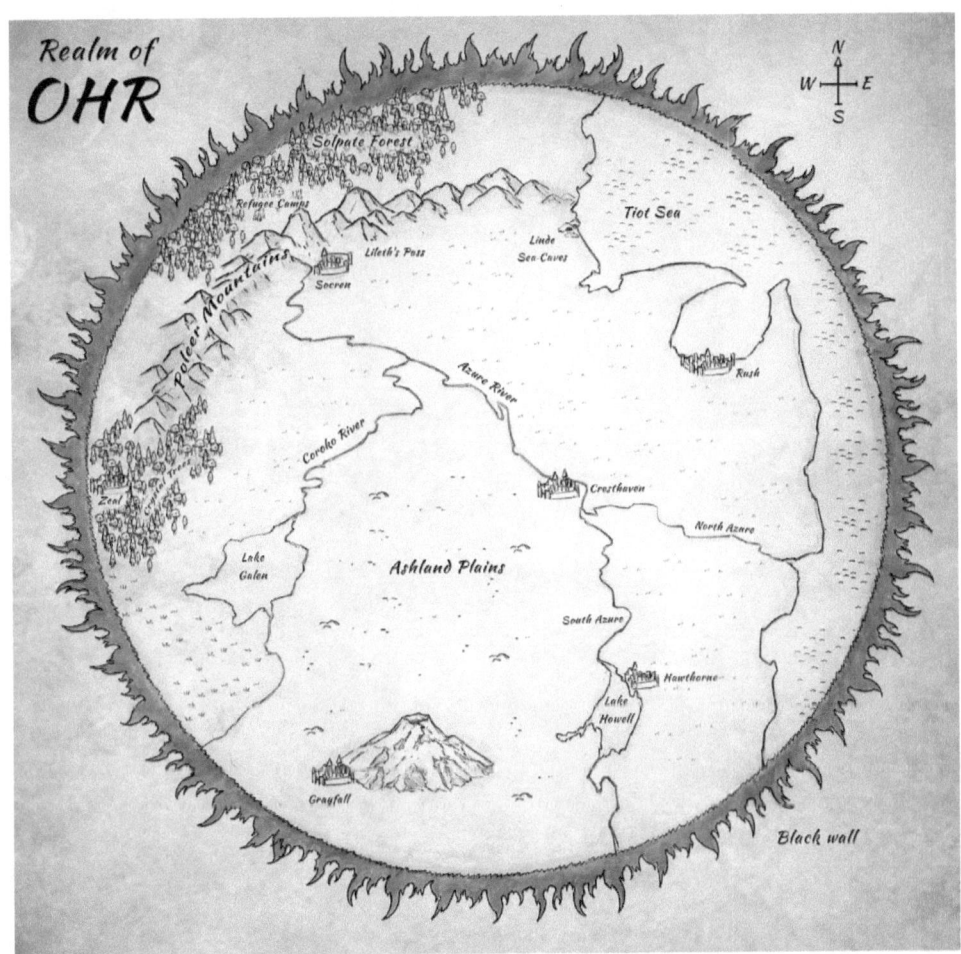

Realm of
OHR

Solpate Forest

Refugee Camps

Polear Mountains

Lileth's Pass

Socren

Coroko River

Azure River

Linde
Sea-Caves

Tiot Sea

Rush

Cresthaven

North Azure

Zeal

Lake
Galen

Ashland Plains

South Azure

Hawthorne

Lake
Howell

Grayfall

Black wall

CHAPTER 1

Fresh, salty air. That was what Leo sought as he climbed the cliff overlooking the vast waters of the Tiot Sea. Nothing like the monotonous crash of waves to soothe the mind and make him forget the worries that lay vividly over his shoulder.

The liberation leader refused to look back. His boots slid on the eroded and crumbling rock face. Leo caught himself on a boulder before he could scrape a knee. The small hike may seem ridiculous to anyone else, but Leo needed it.

The last month had been filled with endless worry prepping for the war to come—inevitable and creeping. He always knew the day would come when Ohr's people must fight for survival. Only, he thought he'd have more time to prepare. To recruit. To pull resources. If he could only free himself of the burden of leadership for a fraction of time, he might be able to figure out their next move.

Leo planted his boots on the plateau marking the peak. The briny taste of the sea set on his tongue as he took a deep breath, and for a moment he found silence in his head. A calm. But not peace. Never peace. Not at a time like this. Not when the clanking of steel and the scent of burning coal echoed at his back.

What little serenity he'd found was cut short when his name carried on the wind from below. Instead of turning, Leo waited there, soaking up the view of the swelling waves. Rise and fall. Rise and fall. Like a breathing chest.

It was hard to believe that at one point the people of Ohr sailed across the sea to lands beyond. Few ships traversed these waters now, for nothing lay on the far side of the ocean any longer. It had been swallowed whole by black flame. Leo had books depicting the lands and cities that once existed there, but they were old texts written by his forefathers. Those same flames had uprooted his city. When he had received a tip that the black fire would move on Socren, he'd had no choice but to relocate. He'd stood there, alongside his people, and watched his city burn.

"Oi, boss!" Two voices yelled in tandem. The accent made it all too clear who scurried up the cliff.

Leo turned.

Two hefty teens barged up the rocks. With such thick necks of muscle paired with thin faces, it was hard to detect the twins' jawlines, especially from this distance. Criz and Boogy had far exceeded Leo's expectations this past month. Usually, Leo needed those of cunning and strategy in his inner circle, but moving an entire city of people miles east to the coast had highlighted the brothers' unhindered positivity. They truly acted as beacons of hope for the people of Socren, who now crammed into quickly propped up tents at the cliff's base. Even the boys' physical prowess proved invaluable in setting up the massive temporary city.

A glint of metal reflected in Criz's hand. Gold. The boy held it out to Leo. "Just got in a couple minutes ago."

Before Leo could reach for the spherical trinket, Boogy punched his fists into his sides and huffed. "We said *you* could carry it up, and *I* could hand it over. We agreed on that."

"Sorry. Forgot." Criz shrugged. His apologetic eyes moved from the bauble in his hand to his brother, and then to Leo. When Leo moved to take it, Criz swung his palm to his brother instead, who gave a broad grin.

Boogy plucked the golden sphere from Criz then presented the thing to Leo while repeating, "Just got in a couple minutes ago."

"Yes, thank you both." Leo had learned a higher patience while traveling with these two. Though they meant well, things never ran to protocol when the twins were involved.

Leo took the bauble. He'd developed the spell years ago, trapping his voice within a hollow object, and shared the technology with his allies across Ohr. A symbol graced the top, signifying the sender. Leo's body temperature dropped. His thumb hovered over the engraving, knowing the message within could win or lose the war before it ever began.

"Wait!"

All three looked down the slope at the newcomer.

Thomas strode up to them, an easy agility in his steps. That all-too-familiar dark glare set on the twins, and he pointed an accusing finger their way. "They took it right out of my hands."

"Bet you're glad we did. We got here a whole minute before you." Criz smiled as if impressed by his own speed.

Boogy nodded in agreement with his brother. "Leo needs things as fast as possible."

"You blindsided me." Thomas straightened and wiped his long black hair from his face. "If it were a fair race, I'd—"

"Settle down. It is all right." Leo waved a hand, and the boys quieted. His group of mighty liberation members had dwindled down to these three. Leo had thought Thomas would step in as the next natural leader, but he sorely underestimated the chaos that was Criz and Boogy, who did what they wanted when they wanted. Only Leo's direct order could sway them.

"Who is it from? Is it the Yamani?" Thomas asked. The small sliver of face visible through the split in his curtain-like hair showed a red flush. Whether from the sprint up the cliff or the blow to his ego, Leo could only guess.

Leo wished for the message to be from the stone people of the south, but the crest signified the sphere traveled from a further destination. He lifted his thumb one last time to note the sigil, which depicted a hammer clutched in a fist. "Zeal."

"Zeal? Ain't that where—" An elbow to Criz's gut made him choke on the last part of his sentence.

"You know he doesn't like us speaking about it," Boogy scolded. "Makes him sad."

"You may speak of whatever you wish. News is only news." Leo pressed his finger on the sphere before any fleck of emotion could push its way to the forefront. The last message they'd received from the far-off city two weeks ago bore grave news: a war won at the last moment through a great sacrifice. When the thought threatened to creep up from where Leo had buried it, he focused his attention on the bauble. A crack appeared around the ball, and it popped open like a hatching egg.

A voice permeated the air with a tone of command. "From Tena of Zeal to Leonardo of Socren." Something shook in the sound of her words. Leo braced himself for the message to come.

"Zeal's first brigade marches toward you. They should arrive within the week. They bring new weapons that need special training to use. I have appointed generals to instruct your people to handle them. Whoever you see fit."

A pause of still air, then a deep breath came from the sphere as Tena continued with a grim heaviness.

"We have no word of Kole."

There it was. Those words echoed on the top of the cliff. The boys' shoulders all sagged forward, frowns growing deep. Leo found himself doing the same. This was what he had dreaded.

"My colleague continues to open the portal every sunset, but hope can only hold out for so long. War is coming. We cannot wait forever. Our preparations will shortly come to an end. When the month closes out, I have instructed all to leave their posts and follow the first brigade to your location. We have power left. Just not all that we had planned on." One more stillness before Tena closed out the message with, "May the lost find their way."

Then the golden ball snapped closed, and Zeal's sigil vanished from the metal plating.

"May the lost find their way," the boys repeated.

Leo closed his hand around the sphere, squeezing it firmly. Two weeks Kole had been missing. The boy who could speak with the gods — the only one who could ensure the world's survival — had crossed the black flames. Was he lost? Or had something terrible befallen him?

"May they find their way, indeed," Leo echoed the sentiment. "For all our sakes."

CHAPTER 2

Kole squeezed his legs and hugged tighter around the stag as the leap sent them flying past licking black flames. The moment the animal's hooves touched down on land again, Kole felt a shudder pulse through his mount's body. Legs buckled, and the stag pitched forward into a roll. The momentum flung Kole off and sent him soaring.

The ground came up too fast for Kole to catch himself, and he landed hard on his side. Pain shot through his shoulder and hip. The world turned two more times before his body came to a stop. He lay there for a moment, testing his fingers and arms then toes and legs, assessing his injuries. Thankfully, he found his body to be in working order. *No worse than normal.*

A deep-seated ache throbbed on his right hip and shoulder, straight to the bone. They moved for him but with great protest. No doubt his whole side would bloom black and blue in a few hours. After a groggy minute, he pushed to his elbows and scanned the area for his companion. The magnificent glowing stag lay a few yards off, still on the ground. Red stained the radiant fur.

"Caradin!" Kole scrambled to his feet, then immediately regretted the quick movement. His head spun, vision black and dotted. Still, he pushed on in his daze and collapsed next to the stag. Back on hands and knees, his head settled, and he probed the beast.

"Caradin? You okay? Talk to me!" Kole shook the animal until a voice came soft in his mind.

"Safe, master Kole. Wounds closing." Caradin lifted his massive set of antlers and let one round eye take in Kole.

The stag was right. Kole passed his fingers over the bloody fur and found untouched skin beneath. The gashes from the fall had vanished as if they'd had months to heal. Not even a trace of a scar stayed behind. Bloodstains stood as the only clue the injuries had ever existed. Kole should've known better than to worry. The stag was more than mortal, after all. He was a god: one of the Seven Souls who'd created the world. When Kole's brain finally reminded him of that, he let out a sigh, half annoyed, half relieved. *Should've been more worried about myself.*

"Master well?" Caradin touched his warm nose to Kole's forearm as if sniffing for blood. The moisture from the animal's nose smeared his skin.

Kole wiped it away on his pants then stood. "Good enough."

They'd made it. They survived the journey through the Black Wall. Not just survived, they'd done it safely. That alone concerned Kole. He looked back to the spot where they'd entered minutes before. The beam of radiant white light that had cut a path through the fire had vanished. Along with it, the portal back. In its place stood a solid wall of dark flames. *Trapped here.* The black hue held a purplish tint Kole had never noticed before. Then again, he'd never been this close to the Black Wall before. Well, only once before. But his eyes had been burned shut by the blaze.

The mere memory of that day jolted his heart into a trilling pace. Kole found himself unconsciously backing away.

Those licking flames.

One touch of the black fire turned people, animals, tress, even cities to ash.

He had been touched by that fire. That night seared so clearly in his mind. Angry red burns scarred his entire body as a permanent reminder. If not for a god's interference that night—a god like Caradin—he would've died on the spot.

The distant memory sparked an anger in Kole.

"Master?" A worried sensation came from the stag. *"The land...."*

Kole tore his eyes from the wall and turned to take in the landscape that no living creature had seen in centuries. A deep gasp choked Kole. Caradin's worry was a massive understatement.

The earth spread flat and bare from his feet for maybe a mile. Charcoal in color. Scorched. Then the ground broke off in chunks, some pieces no larger than his body, and others that dwarfed the massive towers back in Zeal. Those rogue pieces floated in the air, rotating. Smaller fragments orbited around their larger counterparts like tiny solar systems. Yet how could something so heavy as rock fly?

Even odder, the landscape held an unnatural brightness that seemed to come from every direction. It had been night on the other side of the Black Wall, yet no sun or moon hung in the air above. Maybe behind a cloud. But no. A clear sky spread overhead, embellished with too-bright stars. The shine made Kole squint and shield his face.

"What is this?" Kole whispered. The oddity made him forget all about the flames at his back.

"*Broken land.*" Caradin stepped next to Kole, who wrapped his hand around a looping antler, and they cautiously walked on together.

"The Black Wall did this?" Kole's brow furrowed as he thought back. "But the wall's border has fluctuated near Zeal for years. How did that land only get razed while this is... destroyed to the core?"

A few seconds passed. Kole felt a sense of unsureness roll off Caradin through their telepathic connection before the god finally said, "*Time. Time behind wall. Time without gods.*"

Despite the ill revelation, Kole was pleased at the Soul's words. His grasp on language had improved immensely since Kole found and released him a week and a half ago. The prolonged imprisonment had regressed the Soul's intelligence to that of the last form he took: a feral stag. They'd communicated through feelings and images projected into each other's minds. Now Kole could understand the god with little trouble. Strange to think that in such a short time, they'd grown so trusting.

Even with a god at his side, something in Kole's instincts warned him against going further into the broken land. His gut twisted at the thought of taking a single step forward. "If this is what happens to the land on this side of the wall, we should get this done as fast as possible. I don't want to know what it'll do to us if we linger."

Time. The word made him frantically search his wrist. The leather strap of his watch remained secure, but a crack ran through the glass face. It must've happened when he'd tumbled off Caradin. Dread weighed in his stomach as he buffed the dust from the watch face. To Kole's relief, the hands within still ticked on.

"We have two hours until the portal opens again." Kole peered at the fire dancing over his shoulder. "We should mark this place."

While Kole pulled out his map and scribbled away, adding the shapes of the odd floating rocks to indicate their current location, Caradin prodded the ground with his hooves. A moment later, as Kole finished his drawing, a snap made him glance up. Caradin's head hung low, with his crown of antlers skimming the earth. The strike of his hoof had cracked a long piece of his horn on his crest. One more solid stomp and the bit broke free.

"What are you doing?" Kole rushed over. Had the Soul gone mad?

Caradin snorted and took the long piece between his teeth then stuck one end into the hole he'd dug. Once Kole caught on to his intentions, he circled the stag's hindquarters and pushed the mixture of dirt and ash around the base until the antler stood on its own up to Kole's waist. Though detached from the god's head, the antler still glowed with that same heavenly aura. It stood as an easy beacon against the backdrop of the dark flames to find their way back should they lose their bearings.

"Good thinking. Just maybe let me know before you go tearing yourself up." Kole stroked the elk's cheek and before his eyes, the freshly splintered edge lengthened and grew back to its original state.

The stag's dark eye twinkled at him.

Kole snorted. "Show off."

"*Way to Vara?*" came the Soul's voice.

"The map doesn't help us too much out here." He held open the parchment and slid his fingers over the two lines he'd marked earlier that week, following them until they merged. "The cross-point is southwest of here. That's all we have to go on."

"*Talk to Vara again?*"

"No," Kole snapped. "We can't risk it."

Each time he had reached out to Vara, the connection had somehow triggered the Black Wall into motion. No way he'd do that again. Not when his friends and a whole city lay on the opposite side. One slip and the fire could kill them all.

"*Vara will not shove this time,*" said Caradin.

"How do you know?"

"*Black Wall no longer between you. No need.*"

The Soul sounded confident, yet Kole rolled the map and shoved it into place on his belt. "I won't do it. Not unless it's a last resort." Another look at his watch. Though he'd never learned how to read time, it went by nevertheless. The small hand had crossed another tick, cutting into their two hours. "Let's go. Vienna's still out there with Orla."

The elk knelt, and Kole lugged himself atop the great animal's back. Once Kole curled his fingers through the stag's fur for stability, the beast bounded off.

Kole's shoulder and hip screamed at the quick movement. After a moment, the bruising pain dulled into an ever-present throb. Something he'd just have to live with for now. The bouncing stride didn't help. No doubt Caradin would heal him if he asked, but every expense of energy drained the Soul's pool of power. Kole refused to waste that resource on himself. Not when his friends and all the people of Zeal were caught in a battle on the other side of the wall.

His friend Vienna had been struck. Kole could still recall her scream of pain in his ears as the crazed cult leader, Orla, shot her in the back. Vienna had saved him — thrown herself in front of the bullet. With the cult leader closing in on them, seeking to capture Kole and Caradin to use their divine blood to strengthen her power and control the Black Wall, Vienna had opened the portal through the Black Wall. The only means of escape. The only place where Orla couldn't follow.

But what had happened in these ten long minutes since he'd left Vienna? Orla had been coming straight for her.

She got away. Vienna wasn't any girl. No. Kole had known many girls his age, and they all seemed so ordinary in comparison. She was a member of the liberation, after all. Trained to fight. To survive.

Dark thoughts flickered at the back of Kole's head. Doubts. He gritted his teeth and banished them. *Vienna is strong. She's a survivor.* She had her brother, too. Felix would never let anything happen to her.

Kole clung to hope because it was the only thing keeping him from turning Caradin around and barreling back through the Black Wall. *They have their mission and I have mine. Just hang on. I'll be back soon.*

CHAPTER 3

The sun reflected off the polished marble floor and into Piper's eyes. She turned her head, cursing the absurd obsession the people of Zeal had with looking the part of a prosperous society. Freshly swept floors covered in jewel-toned rugs lay below her feet. Dusted tables topped with useless trinkets cluttered every surface. The council had even arranged for a vanity with a large, ornate mirror be brought in for her use.

Piper brushed a comb through her auburn hair, then pinned up the tresses around her face with a gem-encrusted clip. The entire process seemed as ridiculous as the room. Yet here she sat fiddling with her hair, dressed in a red gown the lead councilwoman, Tena, had provided. She rolled her shoulders and twisted against the tight garb. Granted, Tena had been spot-on when it came to sizing. The dress had fit nicely before Piper decided to wear her pants and tunic layered beneath it. She had opted for her worn leather boots instead of the shining, embroidered heels she'd been gifted. Thankfully, the skirt of her gown hit low on her ankle, leaving only the roughed-up toe of her boot visible. She doubted anyone would notice on a day like this. The attention would be on the dead.

A knock told her it was time to leave.

The door swung open to the hall. Piper nodded her thanks to the doorman, then hurried down the corridor. Thick fogs of cologne clouded the halls, seeping from the cracks of the rooms beyond. The same scent stuffed up her own room. No matter how much they tried to mask it, the underlying notes of scorched stone and dust lingered beneath.

A breeze whipped Piper's hair as she entered the main room. Finally, the scene matched the smell. Open gapes stood where stained glass windows had once been. Remnants of their colorful glory had been swept into piles in the far-off corners. The scene beyond the empty windows portrayed Zeal's *true* state. Piper opened the double doors to the city and welcomed the destruction.

Her boots thudded on the cracked staircase as she sidestepped chunks of missing stone on her way to the road. Two weeks had passed since the cult had attacked and the Black Wall had destroyed half of Zeal. The council desperately tried to clean up the collateral. A useless waste of time. Despite their efforts, the night breeze brought a fresh blanket of ash and dust over the roads every morning. Their energy would have been best served trying to find their missing comrades.

Voices carried from up the street, where a cleanup crew began their daily chore of sweeping the streets and hauling away pieces of crumbled buildings. *Like putting a bandage over a stab wound.* Piper had met with the council several times since her arrival. Some within their ranks earned the title of incompetent, but not Tena. So why was the lead councilwoman going along with the cleanup initiative? Probably to keep people busy. Distraction kept order.

As Piper descended the stairs, her eyes focused on the girl standing motionless at the curb. Wavy blonde hair shone bright against the girl's collared red dress. Piper stopped at her side and dipped her head in greeting. "Vienna."

Vienna's mouth twitched in response, though the rest of her remained stiff. Cold.

"Are you ready?" Piper kept her eyes forward, gazing at the long-caved-in roof of the shop across the street. She wanted to give the girl her space. Coddling, handholding, hugging... Vienna had only ever shown such affections to her brother.

Vienna clutched a pouch at her side, which Piper recognized. That pouch of pellets and the slingshot nestled beside it never left Vienna's side.

"No," Vienna answered with a whisper.

That was what she liked most about her old comrade. Even when they'd been in the liberation together what seemed like forever ago, the girl spoke her heart. No hiding the truth, unlike the cleaning crews shining up the crumbled city around them.

Piper snuck a glance her way. The void blankness on Vienna's face set off an odd feeling within Piper. One she couldn't identify. Not regret. Something else. A dread. Deep agony. In an instant, that feeling swallowed her whole and pressed around her heart. Piper couldn't shake it, whatever it was, so she snapped her eyes back to the half-standing store across the street once more and said nothing until a low hum came from the east five minutes later.

"Does she really think it's a good idea to bring that thing?" Piper side-eyed the strange contraption rolling down the street. "A little ostentatious."

The small silver vehicle, shaped like a capsule, slowed to a stop before them.

"The horse-led carriages are being used to transport the last of the bodies," Vienna said flatly.

Piper sucked in her bottom lip, unsure of how to respond. Somehow, any attempt to distract Vienna from the heaviness of the day ahead seemed to backfire. She didn't know why she bothered in the first place. Consoling wasn't her thing. Before Piper dug herself deeper into a hole, the door of the vehicle swung open, and a tall woman stepped out.

"Hello, ladies." A sorrowful smile pressed on Jax's lips as she rounded the front of her horseless contraption. Upon seeing her outfit, Piper cursed the councilwoman who'd forced her into a dress.

Jax wore a richly embroidered vest of silver and maroon over a blouse with billowy sleeves that tucked tight into straight-cut trousers. Typically stained with oil and grime, Jax's face was clean, and her close-cut hair slicked back from her face. Even her fingernails had been washed. A great feat for the woman.

Jax offered an arm to Vienna, who took it. "Best be on our way, my dear."

After opening the door, Jax ushered Vienna in, then tucked the tail end of Vienna's dress inside the cabin. When Jax had finished, she spun to retrieve Piper, arm outstretched to escort her.

Piper ignored Jax's hand. She looked over the woman's shoulder to check that Vienna wasn't listening, then stepped in close. "Our arrangements with the new cannon?"

The proximity made Jax shift and clutch the door. "I, uh...." a quick glance back at Vienna, "I don't think now is the best time to discuss this."

"Is it done?" At least Jax could disclose *that* much.

Jax nodded, though her eyes never quite landed on Piper.

"Later, then."

"Yes, miss." Jax offered her hand once more. A timid gesture this time, as if hoping Piper would refuse it.

And that she did, opting to climb in on her own.

The contraption had clearly been made for two occupants: driver and passenger. Piper had to squeeze in, hip to hip, alongside Vienna to fit. Even then, Jax had to force the door shut. The handle nipped Piper in the side, though she bit back her curse. The voluminous skirts they both donned cramped them further.

Not a moment later, Jax returned to her own seat, and the vehicle rolled forward with a purr. Piper rested her temple on the chill glass window as they drove past toppled buildings.

Streetlights had been downed like fallen trees in a windstorm. They had been pushed onto the sidewalks to clear the roads; their crystal tops, though, as fragile as they looked, lay fully intact. Moonstone didn't chip or crack like glass.

They passed more clean-up crews on their way to the city outskirts. *Shoveling snow during a blizzard.* She scoffed. And for what? Council Leader Tena had made perfectly clear the city was preparing to leave Zeal in a matter of weeks. Perhaps sooner.

It must've been five miles out before the destruction lessened. The cult of the Dark Hand had focused their attacks near the Black Wall's border, so the far east side of Zeal only held a thin layer of dust from the battle, as if the place were some old, forgotten ghost town.

Zeal's city wall loomed over them. Jax drove through the open gates, patrolled by a pair of guardsmen, and the smooth road of pavers gave way to a bumpy dirt road.

The crystal trees stood before them in all their glory, sparkling more brilliantly than jewels in the gold morning sun. No wood or leaf in sight. These stone-like trees were the heart of Zeal. The crux of all their prized creations. The odd energy within the trunks allowed people like Jax to create the very vehicle they rode in. A harmonious blend of magic and technology.

A mass of people garbed in hues from rust to burgundy crowded around the forest edge. Jax slowed their ride, then hopped out to assist with the door, but Piper pushed it open on her own and exited onto the grass. If she had worn those dreadful heels, she would've twisted an ankle on the knots of weeds. Jax rounded the front and walked past her to aid Vienna. They walked a few steps before Vienna nodded and departed on her own toward the gathered crowd.

Before Jax could scurry away, Piper looped her arm into the councilwoman's, stealing her escape. The tension in Jax's arm betrayed her discomfort.

"We still have a few minutes before the ceremony begins." Piper tugged Jax's arm. "Walk with me."

"Yes, miss," Jax agreed with a clipped edge, clearly out of duty rather than pleasure.

Piper led Jax in a wide rounded path away from listening ears. "Glad to hear the new specs for the cannon have been completed. Tested, too?"

"Just last night." Though she walked with Piper, arm in arm, her body leaned away like a stubborn mule.

"How long does this beam last?"

"Depends on the size of the trunk. I got it up to an hour during testing."

"Then we do it tonight. Soon as dark falls." The impatience in Piper's voice must've triggered something in the councilwoman, because she ripped her arm free.

"Why are you so eager to make me a murderer again?"

Piper rubbed her arm where it had slipped from Jax's. "He's not dead."

"You don't know that!" Her voice had carried and caught the eyes of a pair of townsfolk. She glanced their way, forced a smile, then clenched her teeth and stepped closer to Piper. "Here in Zeal, we like to *pretend* we know all about the Black Wall. All we really know is how to drive it back when it creeps in on the city. But what if the wall is not a wall at all? What if there is no 'other side'? It could be a land of never-ending fire. I sent Kole into it without knowing... without fully understanding...." Jax's lower lip quivered. She pursed her mouth as if squeezing it shut would bottle up her emotions, but Piper felt them rolling off the woman. "I was foolish. My foolishness has killed a child."

"Jax." Piper grabbed her by the shoulders. "You didn't kill Kole. He's alive. And I intend to find him."

A dull light flickered in Jax's eyes. She clung to Piper's words with a fevered need as if she wanted to believe. But logic and reason compelled the poor woman. "If he's alive, then why hasn't he come through the portal? Every night I light it—midnight, on the dot—and every night he never shows. Our watches are synched up." Jax fished through her vest pocket. A silver timepiece attached to a chain slipped out, and she shoved the glass front at Piper's face. "I made sure they were exact. Kole knows when the portal opens!"

During the battle with the Dark Hand, the cult's leader, Orla, had destroyed the first moonstone cannon Jax had designed to get Kole safely through the fire. Without that cannon, she no longer had the ability to give Kole safe passage back to Zeal, sealing him on the opposite side. It had taken ten days holed up in her workshop for the engineer to construct another. But Kole had expected to carry out his mission and return to Zeal in a matter of hours. If he'd gone back to the marked spot where the portal had opened before, he'd have found only flame. How long would Kole have waited there before searching for another way back to Ohr? It had been nearly a month since he vanished from the battle, which meant something had gone wrong.

"He's lost." *If only.* Piper made sure to keep her other theories to herself. Jax had enough worry and guilt plaguing her. No need to add to the burden. The truth? Piper herself could only guess. All she knew for sure was Kole lived. She felt it. So did the other Souls. "Your new model will help him, Jax. It'll be a beacon home."

Hints of color came back to Jax's tan cheeks. It was then Piper noticed just how much the engineer had suffered these last two weeks. Bags lay like chasms below bloodshot eyes. Her face had slimmed slightly, sharpening her features. And her nails. Piper had thought she'd scrubbed them clean, but they had been chewed so close to the nub, grime had nowhere to cling. The outfit, the hair: they merely acted as a bandage on the walking wound that she had become.

Piper took Jax's hands in hers and squeezed. "Tonight. Light your new cannon for me. I will find Kole and bring him back. I promise."

CHAPTER 4

The ground raced by. The stag's gait irritated Kole's hip and shoulder, but he gritted his teeth and held strong. He should've been focusing on the strange land of floating rocks ahead, but his thoughts strayed to the last moments before he and Caradin had jumped into this desolate land.

Vienna's eyes. That look she'd given him as she pleaded for him to run. It was more than fear... more than terror.

Heat welled up in Kole's eyes. He nestled his face into Caradin's fur and took in a deep breath of the animal's musky scent: moss and cinder. It grounded his thoughts.

Why had he listened? Why had he run when Vienna had told him too? He could've stayed. Made sure she was safe. Brought her with him through the wall.

No. She'd never let him take her. Not with her brother missing. *She'd never leave Felix.*

Kole knew why he had listened. Deep in his soul, he did. And in that quick flash of a moment when Vienna had told him to run, he'd realized it then, too: Ohr's survival was linked to him. He'd *had* to go.

One last inhale of Caradin's fur soothed him. No matter how much he fantasized about doing things differently, this was the path he was on, and he had no way of changing it.

A jerk in the elk's stride pulled Kole from his thoughts. His stomach fluttered as if falling from a great height. The sensation made him squeeze his eyes shut. Then, as quickly as it had set on him, that feeling vanished, replaced with an odd lightness. Kole opened his eyes, figuring Caradin had merely tripped, but his jaw dropped at the sight of the animal's hooves dangling midair over the ground.

"Caradin?" Kole's voice quivered. "Is this normal for you?" The elk was a god after all. Maybe some new, previously untapped power? The Soul had been nearly mad when Kole first released him from his prison a week and a half ago. Every day, the god gained more and more sanity and strength. Could he add flight to Caradin's list of powers?

When the fabric of Kole's shirt lifted from his skin and rose in a ripple around him, he knew the answer before Caradin confirmed.

"*Ground falls from my feet.*" The stag's voice rang in Kole's head with a tone of curiosity rather than the panic that consumed Kole.

"Not normal. Got it." Kole patted his shirt down. The moment his hand lifted away, it drifted up again. Even his pants pulled upward and billowed about. A vaguely familiar sensation. But what?

Then his pendant slipped from his shirt and bobbed up and down, held in place only by the chain clasped behind his neck.

Floating. That's what it reminded him of. Submerged in water. They drifted up and away, further from the earth.

"It's not falling away from us. We are the ones moving." Kole frantically searched for anything to grab hold of. No shrubs or branches to cling to. How long would they sail up? His gaze went skyward. Nothing but empty space above, save for the beating light of the sun. A fear of floating into that nothingness made Kole's stomach clench. "Can you get us down?"

Caradin pumped his feet into a heavy gallop. The motion tilted the elk sideways.

Still, they drifted up. Too high for comfort. Kole's hands shook as panic set in. Maybe if Caradin transformed into something heavy the weight would sink them. Kole dismissed the idea. Islands of rock floated in the same way off in the distance. That land was heavier than anything the god could change into.

Then, faster than his speeding heart, Kole and Caradin dropped from the sky.

Kole's stomach lurched into his throat as he plummeted back to the ground. His hands grasped at the stag's fur, keeping his body secure to the animal. The landing would break bones—break bodies—from this high up.

With the ground rushing up, Kole wondered if this was how it would all end. Dead on the far side of the Black Wall. No one to know what happened to him. He wished to fly like the birds back in his forest. The ones who could swoop out of a full dive and flutter on easier than breathing.

Something soft brushed against the back of Kole's legs and burst into his peripheral vision.

Feathers. Hundreds of them.

Sleek silver wings grew from Caradin's back. They arched up then beat hard and fast until they slowed the dangerous plumet.

Caradin's hooves hit the ground in a gallop, the great wings arcing back to act as a sail against the wind and slow momentum. Their moment of peril ended in a lively trot from the stag.

Kole's lungs released in relief. Once they'd stopped, he reached out to stroke the silken feathers that glowed with the same internal energy that radiated from the rest of the god's body.

"Since when can you fly?" Apparently, the god *was* capable of such a feat.

"Master requested it."

Kole opened his mouth to question him but snapped his lips shut. Though he'd never voiced a command or a wish, he'd certainly begged for it in the moment. How could he forget Caradin dwelled in his head? The god could hear Kole's thoughts if he allowed it. Usually, he kept a barrier up. The imminent danger must've weakened Kole's defenses. Thank the Souls it had.

"What else can you do?" Kole had seen him take other shapes before. The god had become a weasel small enough to hide away in Kole's pocket, then a valiant bull when they'd needed to barrel down a door.

"I choose forms of animals I have created. Or combination." The Soul spread his wings to their full extent, then tucked them carefully into his sides. The down feathers hugged Kole's legs, bringing a welcomed warmth.

"That'll come in handy. Anything to keep us grounded?"

The elk lifted a hoof, and the polished surface elongated. Three prongs in the front and one in the back. Reptilian scales settled over the skin. Talons formed to sharp points. Caradin placed the lizard claw on the ground alongside the others that had transformed. All four feet gripped the dirt.

If Kole had ever encountered such a creature, he would have run in fear. But these new claws solved their problem should they encounter another shift in gravity.

Each of the seven gods had their own power: a mastery and control of whatever they created on Ohr. His old mentor, Russé, the Green Soul, created plants, and he had allowed Kole and others to share in the ability to move trees at their will—uproot them and use them for travel and protection. Now Caradin, the Orange Soul, allowed Kole the same. He wondered what else Caradin could share of his power. Could he learn to understand the beasts of the land like he did with the walking trees? A theory to test out when they left these dead lands.

Kole pulled out the map Vienna had left him and checked their location. They'd travelled a few miles from the Black Wall, but when he looked back, the fire still looked so close. He checked his watch. A half hour gone, and they still hadn't found Vara's prison. Things needed to move quicker if they hoped to get back to the portal on time.

Speed wasn't the issue. Now that Caradin could fly, they could travel faster than ever. The issue came with direction. They needed a scout. Someone to guide them.

He needed Niko.

Kole closed his eyes and summoned the ghost of his old friend.

"Wh-where did you bring me?" Niko's voice cracked, betraying his fear.

Kole opened his eyes and smiled at the image of his burly friend. "I thought you'd sworn off being scared. You can't die twice, remember?"

"That's a *recent* epiphany." Niko whirled around, taking in the landscape. "It still takes time to get used to."

Given his stubbled jaw and muscly physique, any outsider would've guessed the fifteen-year-old stood as the fearless leader between the two. Far from the truth. While growing up, Kole had been the adventurous one, always pulling a resistant Niko along with him. His friend had a knack for numbers and books. The brain of the pair, some would say.

Niko must've just noticed Caradin, because he squealed and zipped behind Kole. "What in Soul's name is that?"

"Easy there." Kole leaned to one side, allowing Niko another glimpse over his shoulder. "It's exactly what you called it. Caradin has taken a different form is all."

"Caradin?" Niko hovered forward, casting an examining gaze over the creature. Then his head tilted down at the freshly formed claws. "But how? A cold-blooded creature mixed with a warm-blooded one. Impossible."

Leave it to Niko to find the flaw in divine magic.

"I think being a god forgoes reason in this case," Kole teased. "Not much of anything makes sense anymore, does it?" He gestured to Niko's spectral form.

Niko passed a hand through Caradin's wing. "Guess not."

Another quick look at his watch. That hand refused to slow. "I think you might like this place, Niko." When Kole finished recounting their near-death experience, Niko's jaw clenched. "Any idea what's going on?"

"Caradin is right. The land here is blocked off from the main continent. The imbalance from the Souls seems to have a physical impact." Niko pursed his lips, then held up a finger signaling Kole to wait.

The ghost shot straight up into the sky until the spotlight-like sun made him shield his eyes. Not a moment later, Niko returned.

"There's less land the further you go. Like its... dissolving away. Are you really going out there?"

"If that's where Vara is." Kole rubbed his arms and thumbed the corded flesh of his burn scars on his bicep. "That's why I called you."

"Don't' tell me you need a pep talk? I thought those were always saved for me," Niko mocked. His dark brows tilted in amusement.

Kole managed a half smirk. "There's always a first."

The heaviness of the situation pressed down on Kole's shoulders. He let his smile leave him.

Niko hovered a hand on Kole's shoulder, his expression reflecting Kole's. "You didn't summon me just to keep you company."

"No." Kole retrieved the map and rolled it out for Niko. "Vara is somewhere in this area, but I need a more exact location. Thing is, I could do that on my own, but the times I've reached out to her before... well, it triggers the Black Wall."

A painful subject for both of them. That same night Kole had received his burns, Niko had died along with dozens of other orphans.

"I won't risk it," Kole said.

Niko turned somber. "This isn't your fault, Kole. *I'm* not your fault."

The words sent a wave of remorse through Kole. "Then why does it feel that way?"

One more glance at the map, then Niko said, "I'll find the soulstone. Let's finish this whole mess and go back to how things were. Just like Aterus promised."

Kole ground his jaw to fend off the sudden grief, then nodded. He wanted nothing more than to return to the forest with Niko. He'd bring Felix and Vienna along, too. Awe them with Solpate's beauty. The thought of the four of them together... *that* was true happiness. Though try as he might, he couldn't quite form the picture in his mind.

Niko retreated until his translucent formed faded too far for Kole's squinted eyes to see. With his friend on the task of finding Vara's prison, his nerves soothed for the first time since his last full night of rest three days ago. Still, he wished his friends were with him. A god, though he trusted Caradin more than most, provided little comfort. A pang of loneliness cut through him in the brief silence.

This is no time to mope. He had a job to do. Niko would go on ahead, but the stag could still cover ground.

Kole stiffened his back and gripped a wad of fur in either hand. He looked to the barren land of rugged rock and floating islands. Just as he urged Caradin on, a shape in the distance caught him off guard.

A silhouette. Unmoving.

Niko had stopped? Maybe Vara lay closer than he expected.

The stag snorted and stamped his hooves into the rock nervously.

"What's the matter? It's only Niko." Kole waved a hand at his friend to signal he'd seen him, but the figure remained still. Caradin planted his feet, refusing to move on Kole's command.

"*Stranger.*" Caradin sent the word blaring into Kole's head.

Kole gripped his legs around the elk's belly to steady himself. "We're in the desolate region, there's no one...." As his eyes took in the silhouette, even from a distance, Kole's stomach clenched. The form stood solid — flesh-like — unlike Niko's translucent spirit. "...out here," he finished.

But how? How could someone cross the wall without meeting death? No one had jumped through the portal with Kole and Caradin. *That* they would've noticed. So, who? Or what?

The figure turned and ran.

"Go Caradin!" Kole urged the stag.

This time the Soul obliged. His thoughts had merged with Kole's, and a deep curiosity replaced his earlier trepidation.

They bounded forward. The stag followed the land a few yards until it gave way to a massive fissure where the earth had crumbled away. A running start gave Caradin enough momentum to make the leap across.

Kole had been so focused on keeping sight of the escaping figure, he forgot to brace for the landing, and his face slammed into the elk's neck. Floating black spots filled his vision. He shook his head and cleared them away. When he looked again, the figure had disappeared.

Before Kole could pose the question, Caradin answered, "*Climbed down.*"

The feathers nestled behind his thighs shifted. Caradin's new great wings opened and caught the air with a handful of whooshing flaps. They gained altitude. Kole peered down, but only empty land stared back. Fortunately, Caradin seemed to know where to go, because he tilted left and dove for a crack between two floating islands that had broken off from the mainland.

"*Down there,*" came Caradin, attention on the crevice.

Kole's core tickled as they swooped down and landed gently on the ground again. His head spun from the flight, but he threw his leg over the stag's back, found his feet, then raced to the edge Caradin had pointed out.

On hands and knees, Kole craned over the ledge.

A black void lay below. It sunk far beyond what Kole's eyes could perceive. Nothing but darkness and rock face. Where had it gone? No one, no matter how strong, could climb out of sight so quickly.

"Are you sure it was here?" Kole's instincts screamed at him to get as far from that ledge as possible, so he shuffled backward.

"Footprints." The stag scratched the silt piled up on the rocky surface.

Kole hurried over to inspect the familiar shape. Five toes. The usual pad and heel print like his own. *Barefoot?* Odd. Then again, what wasn't out here? He placed his boot alongside it. A bit bigger, but nothing significant. More importantly, the physical evidence left no possible way it could be Niko.

They'd seen something. Some*one.*

"It doesn't make sense. Who could be out here?" Kole followed the tracks to the fissure where he'd been a moment before. He studied the distance from where he stood to the island across the way. Too broad for anyone to jump, even someone athletic like Felix. He doubted Caradin could make it without using his wings.

Even if that jump could be made, there'd be a line of footprints leading away. The undisturbed ash on the far side told Kole the figure had indeed gone down the side of the rockface into the darkness. Whoever it was seemed to know the land well. That thought sparked its own question. How long had they been there? And were they alone?

"Nothing survives the Black Wall," Kole said, hoping to shield his sanity. He'd seen it several times firsthand. A touch of the flames doomed one to ash, be it human, creature, or building.

The sound of sniffing pulled Kole's attention back to Caradin. The stag had its nose trailing the footprints. Kole let his mind mingle with the god's. A wave of confusion hit him.

Kole returned to the elk's side. "What is it?" Though he could easily read the Soul's thoughts, some things, like emotions or feelings, proved harder to decipher.

Gray soot caked Caradin's nose when he lifted his head. *"He smells familiar."*

Kole gaped at him. "He?" There was something else the Soul held back. Kole clearly sensed a hesitation, but unless Caradin put the feeling into a cohesive thought, Kole couldn't decipher it further. "Tell me."

"Smells like you."

CHAPTER 5

Chairs were lined up in neat rows on the edge of the forest. Hundreds of lanterns surrounded the small platform that had been erected to serve as a stage. That was where Jax had hurried off to after talking with Piper. The engineer seemed eager to meet up with the rest of Zeal's council. Either that or the woman wanted to be free of Piper's company. She did have a way of putting people off.

Light reflecting off the crystal trees gave the whole place an ethereal aura. If Piper let her mind drift for a moment, she might think she were trapped in a dream. The bite of winter wind told her this was no such fantasy.

Piper spotted the lead councilwoman, Tena, propped up in a wheelchair at the middle of the stage. All the fresh-pressed satin in the world couldn't distract from the misery on the old woman's face. Her hands gripped the arms of her chair so intensely the tan skin appeared pink.

The battle with the Dark Hand had claimed Tena's legs. They'd dug the councilwoman from the rubble of the collapsed City Hall. Piper hadn't seen the tower fall, but she'd witnessed the aftermath. So much destruction at the hands of the cultists. Decades to recover the city. But what they had done to the people? They'd stricken them more severely than anything Piper had witnessed in her prolonged life. Generations to come would live through the turmoil.

It's only the beginning. That thought lingered on the edge of her mind. It had swirled around inside her for weeks. Zeal's destruction would act as a catalyst to the lands of Ohr. No one was safe. Either the battle here would unite the people in this world, or it would divide them. Piper had been counting on Kole to provide that unity. With him gone, she feared the fate of Ohr dipped toward doom.

Piper moved down the main aisle of empty chairs, letting her fingers trail on the backs as she walked. Vienna would surely want a seat at the front. A good person would stay by a grieving friend's side, but they weren't friends. Not really. *Allies.* Two people with mutual goals and experiences. A front-row seat would put Piper in prime view—something she wanted to avoid—so she turned down a row and sought the farthest chair. A place where she could survey the entire ceremony.

She sank into a seat and studied the scene. The same somber emptiness was plastered over every face. After seeing so many, they all started to blend. Then her gaze locked onto a vibrant pair of blue eyes staring at her.

The scent of wood and morning dew hit her nose as the old man approached.

"Were you even going to tell me?" The raspy voice came low and stern as the man took the empty seat next to Piper.

"Does it matter? You managed to find out anyway." Piper patted her skirt into place as she set her eyes straight ahead. Jax couldn't have let it slip. They'd only arrived ten minutes ago, and she'd been occupied with the council the whole time. Maybe he'd gotten into her head.

"You cannot go about this on your own. We need to act together. I know you have your own abilities, but that might not be enough."

"It's gotten me this far." Her calm demeanor must've dug under his skin because he leaned forward, forcing himself into her view.

Everything about his appearance screamed human. From his deep-wrinkled face and sallow complexion to his thinning gray hair and ever-present slouch. Anyone would think him a frail old grandpa at a glance. But those eyes. Too vibrant. If you stared long enough, the façade fell away. Though Piper gave him credit for the act. By far, the Green Soul blended the best with humans. Those ten long years he'd holed up in the refugee camps with Kole and the others had taught him well.

"I'm going with you," Russé snapped.

"No."

Their raised voices caught the attention of a pair of mourners. Piper gave her best somber smile. It seemed to placate the couple, and they continued past. After a quick glance for any others in earshot, Piper hissed, "What would you do if you found him? Tell me that, Russé. Drag him back kicking and screaming? He's chosen this path because of you. You see that, don't you? His faith in the Souls is lost. He's not a child anymore. He won't follow you blindly. The trust you built in that forest is gone."

Her last words made Russé flinch. The Green Soul settled back in his chair. Whatever anger he'd been clinging to drained away along with the color in his face.

Silence drew out between them.

The seats closest to the stage began to fill. More reason to sit on the edge if Russé wanted to have this conversation now.

"His faith isn't lost in all the Souls. I fear Aterus has gotten to him. Kole has changed sides." The pain in his tone sent Piper's gut rolling.

"You know him well enough not to believe that," she scolded. "Kole is smart. He'd never trust Aterus. Not fully. He's lonely and confused and their goals align." Piper slightly regretted being so harsh before. So much time with humans had made Russé soft. She knew because it had done the same to her.

"Without Kole...."

"I'll get him back." Piper felt a wallop of heat against her back. She twisted in her seat at the sensation. Two eavesdroppers. She should've guessed they would be close. Ever since they escaped their prisons, they'd stuck together like bloodstained cloth.

The Red Soul, Obell, and the Blue Soul, Issira, had taken human forms upon Russé's request. Unlike Russé, they stuck out vividly in any crowd. Obell's bear-like build stood a head taller than anyone in attendance. His irises shone an orange-gold like a dawn sky, and his dark complexion and matching hair only made those eyes more apparent.

Where Obell was the wild essence of the fire that he controlled, Issira embodied grace with every breath. Even motionless, her long, pin-straight black hair seemed to dance. The angles of her cheek bones and chin alone gave off an unworldly aura. Beauty beyond perfection.

The two Souls dressed in their preferred colors: Obell in black with flame-colored trim, and Issira in a blue that reminded Piper of the deepest ocean waters. She only now noticed Russé had done the same in his own evergreen tunic. Leave it to the gods not to know the cultural colors of a Zealian wake.

"There's a better cause you three will need to attend to," Piper whispered as the crowd hushed and settled, waiting for the ceremony to begin. "Kole is merely a piece in all of this. When I bring him back, there's still a chance Ohr will fall. You've relied on him too heavily as it is. If you continue to put this pressure on him, he may abandon us entirely."

"Losing Kole will doom humanity." Issira's eerie sing-song voice rose the hairs on Piper's arms.

"It may," Piper confirmed. "But we have three gods at our disposal," she nodded to each of them, then dipped her head, "and one demigod. If we build up enough strength throughout Ohr, we can contend with my father."

"A united front." The temperature spiked when Obell spoke. "War."

"Ohr is anything but united. Socren is destroyed. Their refugee camp on the coast is barely scraping by." Piper jutted her chin to the stage, where the council began to sit for Tena's opening speech now that the seats had filled. "Tena is the only reason Zeal will join in the battle, but even with the fancy weapons Jax has created, we have too few numbers. We need every city with us if we hope to bring down Aterus."

"Is it wise to bring them all together? So many humans in one place?" Russé asked.

Piper knew what the Soul hinted at. When she'd last upset her father, Aterus had moved the Black Wall over Socren as punishment, obliterating the thousand-year-old city to dust in a matter of seconds. If not for Piper's warning to Leo a few days prior, they would've faced the same fate.

"It's a risk," she said flatly. "Aterus' power is divided between my mother and the wall. When her health declines, he pours his powers into her. That's what makes the wall unstable. He holds her above all else in this world." *As do I.* She almost let those words slip out. The mere mention of Evangeline made her heart swell. Sorrow churned her gut. Piper shoved her mother's face from her mind. "And that's exactly why they should join us. He will use the wall before the end. All the more reason to clear out the borders of Ohr. But there is a way to weaken him. Distract him. It could buy us time. Leave that to me."

"It seems everything is up to you," Obell barked. "Would you have us stay behind and twiddle our thumbs? We are not servants to be ordered around."

"Maybe you should be."

Those inferno-like eyes smoldered. When he took a step toward Piper, Issira grabbed his elbow and a faint blue glow bloomed from her hand. The touch dimmed the Red Soul's eyes to their original color, and his puffed chest deflated.

The calming powers of water appeared more potent when applied to the fire god. Piper was suddenly grateful Kole had released Issira before Obell. Without the balance, the fire god's ill-controlled rage could've cause trouble.

Russé sent a disapproving frown to the both of them, but Piper looked away.

"You and your kin had the chance to fix this a long time ago." Piper let the bitterness flow freely in her tone. "Maybe it's time you took a back seat. Isn't that what you all intended to do before my father locked you away? You meant to ascend. To stop interfering in the lives of your creations."

A heavy silence weighed over the Souls. Then Tena's voice permeated the crowd. The ceremony had begun. Piper spotted Vienna in the front row. Fresh tears streaked down her cheeks, but her face held solid as stone. Piper made a note to speak with her after, though she knew little about how to console another.

"That was our intention, yes," said Russé. A quick glance at his kin, then he turned back to Piper. "I have been following my own mind for far too long. Look where it's gotten me. Where it's gotten all of us...."

The way he said it gave Piper the indication that he spoke of Kole. Maybe the bond Russé had formed with the boy ran much deeper and more genuine than she had initially thought. Kole wasn't just a tool to the Soul but something more. Strange to think a god could love like that. Piper had only ever known her father, and his 'love' was conditional at best.

"You are gods," Piper said. "The people of Ohr worship you. Let yourselves be known. Flaunt your titles. Convince every able-bodied man and woman to join in this war. It could be the last chance they have at true freedom... away from you." As Piper surveyed their faces, she caught micro expressions: the twitch of a lip, a narrowing eye. They were holding a private conversation through their telepathic connection.

A hymn rose from the mourners, led by the council on stage. Their delicate harmonies echoed off the trunks of the crystal trees, whose glowing light seemed to pulse with the sound.

Mid-chorus, Russé turned back to Piper. "We will do this," he said, his voice a low bass hiding within the notes of the mourners. "We will leave at dawn and go our separate ways to cover more ground."

It worried Piper that Obell would perform this task on his own. Issira and Russé had shown their diplomatic sides before. More than capably. But Obell's quick temper might do more frightening than persuading. She pitied the towns he would visit. To cultivate as many allies as possible, they'd need to be strategic as to where each Soul visited.

Obell had been banished from the lands of Grayfall almost as soon as he'd been released from his prison there in the volcano. The Yamani people had disowned their own maker. Obell's careless haste when creating the stone giants had caused mutations in their genes. Their offspring turned into feral monsters: bloodthirsty and hungry. No doubt the Yamani would drive the Red Soul out of their city again if he should step near it.

But there was *one* who would meet with Obell and keep a straight spine.

"Do what you will, but Obell must go to Cresthaven. He'll have the best shot at being welcomed there." Their leader, Azmali, had a reputation for stubbornness. Persuasion and pleading would never sway her. She'd close her doors to even a Soul. But Obell... his no nonsense matched Azmali's. He might have been the only one who could lure the reclusive woman and her army from the safety of their self-contained city.

Russé nodded in agreement. The Soul had passed through Cresthaven on his journey to the volcano with Kole. Piper knew because she had followed them there.

"Issira will go back to the Yamani. There numbers may be low, but their species is powerful," said Russé, then he turned and took the Blue Soul's hand. "They may not need much convincing, but their spirits will need settled from our last encounter with them."

"To the coast then?" Piper guessed of Russé. "Where you can show your talent?"

Russé's control over plants and trees only came in handy when he had access to them. The Souls, in their fragmented state, could only manipulate the elements, rather than create them.

"If it is necessary." The skin of Russé's hand paled as his fingers tightened around his walking stick. Of course, the god had no trouble walking, merely a prop to keep up appearances in his unassuming "old man" disguise.

"Then it is settled," Piper whispered under her breath, then turned back to the stage. People started to rise and add their voices to the beginning hymn. She followed suit and stood. "We part ways tonight. Be ready." Then she fell in tune with the lyrics, wishing the dead safe passage to the afterlife.

CHAPTER 6

"I'm going," Vienna growled.

"Just look at you! You are in no shape to do anything but lie in bed with your own misery," Piper snapped back at Vienna. After the words had left her lips, she realized how harsh it had come out.

Anguish glazed over Vienna's eyes. Her perpetually puffy face turned maroon, and she let out a wild sob.

This wasn't the Vienna that Piper knew. The fearless, clever right hand to Leo seemed so far away, drowned in grief. *The misfortune of a fragile human heart. Feeling everything.* Piper hadn't known Vienna when her parents had been murdered, but if it was anything like this.... It had been weeks since her brother's death, yet the wound bled as fresh as the initial cut. It pained Piper to see Vienna so broken.

Piper took a quick scan, hoping the scenery would grant her a little clarity. Dusk had fallen quickly since Jax had taxied them to the city's perimeter in the wheeler. The reach of the night's chill stopped short here. A fiery warmth surrounded them as they stood nearly a hundred yards from the Black Wall. The flames roared and licked. It seemed ridiculous standing so close to the embers of certain death with a weeping girl.

After a sigh, Piper took Vienna's hands in her own. This is what she was here for, after all: to keep shit together. *Someone must do it.* She rallied her softest voice. "I... didn't mean to snap. It's just that...." She chose her words carefully. The last thing she needed was Vienna going rogue on her. "We don't know what's on the other side. If we switched places, you may never reach Kole. And Jax can't stay here with the cannon. I need a way back. *Kole* needs a way back. Think about it."

Vienna stopped her crying and met Piper's gaze. A flicker of that hardened soldier showed itself for the briefest moment behind those fierce green eyes. *Same as Felix.* Same eyes, same freckles. When her mouth opened to speak, Piper feared another wave of emotion would come rolling out.

"I don't..." Vienna started. Her hands clenched at Piper's, drawing strength. "I don't want to be alone."

"I know," she said, returning the squeeze. "Look." Piper lifted Vienna's chin with a finger. "You are strong. I've seen it. I know it's still inside you underneath everything. I need you to find it. Use it. I won't be long, I promise. And when I do return, Kole will be back, too. Keep your thoughts on that."

Jaw flexing, Vienna wiped her soggy cheeks then pushed away and straightened like a soldier awaiting a command. She reached into her pocket and pulled out a pouch. The vivid embroidery made it immediately recognizable. "He wanted Kole to have it." She offered it up. "Will you give it to him for me?"

"No." Piper closed Vienna's fingers around the small bag. The jingle of metal was muffled beneath the cloth. "You'll give it to him yourself. That's what he wanted. Not from me."

"This baby is ready to go!" Jax's voice rose above the roar of the dark wall of flames. "Come, Vienna, I'll show you how to tame it."

Piper nodded as Vienna returned her brother's things to her pocket, then they both approached the cannon.

The contraptions Zeal had constructed to fend off the Black Wall from devouring their city had been a simpler design. Since the wall had moved that wretched night—the night Kole left Ohr and it claimed half of Zeal—Jax had put her blood and sweat into recreating the moonstone cannons they'd lost. Better versions. Stronger. Devastating. This particular cannon, though, a monstrosity. A weapon that declared Jax's dominance over the strange mesh of technology and magic she'd honed her entire career.

The moonstone cannon stood as tall as Piper. The size of the barrel alone spanned ten lengths of the average man, shining a bright, steely silver in the moonlight. The problem with Jax's previous version had been the longevity of power. Sure, it could create a portal straight through the Black Wall, but the window had been short. A matter of seconds if Piper recalled Jax's words correctly. The solution? The great inventor had tripled the size of the ignition chamber. More fuel meant a longer lasting beam. That came at a cost though.

"Help with this, will you?" Jax hunched over a hunk of moonstone. "Just on its side. I can roll it from there."

Piper and Vienna heaved the cylindrical chunk for Jax to roll like a giant wheel toward the cannon.

It was a shame to see the crystal trees be cut down. Zeal thought it a sacred place. The gem-like trees had always been protected. The council had made sure that the use of their power was only taken when needed. Preservation had been a priority. After the attack, Lead Councilwoman Tena had okayed their free use. In that first week, a hundred had been cut down and repurposed for weapons of war. This cannon included, it seemed. Not a hunk of stone that Jax loaded into the cannon, but a crystal stump. Rings and all.

"You do it like this." Jax had Vienna repeat the steps as she moved through the loading and ignition phases.

All the while, Piper walked the length of the tapered barrel to the end, from where the white beam would eventually erupt. The telescope-like design concentrated the ray to a smaller point. The intensity held enough power to pierce the fires and allow Piper safe passage. The beam had no effect on the skin, so she was told. Kole had walked right through it without harm. *Apparently.*

Piper harbored no fear of the beam. And less than she should for the wall. It was the thought of the land beyond that sent her intestines twisting like a pit of snakes. A hellscape awaited her for all she knew. It took great effort to shake the thoughts away. Dwelling on them would do her no favors.

"Take this with you." Piper jumped at Jax's voice. The woman had managed to sneak up on her — no small feat. In her hand lay a pocket watch.

Piper grabbed it.

"The portal stays open for an hour at least. If you don't come back through before the fuel is up, I'll put Vienna on a nightly schedule. Midnight. Just like we had with Kole." She tapped a short, grime-filled nail on the glass face. "Less likely she'll be spotted coming in and out of Zeal. We evacuate come dawn, but there's always a few who choose to stay. Usually of a particular sort. Best not entice their grubby hands with this." Jax patted her cannon with pride.

"She'll remain unseen." Piper jutted her chin toward Vienna, who studied the weapon at the opposite end. "She's a liberation member, after all."

"I wouldn't entrust my baby with anyone less worthy." Jax grinned. A twitch on the side of her mouth unveiled an underlying tension.

"What is it?"

The woman's cropped hair rustled as she shook her head. "It's nothing."

Piper slipped the watch into her pocket, then lowered her voice so it stayed between the two of them. "Jax," she tested.

Those brown eyes held hers. "I put him in there. This machine, it...." Jax paused, lips pursed before continuing, "I'm responsible for getting him out, but I'm leaving for the coast with the army. I'm abandoning him."

"You're *delegating*," Piper corrected. "It's what great leaders do when they are needed elsewhere. And you *are* needed elsewhere." She folded her arms. "I'd tell you not to worry, but you seem like the type that's going to anyway."

Jax gave a sheepish shrug.

"Go. Get some sleep. You travel across the continent tomorrow."

The engineer dipped her head then returned to Vienna, Piper on her heels. "I'll leave you with my vehicle. It'll make the trek easier."

Jax had given them both a crash course on how to operate the four-wheeled contraption on the way out here. She'd been all too excited to share her inventions with them. Piper got the feeling the council of Zeal considered the cannons her only viable invention, leaving Jax jumping at the chance to show her others to anyone with the faintest of interest. This vehicle she'd built ran on the power of moonstone, too.

Vienna gave the woman a quick embrace. When she pulled away, Jax held her firmly by the shoulders.

"The beam should last around an hour with that hunk of moonstone." She handed Vienna the key to her vehicle. "I've set aside more back in my quarters. Afraid my wheeler can only handle the weight of one at a time."

"I can manage," Vienna croaked, then stowed the key in her pocket.

"That a girl." Jax gave one final squeeze. "I must return and finish packing. If anything should go wrong, catch me before we march out." She turned to salute Piper. "May the lost find their way."

"May the lost find their way." Piper and Vienna repeated Ohr's customary, hopeful phrase.

Piper stood by Vienna's side as Jax lugged a bicycle from the back of her "wheeler," then road back toward the city.

Once the inventor had faded with the darkness, Piper turned back to the Black Wall. She'd always wondered what lay beyond its borders. Fear tingled in her core, but her excitement seemed enough to suppress it. "Ready?"

"Only if you are." Though hesitation laced her voice, Vienna proceeded to the back of the cannon.

"Midnight." Piper took both their watches in hand, checked they were synchronized, then handed one back.

"Midnight," Vienna confirmed. Some of the assuredness in her voice returned when taking orders, which settled Piper's nerves.

As long as Vienna keeps her head.... She'd have to. This was her and Kole's only way back to Ohr. Vienna would never abandon them.

"Give me a few minutes to get closer, then pull it."

A nod.

Piper faced the flames. She set off in a jog, straight out from the cannon's trajectory. Every now and then, she glanced back, ensuring her path stayed true. The heat burned against her flesh like she'd sat too long on the edge of a campfire. Still, her feet pumped beneath her, pushing her closer.

Anytime now, Vienna. As if on cue, a blinding light enveloped her; the ray a cold splash against her skin. Like a barrier, the moonstone beam negated the heat and lit a narrow path to her destination. She followed it to the wall.

Black flames licked and sizzled at the light as she neared the end of the tunnel. Though the ray stood plenty wide for her to run comfortably, Piper found herself clenching her elbows to her sides and minding her steps as if walking a narrow plank. Demigod or not, a single touch of ember could send her to her death. Her corpse merely another spray of ash on these Soul-forsaken plains.

The portal's end came into sight. Piper hastened. The sooner she made it, the sooner she'd find Kole and this war could finally come to an end.

Piper dove through the Black Wall.

CHAPTER 7

The beam sputtered out and with it, any sign of Piper. Not that Vienna could see that far in the dark anyway. Now that the light had gone, her eyes strained to see anything further than her hands. A giant ball branded her vision.

She spread her palms on the cannon and felt her way down to the fuel compartment. Fingers found the lever, and she unlocked the hatch. A wave of fumes hit her nostrils. It carried an unexpectedly pleasant scent: a mix of firewood and cool earth. Still, she swatted the vapors away before taking a cloth to the tank and cleaning out the residue as Jax had taught her. The cloth picked up the faint film of white dust. That strange residue made the cloth glow pale in her hands. Her skin, too, fell victim to the radiance, where flecks had fallen on her knuckles. Just as she finished the last swipe, a swift breeze caught the hair on the back of her neck.

Vienna stiffened.

She couldn't quite pin down why, but an alert blared in her head, and she stilled, focusing on the sounds around her.

The night had been quiet since sundown. No wind. And this breeze had been quick and fading, as if something had swept behind her. The roar of the Black Wall did her no favors. Try as she might, those mighty flames obscured any noise she'd hope to catch.

Vienna knew better than to dismiss the feeling. *Never ignore your instincts.* Leo had taught her that the moment she entered the liberation. Whatever it was, friend or foe, it hadn't acted yet. So, she forced herself to remain neutral, standing like nothing had happened.

Luminescent dust puffed off the rag as she shook it clean then folded it neatly against her stomach. All the while, she scanned the darkness. No person or animal in sight. Even as she shut the fuel tank and turned back to the wheeler Jax had left for her, nothing caught her attention. She made the quick walk to the door, hand twitching at her side, where her dagger hid under the fold of her tucked tunic.

She opened the vehicle without incident. If anything moved on her, it would do so before she closed herself inside the safety of the metal wheeler. Vienna hopped in the seat and slammed the door shut. The small capsule gave her refuge from the growling flames. She held that moment of tranquility and sighed. *Maybe I'm losing my touch.*

The moonstone key to her right lit the small space. She tossed the rag in the back, seat squeaking as her weight shifted, then twisted the stone. The vehicle came to life with a small rumble. Vienna placed her hands on the wheel and looked up. That was when the blood drained from her face. Her skin ran cold.

A Kayetan stood in her way, head cocked to one side as it stared straight through the window at her.

CHAPTER 8

"He smells like me?" Kole glanced at the footprints then back to Caradin. "What are you talking about?"

"Similar."

"You mean human?" Kole had guessed that from the shape of the tracks.

"More than human. The scent...." The stag's nose inched closer to Kole. Puffs of hot, moss-scented breath tickled his face before Caradin's nose twitched and he answered, *"like the Souls."*

A shock of panic struck Kole like a bolt of electricity. Kole had been told before by a Yamani that he smelled like a mutt, a conglomerate of human and Souls. But that was because of the fragments of the gods that lay in his head. Any others who possessed the same mixed scent meant only one thing: blood drinkers. Blood Sorcerers like the cult leader Orla.

Caradin must've sensed his fear because the great animal lowered his head to eye level. *"Not Orla."*

The words eased Kole's prickling worry. But it still left a notable question.

"Then who?" Kole had never considered someone surviving the black flames with Soul's blood in their system. The substance could heal even someone on the brink of death. Kole had witnessed it firsthand when Piper had force-fed it to him after he'd been brutally beaten by a cursed creature back in Grayfall. If there even existed a way to survive the flames, that was it. Kole instinctively rubbed the scars on his forearm.

"Vara."

Then Kole understood. "You think she's doing this through her prison?"

Just as Russé had done with the trees of Solpate Forest, where the magic seeping from his prison caused them to uproot and walk. Vara would have a similar effect. But the phenomenon had seemed linked to each god's creations. Russé with his ramblers... Caradin turning the wildlife hyper aggressive. But what he knew of Vara, the Violet Soul, and her control over the seasons... how did that play into strangers who smelled of human and Soul, or the anomalies in gravity? How much of this came from Vara?

"*Her and the Black Wall*," Caradin said.

Kole kept one hand on Caradin's hide as he circled the elk to get another look at the fissure. "Don't you think it's dangerous?"

"*It ran.*"

A slight lean over the edge to peer down into the pitch. The shadow lay thick below, concealing even the walls of the fissure a handful of yards down. "Maybe not." The stranger could be hidden just beyond Kole's vision, staring back up at him. Waiting. Assessing. The thought sent a chill up Kole's spine.

"Kole?"

The voice made him jump. He swiveled around to see Niko floating beside Caradin.

"Whoa, I didn't mean to startle you. Are you all right?"

Kole shook his head clear. "Fine. Just a little spooked. We saw someone."

Niko cocked his head. "Out here? But that's—"

"Yeah, I know, we've already established it's impossible. But we both saw him. And look." Kole led him to the footprints. "It's human. Well, we think, anyway."

Niko stared at the ground for a moment then his mouth scrunched to the side. "Look at what?"

"The footprint." When the wrinkles around Niko's mouth deepened, Kole dropped to his knees and drew a circle in the ash around the print. "Right here."

"I see your circle...."

"*Inside* the circle." Irritation cracked his voice.

Niko remained silent.

"You don't... see it? There's a line of them straight to the ledge. Caradin?" Kole asked to confirm, and the animal dipped his head in acknowledgement. "He smelled him, too!"

Niko swirled around Kole, his eyes slinking up and down, assessing. "Are you sure you're all right?"

"'Course I am," he snapped back. Kole wiped his brow. Though his burn scars prevented him from sweating, he still found himself doing certain things out of habit. All this fuss had worked him up. He took a moment to slow his breath and let his heart rate settle or he'd risk overheating, which had become a frequent problem since he'd burned. Fainting would cost them precious time.

Kole grabbed the waterskin from his belt and chugged its contents. The cool liquid cleared the lump in his throat.

"I don't think you're lying, Kole." Niko shrugged, holding his arms out apologetically. "I just can't say I see something when I don't."

Kole replaced the waterskin and smirked. Nothing more Niko than that. The guy who always had a book in hand, jotting notes and making sketches to study the anomalies of the walking trees that ruled their home.

"I know. I guess it tells us something about this place, too."

His friend shifted and leaned in, eyes twinkling with interest.

Despite his revelation, Kole found it hard to say the words. "Uh, well, it seems like the living can see it, but not the... you know."

"The dead," Niko finished. His brows came together in thought. "You might be on to something. Some phenomena out here could be affecting your brain. Making you see things." A nod to Caradin. "Smell things."

"All the more reason to hurry, then." Kole checked his wrist for the time. "If this place *is* messing with us, we should get out as soon as we can before it does anything more sinister. Any luck finding Vara?"

A gleaming smile took over his ghostly face. "She was hard to miss. Come on, I'll take you."

The next few minutes blurred. Kole sat atop the stag, wings beating the air as they flew up and over the land, swerving between floating rocks that bobbed as if submerged in the depths of an unseen ocean. Though impressive, nothing could pull his thoughts away from that stranger. How real it had seemed.... Could something about this place be messing with his vision? His mind? Perhaps something in the air. It certainly had a hold on the land and gravity, so why not? No one knew all the secrets of the Black Wall, especially what lay on this side.

A figment of my imagination. That's all it was.

Still, he found himself looking down, spying for another glimpse at the stranger.

"There it is." Niko's voice on the wind made Kole abandon his search.

There it was, indeed. Just as Kole had seen in his vision a few days ago. In person, right before him, the sight made his jaw slack. "For the love of Souls," he whispered.

A massive chunk of floating earth suspended in the air. Multicolored veins of light encapsulated the floating island in rings of green, yellow, orange, and white. They glowed like brilliant stars. *Magic? Pure energy?* Kole could only guess at their true nature.

"If that's not it, I don't know what is," Kole mumbled.

"*I feel her,*" Caradin confirmed.

Budding pressure in the back of Kole's skull signaled Vara's presence. He'd need to keep up his defenses if he wanted to hold his composure. The aching pulse spreading to his neck told him Vara sensed him too. But would she act on it?

When Kole had approached Obell's prison back in the Ashland Plains, the god's anger had overwhelmed Kole and smashed through the barrier between their minds. The Red Soul had taken over Kole's body and thoughts, using him as a puppeteer would. It had happened with Issira, too, but not to such extremes. He sent his worry to Caradin, and an immediate warmth bloomed in Kole's head around the door that linked Kole to Vara. The extra defense set Kole's nerves at ease, if only slightly. Then he looked up, and that second of calm skittered away.

A strange black hole poised in the sky directly above, pulsing like a beating heart. The anomaly seemed to suck out the light from those colorful rings. Just looking at the thing made Kole's hairs rise. *Nothing good, that's for sure.* For once, he wished a god's prison to be in a field of flowers full of sunshine and maybe a warm breeze. He sighed. There would be no easy release. They never were.

One gentle tilt of his wings and Caradin changed course for landing. When they closed in on the rings, Kole's stomach lurched again.

Gravity shifted.

This time, instead of making them weightless, Kole's bones turned into boulders. His body slammed down into the stag's neck, pinning him to the soft fur.

Caradin bleated. The force pulled them both down. Wind assaulted Kole's face as they plummeted. He waited for the flap of wings to rescue them like last time, but it never came. Kole peered out.

The great wings were pinned straight up. Muscles strained in the animal's back, attempting to push them down and let the feathers catch the wind, but Caradin's strength failed. They fell too fast. No. Not falling. Something pressed them down—*forced* them down.

Kole's mind raced. It had to be like the other distortion. A pocket. If they could only find the edge....

"*Dip your head forward.*" Kole sent the command into Caradin's mind. Without hesitation, the god complied. "*Tuck your legs in.*"

They pitched forward. Kole squeezed his arms tighter around the elk's neck as they rotated into a nosedive. Instead of the skyline, he now stared straight at the land below. The new vertical position allowed Caradin to tuck his wings, and they dove faster, like a shooting arrow.

The pocket has to end somewhere. But where? How could he find the invisible perimeter? Despite the wind buffeting his face, he tore his eyes from the fast-approaching earth and peeked up. He didn't know what he was looking for, but when he spotted a floating pebble a few yards ahead, Kole instructed Caradin to pull up on their angled trajectory, setting sights on that small stone. In those next few seconds, Kole guessed his heart pattered a hundred times. Had he been wrong? *What a stupid plan.*

Just as those intrusive thoughts leaked in, the force pressing on Kole's back vanished. They hovered there, midair, freed from their swan dive.

Kole sucked in a long breath and all but collapsed on the Soul's back. The excitement had made his blood churn. The heat from his terror went to his head. He needed more water and a rest soon or risked overheating.

"We need to be careful. My body can't take much more of this," he said. If not for his blasted scars, he'd simply shrug off the adrenaline rush. But now, he'd soon pass out. Not good when riding a flying beast. "Up to the island as quick as you can."

With a flutter of wings, Caradin ascended. Kole kept his eyes closed focusing on keeping coherent—awake. It only took a short time, but Kole kept stiff in anticipation, waiting for another pocket to thrash them about. He worried for not. Claws touched down and curled into the earth, anchoring them.

Once on solid ground, Kole rolled off. His wobbling legs took him a few steps before buckling, and he tumbled onto the dirt. He rolled to his back and stayed there, breathing—in, out, in, out. The deep breaths helped a bit. Only time would calm his body—something he had in short supply. The small tick of his watch fell in time with his pulse. Laying here... wasting away....

"Oh, Kole! That was a close one!" came Niko's voice. "This place is as wild as Solpate."

"Yeah, wild. I'm just glad to be in one piece," Kole slurred, but he opened his eyes to his ghostly friend and Caradin hovering over him. "Never better. Promise," he added at Niko's skeptical gaze.

His friend said something in response, but Kole ignored it at the sight of his new surroundings.

The vibrant rings of greens and yellows shifted—no, *flowed*—like running water around the floating chunk of earth. The sight awed him. Beautiful, however strange. The urge to touch them overwhelmed him, yet with all the chaos that he'd lived through to get up here, he knew better than to get too close.

Kole rose to his elbows, his friends still hunched over him. "What is that?" The dark hole drew Kole's attention.

"Vara. She's there." Niko pointed up at the black hole that lay at the apex of the glowing rings.

Kole stared at it. "That?" He'd seen soul stones before, and this, well, this looked nothing like the others. "Are you sure? It's supposed to be a crystal-looking thing."

"Did I have a stone, Master?" Caradin's voice echoed in Kole's head.

"Well, no, but you were different. Your prison was unlike the others."

"Maybe Vara's is different, too."

Kole frowned. *Would it kill Aterus to have some consistency?* He rolled his eyes. If he could perform the ritual, fine, let the prison be a cloud for all he cared. Getting up there would be easy now that Caradin could fly. The difficult part lay in the unknown. Seeing the anomaly up close, it did indeed suck the light from the rings. Absorbed. His fingers twitched at the thought of touching it.

Kole clambered to his feet. "Take me up."

Caradin dipped his head in response, then sunk into a bow for Kole's ease. Before climbing up, Kole grabbed a handful of pebbles off the ground and stashed them in his pocket.

"You're going now?" Niko's voice pitched with alarm. "But we haven't studied it yet. How it works."

Kole let a smile creep over his face. "Don't get your trousers in a twist." He pulled one stone from his pocket and bounced it in his palm. "I've lived with you long enough, haven't I? Gotta test things out, right?"

Niko's brows raised. *"You?* Testing things? What happened to barreling straight for danger?"

"I learn sometimes." Kole patted Caradin's back in signal, and they took flight for Vara's prison.

As they flew closer, sweeping past the rings of light, the temperature fluctuated. They charged through pockets of frigid air, like the depths of a winter's night, only to meet a breeze of a scorching summer blaze on his cheek in the next moment. At this point, little surprised Kole. As long as he sensed no danger, the grip of concern loosened. It sparked a clue, though, these cycling temperatures.

All four seasons. That was, after all, among the powers of the Violet Soul.

Closing in, Kole pulled one of the stones he'd collected from his pocket, then chucked it at the black portal. The rock zoomed through the space. When it approached the darkness, it slowed and bobbed midair as if it had landed on the surface of sludgy swamp water. The darkness caressed the stone, fondled it, then sucked it up, nowhere to be seen.

He predicted as much. With the rings trailing into it, the black hole all but screamed its importance. Kole sent a couple more stones at it, just in case. All ended the same. Consumed. He worried less about where the stones led, but rather, if they could return. Before the growing shudder could claim his bones, Kole tapped Caradin's neck, and they plunged back down to meet Niko.

"How's it looking?" Niko had leaned back, his body floating at an angle.

Kole dismounted. "Like a one-way trip."

Niko's mouth dipped into a frown as Kole explained. Once finished, Niko idly scratched at the stubble on his jawline. "But Vara is inside, right?"

"All signs point to yes." Kole side-eyed the stag to be sure. The animal gave a certain nod.

"I wouldn't worry about getting out," said Niko.

"You've got to be mad."

"There's a god in there. It's her prison. She'll know how to get you out." Niko gave a grand gesture to Caradin when Kole scrunched his mouth in doubt. "Just look at what *he* can do."

"I'm glad the one staying out of harm's way is so confident," Kole mocked.

"I know, I know." He patted a hand on Kole's shoulder, but his ghostly form passed on through. "I'd offer to go in myself, but it doesn't work that way. Just... take all the time you need."

The words were meant to comfort, yet it only made Kole look down at his watch. One hour left before Jax would open the portal for the return trip to Ohr. Taming his nerves wasn't a luxury he could afford.

Kole pulled out his knife, clenched his teeth, then pressed the cold metal into the pad of his palm. The skin split. A small yelp escaped his lips, but he kept his jaw firm. He'd done this before, and he'd have to do it once more for the last imprisoned Soul. *His* blood was the trigger—the offering he'd need to shatter the prison walls. Better do it now, down here where he knew he was safe. The flying boulders in the distance changed his mind. *Safe-ish.* Who knew what lay waiting for him in that black hole above?

"Let's get this over with."

The wound on Kole's hand burned. Blood trickled into the creases of his palm. He closed his hand in a tight fist to keep it contained, but red seeped out and stained the stag's silvery coat. Kole gritted his teeth against the pain as he and Caradin soared up to the black hole.

"Be ready," Kole warned the Orange Soul.

"I will protect Master."

A warm pressure enveloped Kole's mind like a giant hug. Caradin had fixed his attention and energy on Kole. The sensation eased Kole. He felt strong with the Soul on his side. A flicker of confidence blazed through him. *I've done this before; I can do it again.* Repeating the mantra eased his nerves.

One last look down at Niko, who had stayed back on the island, then Kole set his focus on the rippling dark portal.

No hesitation. If he thought too much about it, his fear would overtake him. At least he didn't go it alone.

The stag flapped his wings harder, picking up speed. As they narrowed in, Kole tensed, flexing his legs hard around the animal's ribs. The urge to hide his face consumed him, but he fought against it, forcing his eyes on the target.

The moment they came within arm's length, Kole and the stag paused mid-air; floated there as if the black hole had a mind of its own, as if it judged and weighed them before it allowed entry.

Caradin's crown of antlers touched first. Like rippling black waters, the portal caressed the beast, but to Kole's surprise, it didn't consume them like the rocks before. The portal pushed against the Soul. Repelled him.

"Go higher!" Kole yelled. If the portal refused to take them freely, they'd have to force their way in.

He reached up in hopes of finding something to help pull them in. The darkness touched Kole's fingers. Instead of shielding him off, it drew him in. Kole's rump lifted off the stag's back. He flailed as the hold of the black hole's gravity tugged him free. Panic welled up Kole's throat. He swiped for an antler. His hand landed, but the blood from his wound sabotaged his grip, and he slipped free. Second by second, he floated further from Caradin.

Worry shone in the animal's deep eyes. Those wings anxiously flapped, yet whatever power the darkness held pushed the god further away. The tug went deeper than physical. The connection between Kole and Caradin pulled taut, thinned. Then it diminished entirely. The portal banished the Soul—separated them.

Dark tendrils wrapped around Kole's limbs. Their touch paralyzed him—every muscle tense and frozen. Before Kole could blink, his vision went dark.

The portal swallowed him.

CHAPTER 9

Four days had passed.

Vienna stood at the edge of the Crystal Forest. Before Council Leader Tena set out with the soldiers and people of Zeal for Leo's camp on the coast, she'd appointed a sculptor to carve a memorial for those who'd fallen during the battle with the Dark Hand. One of the larger stone trees on the border had its trunk covered in the names of the dead and the missing. She circled around the side, tracing her finger over the letters, until finally stopping at one.

Felix Hallas

They hadn't used their last name since their parents died and Leo took them under his wing.

"Hallas. Felix Hallas." It sounded weird on her tongue. Like foreign words. The name sent a lump to her throat, but she swallowed it back.

She hated it here. The abandoned city. All alone. And the *quiet*. It gnawed on her.

Nothing to do during the day but wait until nightfall and return to the cannon to perform her duties. She'd holed up in her room on the first day, but restlessness quickly overcame her. The last couple of days, she'd spent wandering the streets, examining the tools and contraptions Jax had deemed unfit to bring to the coast, and walking the forest. No matter how she spent her time, she found herself back at this tree. The name written here called to her.

"I've brought mead tonight." Vienna lifted the bottle she'd found in the collapsed basement of an old house toward the memorial, then placed it at the base. "Your favorite." A bit of dust had settled on the blanket she'd set up the previous night, so she wiped it off before sitting. One by one, she pulled her supper feast from her pack: dried plums, jerky, and cheese. Jax had set her up with a week's worth of food. After that, she'd have to hunt to fill her belly.

She waited until the last light of the sun surrendered to night before starting her meal. Nightfall marked the awakening of the forest. A white glow birthed in the heart of every trunk. The darker the night became, the brighter they gleamed, until every branch and root, peeking out from the earth, assumed the luminesce of a full moon.

"It's no dumpling, but it'll do," Vienna said with a laugh, then bit off a piece of jerky.

The evening stayed still. Even the noise of the birds had gone.

Mouth full, she slurred, "Aren't ya comin'? I saved ya a seat." Vienna swallowed and paused. "Don't tell me this feast ain't good enough for ya." Her city accent slipped out and she smiled. The sound of the clipped words reminded her of him—of those early days of her childhood cramped in that small house with her family.

In answer, a cloud of smoke slithered through the air in the distance. Like a snake, the jet coiled around the crystal tree trunks, slipping from shadow to shadow as it lazily made its way to Vienna's picnic blanket. She smiled as the shadow took shape. The outline of a young man, lithe with puffy curls for hair formed before her. Though the smoke-like form seemed like something between ghost and demon, Vienna's mind filled in the featureless face down to the very last freckle dotting his cheeks. Instead of two concave bottomless holes for eyes, she pictured the sly green ones that always flashed with mischief. The will of her mind shrunk the blade-like claws hanging by the demon's side and transformed them into human hands with the manicure of an anxious nail-biter. The penumbra took on every quality she deemed.

"Hello, Felix." Vienna offered a plum to her brother, but when he made no move to take it, she rolled her eyes. "All right, I know you want the meat. I'll share. But don't eat it all." After setting aside a piece for Felix, she leaned against the trunk.

Felix swayed in the distance, keeping to the darkness; head trained on her.

"I wonder what it was like here. You know, before the cult and the battle and everything." Vienna gazed at Zeal's grandeur. Despite the destruction, many buildings around the eastern wall lay untouched. Their spiraling towers gave off an ethereal aura in the dim light. "More advanced than Socren, for sure. I suppose it would've been nice to live here. You and me. Kole, too, of course." Her mind conjured happy moments of the three of them. "We'd open a shop." She smiled at the idea, then patted the space next to her. "I'd sell flowers, and you'd sell your embroideries."

The Kayetan cocked his head.

"Oh don't you start." Vienna waved to the vibrantly stitched pouch looped on her belt. "They're too good for you to hide them. Who cares what anyone else thinks? And if they do judge, you know we can always handle them your way."

One of the sunken eyes held a twinkle at the mention of mischief. A wink.

After that, the meal went on in silence as they all had since Vienna had first discovered her brother's Kayetan. The shadow demon couldn't speak, least not to her, but she enjoyed the company nonetheless.

Once Vienna had finished, she reached to collect Felix's portion. Untouched as usual. The shadow never ate, but she still found herself offering him a ration. It felt wrong not to. She packed up the leftovers and loaded them into the vehicle Jax had left for her use.

"Let's get going. Wouldn't want to miss Kole." The first night, Vienna had tried to get her brother to sit inside with her but quickly realized the moonstone core that powered her transportation left no shadows in the small compartment. Felix couldn't enter even if he wanted to.

The shadow remained outside while Vienna started up the wheeler. As always, the moment she pushed onward, the Kayetan followed, zipping along outside the driver's seat.

A short drive later and they had arrived.

Vienna lugged the moonstone stump into the cannon's tank, then locked it as Jax had instructed. "The seal is important. Make sure it clicks or the thing will explode," she echoed Jax's warning as she tugged on the handle. Two clicks sounded before it satisfied her.

She'd come earlier and earlier every night, hoping for....

What am I hoping for? A sign Piper and Kole are waiting on the other side?

No. That surely would ease her worries, but it wasn't why she'd come two hours before midnight. This outing—this job—kept her thoughts occupied. She'd been taking orders all her life. Serving others. That was her *purpose*. What she thrived on. Back in Socren, under the Warden's reign, every day had been a struggle to survive, fearing for her life or the lives of the poor villagers and farmers at the mercy of a madman. It was all she could do to keep people safe.

"It's tonight. I can feel it," Vienna said to Felix. "We'll all be back together. Like nothing ever happened."

Felix's Kayetan never approached the cannon. The creature hated the light of the moonstone. That internal glow reminded her of the weapons

Leo had created to extinguish these demons when they had tormented Socren at the warden's command. Though details remained vague (she was no sorcerer), Vienna knew Leo had imbued fire into the obsidian stone to create sunstone. One stab to the shadow's heart with a weapon like that vanquished a Kayetan. No wonder Felix kept his distance.

After what felt like forever watching those hands slug around the clock, midnight finally came.

"Come back to us Kole," she whispered, then pulled the lever.

The machine roared like an angered lion. And from its mouth a brilliant moonbeam burst out into the darkness.

Vienna stood, gazing at it. The smallest flicker of shadow... that's all she needed. Something to tell her this was the night. That they were walking back through the bridge between worlds.

Ten minutes in, she found her feet on the move. She walked the length of the cannon. Then past it.

It had been days. *Days.* What was taking so long? Piper had promised to return with Kole and Caradin. Vienna wanted to go in after them herself, but what could she offer in aid that a demigod could not? Still her feet pushed her forward—closer to the wall.

A pit of awful dread weighed in her core. Jax's prediction. Could she have been right? Nothing but more fire lay at the end of this beam. Anyone who passed through it met instant death at the end.

A tug on Vienna's arm stopped her.

Felix's Kayetan had its claws wrapped around her elbow. The shadow held her in place.

She looked to Felix, then back toward the birth of the beam. She'd followed the light nearly a quarter mile out.

The cannon suddenly sputtered off, leaving her in complete darkness.

The Kayetan tugged again, but this time she realized not back but down, trying to guide her to the floor. She hesitated until a yell carried on the wind.

Someone was out here with her.

A whiz raced past her ear. Another, then another. Vienna had been on the receiving end of weapons like this before. She dove to the floor. The flat, barren land offered no cover. All she could do was stay low and hope the night would conceal her, especially now that the cannon had been extinguished.

Lights from the wheeler lit up the land, giving sight to a handful of silhouettes gathered around the cannon.

Shit. Jax had warned her of looters. She'd seen a couple in the city every now and then, but they'd mostly been ransacking the abandoned buildings. They'd either followed her out here, or the ray had lured them. This was, after all, the last working cannon in Zeal. The only defense Zeal had if the Black Wall moved again.

Vienna patted her belt, home to one dagger, Felix's old slingshot, and holstered on her left hip, a pistol Jax had gifted her on the day she'd left with Zeal's forces. Though Vienna had received a brief lesson on how to use it, her aim was probably better with the slingshot. She'd need to get closer to use either one properly.

With her chest pressed close to the ground, she crawled through the blanket of ash and dirt. She'd only managed a few yards when another round of shouting carried her way, followed by clangs of metal. *The cannon!*

When Vienna thrust herself to her feet, the Kayetan forced her back down, pinning her to the ground. Another few shots whistled overhead.

"You can't keep me here and let it be destroyed. It's Kole's only hope." Vienna ripped from Felix's grasp. "You handle it, or I will."

The demon lingered for a moment. Vienna could see the creature weighing the options. Whatever bond the demon once shared with Felix had transferred the protective brother trait over it seemed, because the shadow hesitated, keen on defending her.

"Felix," she scolded.

That final urge made the demon's shoulders cave. The Kayetan zoomed away, a trail of shadow shooting straight for the cannon.

Screams echoed. Shots fired. The whinny of a horse.

When the lights of Vienna's wheeler swung across the plain, she scrambled to her feet and pushed into a dead sprint.

Too late.

The vehicle raced off. Dust and ash clouded the air behind it.

Vienna slowed. No amount of speed could catch up. She bent over to steady her breath, her hands resting on her knees. "Not the wheeler," she groaned. *How am I supposed to get back?* Or worse, lug the next moonstone trunk out there to fuel the cannon?

The cannon! All that racket had hopefully come from the looters commandeering the wheeler. She raced back to the contraption. Footprints around the cannon ignited her worst fears.

"No. For the love of Souls, please no."

A wind touched her back announcing the Kayetan's return. The demon lingered by her shoulder as she rounded the weapon and surveyed the damage.

The fuel tank had been pried open; hinges bent and warped. Forcing them back into their original shape would prove simple enough, but the holes where they connected to the tank, along with the screws, were stripped. She opened the lid. Empty. They'd stolen the moonstone.

Vienna slammed her fist on the barrel of the weapon in a huff. Tonight was over. Even if she could get the stone back, she needed the tools in Jax's old workshop to fix the tank. Without the wheeler, she'd never make it back in time. If Kole meant to return tonight, he'd find no passage.

"Follow them," she ordered the Kayetan. "Find out where they're taking the wheeler."

The tone of her voice must've relayed a sense of urgency because the shadow left in a rush, leaving her alone in the desolate plain.

Vienna gathered any materials that had been scattered in the raid, set them safely under the cannon, then stuffed her hands into her pockets and began the long walk back to Zeal.

CHAPTER 10

Kole floated in the nothingness. Once within the portal, his body was his own again. He flailed, hoping this space possessed the same qualities of water and he could swim back to the portal.

The portal.

Where is it?

Kole twisted and turned. Every direction darkness. Which way was up? Or down? No sun or earth.

"Caradin?" He tested the words in his mind, but they echoed around. When he tried to feel for the door in his head that linked his thoughts to Caradin's, he found it shut. More than shut, he realized as he tried to push against it. Blocked.

A deep-seated feeling rooted in Kole's core. He got an eerie dread that the portal had led him somewhere far from Ohr. Something of Vara's creation? If that were true, where was the soulstone?

The dark sky—if he could call it that—swirled with purple and blue light. The colors pulsed in sequence like an assortment of synchronized hearts, beating blue, then purple. The display entranced Kole.

Something in his head wriggled. A whisper came to him.

"Stay with me," her voice said. *"Watch the wonders I can create."*

Once the voice quieted, the lights danced, invigorated. Though soundless, the show reminded Kole of a song. The vibrant purples took the lead role while the deeper hues supported the solo. Every now and then, a blue glow swelled and embraced the other colors.

Kole watched. All his cares drained away. No thoughts of Ohr, the Souls, his mission, or the battle weighed him down. He only thought of the fantastical lights and wondered how their show would develop next.

The shine of metal glinted under his nose, but he ignored it, mesmerized.

"I remember this."

Only when the voice spoke again did Kole's wits return. His pendant floated before his face. Gravity turned the medallion to and fro. Kole grabbed for it, but the chain pulled taut as if an invisible hand held his trinket in place.

"I think I'd like to keep it."

The chain pulled free from Kole's neck, and his pendant drifted away.

"That's mine." Kole had meant to say it, but the words he formed ended up in his head.

"Not any longer." A pressure touched Kole's chest, shoving him away from the amulet. Then a tug to his hood and a tap on his boot. *"You already have so many things."*

She kept poking at him, exploring the trinkets and weapons he carried, but her visage never appeared. Kole didn't need to look upon her to know her identity. He'd traveled across Ohr and through fire to find her. It could be no one else. *"Vara."*

The nudges paused. *"Kole,"* she said his name with such warmth.

"I'm here to save you," he said.

"And you have." A gentle forced lifted Kole up and spun him around. *"I am no longer in pain because I am no longer alone. I have you for eternity."*

Great. Another delusional god. Caradin had behaved strangely when Kole had first found him. The Soul had been in animal form for so long, the beast had taken over his mind. Only after Kole had released him from his prison had the Orange Soul gradually regained his old self and learned to communicate again. It seemed the isolation had cracked Vara, too, though Kole wondered to what extent.

"I can't stay here. And you can't either. I can release you, Vara. You can be with me and all your kin. Caradin waits —"

"No!" The lights grew to an angry shade of deep violet.

A tight, invisible force gripped Kole, squeezed him. His arms pinned to his sides. Try as he might, his lungs struggled to expand and gather a full breath. Blood rushed to his face, but his lack of air was the last thing on his mind as a terrible sight formed.

The blazing lights merged to form two giant rings of indigo. *Eyes.* The deep, inky centers settled on Kole.

"I will not share. That's what got me here in the first place." The roar in Kole's head sent his bones rattling. A few more moments with this crushing weight on his chest would have him unconscious. *"You are mine now."*

Kole thought back to when he first made contact with Vara earlier that week back in Zeal. She'd pleaded with him to find her — save her.

Not that he had a choice in the matter, Vara had to be released, but now he understood her true intent. Vara had lured him. The Violet Soul didn't seek freedom; she sought a remedy to her seclusion.

Something pulsed in the depths of Kole's mind. The door that linked him to Vara rumbled. The Soul wanted in his head. Probably to overtake his body and force him to stay in this strange void. Kole summoned all his energy to fortify the barrier between them. The massive eyes narrowed on him, burning angry at his defiance.

"If you keep me here, all of Ohr will die."

"Ohr is already doomed."

The concentration it took to keep her at bay took too much of him. Gasping for air inside her clutches made things harder. "I can't breathe."

"I only need your mind to keep me company."

He needed to change tactics. Four Souls he'd released thus far, and he'd managed to survive the encounter. No way he'd fail when the end of his mission lay so near. How could he appeal to her? A few more moments with this crushing weight on his chest would have him unconscious. If that happened, he'd be at her complete mercy.

"I will stay with you, Vara," Kole tried. "I won't leave."

It must've been what the Soul wanted to hear because the pressure around him eased. Kole sucked in a fresh breath, and immediately his internal temperature cooled. Step one had worked: he was free for the time being. Now he had to put his silver tongue to the test. *Just keep telling her what she wants to hear.*

"It'll just be you and me, right? That's what you want?"

"Yes," she purred.

"But why me?"

"There is no other who can hear me. I only feel you."

The slightest bit of sympathy touched Kole's heart. When Aterus had imprisoned the Souls, they'd been cut off from everything: Ohr, their creations, and one another. The gods, though distinct in their powers, balanced out their other kin to form one fluid power. Russé had said that he and his kin could share thoughts and emotions freely. The abrupt change had clearly taken a toll on all the Souls. Vara's extreme made more sense now. With that knowledge, Kole fiddled with how to navigate her.

"It won't work like this. The others are in my head." Kole began his plan. One thing Kole had gleaned thus far was, by Vara's reaction to the mere mention of Caradin, she didn't trust her kin. "It can never be just me and you. But I can cut them out... if you'll help me."

"How?"

Kole clenched his stinging fist. Blood dripped off his knuckles into the void. *"I know a spell. For it to work, I need your soulstone. It has the power I need to banish them."*

A moment of silence. The lights had dimmed to a relaxed glow.

"Will you help me?"

The great eyes blinked. A sparkle came from the depths of one of the pupils, and out floated a stone of four swirling colors. It bobbed at arm's length before Kole. At a distance, his skin picked up on the rotating temperatures from cool to warm and back again.

Sure, he still needed to convince Vara to agree to Aterus' proposal, but that was for another time. Preferably when there was no risk of being squeezed to death or threatened with floating in a void for eternity. Goal one: get Vara released without getting himself killed. If her wrath rained down on him after that... well, he'd figure out how to deal with it then. Kole hoped freeing her would sweep away her madness like it had with Caradin. *Only one way to find out.*

"When my soul detaches from me, I need you to return it. Then we can be together. You and me."

"Kole and Vara."

"Yes, Kole and Vara," he repeated. Here goes nothing.

Kole lifted his bloodied hand and seized the soulstone before his nerves could stop him. Though he knew exactly what came next, he'd never get used to the feeling as death came for him.

All went dark—darker than the void, darker than nothingness. His body fell away along with his senses. No eyes to see or skin to feel. Only his mind remained.

A fragment of each god's souls lay in Kole, twisted to his own. To release a Soul, he had to die momentarily. Once his life force left his body, the imprisoned god could take back their fragmented piece that lay in Kole and use it as a tether to break from their prison. After the god was released, the Soul needed to return the fragment back to Kole to revive him. If they refused, Kole's journey to death would be permanent, and with his demise came the end to any hope at releasing the other Souls.

Kole's fate lay in the hands of the gods each time. Not every Soul had been as willing to comply as Issira and Caradin. After a millennium trapped away from the world, the Souls wanted nothing more than to feel their freedom and regain full power. Sending their fragment back to Kole meant stunting their abilities.

Now Kole's fate rested in Vara's hands. Had he done enough?

Then, Vara's voice echoed around him. *"I feel the enemy in you. He's lurking."*

Try as he might, Kole had no way to respond.

"Poison. Betrayer. Liar." The words permeated.

Time meant nothing outside of his body. It could've only been seconds, yet it felt like an eternity. The longer he stayed in the void while Vara decided, the longer Kole's physical body lay cold. If she took too long, he wondered if he'd have a viable body to come back to.

He wished Caradin was with him. Or Felix and Vienna. He'd feel safe with them by his side. They'd find a way to convince Vara. To help him.

Russé.

CHAPTER 11

Just as Kole's hope waned, a force yanked him from the ether. He slammed back into his body. An immediate shudder took him. Stiff fingers and toes told him he had indeed been away from his flesh far too long. His heart throbbed slowly behind his ribs, battling to circulate his thickened blood.

Something warm — no, sweltering — pressed against his side. It burned. The temperature was too much. He shifted away from it, but a pair of hands pushed him back. *Russé?*

"He's awake." But the voice was not Russé's. Familiar, though. Female.

"Vienna?" Kole mumbled. The icy hold had conquered his throat, too, making him sound low and raspy.

"Happier to see her, I'm sure, but with all due respect, no mere mortal could've pulled you out of that one."

Kole finally pried his eyes open. White, glowing fur took up most of his vision. Caradin curled up next to him; his feet had reverted to the natural hooves of a stag rather than the claws he'd last seen the Soul don. The buck nudged Kole with his wet snout. The hot breath felt like fire on Kole's skin. He shouldered away from it, though he knew warmth was what he needed.

"Piper." Kole took in the demigod who sat across from him. Last he'd seen her, she was jumping off a rambler on a murder mission. "Been a while since the volcano," he managed. Violent shivers commandeered his body and sent his teeth chattering. He clenched his jaw in hopes to calm it to no avail.

Piper's face sat expressionless. Her auburn hair shone eerily bright against the dull grays of the land. The richness of those strands made his eyes burn. "It was harder to track you down than it was to kill Savairo."

The name sent a wave of hatred through Kole, warming him from the inside. "So he's dead then?" It felt so long since the warden had chased him through the Ashland Plains. Savairo had meant to capture him, but Piper intervened, allowing Kole and his friends to escape the erupting volcano. Things had gone so fast since then, with Zeal and the cultists, he'd never given a second thought to Savairo's fate.

"Yes, he's dead." Something about her tone betrayed her. A deeper meaning lay in her words, but Kole didn't know Piper well enough to determine what.

Kole shifted to his elbows and propped into a sitting position against Caradin's velvety stomach. "Vara? Did she—"

"Left you to die," Piper finished, then craned her neck upward.

Kole leaned back and followed her gaze. That black portal hovered above, unchanged. "Why did she...? She said she'd...." Exhaustion kept him from finishing. *I feel the enemy in you. He's lurking.* That's what Vara had said before refusing him.

Piper returned her stare to him as he recovered. "I was hoping *you* knew why."

Aterus, he wanted to say. Vara had rejected him and left him to die because she sensed her jailer within Kole. The cold and exhaustion made him careless, and he felt himself frowning.

"You *do* know," she said plainly.

Kole sucked in a breath, prepared to lie, then decided against it. *No use now.* "She doesn't like my... connections."

"Neither do I." This time a growl lay under her voice.

"How did you get out here?" Kole blurted before she could cling to the issue.

"Same as you. Through the moonbeam. Don't change the subject."

Kole perked up. "But the moonstone was only good for one charge. How did you get another so soon?"

Her mouth opened. Closed. Thoughts ticked behind those calculating honey-colored eyes. Kole wished he could read her as well as she seemed to read him. She took a long breath, then looked to her wrist, where her own timepiece rested. "How long has it been since you passed through the Black Wall?"

A wave of anxiety bubbled in his gut. How long had he been knocked out? By the hands on his watch, he'd lost ten minutes since entering Vara's domain. "A little over two hours. We don't have much time before Jax opens a way back."

"Kole...." Piper chewed her bottom lip. A stranger could've picked up on her apprehension. It so clearly marked every muscle in her face. "You've been gone for weeks."

He folded his arms. "What are you talking about?"

"Everyone thought you were lost or dead. I came here to bring you back."

Kole tapped his nail on the watch. Had he broken it when he fell? "It's not possible."

"Apparently it is."

"But it doesn't make sense. Even if this thing stopped working, I'm not hungry. A little thirsty, sure." She passed him her waterskin, but he knocked it away. "I haven't slept. No one can go that long without that stuff."

Her mouth scrunched to the side, mulling it over. "It seems time works differently here. Either because of the Black Wall," Piper pointed a finger to the portal, "or her."

It was his turn to think it through. Weeks, she'd said. He had difficulty wrapping his head around it. "Say it is true. That would mean...." Whatever warmth had returned to him drained once again. "The battle! Vienna! Orla shot her." Kole thrust himself at Piper and clung to her arm. "What happened? Please tell me she's safe. And Felix! He went missing after the building collapsed."

Piper's muscles tensed under his grip as if she fought the urge to pull from his touch. "Vienna is alive." Her voice came low. Eyes held sternly on him. "Listen, I — there are things you should know. This isn't the ideal place to tell you, but if I keep it from you, I'd be making the same mistakes Russé did."

The knot in Kole's belly grew into a cannonball. The worst thoughts skipped through his mind; the Black Wall overrunning Zeal, his friends burning in agony, the war lost. "Tell me what happened."

"Zeal won the battle." Her hands braced his as she spoke. "You know better than anyone, survival comes at a cost."

Cost. That meant life. She already said Vienna lived so that meant....

"Who died?" he asked, though the answer burned bright in his head before she said it.

"Felix sacrificed himself to kill Orla."

"No."

"If it hadn't been for him and his Kayetan, the battle would've taken us all. It was the only way."

A numbness overcame Kole, as if winter's bite had seized his flesh. "It can't be...." he began, but stopped himself. It absolutely *could* be. The way Felix and Vienna had viewed the war — even Kole's role in everything — they'd always been clear where they stood. Nothing would get in the way of saving Ohr. They'd both give their lives fighting if it came down to it. The worst part was Kole hadn't even been there. He'd abandoned the siblings to fight Orla on their own. Why had he listened to Vienna? *I shouldn't have come here. I should've taken Orla down first. Protected them.*

A wave of overbearing calmness—not of his own—eased through him. Kole pushed away from Caradin. The stag may have meant well, but the Soul's interference only angered him further. Kole shoved Caradin's presence from his thoughts and barricaded him out as he rose to his feet and stormed to the edge of the island.

He wanted to rush back to the wall and return to the city. Every fiber in his body willed him to forget Vara and start running for Zeal. But what good would it do? It may seem like hours to Kole, yet Felix's death had been sealed for weeks... his body cold in some grave.

"Tell me how it happened."

Footsteps padded up behind him, but he refused to turn.

"Orla had consumed your blood. It gave her the power to command the wall itself. Not just move it. She summoned the flames to her—siphoned them off from the wall—and began attacking the city. With your blood in her, she was too much for even me." Her voice came closer. She must've stood right at his back. "Still, I was going to try, but Vienna had been badly wounded. She was fading."

"Orla shot her right before I left," Kole added. The muscles of his face twitched. He expected the tears to come. They didn't.

"We tried to distract Orla and use the moonbeam cannons against her. Our last hope. It wasn't enough. Felix, he—" Another step closer. A phantom feeling touched his arm as if Piper hovered her hand there, wondering if she should comfort him. "Vienna was his priority. I stayed and healed her at his command. He played the bait while his Kayetan made the killing blow."

"Bait?"

"Orla got him with the fire."

Touched by the flame. Kole held his hands open. The burn scars over his arms stood out as angry reminders of his own encounter with the Black Wall. The heat. The unbearable scorching of flesh. *That* was Felix's last moment?

Kole let his hands fall. Balled them into fists. The wall had taken everything from him; his home, his body; his friends....

My friend.

A sudden spark of hope birthed in him. "He's not gone. Not fully."

"Kole...."

He turned to Piper. "Felix doesn't have to be gone." His smile must've caught her off guard because she flinched away. "My *connections* can save him."

"You mean Aterus?" She said his name like a curse.

"I made that deal. Vienna and Felix didn't care for it, and neither do you or any of the Souls, I know, but he's *helping* me. Aterus has promised me my life back and more. I might be able to negotiate Felix into it, too."

Piper's eyes focused hard on him as if her stare cut straight to his thoughts. "What have you negotiated?"

"Niko," Kole called. At his voice, his ghostly friend appeared beside him. "I know you can't see him, but—"

"I can see him," Piper cut him off. She stepped away, hand over the dagger on her belt.

"He won't hurt you. He's just a ghost." Despite that fact, Kole found his hands up in a protective barrier in front of the specter. "This is Niko. He was a refugee in Solpate with me. We've known each other since we were kids." Kole took his friend in, who stared just as intently at Piper—two vipers ready to strike the other down. Niko had never acted this way before, even when they had faced down the Black Wall. His chest puffed out, and the muscles of his jaw rolled under the skin like he was grinding his teeth. Hostile, if Kole had to pinpoint it. "H-he died along with the rest of the orphans when the Black Wall burned our camp. I couldn't save him then."

"And how did he come to be here with you now?" Piper asked.

"Your father and I made a deal. I get him the Souls, and he gives me Niko and my body back. If he can bring *him* back, there's hope for Felix, too."

Her face scrunched in disgust. "You're a fool, Kole. A naive fool. You can't negotiate the dead."

Niko floated closer to Kole. Whatever antagonistic nature he'd held before subsided. "Is this a friend? She doesn't seem so nice." That old tremble in his voice returned.

"Forced allies mostly," Kole answered through his teeth before turning on Piper. "It seems like I can. And why wouldn't I? It may not be... *natural*, but neither is the Black Wall. It's taken everything from me."

Her features softened a fraction. "You're not a fool for wanting them back; you're a fool for believing it can be done."

Kole shook his head. "Of course, not now." She clearly didn't understand the deal like he did. "When Aterus has the *combined* powers of all his kin, he'll be able to do anything."

"You've been deceived." Piper's eyes flickered to Niko and back again. "He's got you under his thumb and you can't even tell, can you?"

"What are you talking about?"

"Even if my... *father*," she spat the word as if it were poison on her tongue, "even if he possessed every power in the world, he couldn't do that—*wouldn't*."

Was Piper hinting Aterus would turn on him? The mere thought sent a hot rage through him. His fingernails pressed hard into the skin of his palms as he clenched his fists. "I'm the one making the deals. I'm the one Aterus must please if he wants his power."

"The dead cannot be brought back. It simply isn't possible. It's why he has kept my mother alive all this time. If she fades, she's gone forever."

Evangeline. He'd heard about her before. It seemed like forever ago when Russé had told him how Aterus had fallen in love with one of his own creations: a human. That relationship was the catalyst for the downfall of Ohr.

"It's the spirit." Piper tapped a finger over her heart. "Once it leaves your body—*true death*—there's no returning it. Sure, the body can be remade and transformed, down to the smallest birthmark. I have no doubt Aterus could erase those." She nodded to Kole's scars. "And he can bring your dead friend's physical form back, but it'd be a hollow chunk of flesh, not the real thing."

Kole tried his best to follow her words. "He'd be making a copy?"

"Yes."

"But that copy is still Niko."

"That copy will have a brand-new spirit. No memories of you. No personality. Like a newborn freshly birthed from the womb. It'll look like your friend, but it will never truly be him."

Kole had witnessed firsthand his own spirit leaving his body during each ritual to release the Souls. Not a true death but a partial one. Kole remained himself afterward. Niko, on the other hand, had perished in the Black Wall months ago. One thing seemed off, though. "But Niko's spirit is right here." Niko nodded beside him. "Aterus must have knowledge you don't."

"Why can't you see it?" Piper seethed.

"I don't need a lecture!" Kole snapped.

Niko placed his spectral hand on Kole's shoulder. Though meant to comfort, it only made him feel claustrophobic, so he shrugged away.

Piper watched him. Her silence only infuriated him.

"I don't think she'll ever be able to understand," Niko whispered in his ear. "She hasn't lost like we have. It's not her fault."

Those amber eyes of Piper's burned on Niko so intensely, Kole half expected the specter to burst into flames.

"If she's right about this place, though," Niko continued, "we are wasting more time than we think. You need to try again with Vara."

"Venom." Piper's head tilted to the side. Something behind her eyes lit up, and she stepped closer. "Poison."

The way she started at him made Kole retreat, but the ledge of the island came up quick, halting him. "What are you doing?"

"If you won't get rid of the parasite, I will." Piper still came for him, firm confident strides.

The way she spoke prickled the skin on Kole's neck. He let the barrier between him and Caradin's thoughts fall away, then summoned the stag. In an instant, the Soul scrambled to his feet and took a place next to Kole's side, head tilted down with the massive antlers pointed for Piper. One word from Kole and the beast would charge.

The threat of the stag did little to deter her. "Once you have what you want, you'll toss him aside like the rest of them. Like me. I won't let you have him."

But Piper's gaze focused past Kole. He glanced over his shoulder to Niko, who hovered higher in the air, an unnatural sneer hanging from his mouth.

"For Soul's sake, Piper. What are you talking about?"

"Your *friend*. Niko, is it?" Piper slowed when she got within arm's reach of the points of Caradin's crown of antlers. "Do you have a last name? Siblings?"

"They're dead," Niko said stoically.

"Can you name them?"

"'Course, he can," Kole defended. "What are you getting at?"

"Let him speak, then." She pressed her stomach against Caradin's antlers as if she dared Kole to signal the command.

"She's lost it." Niko's ghostly form shook. Whatever bravery he'd summoned earlier when he'd boldly scouted the land had vanished. His eyes held wide like the day he and Kole had encountered the Black Wall.

"Don't worry, Caradin will keep us safe," Kole assured him with a whisper. "Plus you're dead, remember? The only one in any real danger is me."

"Kole...." Though her stance remained tense, her voice held a tenderness... and a warning. "Listen to me. I know how much you want to believe it's true, but Niko can't be returned to you. Not even his ghost. It's Aterus who stands beside you, not your friend."

"What?" Kole flinched at the accusation.

"Think about it." Piper gripped the antlers like prison bars. "He appeared after your agreement. Aterus summoned him."

"Of course he did. That was the deal!"

"How do you know it's truly him?"

"Stop. Just stop." Kole's face warmed with his rising anger. "You don't know what you're talking about. What is it about the Souls? You're only half god and still you act like Russé." No matter how much he explained himself to anyone, no one seemed to understand. *They don't want to. That* was the purest truth. Because in their heads Aterus was the devil, and how could Kole ever choose to align with him? "I know Niko better than anyone in my entire life, and you think I can't recognize him? If you *must* know, yes, we've talked about our past. Things no one other than my best friend would know about." Kole sent his anger into Caradin, who in turn pushed his antlers harder into Piper. Not enough to injure, but hard enough to get her to back off. "You're just like them. Trying to manipulate me. I know the game all too well, now. It won't work."

"But it *is* working, Kole. Except it's not coming from me. Aterus is in your head. He can read your thoughts, your memories. What better way to play the role of your best friend?"

"Hasn't he been through enough?" Niko shouted. "Leave him alone."

The boiling rage made Kole's body shake. "If this is your play, then just leave. I trust Niko more than I could ever trust you," he fumed. The encounter with Vara had left him weak. All this yelling drained him. He had to get his heart rate and temperature under control, or he'd risk passing out and losing more precious time.

"If you don't leave, Caradin will make you." One thought sent to the Soul and the stag dragged his claws over the rock, bracing to charge.

"Why not put it to the test then? If you're so sure."

"He doesn't have to prove anything to you," Niko snapped.

Piper finally released her hold on the stag's crown. Two steps back. "I am on your side, Kole, even if you can't see it. When I spoke with Russé and the other Souls, I told them I would support whatever path you choose. I stand by that. But that path needs to be free of corruption. It's time for you to be in full control of yourself."

Flashbacks rushed through Kole's head; all the times when Russé had made decisions for him, lied to him, led him along with half-truths.

Aterus was a Soul with a trail of deceit in his own past as well. *They're all the same.* Kole had said it himself. Maybe Piper was right. *There's no shame in checking.* If nothing else, he could prove her wrong.

"Get back." With the last of his strength, Kole pulled himself onto the stag's back. Caradin cautiously retreated from Piper and Niko, head still low and ready to gouge.

"Kole?" Niko's spirit began to float after them. "What are you doing?"

"Both of you get back," Kole warned. His limbs shook so violently, he could barely keep mounted. Wings flourished up from the animal's back, creating a barrier on either side of him should he pass out.

Piper let her defenses down. She stood, hands at her sides with open palms. "Block him out. Block everything and everyone out. Let it be just you. Then ask something only the both of you would know."

"You can't really be doing this." The pain on Niko's face broke Kole's heart. "You believe her over me?"

"I don't know what to believe anymore. But whatever is happening, I'm going to get to the bottom of it myself." Muffled voices reached Kole's ears, Niko saying something, but he had already closed his eyes and begun to isolate his thoughts. He tore Caradin's closely intertwined aura from his and sent him behind the door in his mind. Locked it. The other Souls he'd long locked out before, but he checked again. Aterus' gateway had stood open since they'd made their deal. That, too, he slammed.

Totally alone. Silence. Then he opened his eyes and set them on the specter. He knew exactly what to ask.

"How many anchored ramblers made up the northern camp?"

CHAPTER 12

"Do you understand?" Vienna knelt beside the map she'd drawn out in the dirt, her finger lingering above the spot she'd deemed their base. Felix's shadow tilted his head. Unsure if that meant a yes or no, Vienna sighed and rolled up to her feet. "You know what? It doesn't matter. Just lure them out. I'll take care of the rest." She wiped her hands clean on her trousers, mumbling, "You never have trouble finding me every night regardless."

She still wondered about that. Their first encounter had been at the edge of the crystal trees. For a while, she'd wait there each night until the shadow arrived, but after a few cases of poor time management, Felix had sought her out in the city. Since then, Vienna hadn't bothered to travel to the forest, instead having Felix come to her, like she had tonight. *For the better.* Her strict schedule made her predictable. Probably how the raiders knew where she'd be and when. She shivered thinking how long the bandits might've been watching her.

"Let's move." Vienna erased her haphazard map with a boot, snuffed out the candle she'd set on the floor, then headed for the door.

Wary of unwelcomed guests following her back to her more permanent location at Jax's lab, she'd opted to hole up in a half-crumbled building since the raid last night. The wreckage here hinted at a family home. A chest of toys lay in one corner of the main room alongside a reasonably padded couch, where Vienna had slept with a blanket she'd managed to tug from the debris. Like all who had abandoned Zeal since the cult's attack, this family only took what they could carry.

An archway led to the other side of the house, but the ceiling had caved in leaving it blocked off. *No chance to scavenge food.* Vienna's stomach growled at the mention.

"The lab first."

All her supplies were stowed there, including the tools she'd need to fix the cannon. So much to do in the four hours leading up to midnight:

steal back the wheeler, load up another moonstone trunk, and make it back to the Black Wall to fix the cannon. A hefty goal. One she had to meet.

Vienna cracked open the door leading to the street. "We'll make it to Kole. We're not going to leave him stranded."

Something came up behind her and tickled her ear. She paused. Wind? No. More like a vibration. It had slid in her ear. She looked over her shoulder at Felix's swaying shadow.

The sound. *That* sound. A hiss—no, a whisper. Rewinding the sound in her mind's ear, she played it back.

Kole. Felix had said Kole.

She'd heard of this before from a Kayetan—*one* Kayetan in particular. One that had the unique ability to speak.

Butterflies stirred in her stomach. "Felix?" she posed.

The shadow merely hovered.

"That was you, wasn't it? Can you... speak?" She waited; teeth clenched for a response. Maybe not a sentence, but a word or phrase. Hell, any sound other than the typical Kayetan shriek would be enough for her.

Seconds passed. Nothing.

Until....

"Kooooole." The name came long and soft in the small room.

"You can talk." Trying too, at least. Her mouth tugged open in a smile; an expression she'd gone so long without, it strained her muscles to hold it longer than a moment. Hope warmed her at the thought of potentially speaking to her brother again, whatever that might look like. Sure, the demon would never be Felix, but still... she'd take a piece of him over nothing. "Yes, we're going to get Kole back. Help me?"

The Kayetan slipped through the cracked door in answer, Vienna quick on the shadow's trail.

Not a ten-minute walk from her temporary hideout and they were closing in on her former abode.

All stood quiet.

The eastern horizon glowed a silvery white with the aura of the crystal trees a few miles away. A few moonstone lanterns, unharmed by the battle, lit the road in spots. Vienna evaded their light and stuck to the darkened alleyways to avoid detection from the looters she'd seen last night.

A quick check ensuring an empty path, then she hurried across the cobbled road. Felix matched her pace up the crumbled steps to the entrance, where she halted.

The door hung open at an angle. "Not how I left you."

Splinters littered the ground at her feet. The hinge had been ripped away from the bottom and a large indent marked the middle of the wood. Bashed in.

Looters. No doubt the very same who'd vandalized the cannon.

"Shit." At her curse, the Kayetan slithered in through the gap and disappeared. "Felix," she said in a harsh whisper, "get back here."

The damage could be fresh. No real way of telling. So, Vienna backed off and retreated to the side of the building. Her best bet at getting in was through the window to her room on the southern wall. Careful steps kept her approach silent. The glass stood dark. A good sign. At least no one currently occupied the space.

Vienna nudged the pane open. It stuck halfway up. Hard as she tried, it refused to budge. She weighed the small gap, wondering if her hips would fit. Worth a shot. A pull on the sill gave her enough momentum to lift her upper body through the opening. Just as she guessed, her hip bone caught on the edge. Thankfully the room was indeed empty, so she braced her hands on either side of the window for leverage and wiggled inside. She tensed as she landed on the wooden floor with a thump.

Still silent. She let out a breath of relief. As she lifted to her feet, a silhouette in the doorway to the hall caught her eye. Her heart skipped a beat before she recognized the familiar outline.

"Oh, for Soul's sake. You have to stop popping up like that." Vienna dropped her hand from the blade hung on her belt.

Felix's relaxed posture told her the building was clear.

"Gone, huh?" The quiet should've been a dead giveaway. The looters hadn't been exactly stealthy while ransacking the cannon. Better to err on caution.

Vienna moved to the bedside table for her lantern only to find a ring of dust where it had once sat. They'd been here. Unease stirred her stomach. What where the odds of stealing a single lantern? *Pretty low.*

She may be without a lantern but not without any light. Vienna retrieved the flint and starter from her pouch and scrounged around the room for items to use as a makeshift torch. The curtain would work nicely. A few sawing motions from her dagger gave her a useable scrap. She settled on winding the material around a picture frame she'd pulled from the wall and stomped into pieces. A little oil from her flask and her torch sparked to life; the flame more intense than she'd anticipated.

Felix hissed and recoiled to the safety of the shadows behind the door.

"Yeah, sorry about that." She'd kept the light to a minimum thus far knowing Kayetans feared fire and sunlight. "You're going to have to deal with it. Not like I'm going to stab it at you."

The warm light exposed the room. More than her lantern turned up missing. The bedroom's vanity, which had once housed an array of bottled perfumes and creams, lay bare. The bed had been stripped of linens, and the armoire formerly stocked full of fine dresses stood vacant. Anything of value gone.

The work of a large group.

The pilfered frivolous items gave her no concern. She swiveled toward the chest at the far side of the room and let out a curse.

The lid had been flipped open and the lock lay in a twisted piece on the floor. She rushed over. Her throat plummeted to her stomach as the wood bottom stared up at her. Every one of Jax's tools gone.

Vienna slumped to her knees, mind numb. How was she supposed to get everything back? Were these even the same looters, or did the culprits belong to a different group? No way her original plan would work now. Even if Felix *could* distract them long enough to raid their camp, she had no idea which tools she needed to repair the cannon.

Jax had spare tools somewhere. Her workshop most likely, but that building probably would've been first on anyone's list to wipe clean. That place held scrap metal, oil, specialized trinkets, and all sorts of valuables. If worse came to worst, she could scrounge up tools around the city, but that could take days. Either way, one thing was for sure: the cannon would stay dark tonight.

The vital component, though, the moonstone trunks, Vienna desperately hoped remained untouched. They waited in a hidden safe only opened by the key in her pocket. Worry forced her to her feet, and she sped down the hall to check, Felix stalking after.

The door to Jax's room had been kicked open. Same as her area, the place had been cleaned out. Her lips pursed at the ajar closet door. She opened it wide until the handle hit the doorstop on the back wall. A shove and the knob snapped inside a small indent in the wainscot paneling.

Vienna dug the key from her pocket. Her trembling hands gave her a bit of trouble pushing the key in, but once she managed it, she turned the lock. A satisfying click echoed in the room. She yanked the door open along with the cut out in the wall. The trunks nestled in the hidden closet, untouched. *Now to get one of these guys out to the cannon.* She had to get that wheeler back.

A clang sounded. The hairs on Vienna's arms rose at the noise.

Distant, but close enough to concern her. She hurriedly relocked the closet. The thought of leaving all the trunks here only protected by a false wall triggered a jolt of anxiety. She'd wanted to relocate a few in case anyone else poked around in here again. But she had to have faith in Jax's hiding place. The fact that they still lay undiscovered after the first raid settled her nerves, if only a bit.

Voices carried in from the shattered window on the far side of the room just as she replaced the key in her pocket. Keeping low to the floor, she crawled over to the sill, then risked a peek over the lip.

The street lay dark. No sign of life. She craned her neck for a better glimpse down the road.

A glow reflected off a window a block down. The way the orb bobbed told her the source came from a handheld lantern. Raiders.

They continued her way. Vienna found it hard to tell how many made up their party by the lights and voices alone. *More than two, that's for sure.* Beside her, Felix stood in full display at the window.

"What are you doing? Get down." Her initial reaction was to yank his arm, but her hand passed straight through the shadow's body. Instead of following orders, Felix zoomed like a streak of smoke through the shattered glass of the window. "You've got to be kidding me," she muttered, rolling her eyes. The Kayetan proved just as rebellious as his former host.

Try as she might, squinting with her nose pressed on the glass, she lost sight of the shadow immediately after he flew out of the panes. A minute passed. Then two.

The voices came closer. The formerly muffled words came clear every now and then: mundane stuff. Then a single word perked her ears.

Moonstone.

She'd heard it clearly. Panic pinched her. Did they mean to come here looking for moonstone? Did they know of Jax's hidden safe?

Before she could think to react, four people stepped into the light at the edge of her vision. Two buildings down walked three men and a woman. They spread out as they went, quickly peering through each abandoned building they passed. Either looking for something — valuables — or checking the area was clear. Whichever, Vienna's spot would likely be next.

The raiders wore a hodgepodge of ill-fitting clothes layered with thick pieces of leather over their chests. Poorly made armor. Each held a long metal rod in their hand that reminded Vienna of a cattle prod.

Only one building away from her position and with Felix yet to return, Vienna searched for a place to hide. The couch or bed would suffice, but she wanted a clear view of the window. Off in the corner stood a floor-length mirror. Perfect. She hurried over and squeezed behind it, leaving one eye beyond the elaborate wood frame to spy the raiders.

Footsteps crunched by the sill. The light of a lantern swung into view. Just as Vienna had hoped, the light reflected off the mirror and illuminated a striking face. Slick, dark hair came to a blunt edge at the woman's sharp jaw.

"The more we comb the city, the more shit we find," the woman said. "Those bastards."

Someone grunted in response. "You think they'd give us all a cannon? Be real. The counsel wanted us suckling like wee pigs."

Her eyes scanned the room, passing the mirror without hesitation. "Ain't this that engineer's place? We got a lot of good stuff last night. Bet that witch is hiding more."

Vienna tightened her grip on the frame and instinctively slid her eyes to the wainscot wall. Any other time, she felt confident she could hold her own if a scuffle broke out, but four versus one... the odds weighed against her without back-up. Where was that Kayetan?

"We have all we need at the factory," one of her unseen comrades answered. "And the only thing I'm gonna lug around for you is one of those pretty moonstone chunks. So, unless you think Jax has a tree in there, we need to get to finding that girl."

The woman scoffed. "If it was just the tree we needed, we'd have a whole forest to harvest. We need the refined stuff." The raider withdrew her lantern and darkness reclaimed the room.

It took a moment for the floating spots to leave Vienna's vision and her eyes to reacclimate. Her ears remained sharp, picking up a bit more of their conversation as the group moved on to the next building.

"That damn woman took everything with Zeal's army, dismantled the rest. Gonna take a real smart one to reconstruct anything," said another male voice.

Vienna guessed the "damn woman" they spoke of was Jax again. By now, her eyes had adapted to the dark enough to feel her way back to the sill.

"That girl knows something," a man growled.

"Even if we don't find her tonight, she'll show herself soon enough. Whatever she's been doing out there by the wall... well, she'll need that wheeler if she wants to go back. Just a matter of time."

Vienna lost the conversation soon after as the raiders made their way for the next building. Alone again, she released the tension she'd been holding.

"Trying to bait me, huh?"

Knowing their intentions gave her an advantage. The raiders not only had a scout party looking for her in the city, but the wheeler no doubt had its own guard or two. If *she* was their target, it likely meant the vehicle was still intact. All the talk about parts had made her worry she'd find the thing in pieces, like they'd left the cannon.

Eavesdropping had confirmed her next move: the factory. Before she left, Vienna returned to the hidden closet and rolled two of the moonstone chunks under the bed. Anyone poking around would find exactly what they wanted and hopefully stop searching. Sacrificing a few seemed like a better idea than letting the raiders get the whole lot.

"Felix," she dared to call above a whisper.

She waited.

No response.

Apparently, Felix had his own plan.

CHAPTER 13

"How many anchored ramblers made up our camp?"

If Piper was right... if there was a chance Aterus was playing a role, then the question had to be so mundane it would be overlooked. Data and numbers. Niko swore by them. He took down notes and remembered them all.

Kole held his breath waiting for the answer. It had to be Niko. It had to. The things they'd talked about... the way his friend had comforted him these last weeks. Nothing could fake that. Ghost or not, he knew Niko's soul. This was him. But an edge of doubt gnawed him no matter how much he tried to shake it free.

"After all we've been through. You don't trust me?"

"Of course I do. I just need to hear it."

"Kole...." The pain in Niko's voice sent a dagger to Kole's heart.

"Answer it!" The shout sparked a dizzy spell. His vision blurred, but his anger snapped him back. "Please answer it. You know this."

Kole had to believe it was Niko—*his Niko*. As the stillness lingered, Kole and Niko locked in a stare, he wanted nothing more than to whisper the answer.

It had to be Niko. *Had to.* Because if it wasn't.... If it wasn't, Kole would have to face something more painful: Niko was gone forever.

And so was Felix.

"Say it!" Nothing could hold back the tremors. Even Kole's voice shook. "Please say it. Niko... come on, please."

Something flipped in Kole's brain. An alarm. A pressure built on the outskirts of his mind. He raced to the doorways between the Souls. All steadfast save for one. Aterus' gateway swelled inwards. The Soul pounded against Kole's brain, trying to force into his thoughts.

"No." Searing anger pulsed through his veins. Eyes leaden with tears, Kole collapsed against the fur of the stag's thick neck. "It can't be true. You promised me!"

Niko's form lowered to the ground. Once his feet touched down, the ghost shimmered, changing and morphing. No longer Kole's dark-haired, inquisitive friend. A new image formed. A tall, middle-aged man with salt-and-pepper hair stood where the ghost of his friend once had.

"Aterus," Kole breathed. Rage sent his heart pounding against his ribs. Fooled again. "We made a deal."

"A deal that you haven't been able to uphold," came a deep and gritty voice that sent chills over Kole's skin. "You've freed Caradin but failed to promise him to me." Aterus glanced toward the stag, who snorted at the mention of his name. "And your encounter with Vara is a failure." He took a step toward Kole.

Piper grabbed Kole by the arm and yanked him back, her stance protective, like a bear guarding its cub. He stumbled but caught the back of her shirt to steady himself.

"Stay back," she warned her father.

Aterus' form appeared different than Niko had. No longer sheer and faded, but solid. Rock and sand shifted underfoot. The breeze moved the man's hair. Kole had only ever seen the Soul in his mind and thoughts. Only ever an image. Here, Aterus stood as real as Piper in Kole's eyes. Part of Kole's head formed questions of how, but the reality of the danger swept them aside.

The Soul's glare trained past Piper's shoulder to Kole. "I knew I had to keep an eye on you. How easily your mind is swayed." Still, Aterus pressed toward them.

Caradin lunged into the space before Aterus. The animal's body shimmered. The fur rippled head to toe, and the stag's shape enlarged to a bull with curling horns thicker than Kole's legs.

Aterus pursued without a flinch.

"You lied to me," Kole shouted over Piper's shoulder. With every step Aterus advanced, they took their own in retreat.

"I made you hopeful — gave you purpose."

"False hope," Kole snapped.

"You have been quite happy with my version these last few weeks. Built on the memories in your head, I have remade him."

It was true, Kole hadn't suspected a thing until Piper had made her accusations. Aterus had made a convincing version of his friend, but.... "It's a copy. Not the real thing. It's not *him*."

"Would you rather have the alternative?" Aterus cocked his head. "Your friend forever gone from this world."

A ghost. That was what Aterus offered. A shell of what his friend once was. Niko would forever be frozen in time as a teenage boy. Never growing or changing. If Kole wanted to look back on his friend, he could do it himself. This version—Aterus' version—violated Niko's memory. And it all became clear. "Piper's right. You can't bring him back, can you?"

The Soul's silence said more than any words could. An ache spread in Kole's chest. Old wounds he had nurtured these last few months, shoddily sewn together so he could function, unraveled at the seams. His heart could no longer take the abuse. Niko was lost forever. Now Felix, too.

"How could you?" Kole growled.

Aterus stopped his approach right at the tips of Caradin's fearsome horns. "We all want something. Some of us are willing to do anything it takes to get it. Even if that means using others in the process. You are a child, Kole. You know nothing of the world, or the gods. And you never will. But you have something I need. And I will have it."

Though Aterus knew the location of the Souls' prisons, he had no means to free them. Only *that* leverage could get the Gray Soul access to the power he wanted. He needed Kole for that. Everyone needed Kole for that....

"I will never help you," Kole hissed.

"Maybe not willingly." Aterus lifted a hand toward the raging bull and wrapped his hand around a horn. Caradin roared. The great beast sunk to his knees.

"Stop it!" Kole sprung to help Caradin. An arm stopped him in his tracks.

Piper turned on him, a hellish fire in her amber eyes. She held him at arm's length strong as a vice. "Brace yourself." Faster than he could blink, a glint of silver shown in her hand. The sharp edge of her blade pressed down on Kole's exposed shoulder.

"What the hell are you doing?" First Aterus, now Piper. Kole struggled against her iron grip. "Let go."

Piper pulled him close, nose to nose. Her breath held the scent of cinder as she spoke. "If there's one thing you can trust, it's that you are too weak to take him on alone." With one swift pull, the blade sliced his skin.

Kole cried out at the fresh heat trickling down his arm. But the shock of Piper bringing the blood-stained steel to her lips made him forget his pain. She licked the blade, then tossed it aside. His eyes lingered on her in horror. *Blood sorcery.* Kole cupped his wound.

A thud shook the ground. Behind them, Caradin had fallen. The bull lay prone, muscles twitching in agony. Aterus had kept him in some strange hold.

The Soul stepped over the body. "You can't refuse me. My blood runs in your veins."

Kole sent a glare to Piper. She'd been the one who'd forced the Soul's blood down his throat back in Grayfall, linking their minds. For all the trouble she'd caused, Piper now had the audacity to ask him for trust.

She met his scowl. Instead of a forlorn expression, her eyes burned bright with the effects of his blood. A rabid wolf on the prowl. Piper grabbed Kole's hand then turned to face her father.

"Your mind is mine should I wish it." Once the words had left his mouth, Aterus sneered at Piper. "Grasping a loose thread." He tutted. "She can't help you, Kole. Neither can Caradin."

A sudden pressure struck the base of Kole's skull. He stumbled back, but Piper kept him firmly on his feet. That place in his mind — the spot at the end of the road where Aterus' door stood — ached.

"You will hold up our deal because I will make you."

Just as Kole summoned his strength to barricade the portal, Aterus bashed through. The door exploded. The Gray Soul forced his way into Kole's head. Every thought and feeling. Every memory. Private, precious, and terrible ones alike. Aterus claimed them all.

The unbearable anguish sent a darkness over Kole's vision. With a scream, he crumbled toward the floor. Arms caught him.

Piper.

She held him up. Her voice came harsh in his ear, but the words ricocheted off in the midst of his agony.

The fingers of Aterus' consciousness raked over his brain. The touch made his muscles twitch and spasm. The Soul gradually claimed Kole's body.

Hands first. They clenched and flexed despite Kole never commanding them to. The chill from his fingers ran up both arms and flooded his chest. A fear welled up inside him. If Aterus took his body, Kole might never get it back — forced to play spectator from the dark depths of his own mind.

Little by little, Kole fell away. His attempts to push back the Soul proved meager.

From the very moment he was thrust into this mess with the Souls — with saving the world — it had been fight after fight, struggle after struggle. And for what? The tiniest step toward saving Ohr? Was all the death and sorrow he'd endured worth that miniscule victory, which had always seemed so insignificant and short lived? Kole stood at the heart of every one of those battles. Battles he stood no chance against. Him versus a god. How could he possibly win? Not without Russé. Even Caradin, Kole's only backup, lay incapacitated on the ground.

So, he stopped fighting.

He let go.

What was the point?

He'd never have Niko back. Never see Felix again.

With his surrender, Aterus worked fast. Kole's muscles no longer moved at his instruction. His mind quieted as he retreated to a hidden corner and cowered, watching the inevitable conquering of his brain.

One last piece of Kole's mind remained untouched. Aterus concentrated on it, yet the piece did not bend to his will. The Soul's frustration flared in Kole's body.

From his corner, Kole probed the area. Sure enough, a strong force enveloped it. But Kole had surrendered. Every defense gone. So how could it be?

Unless it came from someone else.

Aterus forced Kole's eyes open to the sight of Piper's face, scrunched in fury. Her hands gripped either side of his face, though he could no longer feel the touch on his skin. *She* was the force in his brain keeping Aterus from full control.

"Is this really what you want?" Her brows furrowed deeper as she spoke. "If it truly is, I will let you go."

With his mouth and voice no longer his, Kole had no way of answering her.

But his voice came with a threat from Aterus. "Release him or you will never see your mother again."

Piper ignored the words. She seemed to understand Kole no longer had hold of his body, because she answered in a strained tone, "You fight for those who are gone. You fight for others in danger, and you've fought because someone told you you should. What about you, Kole? When will you start fighting for yourself?"

For himself? Isn't that what he'd been doing when he'd turned from Russé and pursued a deal with Aterus? He'd been taking back control. Hadn't he?

"You are important to this world, with or without your links to the Souls. You, Kole. You." Piper winced as if a punch had caught her in the gut. It took her a breath to recover. "I can't hold against him much longer," she said through clenched teeth. Drinking Kole's blood had given Piper the boost in power she needed to fend against Aterus, but it only lasted so long. He was draining her, and it showed all over her face.

Sweat beaded on her temples. Muscles twitched beneath her reddened skin.

It was there, while gazing upon Piper, that her words struck him. His whole life, someone had told him what to do—which path to take. Sure, he'd rebelled and tested his limits every now and then, but he'd lived by someone else's rules. To please.

Yet here, in this moment, Piper fought for *him*. She had her own motives—ones that aligned with his own and others that didn't. Even still, she gave him control.

World at stake or not, she allowed him to *choose*.

Aterus' deal... Kole had made it in an act of rebellion. Retaliation. What he thought was taking back power over his destiny ended up thrusting him into another conniving cycle. The Souls kept pitting him against the others.

That cycle had to end.

Kole crawled from the small space of his mind and flung himself at the stronghold Piper kept. She allowed him entry. He felt her relief wash over him through their mind-link.

"*We have one chance,*" Piper's voice sounded in his thoughts. "*His mind is here, but not his body. It's a weaker connection.*"

"*What do you have in mind?*" Kole asked.

"*Push him back out the way he came. Your blood in my system gives me a temporary link to all the Souls' strength. It may be enough to force him out. If we get him past the threshold, you are the one who must close it. It's your mind, not mine.*"

Use the Souls against Aterus. A thought sparked.

"*Be ready to drive him out,*" Kole instructed. "*I'll tell you when.*" Before she could answer him, Kole withdrew into a calm, focused state how Russé had trained him. He knew his mind better than ever since embarking on his quest to release the Souls. If he hoped to pull this off, he'd need to trust in that knowledge. So many pathways. He hastily reviewed them before he embarked.

Six doors served as direct connections from his head to each of the gods. They all lay locked, but Kole was the key. Opening them one by one would take too long. Aterus would catch on. It left Kole with no other option than to try something he'd never attempted before.

"*Now,*" Kole ordered Piper.

She burst out from their small haven and fought back against her father. The blood she drank must've settled in her system because that first initial shove not only gave Kole the distraction he needed to sneak out undetected, but the feeling in his fingers returned, no longer under Aterus' control.

Kole pressed on until the road at the center of his mind split. He'd take not one path, but all. *All at once.* Balling his newly restored fingers, Kole released and let his consciousness spread.

The initial move proved difficult. He stretched thin like dough— pulled in each direction until he finally divided and shot down the paths to the Souls. The barricades easily fell away at his order, exposing the doors to him.

He called to them.

"Russé. Issira. Obell. Caradin. Vara. Braxus."

The seams around the doors glowed as they answered his call. He grabbed the knobs, then unleashed their light onto his mind.

Their energy poured in. Kole harnessed each one, careful not to allow any to roam unchecked in his mind like Aterus. He'd done something similar once before, and it almost ended in his death. Now he knew what to expect.

"Kole!" Piper's warning echoed a split second before a pressure shoved back against the Souls' doors, trying to close off the connection.

Aterus had caught on to their ruse.

But it was too late.

Kole harnessed his allies' energy and forced them onto the intruder, entangling him. The moment they all crashed into Aterus, working as a combined front, a shudder ran down Kole's limbs. Aterus' grasp on him waned. Though the fingers of his power scratched and clawed to remain in Kole's head, the Gray Soul's hold slipped.

Now Piper joined in. She navigated her way around the edges of her father's presence and shrunk him down along with Kole and the other gods.

Aterus trembled with rage.

But with every passing second, Kole leveraged Aterus from his control. His skin prickled as the nerves reawakened. Soon Kole had full power over his body and mind.

Just when Kole thought the Gray Soul would fight back, the god did something that shocked him: Aterus fled.

The move sparked Kole's hunting instincts. He stalked his prey. If the god truly sought to flee, Kole knew where he'd run: the same door he'd slithered in from.

Kole raced to it, cut the Soul off, then slammed it shut before the Gray Soul escaped.

"What are you doing? Push him out. Be rid of him." Piper's voice resounded in his head.

The moment that portal between them stood blocked, Aterus' rage shifted into panic.

A cornered animal. Kole thought back to all the rabbits he'd hunted back in Solpate Forest. Fear radiated from his prey just like those wide-eyed creatures. With the power of the Souls at his command, something awoke in the depths of Kole's core. He didn't want a chase. Kole wanted pain. Torture. Death. Craved it. He could end it all now — Aterus' hold on him *and* Ohr. A final shove and Kole hurled all his strength at the corruption.

An agonizing cry pierced the air on impact. Not within Kole's head, but a real voice. One that drilled into his eardrums.

Kole opened his eyes.

Piper lay on the floor writhing. "Stop it!" Her hands gripped her head, pulling and ripping at her auburn hair.

"Piper?" Kole knelt. The moment his focus shifted from his onslaught, her thrashing ceased. Still, her breaths came heavy. In the back of his head, Aterus' presence lingered, slithering around at the distraction, looking for a way out. Kole pinned him in place in case the god tried anything.

Piper placed a hand on Kole's arm, a desperate plea in her eyes. "You can't kill him."

"We have to do it now. You felt him. He's weak in this state. All of us together... we can do it here and now."

"It would destroy everything." Blood trickled from her nose. She smeared it with her sleeve. "Let him go. Banish him from your mind. It'll keep you safe."

Kole stared at Piper. She lay there prone but not from any attack from her father. It had come when Kole had targeted Aterus. *Father and daughter.* The two shared a familial link. Could the bond go further than that? Attacking Aterus in this way meant harming Piper, too?

"Let him go," Piper pleaded.

The truth would have to wait. Kole could only sustain this borrowed energy for so long. It already exhausted him. He closed his eyes and withdrew back into his mind to find Aterus squirming in his clutch. *Banishment it is.*

Kole called on his power and rammed Aterus into the portal through which he'd come. After every last whisper of the Gray Soul's presence passed the threshold, Kole focused on the door. Closing it — barricading it—wouldn't suffice. Aterus had weaseled his way in before. No doubt he could slip through any crack.

Annihilation. The link had to be destroyed.

"We are here with you." A familiar voice, deep and soft, sounded in his head. Though it had been weeks since Kole had last spoken with his old mentor, no animosity laced the Green Soul's words.

"Russé," Kole answered. *"I know you warned me against leeching from your powers, but—"*

"Use us as you will." This time a chorus of voices joined Russé. Kole could pinpoint most of them; the melodic whine of Issira, the gravelly tone of Obell, and the calm whisper of Caradin. Vara was there, too. And the last belonged to the Soul he had yet to meet, Braxus.

Once they submitted themselves to Kole's use, he found the wildness of the energy he'd siphoned from them turned docile—malleable to his will. Kole gathered their energy and concentrated it on the perimeter of Aterus' portal.

An initial pain made Kole shudder. It seared his brain as if a hot branding spike impaled his skull. Stupid of him to think the act would be painless when he sought to eradicate a piece of his consciousness. Still, he braced himself and pushed onward.

Arms wrapped around his torso and slowly guided him to the ground. His eyes may be closed, but he knew Piper stood alongside him, protecting his body the best she could while he worked.

And it *did* work.

Gradually, that door shrank.

"You're doing great. Finish it," Piper said in his ear.

Kole took a great breath then tensed his core, ready for the final blow. The last of his energy hit the center point and blasted it away.

It was done.

Relief drowned him like a frenzied tidal wave. A sudden lightness filled his being. Kole probed the new, vacant spot in his brain. Was Aterus truly gone? He flicked his eyes open to be sure. Piper still clung to him. And beyond, Caradin roused, clambering to his feet.

No sign of Aterus.

Kole released the tightness in his body. For a brief moment, he allowed himself to revel in his victory. He'd done it. Aterus may not be gone, but the Soul was gone from *him*.

Now the threat had passed, Kole sent Russé and the others back through their own doors. This time, though, when they crossed over, he left their portals unbarricaded.

CHAPTER 14

Vienna crouched behind a pile of rubble in the alley across from the old cannon factory. She'd been in there before with Kole. Though the visit had been quick and in the midst of the battle, she vaguely remembered the layout. Lucky for her, glass windows dominated the side of the building, granting her a clear view of the interior.

Dozens of moonstone lanterns hung throughout the building, even a few floors up, and just as many people lingered inside. Not on guard but working. Some gathered around tables, hunched over what she guessed was metal scraps, others towed parts up and down the staircases. *Raiders?* Except they wore no mismatched armor like the group she'd encountered earlier. They looked more like Jax-type of people — engineers or builders — with their protective goggles and gloves.

No one minded the wheeler parked in front of the entrance. Not more than twenty yards away. Just sitting there... toying with her. Vienna searched the road, then let her eyes wander up the building. She *knew* guards watched the wheeler; she only needed to find out where. *Wouldn't be much of a trap if they hung around in the open, now would it?* As far as traps went, this stood out as almost too obvious. The raiders had the keys. They could afford laziness. Not like she could push the damn thing down the road herself.

Vienna lurked back down the alley, away from the factory, and took a wide path around for a better look of the west side. She needed another way in: an open window, a back door, or perhaps a hatch to a cellar. This end of the building appeared more vacant. Only a few lights illuminated the first floor, leaving the upper levels dark and empty. Certainly a better option.

The chill of the brick wall at her back seeped through her clothes and made her shiver. Her breath left a thick fog in the winter night. Yet she waited, braving the cold until the opportune moment finally presented itself. Just as her nose and fingers numbed, one of the two engineers left their workstation and exited the room.

One more assessment to ensure no unwelcome eyes lay on her, then Vienna sprang from her dark nook and narrowed in on the glass building. She reached up to climb. The panes felt like ice against her bare palms, and the film of dew made them just as slippery. Her hands found purchase on the iron muntins, and she pulled herself up. The tips of her boots fit just enough against those bars to serve as a step. She used the windows as a sort of ladder and climbed the first few yards, all while splitting her focus between her holds and the engineer still enthralled in their work at the table just inside.

Slow and steady.

If she could just make it past the fourth row of windows, the second floor would block her from view. Vienna pushed on and grabbed the next ledge. As she pulled herself up, her hand slipped. Shards of ice sprayed her face. She stumbled. Her stomach clenched as her body slid down the glass. She scrambled for another hold. The muntins nicked her chin and knees on the way down in a cacophony of sound. She braced her body, ready for the hard landing. It'd hurt, but her real dread lay in being spotted. However much it stung, she'd need to bite back the pain and retreat before anyone had the chance to investigate.

While she waited for the hard strike of the ground, something grabbed her by the collar and dragged her skyward. She soared like a flying arrow past the windows. The moon cast her silhouette against the clear glass. A shadowy form loomed behind her in the reflection.

Felix.

"The second floor," she ordered. "Get closer to the building."

The Kayetan zoomed them both up to the destination and hovered there with Vienna pressed to the glass.

"Stay still." Vienna arched her neck down, eyes pinned to the spot where she'd bumbled her climb. As long as they hugged the glass above, they'd stay out of view. The engineer appeared; his brows held low as he inspected the noise. The man frowned, then turned away.

"Think he blamed it on a bird?" Vienna offered with a shrug. "Guess we'll know soon enough. Get us in there, but be quiet about it." She had planned to use the hilt of her knife to break a pane, but Felix's claws would substitute just as well.

The Kayetan switched Vienna into one arm, her feet dangling midair, while the other hand traced over the glass in a circular motion. The wailing screech of the cut made Vienna clamp her jaw. She hoped the commotion of work inside would be enough to cover their entry. With the cut finished, Felix pulled out the glass and drew Vienna closer to the human-sized hole. She felt very much like a kitten held by the scruff in its mother's mouth, except in this scenario, that mother was Felix. Vienna rolled her eyes at the thought. Felix was probably getting a kick out of this.

Vienna gripped the glass. The edges nipped her skin. Guided by Felix's hand, she half crawled, half launched through the hole. Vienna sprawled her hands out, catching herself before face-planting the floor. Warmth radiated from her left palm. She thumbed it. Just a bit of blood. A wipe to her pants along with the cold would handle it well enough.

"About time you showed up." Vienna hopped to her feet then spun on the Kayetan. "You ditched me back there."

Felix slithered through the hole and tilted his head as if casting a judgmental glare at her.

"Yeah, I know. Not like I've never done that to you before." Vienna took out her dagger and moved to the spiral stair. She paused before the first step. "Thanks for catching me."

Within the blink of her eye, Felix had flown in front of her, blocking her way down.

She swerved to go around, but he shifted again, right in her way. "I could just walk through you, you know?"

Felix hovered there, the wisps of shadow coming off him like fire. Despite the sunken, empty holes of his eyes, Vienna held no fear. With her mind, she merely replaced the hollows with the sly green irises they'd been when he was alive.

She sighed, then whispered. "Why should I tell you the plan? You might decide to abandon me again midway." A beat, then, "I need the keys. I'm assuming that's not what you were looking for on your midnight stroll?"

A shake of his head.

"I need some tools, too. Pliers to bend the cannon screws back in shape, a hammer, maybe more. If you're going to help, how about taking out anyone stationed around the wheeler?" A glance back to the window, where an icy breeze streamed in. "Have a feeling I'll need another way out, but I've got a plan. Find me when you're through?"

The Kayetan vanished from the stairway.

"For the love of Souls," she cursed. "Guess that's a yes."

Vienna gathered herself, then crept down the spiral path. Halfway down, she hesitated. The engineer had left his station. *Please don't be reporting the noise.* On the other hand, this might turn out to be a blessing. Tools were scattered along the table and bench. The pliers stood out. She tiptoed down the remaining steps and crossed the room. Pliers first. She tucked them into her waistband. A few loose screws lay around. *Better to have more than I need.* A handful went into her pocket.

As she looked around, she stopped to study the contraption the engineers had been fiddling with. The thing was a conglomerate of metal boxes and tubes. What looked like a leather belt ran on one side. She first thought it had to be a piece of a cannon—something internal—yet the more she scrutinized, the more she knew that to be false. The thing held stains where the ghost of a missing piece had imprinted.

Not a creation. A dissection. It made since. The raiders had been talking about their frustrations over Zeal not sharing technology with its citizens. The engineers were learning what made this thing tick, which left no doubt they held at least a partnership with those raiders Vienna had met earlier tonight.

A scroll of parchment lay open on the far end of the table. Upon seeing the sketch, a curse slipped her lips. A detailed diagram of the wheeler took up the middle, labeled in ink. Jax's handwriting. They'd stolen her blueprints. Below the drawing sat another that matched the hunk of metal on the table and beside it, the label: engine.

Vienna's body drained. She slumped forward and let her elbows fall on the worktop as she put it all together. They had removed the engine. *How in Soul's name am I going to get those moonstone trunks out to Kole?*

"Hey."

The voice made her snap up. The engineer had returned. His eyes trailed down her arm to the dagger held in her hand, and he took a hesitant step backward. Before he had the chance to open his mouth and call for help, Vienna raced across the room. The engineer had turned to run but only gotten as far as the corner before she had her hand clamped over his mouth, muffling his weak cry.

"Calm down, you'll be fine." Not like she could kill him. The only thing he'd done wrong was disassemble her wheeler, probably under orders. A desperate idea crossed her mind. She slipped a hand to the pouch at her side. A smooth vial grazed her fingertips. She drew it out, then wrestled the engineer to the floor. The man put up a decent fight, but his body, thin and gangly, left him wanting in their battle of strength.

In their struggle, Vienna's palm had moved from his mouth and his grunts resounded in the open room. Sounds from the entrance covered it well enough for now, but if she couldn't get him under control, she'd have backup to deal with.

That was where the vial came in.

Vienna pressed her knees into the man's chest, pinning him down, then worked quickly. A flick of her thumb removed the cork. She tilted the vial over the engineer's mouth and poured. A small dose would do, but the man wriggled relentlessly, now shouting for help. She shoved her hand over his face, trapping the liquid in, and waited for his inevitable next breath. How had Felix made it look so easy when he'd used this stuff? Perhaps sneaking up on an unaware victim would've offered a better route. *Desperate times.*

Finally, the man sucked in a breath. Vienna could tell the drops had gone down his throat when his body stilled, and his pupils dilated.

"That's it," she cooed. Once in his trance, she lugged herself off him, then grabbed hold of his ankles and pulled him to the dark corner of the room behind a crate. "You felt tired and needed a quick nap," she said to him as she removed his goggles, gloves, and shirt. They fit well enough on her, though the hem of the tunic swept the tops of her knees. She tied the bottom in a knot at her hips, then settled the goggles on her forehead.

For all the times Vienna had ripped into Felix for using the same technique, she was glad his Kayetan hadn't been around to witness it. The Taliroot mixture was a concoction of Leo's. When used properly, given to a subject beforehand, the recipient's memory could be adjusted to whatever the user spoke: a preventative measure for interrogation. Everything in Felix's hands went a bit askew. Instead, he used it as a tool to manage the aftermath of botched missions. A drop proved more than enough for a single dose. The guy stared blankly at the ceiling. She might've gone a bit heavy handed. Vienna used her fingers to pull down his lids so it at least *looked* like he was sleeping. She didn't want to hurt anyone if she could help it. Especially this bloke. Though he may work with the raiders, he hadn't tried to attack her. After nestling the vial into its proper place, she assessed the room.

A leather satchel sat tucked away under the workbench. She seized it and stuffed any other tools she thought she may need into the pocket alongside the journal already inside. Just as she closed the flap, a scream rang throughout the building.

She froze.

No one had eyes on her as far as she could tell. The cry had come from the front set of rooms near the entrance. The sound of shattering glass accompanied the screams.

Time to go.

Vienna slung the satchel over her shoulder and took the spiral steps by twos. Already the broken window had chilled the room. Her breath came in a thick fog. With her new leather gloves, she confidently threw herself at the hole and climbed through feet first. She set her backside against the glass and prepared to slide down the side of the building when Felix came zipping around the corner. She let go. The breath shot out of her lungs as he caught her and carried her away.

The rooftops raced below. Vienna glanced over her shoulder as she dangled from Felix's claws. A few people stood in the street around the wheeler, one with a hand pointed to the sky, shouting something. They'd seen their escape.

"I thought you were the stealthy one," Vienna said. She thought she heard a grunt of annoyance in response. His empty hands only gave her more fuel. "Didn't even get the keys? You're losing your touch, Brother."

CHAPTER 15

Piper slipped her hands from Kole, releasing him. "That was impressive, even for you."

Every ounce of strength had left him. He let his body collapse on the ground, and he rolled to his side, taking in Piper. Her red hair clung to the sheen of sweat on her temples, and dark bags draped heavy under her eyes. It looked like she'd put up quite the fight, as well.

All he could think to say to that was, "You're still on your feet."

"Demigod." She straightened up, a hint of humor behind her gaze. "It has its perks."

"Lucky you." Kole had meant to play it as a joke, but his raspy monotone made it come off as a jeer.

Her face fell a bit. She sat next to him and fiddled with something at her side. Before he knew it, she'd made a tiny cut on her palm and poised it by his mouth.

He pushed it away.

"It'll return your strength."

"I'd rather get it back the old-fashioned way."

"Not that I don't appreciate your effort to abstain," that edge returned in her voice, "I will just remind you that a minute in this place could be half a day in Ohr." Piper offered her hand again. "Willing to risk a couple of months for a nap?"

Kole's shoulders slumped. She had a point, though he grew tired of her always being right. Reluctantly, he pulled her hand to his lips, grimaced, then drank. The warm metallic taste made his insides churn. He took as much as his stomach could bare, then reached for the waterskin, hoping to rinse away the vile taste. No matter how much he gargled, it lingered on his tongue.

Warmth bloomed deep in his core. Either from the blood or the lump of fur that had settled in next to him.

While Kole had been taking his dose of Piper's blood, Caradin had awakened and lain beside him. "Master is safe," the words came to Kole's ears instead of through his thoughts. The Soul must've returned to his stag form, because a soft nose wiggled under Kole's head, acting as a welcomed pillow.

"I am not your master, Caradin. Not anymore, and I never should have been," Kole whispered. "I'm your friend." A deep rumble resonated from the animal's chest. Kole closed his eyes, allowing the vibration to ease his aching muscles. The blood worked fast as the fatigue on his body began to ease.

"I thought I lost you back there." Worry tinted Piper's tone. "That you'd finally given up."

Kole cracked his eyes open. The demigod sat across from him. Though he regretted admitting it, he said, "For a second there, I did." His bottom lip quivered and bent into a frown. It'd only been a moment ago when he'd nearly surrendered himself to the enemy—giving up all autonomy over his body and spirit. He regretted that dark state. *Never again.*

"Do you want to talk about—"

"No," he snapped. "I think you're the one who needs to talk."

The reversal made her flinch. He could practically see her guard raise.

"How did you find me?" Kole pressed. "When I attacked Aterus why did it hurt you, too?"

"I don't know what you're—"

"Don't pull that on me. I've heard it from Russé too many times before." His heartrate sped as his annoyance bubbled. A long inhale calmed him. "If you want me to trust you, I need answers. Full transparency. No omissions. Nothing less. I know everything you know, or *this*?" Kole wagged his scarred finger between them. The red, blotchy skin of his burns stood like a beacon compared to the demigod's pale complexion. "This alliance isn't going to work."

The moment passed with only the hum of Caradin's heaving breaths filling the air. Kole spat trying to rid himself of the nasty tang in his mouth.

Piper's jaw clenched and re-clenched as if mulling it over. "I am more like you than you know."

Her admission made old suspicions resurface. "You'd be surprised what I know."

That made her lips scrunch to one side. He could tell by her wary gaze she wanted him to elaborate, but he'd rather hear the truth straight from her.

"I was born a demigod. Aterus, the Gray Soul, my father," she spewed the endearment as if it had scorched her tongue, "and my mother, Evangeline, a human. I am a true division: half and half. I always have been, since I was born centuries ago. Until...." Her head tilted, and a peculiar expression took hold of her face. Regret? No. Something between that and sorrow.

"Until?" Kole urged.

"Until you."

"When I released Russé." The catalyst of everything: when his five-year-old self touched a grand red tree back home in Solpate Forest.

She nodded. "You know this." A statement rather than a question. When he kept quiet she continued. "A piece of Russé's soul was transferred to you. It brought you back to life. And what happens to one god—"

"Happens to all," Kole finished.

"Such is the order of balance," she recited.

"I have a piece of *six* of the seven Souls inside me. Not Aterus'. He was only able to contact me when you fed me his blood. That's what opened the door between us."

"Correct."

"When I released Russé, I fragmented Aterus' soul, too. And if his fragment isn't in me, then...."

"It latched on to the nearest combatable life-form at the moment of splitting." Piper looked away.

The pain on her face made Kole bite his tongue. He had guessed the truth when he made his last deal with Aterus—used that piece of knowledge to leverage himself a better deal. Though Aterus did not confirm it, the god's quick acceptance of Kole's new term had sealed it.

Kole finally understood. All the way back to the first time he'd met Piper in the liberation's hideout; the scorn she'd held for him and Russé, her recklessness in battle, her secrecy and acting as Aterus' servant for a time. He'd thought her the enemy at one point because of her demigod blood. Had her connection with her father made her follow his orders? Kole would be lying if he said he'd never felt a compulsion to follow Russé and the others. "So is that how it works? Attacking him attacks you."

"Yes," she growled. "I can't hurt him. Not directly, or I risk myself—risk not finishing the job."

"Then how do we even go about defeating him?"

"I said *I* couldn't do it. It doesn't mean someone else can't. Besides, killing isn't on the table anyhow."

The gods were immortal. Whatever happened to one happened to all. Death, if they managed to find a way to do it, would kill all seven Souls. Who knows what that would do to Ohr. The world lay in such peril already, teetering on the tip of a blade—that blade firmly held by the gods. The current imbalance that Aterus created when he banished and imprisoned his kin triggered the birth of the Black Wall. The risks were too great to make rash actions. Without careful planning, Kole could lead Ohr and every living creature in it to annihilation.

"How do you take down a god?" A prickling spread throughout Kole's body. Each muscle it passed twitched with a renewed vigor. He hated using blood as a tool, but it did the job. Too well. That gave him a thought. "What about blood sorcery? Anything we can use there?"

"That's the question, isn't it?" Piper let her head fall back, and she jerked her chin to Vara's prison above. "Release the gods. That's step one. Their combined power should be enough to subdue him. Whatever we decide to do from there... well we better have a plan when the time comes."

Kole stretched his limbs, testing his body's strength. A few pops and cracks from his joints, but other than that, he felt refreshed. Even the heaviness of his eyes had lifted. "There's still one thing I don't understand."

Piper side-eyed him. "I envy you if there's only *one* thing."

At that, he snorted. "All this time I thought Aterus was more powerful because his Soul wasn't fragmented like the others." Kole ran his fingers through Caradin's fur. "But if it's split within you, then he's no different than Russé. How does he have the strength to keep your mother alive? Why can't Russé or even Obell stand against him on their own?"

She leaned forward, elbows on her knees, and rested her chin in her hands. An inquisitive stare scanned over Kole. "Very perceptive. And a fair concern—one I confess, I only have a theory on. That's why I traveled to Socren in the first place."

The truth came out. Kole remembered the story she had fed him back when they first met in the underground liberation hideout. The details remained vague, but she had said something about her parents dying at sea and finding apprenticeship under Leo.

She must've caught the roll of his eyes because she said a bit defiantly, "My father is dead to me. And mother... her coma has lasted years now." She waved her hand as if sweeping away the thought. "I initially sought out Savairo. His work with Aterus gave him thorough knowledge of blood sorcery. I think the difference lies there."

"Wait. You wanted apprenticeship under the warden that kidnapped, tortured, and killed my people?"

"I wanted answers."

"I guess that's where our similarities end."

"Did you not seek an alliance with Aterus for your own answers? Under the hope that he would spare you and gift you back your friends? Not far off, I'd say."

Kole folded his arms, lips pressed together. The scenarios felt completely different, yet the way she worded it made them both sound sordid. He shrugged it off, but it left a bitter taste in his mouth. Or maybe that was still her blood.

"If anyone had the answers I needed, it was Savairo, but I couldn't train with him directly. He knew who I was from working with my father over the years, perfecting his Kayetans. I'd run away at the time, and I didn't want Aterus knowing where I was if I could help it. Savairo would've turned me in." Piper tucked a loose piece of her hair behind her ear. The cut she'd made for Kole had already healed. "I went to Leo instead. I knew of his magical talents, and as bothers, hoped Leo could give me some insight."

"And?"

"And nothing. I got no real answers, only more speculation. But I have a hunch about Aterus' lineage." Piper shook her head at Kole's lifted brows. "No more offspring, I'm sure of that. More about the powers he gifted humans."

"He took those back." As soon as Kole said it, he caught himself. "Orla."

"Orla is an extreme example."

The priestess that had headed the cult in Zeal and orchestrated the attack on the city that Kole had left mere hours ago — or weeks ago in reality, apparently — had bragged about how her ancestors had dodged Aterus when he sought to retract the gifts he'd given to the humans. It meant her raw power was greater than any measly sorcerer. That was how she'd managed to gain some sort of control over the Black Wall.

"Despite my father being an absolute ass, his humans were a miraculous creation. They — we — change and adapt so quickly. I think by the time Aterus went to rescind his gifts, some had melded so much with the new power that it was impossible to take back every sliver of magic."

"Which is why we have sorcerers." Made sense to Kole.

"I'm not going to act like I know how or why it happens, but I think Aterus may be using that somehow to keep his strength up. Like he's siphoning it or something."

"Sounds like what Savairo did with his Red Cloaks."

Piper nodded. "I was afraid to tell Leo at first. I didn't want him knowing who I truly was, but I have a feeling he's always had his suspicions. If he didn't know then, he certainly does now. And I'll need him to sort this all out when we make it back to him. But in the meantime," she stood and held a hand to Kole, "we have a job to do here."

Kole took it, and she helped him to his feet, though with his new energy, he didn't need it. The lightness of his step made him feel like he could jump straight up to the portal himself. This time he'd be ready for Vara.

CHAPTER 16

"Find her!" A woman's voice shouted from the road.

Vienna scooted closer to the wheel of the cart. The spokes provided little cover. Someone only had to shine a light in her direction and she'd be known. But the abandoned wagon stood as the only viable cover on this stretch of street. Even more reason to ditch it. The raiders would know exactly where to look.

Her chest heaved from the dead sprint. When the raiders had heard wind of the break-in, they'd spread word to others already on the prowl in Zeal. After a one-sided argument, Vienna had made Felix drop her off a mile from their destination. No need to lead them straight back to the moonstone trunks. And now the raiders knew to look to the sky in their search, too. Better to go on foot.

"Anytime, people." Vienna squinted through the darkness, trying to time her escape right. Four raiders roamed the store fronts a couple dozen yards north, heading her direction. The sound of the woman's voice matched the group she'd run into earlier that night.

Unlike the engineer she'd left virtually unharmed earlier, she had no reservations in getting bloody with these raiders. Sure, they were opportunist following a leader—not all bad—but she'd rival their aggression if it came to it. Felix's Kayetan seemed to follow her lead. A good thing, too. If Vienna commanded it, the demon could turn the whole raiding party in ribbons of flesh. Right now, outnumbered, she needed to flee.

Finally, the woman's face turned away. Her chance!

Vienna bolted from the cart for the safety of the alley. Her boots clicked on the stone and the stolen satchel full of tools bounced on her hip with a clatter. A far cry from quiet. And a bit louder than she wished because a beam of light swung to her, illuminating her escape.

"There! Go, go, go!"

Felix had thrown others off her tail earlier and had yet to return. Though she welcomed his arrival, especially in this moment, she couldn't rely on his intervention every time she got herself in a bind. Usually, the roles were reversed. *She* was the older sibling, after all. Funny how that worked out.

The pounding of feet tailed her. The moment she passed into the backstreet, her eyes darted for another route. A handful of seconds and the raiders would turn the corner. She needed to be out of sight by then.

Brick wall after brick wall. No ladder, no boxes of ledges to aid a climb for the roof. *Come on. Come on.* Then she saw it.

A gate.

Without a second thought, she swerved toward it. Her hands grasped the iron bars and pulled. It didn't budge. Yanking only rattled it further. A lock secured the latch.

Damn it all.

The glow around the corner brightened as four silhouettes swerved down the alley and charged her.

In that split second, she decided to climb. Souls forbid she ran into another group out in the open and get herself trapped. *Lose them.* That was the only thing on her mind.

The decorative design of the iron gate acted as fine footholds. She heaved herself up and swung herself over the spikes. When she moved to jump down, something pulled on her neck. She twisted back. The leather strap had tangled itself on one of the spikes. She fiddled with the thing, but adrenaline made her hands tremble.

A projectile hit the stone wall to her right. On contact, a flash of electricity exploded. A surging jolt ran through Vienna's body. Her breath caught and her heart skipped a beat at the short burst of pain. At the ground lay one of the cattle prod-looking weapons the raiders carried. White stone, carved to a point, topped the rod.

Vienna pulled at the bag once she regained her bearings, but it stuck firm. Not wanting to risk another shot, she fiddled for her dagger and sliced the strap off on both sides of the bag and tucked the bare pack under arm. The raiders closed in on the gate as she backed away.

The woman approached the entrance—her men at her back—arms open as if yielding. "Whoa, there. Hold on. We just want to talk."

"Your weapon says differently," Vienna barked. The hair on her body still stood on end from the shock. She wanted to pull out the slingshot, but that required two hands. Now that the satchel's strap had been removed, it meant ditching it to fight.

"We're not your enemy," the woman tried.

"Since when do allies cast stones?" An eerie warning fogged Vienna's mind. She got the sense the woman was stalling. To pick the lock on the gate? No one made a move for it, not even attempting to climb it. That feeling made Vienna retreat a few more steps. "It was you at the cannon wasn't it? You shot at me. You sure act like an enemy despite your claim."

"That was a mistake." The raider grabbed the bars of the gate. "You're all alone in the city. We can help you."

One woman. Two men readied behind her. What was she missing? Something felt off. Three raiders. But she remembered seeing four in pursuit. The epiphany drained the blood from her face.

Shit. The woman *was* stalling.

Vienna turned on her heel and ran... straight into the hard body of a towering man. He grabbed her, trapping her in his muscled arms. She kicked at his kneecaps, which garnered a few grunts in response. When that failed, she sunk her teeth into the nearest flesh. The skin broke, and blood filled her mouth. This time the brute released her just as the sound of a swinging gate reached her ears.

Too close and outnumbered. She clutched the satchel close to her chest, then made a break for it deeper into what seemed to be a deserted garden. A dried-up stone fountain graced the center of the plot. The time for hiding had passed. She needed distance. Or Felix. But those prods they armed themselves with... she feared their source of power may be bad news for a Kayetan.

A path of flagstone swerved between the plots of overgrown vegetation. The house obscured the light of the moonstone streetlamps from the road. Vienna struggled to keep up pace in the pitch. She had to stay on her feet. One single falter could get her back in the arms of that man.

But they were quicker. The dim light of their weapons gave them an advantage. Soon, the heavy breaths and pounding feet caught up.

Vienna turned from the path and barreled through the garden. Tangled vines snapped at her ankles. The scent of upturned soil wafted to her noise. The new course may slow her, but she banked on the dense vegetation doing the same to the raiders.

Then she saw it: her way out. A shed sat by the far wall, beside it a wheelbarrow. If she could make it to the roof, she could leap over the wall in one fell swoop. That would give her a moment out of sight and another chance to lose them. She veered left and pushed her feet hard into the earth.

The wheelbarrow sat low enough that a simple step placed her squarely inside it. She sprang for the roof.

A hand snared her ankle and dragged her down. The metal lip of the wheelbarrow nipped her cheek. The hit numbed the right side of her face, and her vision flashed with spots. The cold soil pressing against her back told her she'd been lugged to the ground. A groan escaped her as a throbbing pain blossomed from her cheek bone.

"Gotcha," said a deep voice.

Vienna fluttered her eyes, each blink clearing more of her vision. The man hunched over her, hands on his knees. But something above him caught her gaze.

A wisp of shadow moved over the night sky.

"Stay back," Vienna warned. "Their weapons —"

As the words left her mouth, a streak of light soared for the Kayetan. Another one of the raiders had thrown their prod at Felix, but he deftly evaded it. Still, Felix hovered there, no sign to flee.

"Please go," Vienna begged. Losing him again would break her.

The earth rumbled. Vienna thought it in her head at first, but the brute standing over her perked up and swung his head around.

"Boss?" he said.

"That ain't us," the woman responded. She and her gang had finally caught up.

Drumbeats in the earth — the quick tempo matching the beat of Vienna's galloping heart. The loose soil around her vibrated. No earthquake. She'd been around those before. The volume rose — closed in.

Vienna gasped as the wall behind her exploded. The raiders' cries of surprise faded behind the blast.

Stone rained down like meteors. She rolled to her side and squeezed her knees to her chest, shielding herself from the onslaught.

More screams — not of shock, more guttural. These held an edge of utter terror. How Vienna imagined herself to shriek if she ever saw a ghost. Now that the explosion had settled, she peeked out. And what she saw made the frigid air drill deep into her bones.

A hulking figure of pure stone lumbered across the edge of the garden. One massive arm swung at a raider, hitting him firmly in the stomach. The impact sent him hurling backward and skidding over the dirt even after he'd landed. The next swift blow sent another raider crashing into the fountain with a sickening crack. When the stone creature turned to the last two adversaries, they bolted like terrified dogs with their tails tucked between their legs.

Then the colossal creature turned on her.

Vienna peered up. "Shikar?"

"Yes, small one."

Shikar's sturdy rock body had changed since Vienna had last seen the Yamani. Taller. Larger. *Fearsome.* Those fiery yellow eyes burned brighter, like the core of a flame. Light caught the facets of her sable crystal body, making her gleam. The color was so dark and rich, it strained Vienna's eyes.

"How?" Vienna climbed to her feet in awe. "You died on my shoulder. We buried you. How are you here?"

"I did not die, though I was close." Even the sway of her stance seemed to quake the earth. "Laying me in the earth was the best thing you could have done. The land revived me."

The image of Shikar's former broken body flooded her head. The Yamani had braved the rivers of lava on the side of the Volcano to save her, Kole, and Felix. The act had melted Shikar's feet, leaving her unable to walk. But they were creatures of the earth—as old as the earth. Shikar had said herself that their deaths only came when they deemed it. The very rock and soil that made up Ohr provided their sustenance—kept them strong. The grave Kole had dug must've served as a sort of incubator. Here she stood, her body whole and unscathed.

"As for how I am here. I walked." Shikar wiggled her regenerated feet. "That's why it took so long. But I had a guide." At her whistle, Felix's Kayetan appeared by her side. "She led me to you."

"She?" Vienna stared at the Kayetan. Her vision blurred and shifted. It was as if a veil had been pulled from her eyes. To her horror, the edges of Felix's shadow grew; shoulders broadened, neck thickened, and the lithe form of her brother vanished. The shadow morphed into a duplicate image of the hardy Yamani woman.

No more freckles. No more sly, green eyes and matching grin. No unruly curls.

No Felix.

"She?" Vienna's breaths came in spurts. Hard as she tried to suck in air, her lungs constricted. *It can't be.* The shadow before her was her brother's Kayetan. The way they'd worked together these last few weeks... seamless as old times. The way it moved so much like her brother. It *spoke* to her!

"Once I awoke, I sent her to look for you three. My Kayetan picked up your tracks and followed you to the city. Once it found you, I ordered her to keep watch over you until I arrived." Shikar set her molten eyes on the two men she'd downed, who still lay passed out in the garden.

Though Vienna heard the Yamani's every word, they passed through her ears. She could only stare at the Kayetan. No matter how hard she squinted, the shadow wouldn't return to its former image. Had it been in her head? All of it?

"Arrived just in time, it seems. You've stirred up a whole lot of trouble, small one." Shikar chuckled. The laugh cut short, and the Yamani stepped closer. "Vienna?"

"I... I...." Vienna willed her eyes to see her brother in the Kayetan. Whatever power her mind had given her had vanished at the Yamani's arrival. If the shadow wasn't Felix, it meant....

It meant her brother was dead. Gone from her forever.

Something in her mind broke. All those memories of the battle with Orla came rushing back. How she'd sat there, bleeding and helpless on the ground, as she witnessed her brother's murder at the hands of the cult leader. That streak of black fire touched his back and his body disintegrated into ashes. The pain clasped harder around her lungs. It burned to even try to breathe.

All Vienna could remember was staring at the shadow one moment, and the next, her vision darkened, and the cold feel of Shikar's strong arms wrapped around her.

Felix.

Vienna knelt at her parents' gravestones and placed the bouquet of wildflowers she'd picked on her way out of Socren at the base. Weeds, mostly. This side of the mountain hadn't seen rain in ages.

No names graced the smooth stones. It wasn't even a proper headstone, merely a pile of rocks to mark the spot. But her parents' bones lay below, nonetheless. Leo had made sure to properly put them to rest all those years ago, after her and Felix's home had been raided.

"Leo has given me a task," Vienna said. "I don't know when I'll be back again." In truth, a feeling squirming inside made her wonder if she'd ever make it back. She should be a mile further south by now, but that dread had made her stop here. "I came to say goodbye."

"Well don't I feel like last week's dumplins." Her brother's voice sapped the sentiment from the moment.

Vienna pushed to her feet as Felix came bounding down the footpath. A hawk sat perched on Felix's shoulder.

"Fiona," Vienna scolded low. "You're supposed to keep watch."

"Hey now," Felix cupped a hand around the hawk's head as if it would shield the bird from her words. "She's trained ta spot enemies. Clearly, I'm her favorite. Isn't that right, ya old bird?" Fiona nipped at the fleshy part of his palm. His grimace turned into a strained smile as she flew off. "Love bite."

"What are you doing here?"

"Same as you. Payin' my respects ta Ma and Pa. Haven't seen them since before the battle, ya know. It's 'bout time."

"You never come down here."

"Well it's sad, ain't it? Not like I'm lookin' for more of that in my life. Besides, I'm here now. That's countin' for something."

"Enough," Vienna snapped. "How long have you been eavesdropping?"

Felix gasped with all the dramatics of a tired toddler. "I'd never...." He placed his hands on his hips. When Vienna lowered her brow, he finally gave in. "I'd never snoop if it wasn't necessary. That's on you, Vi. You made me."

"Go home." Vienna turned on her heel and headed south. The crunch of her brother's boots followed her from the grave. "I mean it, Felix."

The steps ceased. "You're just gonna leave me again, eh? No explanation? Not even a goodbye? Maybe if I was six feet in the ground, you'd give me more warnin'."

Vienna stopped. The plains stretched out before her. How unseeming they looked from here. Deceit. This mission... danger lurked ahead. More than she could imagine. "You can't go with me."

"And why not? I know where yer goin'. Chasin' after Kole and gramps. I heard that much. Blondie's my friend, too, ya know. I met him first, and that means I got bigger dibs."

"It's dangerous."

"What isn't nowadays?"

She turned. "That's exactly why you need to stay in Socren. It's safer now. Leo will look after you."

"I don't need lookin' after. I may be yer little brother, but I'm not a kid anymore. Plus, I'm more stubborn than you."

There. That was the moment.

Vienna paused the scene.

She'd pinpointed the moment when she let her heart go soft. The moment when she yielded. She should've been strong. She should've argued. Pushed him away. Scolded him and cursed him to hate her. Anything to make him stay. Anything to make Felix turn back and leave Leo's request to her.

If that one moment had changed, his entire future would've altered. Felix never would've been captured and turned into a Kayetan. He wouldn't have joined her and Kole on the journey to Zeal. And without his presence there, Orla never would've set that fire on him. Felix would've lived.

But the scene played on as it did in reality instead of her perfect fantasy. He followed her to find Kole and Russé at that lake where they'd released Issira.

Vienna reversed the moment until she was back alone at her parents' gravestone. Alone. How it should've been. No matter how many times she wished fate to bend to her will, it replayed over and over again. All leading to Felix's inevitable death.

CHAPTER 17

"You could come in handy," Piper said with a tap to Caradin's side before hopping up behind Kole. "Can he become anything?"

Kole looked over his shoulder and caught her admiring the Soul's wings. "Any animal, or combination of them. So he claims." He settled into the warmth of the stag's back, enjoying the heat while he could. If the second trip wound up being anything like the previous encounter, he'd need to soak it in while he could.

"No need to worry." Piper must've sensed his nerves. "Aterus is no longer within you. She'll sense that. And we'll be in here if you need us." She tapped her temple.

Great. Kole had gotten used to sharing his mind by now. Since he took Piper's blood to mend himself, their mental connection had strengthened. The blood would run its course eventually, and he'd be rid of her once again. For now, though, he'd take the extra ally.

"Let's get this over with," Kole murmured.

The stag launched into a gallop. Wings beat. A heavy rush of wind hit Kole from both sides with each downward stroke. Then the Soul lifted off.

The trio swirled up. Piper had no reaction to the changing seasonal temperatures. Maybe she expected it.

Kole took out his knife and held out his palm. A pale thin line sat where he'd made the mark last time. The demigod blood had done more than give him an energy boost. He reopened the wound, then raised it up to the portal.

He was ready this time. Instead of fighting it, Kole climbed to his feet, balancing on Caradin's back, then jumped for the portal.

The shock of cold made his chest tighten and sent an aching rush to his head, like he'd dove straight into a frozen lake. Inside lay the same dancing lights. Their lazy glow sharpened at Kole's presence. He braced himself.

A throb built in the base of Kole's skull. At first, he thought it Vara on the attack, but this presence felt different—cautious. He followed the source of the ache and tracked it back to Russé's door. His old mentor was reaching out to him. Instead of barging in like old times, Russé seemed to be knocking, requesting entrance. Kole obliged.

The moment he opened the door, Russé said in a hasty voice, "*Don't carry this burden on your own. I can handle Vara. Just be the vessel. I can do the rest.*"

Relief ran through Kole. He had to admit, this task had weighed on him. When he'd freed Caradin, he'd almost lost his life. Vara proved even more headstrong with her twisting words.

"*If you trust me to do it,*" Russé added.

What was there to trust? Russé had done this for him twice before when they'd release Issira and Obell. Kole knew his old mentor could perform the task, and more than anything, the Souls needed him alive. No, it wasn't that. What worried him was the distance. Russé had physically been by his side those last two times. Could he do it purely through Kole's mental link? *Guess we'll see.*

"Do it," Kole accepted. He lent his body to Russé and let him take charge.

"*Lift your hand. Close your eyes and breathe.*"

Kole followed the instructions. That first inhale went smoothly. At the second, a familiar sensation spread through his body. The last thing Kole heard before the feeling overtook him was Russé calling out to his kin.

Death crept his way. No manner of preparation could settle Kole's nerves now. Russé had begun the ritual.

Numbness. Kole's consciousness thrust into the void. He floated there between life and death. He imagined his spirit leaving his body. Vara required it to free herself. The piece of her inside Kole's head needed to detach itself. It acted as a road—a portal between her prison and Ohr. Only then could Vara return. Once she made it back, that piece of Kole's spirit reattached. Until then, Kole remained dead. Or half-dead, anyway.

Time stood still. The exchange could've taken a minute or a year. It felt all the same to Kole. It should've been peaceful. The quiet serenity around him might've calmed anyone else. But the possibility of succumbing to death's embrace sent a rush of fear through him. He drowned in it. If Kole were to die here, stay dead, Ohr would fall.

Just as those dark thoughts settled in his core, a pressure enveloped him like a giant hand. The hand yanked him out of limbo, and he fell back into his body.

Kole coughed on crisp air. His eyes fluttered open. Three figures stood over him. His eyes needed time to adjust, yet despite the fog over his vision, the distinct silhouette of Caradin in his stag form and the fiery-haired girl beside him stood clear.

The third? Vara.

His eyes fixed on her. Little by little the image cleared.

Tight curls of deep mahogany twisted around her head like a crown. Pieces of her hair shone brighter. It reminded Kole of the varied colors of the changing leaves of autumn. Her skin, the deep gold tan of summer, seemed to radiate its own unworldly warmth. And finally, her eyes. They enraptured Kole. He would gaze on them forever if he could. One held the piercing white of winter snow and the other the pale green of a sprout.

Vara knelt before him. "I am sorry for my rash behavior, young Kole." Something about her voice triggered fond memories of his late nights with Niko, whispering to each other from their bunks, far past curfew. She was the Soul he most wished Niko could have met.

Though his mouth opened, no words passed his throat. Kole found himself nodding idly with a half-developed grin on his face.

She gave her own tender smile. "Russé has informed me of the state of things while I was in that portal." Those brilliant eyes scanned the floating island and the land beyond. "I remember the very moment the Black Wall overtook my prison. My mind hasn't been the same since. But now that I'm free and reunited with my kin," Vara placed a hand on the stag's nose, who hummed in response, "I have regained clarity."

"Well, isn't that grand," Piper sneered. "A moment ago, you were dead set on killing the key to Ohr's fate. I'm so glad you've mastered your murderous tendencies."

The venom in Piper's tone stripped any lingering fog from Kole. He sent her a glare, but she ignored it.

"Betrayal and prolonged isolation can do that to the psyche. No matter how much divine power one possesses," Vara retorted. A knowing glint crossed her duel-colored eyes. "Forgive me for wanting to strangle anyone who has a connection to my captor. I'm sure you are more than familiar with Aterus, hmm?"

Piper's jaw clenched. It seemed their new acquaintance knew about Piper's lineage or at least sensed it.

"If we are all done with the pleasantries, we should leave. Time is ticking." Piper tapped the face of her watch, then she stomped off to the edge of the island.

"Don't mind her, she's always like that," Kole excused.

Vara's features softened. "For good reason. I know about the time shift here. I was the one who made it." She offered him a hand.

"I figured." Kole lifted to his feet with her help. "Strange things happen around the prisons. Russé said your powers leak out and affect the land." After Kole filled her in on the walking trees of Solpate, the animated water at Issira's pond, and intelligent wildlife he'd encountered when seeking Caradin, she shook her head.

"Those sound like accidents. Mine was intentional."

They walked side by side with Caradin until they caught up with Piper.

"Intentional? Why would you change the time out here?" Kole asked.

"Not the time, Kole," Piper interjected, "the seasons."

Vara nodded. "I slowed them."

"But why?"

"Because when I sensed the Black Wall closing in, I knew it would destroy everything here, including my portal. Maybe even me. This place," she gestured to the crumbling earth below, "is stuck in slow motion from the very instant the Black Wall passed through."

They all craned their necks over the lip of the island. The fissures drew Kole's attention—called to him. He peered into their rocky depths, eager to glimpse that strange person he and Caradin had encountered earlier.

"I stretched out the moment of destruction," Vara said somberly.

"What does that mean?" Kole forced his attention to the Black Wall, which stood like a creeping nightmare in the distance.

"It means, this place isn't here at all," Piper said. "It's already destroyed and there's no bringing it back. It may take thousands of years, but it will fade away like the rest of the planet."

Kole turned his back on the wall and peered out. "How far does it go?"

"I don't know," Vara admitted.

His vision had its limits, and floating stones spanned the entirety. "So, the land beyond your touch...." Kole began. The Black Wall had birthed somewhere on the far side of the world. It had been centuries since then. He wondered if any records of those first years of terror existed. When that ring had expanded year after year, consuming Ohr— shrinking it—it took out any living creature in its path. The only person who had lived since that day to know the details was Aterus. Questioning that route would most certainly lead to a dead end.

"There is no land beyond," Piper said.

He'd once thought the lost lands sat deserted. No one truly knew, because no one had ever done what Kole and his companions had managed: survived the journey across the flames. To see this.... Quelling the wall would save the people at the heart of Ohr, but nothing could bring back what had been lost. A shadow fell over Kole's heart as he grasped this new revelation.

"You're right, Piper. We should leave." As much as Kole wanted to explore and search for the phenomenon he'd encountered before, time moved against them. Now that he'd broken his deal with Aterus, the devious Soul could move the wall at the slightest whim. And he may, too, in an act of revenge against Kole.

The wall kills everything. What he saw... the footprints, Caradin picking up on a scent, it *had* to be in his head. Though in hindsight, it had been Aterus who'd suggested it. Kole had to convince himself to believe it as fact. War waged on Ohr. He couldn't leave his friends to fight alone on a whim.

Caradin had to double in size to accommodate all three passengers on his back. They soared through the boulder-studded sky, swerving in and out of the obstacles. Once or twice, they found themselves inside a channel of altered gravity, but Caradin deftly eased them away.

"How'd you get up to us anyway?" Kole called over his shoulder after they'd exited the last pocket. He thought he heard her laugh. "Don't tell me you can fly."

"I probably could if I found the right place. I'm tempted to try now." Another chuckle, then, "Caradin heard me calling for you. He taxied me up."

Finally, the wings tilted down, and they gradually descended to the ashen floor. A puff of gray billowed up as the stag flapped and gently touched down.

Kole dismounted. As fantastic as flying was, Kole preferred his feet solidly on the ground. He missed his rambler. He'd planned on bringing the gargantuan tree on his mission to find Vara. What a mistake that would've been. The poor thing had no chance passing through the black flames.

"How do we find a way through?" Vara was the last to slide off the animal's back.

"We used a piece of Caradin's antlers as a marker." Kole surveyed the terrain. They had landed as near to the wall as they dared, yet the place only held dreary hues of gray. "It should be somewhere around here."

"I will search, Master."

The title made Kole cast a stern look Caradin's way.

"Friend," the Soul corrected, before taking to the skies.

Vara paced. "And a door will appear?" Her gold blouse shimmered in the fierce light of the stars. Only now did Kole notice the intricate detail in the hem. The sewn edge looped and curled, depicting the full cycle of a tree from spring buds to shedding leaves, then finally the bare skeleton of winter hibernation.

"That's the plan." The broken watch on Kole's wrist held no use. Even if it did still tick, he wondered how the time difference would work between both sides. "We find the spot and wait."

"He's back," said Piper.

From the ground, Caradin's glowing coat made him appear as a shooting star diving for earth. The stag's hooves thundered into the ground, accompanied by frightful black eyes.

"Kole!" The hysteria poured off the animal and shot straight through Kole. *"The marker."*

He rushed to the animal and stroked his neck. "Did you find it?"

"Yes, but it's not where it once was."

"What do you mean? Where is it?"

"What is he saying?" Piper tapped her foot impatiently. "Did he find it?"

"Yes, but something's wrong," Kole answered quickly to placate her, then he turned back to the Soul. "Where is it, Caradin?"

"A mile back."

"A mile back," Kole repeated. "It doesn't make sense."

"The wall has moved again," Vara said.

"We would've felt it—heard it." Each time Kole had witnessed the event, the wall had roared at deafening volumes and quaked the earth. Nothing of the sort had happened since he'd crossed over. "It hasn't moved since Orla summoned it. Caradin, which direction is the marker?"

The great stag pointed his snout west.

Piper swung her head between the wall and where the Soul directed. The focus in her eyes told him she was grasping at some clue. "When did Orla summon it?"

"Right after the cult attacked the city," Kole answered. "You have a theory?"

Folding her arms, she shook her head, apparently coming to some sort of conclusion. A bad one if Kole had to guess.

"The wall didn't stop moving until Felix killed Orla," Piper said flatly.

The mention of his friend's name sent a gloom over Kole. The fresh news of his death had yet to fully register. To feel real. In his mind, Felix had been laughing with him a day prior. Kole shook the memory away before it consumed him. *No time to grieve out here.* "So, what are you saying?"

"So," a hint of agitation gripped her voice, "you passed through the wall while it was still on the move. It hadn't settled into its new position yet. The marker means nothing. It just tells us where *you* came through. That spot is completely different from where I entered."

Logistically, it made sense, but he still expected to have felt it or *seen* it move once he and Caradin crash-landed on this side. Perhaps Vara's influence was to blame. Kole played with Piper's theory. If it was correct, they needed to find *her* point of entry. "Where did you cross through?" Her scrunched face said all he needed. "You didn't leave a marker." Kole kicked the ash.

"I was more concerned with finding you at the time," she snapped back. "You should be glad I went straight to you. Otherwise, I'd be dragging your corpse out thanks to this one over here."

Vara's mouth sank into a sheepish grin. "I am sorry, Kole. I was not myself."

Kole waved his hand at both, then massaged his temples. "How the hell are we going to find the gate? It could be anywhere around here, and there's only a short window to cross."

"I guess now would be a good time to mention the improvements Jax has made."

"What sort of improvements?"

"The beam lasts an hour, now. Roughly," said Piper. "And since your marker tells us a general location, we can split up and patrol the area. Once we find it, there should be plenty of time to regroup and leave."

Kole sighed, half in relief, half out of annoyance. "That would've been nice to know *before* I thought we'd be stuck here forever."

When she went to respond, Piper seemed to stop herself, then said, "I... forgot how much you've missed."

"Well now that we have a plan, how about we put it in place?" As if trying to cut the tension, Vara stepped between Kole and Piper. "Shall we?"

CHAPTER 18

Vienna sat up with a gasp. A streak of sun blinded her, and she recoiled, shielding her eyes. The sound of dragging fabric banished the ray and plunged the room into a dim gray. She blinked. A tattered sheet lay over her, folded at her waist. No mattress was beneath her. Instead, hard wood nipped at her bones. Her spine ached. She must've been out for a long while.

The last thing she remembered....

Her dream. No, before that.

"Shikar?" she whispered.

"I am here, little one." The Yamani stood by the window drapes, the fabric pinched between her thick fingers, keeping them closed.

The muddy scent of mildew and dust filled her nostrils. "Where are we?"

"Western edge. Raiders don't come this far."

The room, if you could call it that, sat in disarray. The place looked like a temporary shelter pieced together by a hodgepodge of broken wooden pieces, sheets of metal, and whatever else could stand upright. The window and curtain Vienna had thought she'd seen turned out to be a hole in the patched wall with frayed squares of burlap nailed over it.

"Did they follow us?"

"No. But they know we are still in the city." Shikar released the fabric. "My Kayetan kept them distracted while I took you. We are safe."

Her Kayetan. Vienna was glad night had passed. She couldn't bring herself to look at the creature. A kick removed the sheet from her legs. "What time is it?"

"Midday."

Vienna rolled to her feet. She'd hoped to return to the cannon last night to repair it, or at least attempt the task. She would've missed the midnight window regardless, but she'd grown accustomed to her routine. It felt wrong to skip her charge.

The repairs! After a quick scan of the enclosure, her panic swelled. "Where is it?"

"Where is what?"

"The bag. I had a bag with me."

"I saw no bag."

Vienna paced. Four steps took her to the end of the small space, then she turned back the other way. "I can't risk another break in. They'll be ready for it this time."

"It's what you took in that glass building," Shikar guessed.

"Tools for the cannon. Kole and Piper can't get back unless I have them. The raiders destroyed—"

"I know what the raiders did. I was there, too."

Vienna's brows lifted. If the Yamani had been there the other night, she would certainly have seen her. Then, she realized what Shikar had meant. Her Kayetan had been there. They shared a peculiar link, shadow and master, similar to Felix and his Kayetan. Except the ritual that had made the demons had gone very differently between the two of them. Shikar had simply survived the foul ceremony, whereas Felix's had been stopped midway. It left Felix with a deeper physical connection to his shadow; powers he had only just started to conquer. From the time Vienna had spent with the stone woman, she had witnessed the Yamani's own abilities. They could communicate telepathically. Shikar primarily had used her shadow as a scout. And after their brief conversation last night, Vienna imagined every encounter and conversation she'd had with the Kayetan, no matter how personal, had been relayed to Shikar.

Her cheeks heated with embarrassment. The Yamani must think her ridiculous. The fact that she'd treated this Kayetan as her brother, fooled by the illusions of grief.

Thuds shook the floor as the Yamani crossed the room. She knelt on one knee, bringing her face level with Vienna's, and reached a curled finger to her cheek. The cool stone burned against Vienna's skin.

Despite the stiff features of stone, Shikar's face held a sadness. "I have lost those near to my heart. It hurts more than any wound. Do not fear how you grieve, little one. Your mind created what it needed, just as mine did when I lost my daughter." When her hand pulled away, it carried one of Vienna's tears. "I hold no judgment."

Vienna fell into the stone woman and flung her arms around her shoulders. Face pressed into the rocky crevasse of her neck, she cried. "I miss him."

"You will never stop missing him."

The feeling—that deep-rooted stitch gnawing her heart—she knew all too well. It had reared its head when her parents died years ago and had never really left. Now the feeling grew in strength. She feared if she let it run loose, it may break through the cage of her chest.

A long moment passed. Vienna stayed wrapped around Shikar, who never made a move to rush her. *Like a true mother.*

Finally, Vienna found the courage to let go and pulled away. She swiped at her soggy face, took a deep breath, then set her mind on the task at hand.

"We need a way to fix the cannon."

"Sealing the chamber box is all we need?"

Vienna nodded.

"I can keep it closed." The Yamani woman rose to her feet and rolled back her impressive shoulders.

"It's dangerous. If it's not properly sealed, it will explode." Jax had been very specific about that part. *"Don't mess with the fuel tank,"* the engineer had said repeatedly.

"My skin is harder than diamonds, little one. I will keep it shut."

Vienna had to trust her. Going back to the factory wasn't an option. "Then we'll need one more thing."

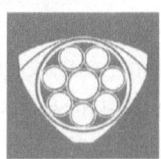

Though Vienna wanted to go by daylight, Shikar insisted they wait until dusk to trek through the streets. A Kayetan scouting ahead made sense. Seeing the creature pained her heart. The Yamani must've guessed at her sensitivity to the shadow because she sent it away as soon as it emerged.

The pair walked the street toward Jax's old quarters without difficulties. Actually, Zeal remained relatively quiet throughout their journey, which perked Vienna's suspicion.

The moonstone stumps lay behind the secret wall, just as she'd left them. She settled on bringing two for safe measure. Propped on either of Shikar's shoulders, they appeared small and weightless.

Vienna relocked the panel door, and they left the building to begin their long trek for the Black Wall.

A ten-minute travel time with the wheeler took nearly two hours on foot. The Yamani was the greatest blessing. No way Vienna could've rolled the stumps this far. They trudged through until the shape of the weapon emerged in the darkness.

Vienna examined the damage once more: bent screws and a bowed lid. As Shikar set the stumps down, Vienna started to wonder if they needed replacement bolts at all. She gathered the mangled pieces. "Can you straighten these?"

The stone woman carefully poised the screw between two fingers. With gentle precision, probably afraid she might snap the metal clean in half, Shikar molded the metal to her will.

"Good enough." Vienna took it and tried it in the hole. It fit. "And the lid."

Shikar got to work while Vienna dusted the lenses and checked for any more damage or signs the looters had made a second visit. Things looked in order.

By the time Vienna made her round about the cannon, Shikar had the lid reshaped and was fiddling with the screws, attempting to reattach it. The tiny elements gave her trouble, and the Yamani huffed.

"I have it from here." Vienna scooted the woman away and threaded the missing screws. The finished product looked useable from an untrained eye, but upon closer inspection, the seal gaped at the corner and across one of the flat edges. She pointed the cracks out to Shikar. "Can you press it down?"

The metal squeaked as the stone woman pressed her weight down. The added pressure seemed to do the trick.

"It's as good as we are going to get it." Vienna's watch read ten minutes until midnight.

They loaded up the stumps, then waited.

Shikar leaned against the weapon, eyes cast toward the Black Wall. "This thing really goes to the other side?"

"Supposedly. We don't really know it works until someone returns." Such had been Jax's biggest fear with her invention. Did it genuinely work? Or did everyone who walked to the end of the beam meet their death? Vienna had to believe it worked, though each passing day without their return sprouted seeds of doubt.

When the hands over her watch joined at twelve, Vienna grabbed the lever. "It's time."

The fuel tank sealed under the Yamani's weight, cutting off the seeping light of the stone within. A good sign. Satisfied, Vienna activated the cannon.

The weapon roared to life. The tank under Shikar's arms rattled but held firm as the radiant white beam burst from the barrel.

The flames of the wall, illuminated by the brilliance, shuddered and extinguished on contact.

The portal was open.

The sight of their success pulled Vienna's mouth into a smile. They'd done it. She gazed up at the Yamani, whose face held an awed expression.

Then the woman winced.

Vienna checked the fuel tank. All in place. Before she could ask what was wrong, Shikar roared out in pain. That's when a spray of rock hit Vienna's cheek. Yet the seal hadn't loosened. The Yamani glanced to her shoulder, where a chunk of her stone body was missing. The injury hadn't originated from the cannon. Vienna spun.

A dozen raiders appeared from the cover of darkness at their backs, approaching in a semi-circle, surrounding them. Each gripped a pistol or spear in their hands, with the ends raised toward the pair.

They'd followed them out.

Shikar snarled as she tried to turn toward them.

"No!" Vienna lay her hands over the Yamani's and pushed the stone fingers firmly on the lid of the fuel tank. "I'll deal with them. Keep focused." When the Yamani nodded in compliance, Vienna slipped the slingshot from her belt and dug out a handful of pellets. "Your Kayetan, call it."

"It can't get close to the beam."

Shit. Shikar was right. When Vienna had last been out here, the demon had kept its distance, only able to pick off those who'd strayed too far from the cannon's light. Maybe that's why they hadn't been warned of the looters. The Kayetan couldn't reach them to report.

Slingshot ready, Vienna slipped out from behind the cover of the cannon and aimed it toward their unwelcome guests. She let out a handful of pellets. They'd made their intentions known firing first, and she wasn't about to surrender. If they wanted to talk, *they* could lower their arms.

Vienna sprinted from the cannon while digging her hand into her pouch for another round of pellets. If she could only lure them away from Shikar, she'd not only protect the portal but give the Kayetan a chance to pick off the lone enemies.

Shots fired at her back. Wind whistled by her ear—too close for comfort. A near miss. It was enough to make her throw herself to the ground. Vienna propped up to her elbows, loaded a pellet, and aimed for the nearest looter. A scream disclosed a direct hit.

Another pellet. She pulled. Shifted her aim. Fired. Another cry.

Two for two. The side of her mouth curled up. She hadn't lost her skill. But the half-smile stretched thin when a glowing light arced in the sky and angled down at her. Vienna scrambled to her feet just in time. The strange spear had struck directly where she'd been not a second earlier.

As her sigh of relief escaped her lungs, her body stiffened. A jolt ran up her legs, making her muscles convulse. The shock couldn't have lasted more than a few seconds, but it was enough for her enemies to close in.

Hands wrapped around her waist and dragged her to her feet. She kicked and screamed. Someone slapped the slingshot from her grip. Her head swung side to side.

Shikar's Kayetan lingered over a body off in the darkness. At Vienna's shriek, the demon zoomed from its kill but slammed to a stop where the last of the moonbeam's vibrant light touched the ash. Restricted to the darkness, just as Vienna had suspected.

A kick at her captor's legs only made the grip on her waist tighten. Three or four raiders encircled her, grabbing at her limbs, trying to keep her contained, but her worries settled on Shikar at the cannon.

A group of raiders had neared. They had rope snared around the stone woman, pulling her away.

"No, stop," Vienna yelled. "Let go of her."

"Shut your mouth, girl," a voice came hot and harsh in her ear.

"No, you don't understand. She can't leave the cannon. It's unstable. It'll—"

A flash of pure light burned Vienna's retinas. The boom that followed pierced her ears, sunk through her skin and muscles to rattle her bones. The invisible blast hit Vienna square in the chest and launched her off her feet. The hands of her captors fell away. She soared, body twisting. The new darkness was so intense, she never saw the ground coming up to meet her.

The wind in Vienna's lungs rushed out as she thudded hard on her side and rolled over the carpet of ash. It should've hurt, but the fresh injection of adrenaline barreling through her veins cushioned her nerves. She lay sprawled on her back, unable to move while her head spun.

All quieted.

"Shikar." Vienna knew she said the name, but the ringing in her ears blocked the sound.

Half dazed, she pushed herself to her hands and knees and crawled. Which way? Spots clouded her vision, and her ears were useless. The bitter smell of burning metal swarmed her nose. She stood on shaking legs and followed the scent.

"Shikar?"

A shape moved in the distance. It rushed her. The Kayetan had grabbed her and swept her into its arms before she could register what was happening. Wind slapped her face, before stilling again a moment later.

The Kayetan planted her on her feet. The short journey had given her senses a chance to clear. She made out the shape of a hulking form collapsed at her feet.

"Shikar!" Vienna fell to her knees and shook the Yamani's face-down form. Despite her best efforts, the woman didn't wake. She ran her hands over the body. Sharp bits of stone poked her palms. The explosion had cracked off shards of Shikar's arm and torso. She balled her fists, dug her heels into the earth, and shoved. The body gave way and rolled to the side as it released a quiet moan. Yellow eyes opened.

"Oh, thank the Souls," Vienna gasped.

A heavy hand lifted to pat Vienna's back. "It'll take more than that to get rid of me."

Vienna slumped back on her heels. A crunch beneath her drew her attention. She slipped a splintered wheel spoke from under her shin; still warm, it smelled of char. Her gaze moved from the Yamani to the remnants of the cannon.

A pile of twisted metal lay where it once stood. Destroyed beyond repair. Jax herself would have sent it away for scrap.

"I've failed." The realization engulfed her.

Shikar sat up, head turned to the mangled weapon. "Is there a way—"

"No. There's no way to fix it and no other way to get our friends back. We'd need Jax to create another one, and she's halfway to the Tiot Sea by now." Even if the engineer could return, the project would take weeks: time they didn't have. A great hand rubbed her back.

"We will find a way, little one. Without your metal weapon."

Maybe Russé and the other Souls could figure out a way. If they worked together and combined their powers.... "The war could be lost by then."

Voices broke through the silence of the plains. Vienna squinted into the night. The raiders must be stirring. Hopefully, they were in no state to fight, either. If they tried to take her now, she might let them, though Shikar and her Kayetan would never let that happen.

Through the groans and murmurs, the beat of a drum built somewhere far off. As it closed in, Vienna recognized the series of pulsing strikes. The beating of hooves. The looters had brought backup.

Vienna leaned into Shikar to aid her to her feet, yet when she scanned the area, nothing new appeared. "Do you hear that?" Maybe the explosion had messed with her eardrums.

"I *feel* it." The Yamani rose. Despite her slight limp, she puffed her chest, ready for battle. "From the wall."

Vienna spun. She found her arms clinging tightly around Shikar's as they both peered out toward the growing noise. That's when she spotted it.

A pale glow. It was as if the moon had fallen from the sky and graced the earth with its aura. Wonder transfixed Vienna. She dropped Shikar's arm and sprinted for the light. Her damaged equilibrium made her stagger, but she pushed on, ignoring Shikar's attempts to call her back.

"Kole," she yelled through the icy wind. It was him. She knew it.

Then the shape of a stag cut through night's obscurity. The crown of antlers stretched wider than she remembered. A beast more magnificent than any memory could serve galloped up to her, its riders basked in radiance.

Kole slid from the stag's back.

Vienna didn't bother slowing. She flung her body into him and threw her arms around his slight form. "You're back," she whispered through her sobs. No winter winds, nor the harshest of blizzards could dampen the warmth in her heart.

"Yes." At first, he flinched at her embrace, but then he relaxed and returned the squeeze. "I have you to thank for that."

CHAPTER 19

Kole noted the scorched scent clinging to Vienna's hair. The light of Caradin's form revealed black dust in her tresses. He set her back at arm's length to take her in. Soot covered her clothes and smudged her face, washed away in streaks by her tears.

"What happened?"

"The cannon exploded. But we are fine."

"We?"

Vienna sidestepped and pointed at the stout silhouette walking up behind her.

He'd know that shape anywhere. "Shikar." His voice cracked, but he gave it no heed. A few steps brought them both together, and she lifted him in a great big hug. The usually smooth, polished finish of her skin now stood rough and sharp. His scarred skin pained in the snug embrace, but he endured it just to stay close to her for a moment longer. "How?" he finally asked once she returned him to his feet. "You were dead."

"I was never dead," Shikar ensured. "There is much you have missed."

Those words made him shudder. Shikar must've blamed it on the temperature because she pushed him back towards Vienna. "We need to get you two inside before you freeze."

"And before the looters come to," Vienna added.

"Looters?" The sheen of metal in the ash caught his attention. What he first thought to be a pile of junk held familiar pieces: a tapering telescopic shape. The carcass of the moonstone cannon. Vienna hadn't exaggerated. "What happened here?"

Vienna and Shikar shared a meaningful look, then Vienna linked her arm in his and pulled him close. The heat of her body warmed his side. "We'll catch up in the morning. You look as drained as me."

"Get them on the stag." Piper, who had dismounted along with Vara, brought Caradin over. The animal knelt for them to mount. An unspoken greeting passed between the girls before Piper assisted Vienna atop the animal and Kole followed.

Propped behind him, Kole heard Vienna's whispers of awe at the sight of Vara. He'd forgotten how a normal person reacted to the Souls. Admittedly, the wonder of meeting another god had been lost on Kole and Piper. Him because, well, he had to die to release them so didn't exactly look forward to the encounter. And Piper, he assumed, had lost her thrill from living so long with her father.

The group set on their way, Vara leading the stag while Piper and Shikar took the rear. Kole caught sight of dark forms lying in the ash, unmoving. Must have been the looters Vienna mentioned. He squinted, though it barely helped. Dead or passed out, he couldn't tell.

"It is a long walk back. You should get some rest," Shikar said to him.

Nothing got past the Yamani. Could she really tell how hard he focused on keeping his eyes open? That and she probably thought it better to keep the scene from him.

As much as Kole wanted answers, he found the urge to sleep even more bewitching. His lids weighed down.

High on the mount in the quiet of night, they traveled back to Zeal — whatever it may look like since Kole had left. But he would miss the grand return to the city. In a matter of minutes, he found himself pitched forward, resting on Caradin's soft fur. Vienna leaned against his back. The sounds of her deep breaths lulled him to sleep.

CHAPTER 20

Kole sat cross-legged in the thick mossy floor of the forest. Apparently, Shikar had thought it best to stay outside the city while the group recharged. Her Kayetan had led the way without incident. Not that Kole would've known, since he'd slept through the entire journey.

The sun had reached its apex by the time Kole woke to the smell of roasting meat. Rabbit. He'd wiped the drool from his mouth, waiting for breakfast, while Vienna caught Kole up on the status of Ohr.

They all sat in a circle silently devouring their meal. Caradin, on the other hand, grazed on the grasses and moss around the crystal trees. Mid-bite, Kole paused, wondering if the Soul took offense to their choice of breakfast, Caradin having created all the animals and such. Maybe that was why the Orange Soul kept his distance.

The thought made Kole reconsider the rabbit leg. When his stomach growled in protest, he gave in.

"Do we know if the people of Zeal have reached Rush yet?" Kole set down the bone he'd picked clean.

"I don't have any way to contact them," Vienna confessed. "With Jax's wheelers, they move quicker than on foot or horseback."

"And Leo? The liberation? Any word?"

Vienna's frown said what she couldn't.

"We know they are safe," Piper said. "Leo has moved Socren to the coast. They are working on our war efforts."

"Has Aterus made a move?"

"My father has been quiet for some time. I'm assuming that silence was because of your deal. Now that it's gone...." Piper shrugged. "He could move at any moment."

"And Russé, Issira, and Obell, are off recruiting soldiers."

Piper and Vienna shared a glance.

"Shikar?" Kole turned to the Yamani.

"Don't look to me, boy." Shikar ate the rabbit, bone and all. "I was hibernating underground until last week. This is all news to me — dismal news at that. It's making me rethink digging myself out of that grave."

"So, let me get this straight." Kole stretched out his legs. "We are stuck on the other side of the continent while a war is waging against a very angry, very vengeful god. Our numbers are undetermined, and our reinforcements, if we *can* convince them to fight, might not make to the battle before said angry god strikes."

"When you put it like that, it makes us all seem very unorganized." Piper's mouth held tight in a line. Kole couldn't tell if it was a morbid realization or humor.

"What would you have us do, Kole?" Vienna asked.

"No. Don't you dare put that in his head." Piper waved her hand at Vienna, then focused on Kole. "Everyone has their job. We cannot deviate. Yours is to release the Souls. That is your focus. And we," she gestured around the circle, "are here to make sure you don't die in the process."

Vienna shrank back and twisted the hem of her tunic at the mention of death.

When the silence extended, Piper leaned forward in her seat. "Victory cannot happen without it."

One god left to release. Braxus. The Yellow Soul. Creator of the moon and earth. Kole would need to open his mind to her sooner or later. As important as his task was, nothing could deny his urge to join Leo and the liberation in Rush. We wanted to be on the front lines, ready.

Vara, who had been quiet thus far, taking everything in, Kole assumed, cleared her throat, drawing the group's attention. "I think it is wise to stay on your path, Kole. You may not have chosen it, but you are the only one who possesses the power needed."

"I know that. I just... I feel like things are messier now than the way I left them."

"That's because they are." Vienna had a dark tone. No need to guess to know what sorrow plagued her mind.

Felix. Vienna had filled Kole in on everything from the battle to Orla, Jax, and the raiders, even her time with Shikar's Kayetan. But she hadn't spoken of Felix. *How* it happened. The why. And her state of mind since then. It had to be bad. Kole knew how she felt, and he'd only known him for a couple of months. Losing a brother must be hard. She must feel like Kole had when he'd lost Niko.

Kole rose. "I need a walk. Vienna?"

She glanced up from her daze.

"Join me?" Kole ignored Piper's eyeroll.

Vienna stood, brushed the grass from her pants, then followed him out of camp.

"Where are we going?" Vienna asked after they'd been walking for ten minutes in one direction.

"To the edge of the forest." Kole's steps hastened the closer they got.

"For what?"

Kole glanced over his shoulder and grinned. "A ride."

Her features softened at that. "I had completely forgotten."

"I hope it's still there." White crystal trunks dominated his vision. He peered around for a darker hue. "I'm not exactly sure what they get up to on their own outside of Solpate Forest."

Then he spotted it. Wood. *Real* wood. The mahogany bark called to him. Kole upped his pace into a run. The scars of his skin pulled tight against his widened stride, forcing him to take it easier than his exhilaration demanded.

Finally, he broke out from the tree line. There it stood in all its glory. His rambler. It had come straight from Solpate, survived travels south over the Azure River, through the Ashland Plains to the volcano of Grayfall, and across the marshes all the way to Zeal.

Kole had last seen it when they'd made it to the city and dropped it off in a hurry, seeking aid for an ailment Vienna had picked up at the volcano. It had stayed—heeded his command—though it had been weeks and Kole had trekked across the black flames and back.

He rushed up and put a hand on the massive trunk. No other trees in Ohr grew as tall as the ramblers. Russé's prison in Solpate Forest had done a number on the plants and wildlife there. Their branches stretched so long it seemed as if they strived to touch the clouds. And Kole's rambler was no different. Although not the largest he'd laid eyes on, it stood well over a hundred feet tall.

Despite the frigid temperatures of winter, warmth radiated from the trunk. A deep hum vibrated beneath Kole's palm. A greeting from the tree.

"Time to wake up, big guy," he murmured, then signaled Vienna to keep her distance.

Kole thought back to his days training as Russé's apprentice. Advancing to a master shepherd had been his only goal throughout his childhood. Russé had taught him well. Little had Kole known at the time, Russé had such impressive control over the walking trees because he had created them. The Green Soul possessed an unparalleled connection.

Now, standing at the base of the trunk, Kole used those teachings to lure the great tree from its slumber.

He thought of spring: icicles thawing and dripping down to the fading slush of snow, where fresh green sprouts pricked through. In his mind, he heard a babbling creek, free of its icy shell. The scent of damp, autumn leaves, half decayed from the carpet of frost, hit his nose. Kole pictured himself back there in Solpate Forest, watching the break of spring, searching for the first bud of life on the skeletal branches. Kole wrapped this feeling inside himself, then pressed it into the rambler.

The groan of wood echoed through the forest.

A creak, then another.

Then silence.

After lowering his hand, Kole stepped back and stood next to Vienna to witness the grandeur.

It took a moment, but when the earth began to rumble beneath his boots, he knew the great tree had finally awoken.

The soil rippled underfoot, like slithering snakes just beneath the surface. Roots sprang up, dozens at a time. Kole and Vienna shielded their faces from the sprays of dirt as tendrils yanked from the earth. Now free, each root pressed down with such force, the trunk lifted from the land and rose atop its hundreds of spider-like legs.

Though noble in its appearance, the ramblers had a deadly past. Any one of those roots could crush a bear. Their danger was the reason the shepherds existed: to protect the refugees from being trampled by the walking trees.

The rambler shook its bare canopy, and a flurry of twigs showered down, pelting Kole's head.

Vienna ducked. Kole could've sworn he heard her laugh.

The way the tree moved, swelling upward, made it appear as if were yawning. When the rambler finally settled, gently swaying, Kole approached. Though he knew this rambler well—had formed a special bond with the tree since embarking from Solpate—a healthy sense of caution drove his advance.

He reached out for a root. Damp soil still clung to the tendril, falling away in clumps at his touch. Through their connection, Kole sent a greeting of his own. A test. No doubt the rambler would remember him, but he had to be sure in his weeks away that the thing hadn't gone feral.

In response, the root curled around Kole's forearm in somewhat of a handshake. Then two other roots snaked around Kole, one poking his side while the other ruffled through his hair. He smiled at the playfulness, then glanced back at Vienna.

"It's safe."

Before he could reintroduce Vienna to the rambler, the root at Kole's side circled his waist and lifted him into the air. Kole gasped at his sudden weightlessness. The tree brought the shepherd up to its trunk and placed him at the base. Kole grabbed a handful of bark and found solid footing before he spun around. He couldn't hold back the smile that threatened to take over his whole face.

Vienna had reached the roots far below. Kole sent his will through the tree, and a tendril scooped her up. Her laughter rang like bells in his ears. The twinkle in her eyes caught his attention. It warmed his heart to see her happy, even if only for a moment. No doubt she'd been driven to a dark place in these last weeks as she suffered the loss of her brother alone.

Closing in on the trunk, Vienna pointed her feet and reached for the landing zone. Her arms hugged the trunk upon release as she found her bearings. She'd always been fearless. More so than anyone Kole had known.

"I forgot how tall it was." Vienna craned her head over, spying the forest floor below. "If you did that to Felix, he'd be screaming like a toddler."

They both laughed.

Kole fondly remembered the first time Felix had encountered the rambler. After all the danger his friend threw himself headfirst into, heights were the thing that got him.

After the initial delight wore off and the memory faded, a gloom rose between them. He wanted to ask her about Felix. Wanted to know how she was doing. *Obviously not great,* Kole lectured himself. More than anything, he wanted her to know that he may not have been around when she needed him most, but he was here now. And he wouldn't abandon her again. He wished to say everything to her, but his lips squeezed tight like a dam. How would he even go about it? And bringing it up now? If she didn't want to talk about it, his inquiries would only remind her of his death again.

Vienna tilted her head back and stared at the canopy above. "It wasn't just heights, you know."

Kole glanced over. Her face held a solemness, yet a distant fog covered her eyes as if she were reliving a tender memory. He feared a single word would break the spell, so he stayed quiet and urged the rambler to still.

"There was this tree out in the farmlands we used to climb. The *biggest* in Socren," she said with a youthful awe. "Our ma would have us run errands at the market. She'd send us off with coins in our hands and tell us not to come back until lunch. So we'd buy her ingredients then wander the farmlands all morning. We'd hop the fences and play with the animals out there, but mostly we climbed this one tree. We did it for years—always seeing which one of us could go higher.

"One day, Felix went higher than he'd ever gone. All the way up to the thin branches. It might've been okay a year prior, but since the farmland had been run dry, the tree had died and dried out throughout the previous summer. A branch broke off on his way up and he got stuck up there."

"How'd he get back down?" Kole asked. All the while, he recreated the images in his head, pretending as if he were there, getting a glimpse into their childhood.

"I went up after him. He'd broken off so many holds, I had to go a different way. The branches were fragile. When I got close, I reached up for him, but the limb snapped beneath me, and I fell and hit my head so hard it knocked me out. He said he screamed for me, but I didn't wake."

Kole looked to her expectantly. Clearly, she'd recovered.

"Some farmhands heard him wailing and took us home. His fear came from seeing me fall and having to watch me lay there unconscious for so long."

Felix had always been protective of his older sister. Maybe that was the event that sparked it.

"I felt like that... watching him from afar with no way to save him. I was in that tree, looking down at him—helpless—as Orla took him." Vienna's voice broke off. "Except there are no farmhands to come save us. No more parents to go home to."

"I should have been there." Kole wanted to be that farmhand for them. If he could go back to that night, he would've never gone through the flames.

"No," Vienna turned to him, "you shouldn't have."

"It could've been different."

"But it's not," she said sternly. "We all made a choice. If you hadn't listened to me, things would have been different, for certain. But it doesn't mean it would've been better. We could have lost more because we were all afraid of losing each other. It took a sacrifice. One that Felix made of his own free will. This isn't some bedtime fairy tale parents tell their kids, where the heroes save the day unscathed and happy. Reality is cold. Heroes don't always make it to the end of the story. I'm scared of what that means for us and our friends."

The thought made Kole's stomach knot. *Who's next?* Those words repeated in his head. The faces of Leo, the liberation, Shikar, Jax, Piper, Vienna, and himself, shuffled in his head like playing cards. Which would draw first?

"I don't have to like it or be okay with it, but I do have to accept Felix's death," she said, distracting Kole from his spiraling pit of worry.

"He's not coming back. I know that, yet my brain keeps trying to convince me otherwise."

"What do you mean?"

Vienna slid her back down the trunk and sat at the base, legs swinging freely in the open air. "Shikar's Kayetan. I was alone when I met it. My eyes made me see...."

Kole sat down beside her.

"They made me see him." She looked at Kole with desperation behind her gaze. "I thought it was Felix's Kayetan. Even though I saw the shadow disintegrate before my eyes along with my brother, I was sure of it. And that led me to hope that maybe... somehow... he could still be alive, too." She scoffed and cast her glare down. "It's stupid, I know."

"No, it's not." Kole touched her arm. "Our minds our powerful things. They can confuse us. Make us believe things that are untrue — see things that aren't there. All you wanted was your brother back, and your mind gave that to you." He tucked his knees to his chest and hugged them. "Like how I was fooled with Niko."

Vienna peered over to him.

"You were right about Aterus." Kole didn't want to explain, but by the shift in her eyes, it seemed she understood.

"I guess we were both duped."

"I'm sorry," Kole said.

"Me too." She leaned over, laid her head on his shoulder, and wrapped an arm around him in a half hug.

Kole froze. The closeness sent a wave of warmth through his body. Surely, she could hear his pounding heart. But the embrace felt lovely. He couldn't bring himself to move his arm, so he let his head fall onto hers.

Their hug out in the plains had been different — a greeting of sorts. This felt... intimate. Friends comforting each other, surely. They both needed someone right now. Kole knew, deep down, he longed for it to be something more. He'd been repressing that feeling for a while now. Yet he knew this wasn't the time. Not when death had made such a fresh wound in both of them. It wouldn't be right. Not now. Maybe not ever.

No matter the intent, Kole cherished the embrace. It soothed his pain if only a little, and he hoped it did the same for her.

Kole hopped to his feet, trying to conceal the blush that most certainly covered his cheeks and neck. He prayed she didn't notice. "I'd like to see him."

Vienna gave a small smile, then pointed north.

Chapter 21

With a root in each hand, Kole steered the rambler up the forest line. He'd missed the thrill of being a shepherd.

The giant tree allowed him full control. It gave Kole power. More than he could ever have after his burns. On his feet — on his own, without a god by his side — he was just a teenage boy limited by the damaged tissue of his scars. Restrained in his own body. He wished to sprint again. Feel his heels dig into the earth. *Oh, to climb and jump and fight unhindered.* It would be a godsend to have his former body back. But even the Souls, he learned, couldn't grant him such a request.

Instead, he had his rambler. Here Kole felt alive. Strong. Unstoppable. At the helm of the gargantuan tree, it seemed like any opponent would fall at his feet.

From his position at the base of the trunk, Kole looked out for miles over the spiky tops of the crystal trees. The sun bounced off each branch, giving them a sparkling finish. The brightness hurt his eyes.

"There." Vienna pointed out the memorial.

Kole saddled the rambler up to the tree. The roots delicately wrapped around Kole's and Vienna's waists and lowered them to the ground.

A thick-trunked crystal tree stood as the memorial. Kole rounded the stone tree, taking in all the names carved there. So many more than he had thought. Should he have expected any less from an uprising and the Black Wall sweeping through the city? During most of the battle he'd been confined underground. By the time he escaped, the streets of Zeal had seemed empty.

Vienna ran her hand over the letters. "This tree is for the ones who couldn't be recovered."

It was the nice way of saying "touched by the wall or entombed under the collapsed buildings." The ones whose bodies were eternally lost.

After encircling the tree, he moved next to Vienna. Her fingers traced the name of her brother.

Felix Hallas

The letters burned into Kole's brain. It had been more than a month since his death, but for *him*, stuck on the other side of the Black Wall... it had only been a day. *One day* since he'd last laid eyes on his friend. He never got to say goodbye. Or apologize. They'd been cross during their final conversation. Felix had held a grudge when he found out about the deal Kole had made with Aterus. *For good reason. Look where that got me.*

The pit in his stomach swallowed up his insides. Kole felt as if he'd fall into himself. He wanted to. Why had that been the last thing they'd said? Why had Orla made the cult strike *then*? He'd never forgive himself. He'd been selfish. "He was so angry with me." Kole pictured the look on Felix's face when he discovered Kole's secret. Disgust.

"No. Not in the end," Vienna said fervently.

"I betrayed you both."

"It was a mistake; the deal, the way we treated you. We all should've talked it out. But we're stubborn. Every one of us." Sounds of rustling came from her, but Kole kept his stare on Felix's name. "There was a moment before it happened," she went on. "He had made up his mind. I think he knew how it would end for him. He gave me this." Vienna held the slingshot in her open palm and the embroidered pouch of pellets in the other.

Felix's prized weapon. For such an innocent-looking weapon, it sure packed a deadly blow. With a keen shot, he'd seen Felix tear a finger clean off an enemy's hand. Felix had used it to save Kole from a guard when they'd first met. His friend had even gifted it to him until taking it back after learning of the deal with Aterus.

"He told me to give it to you."

Tears blurred Kole's vision as he reached for it, but his hand flinched away. "I can't."

"I gave him my word." Vienna took his hands and placed the slingshot and pellet bag in Kole's possession. "Don't make me go back on it."

The handle still had the fabric wrapped around the wood. Kole's scars prevented him from squeezing anything too tightly without pain, so they'd fashioned it to better fit his grip. A bright jingle came from the pouch as the metal balls inside slid around. He thumbed the vibrant seven Souls symbol embroidered on the side. Felix had never mentioned the stitchwork had been his own, ashamed of anyone knowing his love for needlework. While rolling the pouch in his palm, Kole rotated to the back, where a new picture lay. He glanced up to Vienna, curious.

"He loved you, Kole. Until the very end."

The image sewn in the fabric portrayed a red hand, Kole's burned hand, shaking a Kayetan claw. Felix. They'd both faced death and survived. Something they'd bonded over. The image could mean so much: Felix's acceptance of his Kayetan, or it could represent their friendship. But it meant something more to Kole. Forgiveness.

The chance to apologize hadn't been stolen. It stared Kole straight in the face.

And just like that, the pit in his stomach exploded.

He broke.

Kole fell to his knees at the base of the memorial and cried. The slingshot and pouch rolled off into the grass. If Vienna tried to console him, he didn't feel it. Something in his heart burned. It was like losing Niko all over again. The sorrow drowned him. If this continued... if people close to him kept dying... there was only so much he could handle.

Yet the war hung over him like a circling vulture. Death was inevitable. Violent deaths. Massacres. Is that how Felix had gone out? A hero? Or a senseless murder? His friend deserved better. He deserved to live. Wasn't being captured and turned into a Kayetan enough? Why did it have to be Felix to bear the brunt of this burden?

Kole's grief twisted to rage. His very skin warmed so much he thought it had been set aflame. He curled his fingers into the soil, hoping the coolness would quell the heat. But it only fueled him.

"Kole?" Vienna's shaking voice barely registered.

The wrath built and built until he lost control and screamed. A new energy sparked. It ran wild inside him. Kole felt it swirl through his head, meddling. Yet he couldn't reign himself in. Or truly didn't want to.

The doors in his mind leading to the Souls rattled against their hinges until they finally shattered. Kole sucked in their energy like drought-ridden earth soaking up fresh rain. He let the power fuel his rage. His limbs quivered.

"Kole!" She sounded so far away.

What he needed was a fix. A solution. Protection. Something that ensured this wouldn't happen again. A way to protect the friends he had left. Vienna.

Kole snapped his eyes open. Everything had been tinted in white light.

"Kole," came his name again. This time, a man's voice. Russé. *"You're going too far. Come back down."*

Inviting the gods' power into his body had gone poorly before. He hadn't known what was happening then. If he used the energy instead of allowing it to fester inside of him, he was certain he could maintain control.

"You made the others walk," Kole answered. "Help me."

Regardless of Russé's reply, Kole thrust his palm onto the stone trunk and poured forth the Souls' energy. He sent thoughts of rising suns and springtime into the crystal. Just when he thought he worked alone, his borrowed energy shifted.

"Full moon," Russé hinted.

That's right. The crystal trees shone during the night. Kole turned his thoughts to dusk, replacing the sun with a glistening moon suspended in a clear, starry canvas.

The trunk at his palm rumbled. The earth split at his knees, and a stone root peeked through.

Kole released his hold on the Souls' energy and let it return through the portals. In one quick motion, he pushed to his feet, grabbed Vienna, whose terror-filled eyes darted in circles, and pulled her back to the safety of the rambler. At his command, the towering tree set its roots down in a protective cage around the pair.

The memorial tree broke from the soil and stepped up on its crystalline legs. It stayed poised there like a newborn figuring out its body.

"What did you do?" Vienna's face had paled, whether out of fear or fascination, Kole could only guess.

"Called for reinforcements."

While the crystal tree adjusted, Kole cast his attention past it, knowing the awakening had just begun.

The thing about forests, or at least back in Solpate, was that they nestled so close together that their roots entangled with their neighbors. All connected as one.

A tremor shook Kole's knees. He and Vienna held onto the cage of rambler roots to keep from falling. Even their rambler had to drill roots down as an anchor to stay steady.

Birds flocked away from the canopy. Wildlife fled as if a fire had run them out. Glass-like tendrils flung from their earthly prison and met the air. Thousands of legs emerged as far as Kole could see. One by one, the trunks rose, becoming a new kind of rambler.

When the tremors settled, Kole slipped through his rambler's roots and made a break for the memorial tree.

"Wait. Kole!" Vienna shouted after him.

Kole made for the newborn, slowing as he neared. The crystal tree must've noticed his advance because it stood taller on its legs, like a bear showing its strength. He stopped and held his hands out. "It's okay, little guy. I'm not going to hurt you."

The stone tree made no move to attack, nor did it back down.

With his hands still open, Kole took one step at a time. All he needed was a single touch of one of those roots to show his intent and gain control. He wished he had his shepherd tools. A rope would've proved useful about now.

Vienna must've caught onto the weight of the task because she hushed.

A few more steps now. Then he just might reach. Kole stretched out his fingertips. Flesh within a whisper of the root, the tree lashed out.

Kole threw himself to the floor. The tendril whizzed overhead, barely missing his neck. What the new rambler lacked in size, it certainly made up in its strike. A hit with a stone arm would cause more than a bruise or a couple cracked ribs. This thing could be a killer. All the more reason to win them.

Kole's rambler moved to aid its master, but Kole sent his will to the giant to leave him be. He must calm the crystal tree on his own to have complete control. Usually, shepherds worked in pairs in this sort of situation, but the rest of his trained comrades had joined Leo on the other side of the continent. He was alone.

He had one advantage, though. The newborn acted much like a sapling: wobbly on its newfound legs, uncoordinated, and rash. Before the tree could send another swipe, Kole moved quick. Scarred skin resisted his opened gait, pulled and screamed at him to take it easy, but he pushed harder. Instead of a direct path to the tree, Kole rounded it, hoping it would confuse the rambler.

One eye stayed ready for another deadly swing, while his other kept focus on the nearest root. With a creak, the second blow came for him. It arced down, slapping the ground far behind his heels. A poor shot, just as Kole had anticipated. The moment the hit landed, sending a wave ripping through the soil, Kole jumped for the roots. He curled his fingers around the cold surface and thrust his thoughts into the feisty tree.

Though the new rambler acted as a sapling, as Kole navigated, he found the tree far older than he thought. He remembered learning the crystal trees were an ancient species. Their growth and reproduction had been stunted when the Souls were imprisoned. Not only that, but their essence felt alien. The tree part was there, plain as day, but another sense made up their aura. Earth. Stone. The part that made them so different from the ramblers Kole was used to.

They may be different, but they grow from the same ancestors. He needed to find the commonalities and latch on. With that in mind, Kole switched tactics. Where the Solpate ramblers soaked in the sunlight, the crystal trees welcomed the moon. That image alone dampened the hostility.

Now to command it. Instead of forcing his hand to dominate, Kole sent the wild thing his memories of his time with his own rambler. Their bond. Their friendship. A hum came from behind Kole. His rambler vibrated the air, as if recalling the same.

A moment passed.

Kole turned his head, wondering if somehow the two trees held their own conversation. Then, the root beneath Kole's hand buzzed.

The memorial tree lowered from its high roots, falling into a relaxed stance. More buzzing filled the air—surrounded him. His entire body from his bones to his nails vibrated along with the hum.

"It's the forest." Vienna walked out from the safety of the rambler's cage toward the mass of teetering crystal trees.

The sight made Kole feel small. Every stone tree, as far as his strained eyes could register, swayed and hummed. Were they yielding? Allowing Kole to be their shepherd?

Only one way to find out. Kole touched the memorial tree once more and asked it to lift a root. It complied.

Strangely enough, the command rippled through the forest. Each new rambler lifted a root in unison. The sight took his breath away. He'd seen Russé control several ramblers at once, but this was on a whole different scale.

An army. The one they needed to stand against Aterus.

CHAPTER 22

"What the hell is going on?" Piper ran out from the forest line, giving a wide berth to the risen trees.

"How did you find us?" Kole asked.

The demigod pointed to the towering rambler. "Can't exactly hide that thing. It's the size of a mountain."

She and Vara both slipped through the roots, eyes wide and darting as they approached. Shikar, however, touched every tree as she passed them as if admiring the stone beauties. The stag followed, unbothered.

Kole retrieved Felix's slingshot and pouch at his feet, rubbed his thumb over the embroidery, then tucked it on the side of his belt for safekeeping. "How far does it go?"

"How far does it—It's the whole damn forest, Kole," Piper huffed. "Shikar said she could feel the whole bloody place uproot." She seemed almost annoyed that Kole and Vienna were unharmed and happy. "I thought the Black Wall was on the move."

"Just Kole," Vienna said, still taking in the new ramblers from afar.

Out of habit, Kole quickly checked his six o'clock, where the wall lay. Still miles past the city. His nerves rested easy. "Not just me," Kole corrected.

"I felt you tap into my powers." Vara's leaned-back posture gave Kole a sense she was impressed. "A dangerous thing for a human to tamper with us like that."

"I know my limits." Kole's chest had unintentionally puffed up. Though not entirely true, this time felt different. He had felt more in control. Maybe he was finally building confidence in himself. Or maybe it was dumb luck. Either way, he had summoned an army. One that could go up against whatever Aterus threw at them.

"And what are those limitations, exactly?" Piper cut in. "Are these things going to stampede and trample us as we leave?"

"They'll do more than that." Kole patted the trunk of the memorial tree. "They're our ride out of here."

Piper tilted her head towards Caradin. "Looks like the god has been demoted from caravan to pet."

The stag snorted at that.

"Better than walking, I suppose," Vienna said. "We'll all get some well-needed rest."

Vara brushed a coiled strand from her face. "And where exactly are we headed?"

The question alluded to more than their destination. What the Violet Soul actually asked was if Kole had made progress on locating Braxus' prison. "I haven't reached out to her yet."

His companions quieted. Their stares weighed heavy on him.

"I just need some time. For now, we can move the reinforcements toward Rush. I'm sure an army like this would boost morale."

"A worthy army, indeed. A force like this may sway my people into joining the cause," said Shikar.

That sparked an idea. "Then we will send forces there to help Issira in her mission. If you think it would help?"

The Yamani nodded approvingly. "Not even Mikal could deny this sort of strength."

The last time Kole had seen Mikal, the Yamani tribe leader, they'd been fleeing the erupting volcano. No doubt they were still recovering from the explosion of their home. It would be no easy feat to pull them away from Grayfall now. Though Issira's tranquil demeanor may be the best fit to soften Mikal into aiding the cause, the Blue Soul still needed every assistance afforded to her.

"A portion will go to Grayfall," Kole deemed. "The rest will accompany us in search of Braxus." The strength in Kole's voice surprised even him. He felt... in control. And it felt good.

No one argued.

Taking that as approval, Kole approached the memorial tree to give his orders to the crystal trees.

"Wait." Vienna appeared at Kole's left, one arm protectively over the names. "Leave this one here. Please?"

Kole paused and scanned the names. All the dead etched into the stone. Despite the dozens that graced the bark, his eyes kept coming back to Felix Hallas.

"They've seen enough battle." She brushed a light hand over the etchings.

Kole understood. This tree had a new purpose: a grave for the fallen. Not just a memorial but a headstone. And it needed to stay in its rightful place in respect to the dead. He had a sting of guilt for awakening it in the first place.

He closed his eyes and settled the memorial tree. It was for the best not to bring it. Parading around the names would dampen the spirits in Rush. A reminder of the pain of that horrific night.

The tree drilled its roots down and settled. Aside from the upturned soil at the base of its trunk, it looked as if it had never moved. Then, he crossed to the nearest crystal tree and sent out his will.

Like stone spiders, the trees skittered south, while the few dozen surrounding Kole's group stayed put.

The ground rumbled as the forest marched on, eventually fading when the trees shrunk further and further away on the horizon. Kole found it hard to imagine any force to rival the army they had now. And they'd only gain more power.

"We can all fit on my rambler." Kole turned to the Yamani. Her weighty form had slowed the great tree when last she'd ridden it. "Shikar, it might be best—"

"I remember very well. No need to tiptoe." The rock woman strode up to a crystal tree and patted one of the roots. "Much hardier."

Kole had the crystal rambler carry the Yamani up to its trunk. An odd sound resonated from her on her journey up. One of grinding stone. A laugh, Kole realized.

The rest of the company ascended along with Kole to the giant rambler's trunk. Caradin transformed into a silver weasel, scampered up Kole's trouser, and cozied up around his neck. Kole smiled. The winged stag had its advantages, but the rodent form held a place as Kole's favorite. The warmth of the critter, like a fuzzy scarf, banished the grating chill.

"Where to?" Vienna sat on the ledge of the trunk with her feet pumping over the side.

"That's the question, isn't it?" Kole mumbled.

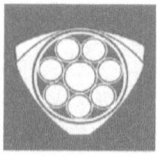

They rode east through the day. The rambler led the way while the smaller trees followed in a large mass. Right as they had set off, gray clouds rolled in bringing a flurry of fresh powder.

Kole and Vienna sat shoulder to shoulder, sharing each other's warmth. While Piper had initially sat on her own, she eventually migrated to them. The way she scooted in, with her chin set the opposite way, made it clear her intention was to warm herself rather than to engage. While Kole and Vienna talked, Piper kept her shoulders turned away, but she would comment every now and then, obviously invested in their conversation.

The time Kole had spent with the liberation in Socren had been short. He hadn't been around Piper to get to know her very well. All he gathered from their brief interactions was her aloof, distant manner. All this time, Kole assumed it came from Piper's lineage. That she thought less of humans and regarded her demigod status as better than. Now, as she interacted with him and Vienna, Kole suspected she felt as much an outsider as he did with his burns.

By the time night came, two solid feet of snow had cloaked the land. The glow of the crystal trees bouncing off the glistening powder made the terrain appear straight from a dream.

"Not bad for a day's travel." Piper pointed to the dark shadows on the northern horizon, then glanced back as the crystal trees began to glow at the moon's appearance. "These ramblers travel faster than any horse."

The Poleer Mountain Range. The sight of the distant peaks soured Kole's already growling stomach with homesickness. Solpate lay just north of the mountains. He yearned for home—his old home. Now Solpate... well, it wasn't what it used to be. So he'd heard. Things had drastically changed. There were reports the ramblers of the forest had rooted for good and no longer walked. The refugees, his people, had been driven out. Nothing of Kole's good memories remained. Even these peaks were alien to him. Though he'd lived next to the mountains for years, he'd never traveled so far south. He wondered what would happen after all this ended. If he survived and succeeded in saving Ohr, where would he go? Where would he call home?

"How long until we reach Rush?" Kole shifted in his seat. The perks of a smooth ride on the rambler had its downfalls. The rough bark rubbed his scars. He found himself changing positions frequently. The only thing he missed about Caradin's stag form was the soft coat.

"Do you still have my map?" Vienna asked.

Kole retrieved the scroll from his belt and handed it over.

After a moment of study, Vienna scanned the mountains, land, and sky. Finally, she placed her finger on the parchment. "It's hard to tell with all the snow covering the landmarks. If I had to guess, we should reach the river by morning." Her hand slid across the map to the far side where the coast lay. "If we keep pace and travel through the night, we could make it to Rush in three days."

"But we aren't going to Rush, are we, Kole?" Piper turned around in her seat to face him.

It was a reminder — a nag, really — for Kole to get on with contacting Braxus. The weasel around Kole's neck yawned. Shikar had fallen asleep on her crystal tree. They had all gotten their rest. Vara hadn't said anything, but her ears perked at Piper's words.

"I'd rather not on an empty stomach, but if you insist," he mumbled. Not that the task was impossible without food; it just brought another distraction.

Before anyone could respond, Kole had a root curl around him and take him up to the canopy for privacy. There, he settled in on a branch and focused on the task at hand.

Braxus. He hoped the search for the final Soul would prove simpler than the others. No riddles or clues he had to decipher. He'd go straight to the location, release her effortlessly, then join the war initiative in Rush. *Here's to hoping.*

Kole opened the door to the god and repeated the name, calling for her.

Something wriggled in his brain. It pounced on Kole. The sudden act took Kole by surprise. He jumped in his seat atop the bough and would've fallen if not for the roots holding him firm.

"Where am I?" the voice said in a high-pitched hysteria. *"What's happened?"*

"Braxus?" Kole tested.

"That is what I was called." A suspicious note laced her words. *"How do you know this? Who are you?"*

Odd questions. Amnesia? But not nearly as disconnected as Caradin was. At least Braxus knew how to speak. *"My name is Kole. I am friends with your kin. I am tasked with releasing you from your prison."*

"Then release me," she snapped.

"I need to know where you are to do that."

"Darkness. I see... I feel darkness. Everywhere. All the time."

Another riddle to solve. Kole bit his tongue to repress his frustration. *"What do you hear?"*

"Let me show you."

A pulling sensation swept through Kole's body. The mountains vanished. His ears left the groans of wood behind and jumped to a far-off place. Just as Braxus had described, the palate of nothingness confronted Kole. Nothing like the darkness he'd encountered before. This was pitch. No moon or stars or sun spread their light here. The vision reminded Kole of his time in the void when he died for those brief seconds while unlocking the Souls. Except the sound was off. In the void, his senses were deleted. Nonexistent. Here... he felt something. A pressure encasing him.

"Nothing moves, nothing changes. I thought death had taken me long ago."

If Kole had never faced those near-death experiences, he would've come to the same conclusion. *"I will find you. Just hold on."*

Kole cut off the connection. So little to go on. He'd need more help this time.

CHAPTER 23

Kole stuffed his face with fish. The moment the meat hit his stomach, his body shuddered with relief. Cool water from his canteen washed it down. When they had reached the Coroko River not half an hour ago, Kole had instructed his rambler to break the thin layer of ice and use its roots to block off a small portion of the water at the bank. Dozens of fish swam in a frenzy trying to escape the snaring roots. No need for a fishing rod when you had the biggest net in Ohr.

The group gorged themselves on seared trout and river water. Kole picked a bone from his teeth.

After her third fillet, Vienna said, "Underground for sure."

"Yes, but that could be anywhere," Piper added.

"She is the god of the moon and earth." Vara's duel-colored eyes held a purplish hue in the early dawn hours. "It might be something related to that."

Shikar grabbed another fish from the makeshift pond Kole had made. "There's plenty of earth to search. Too much. Now, say she's on the moon. That's going to get interesting."

"That can't really happen, can it?" Vienna set her sights to the hazy white moon. "She can't be up there."

"I see the family humor lives on in you." Piper smirked, but her mouth instantly relaxed when Kole scolded her with a glare. "Sorry," she mumbled, then continued in a gentler tone, "It must be somewhere Aterus could go. We can cross out the moon."

"And the wall." Kole jerked his chin to Vara. "The communication was too clear." When he'd first reached out to Vara, her words had come to him clipped and rushed.

Vara nodded. "I would've felt her if she were behind the flames with me."

"I think he should've put her in the moon. It'd be fitting and a smarter choice." Shikar threw the whole fish into her mouth, bones and all, then scoured the bank for river rocks.

"Whose side are you on?" Kole teased.

The Yamani woman's yellow eyes trained on Kole, her arms filled with loose stones. "I just meant if he really didn't want the Souls to be found, it would've been smarter for him to put it in a place where mortals cannot reach."

"Let's be glad you weren't his advisor," Kole poked back.

Shikar took the compliment with a smile, then returned to foraging for pebbles as she popped a few into her mouth.

"We should consult the others," Vara suggested. "We might be able to learn more if we put our heads together."

Piper huffed. "There's no way to figure this out on our own?"

"She put me there — wherever 'there' is. I don't know anything else." Kole leaned back against the root that acted as a lounge chair and propped his hands behind his head. "Unless you have a sudden epiphany as to what it could mean?"

"I'll let you know if I do," Piper said curtly.

Shikar sat back down and munched on her collected rocks while watching the back and forth between him and Piper. Though she winced with each bite, the rock diet had much improved her form. The Yamani had complained before about the inferior taste of stone to "human food." Her kin back in Grayfall had teased that she had gone soft for abandoning the Yamani habits. Their earthen bodies were what they ate, so Shikar had explained. Stone kept them strong as diamonds.

"Stopping at Rush will delay us," Piper posed.

"We'd waste more time searching random hunches." Kole held back the urge to smirk. Oh, how he sounded like Russé. Waiting wasn't Kole's typical style. Jumping to conclusions — acting on impulse — had been more his thing. At least it had been in the past. *That old man might be proud of me.* "The other Souls might have more insight."

"Looks like you'll get your way after all," Piper relented. "To the coast, then."

After they'd eaten, Kole had the rambler form a makeshift curtain out of its roots to act as a personal room on the shallow bank of the river. They took turns bathing as best as they could in the icy river. Now that the sun had risen well above the horizon, the warmth of the day cut through winter's hold on the land.

Permanent goosebumps graced Kole's skin ever since he touched the frigid river water. They all only had the clothes on their backs, so washing them was off the table. They'd either have to wait for them to dry on the rambler's boughs or wear them sopping wet. Neither boded well for frostbite. Shikar, of course, had no issues. The stone woman wore nothing. Kole doubted the temperatures affected her in the slightest. Why did it have to be winter now? Why indeed. Especially when they had the Soul of seasons as a companion.

While everyone gathered their things and readied for travel, Kole found Vara tying down a handful of fish onto the rambler's trunk.

"Isn't there something you can do about this?" Kole waved a hand to the frozen river. "Make it a little warmer?"

Vara turned to him after securing the rations. "There is. But I assume you want an instant change, do you not?"

"Well, yeah."

"Winter has just started. If I end it now, it could have a drastic impact on Ohr."

"Seems like everything has a 'drastic impact on Ohr.'" It was hard to imagine how an entire world could be so fragile. Yet here it was, teetering on existence from the devouring Black Wall.

The blatant disappointment must've tugged her sympathy because she sagged her shoulders and sighed. "A few warmer days won't spoil the cycle."

"Really?"

"I'll see what I can do." Vara held her hands up to the sky and whispered into the air. The words were lost on Kole. Some language he'd never heard.

As she worked, Kole scanned the area yet saw no change. The snow still glittered, and the ice crusted the river like a shield.

When he turned back to Vara, her body hummed with a golden hue. And those eyes. Her mismatched irises switched from white and pale green to emerald and orange. Kole waited to feel a rush of heat, but it never came.

Then she relaxed and smiled at him, an amused look on her face. "Things take time," she reminded him. "Shocking the land will only bring trouble."

Kole nodded. When the other Souls had used their powers, they had made instant, tangible changes. In comparison, this seemed lackluster. On the other hand, Vara *was* trying to perform something that touched the entire region. Just as grand in power, yet not as flashy. Still, he eagerly waited for the slightest trace of warmth. Souls knew he needed it.

With newly cleaned skin and chilled bones, Kole set the ramblers on their journey across the river. Last time they had crossed had been tricky with the strength of the current. Kole hoped to avoid the water and take their army of trees over the road of ice. One step in and that hope shattered along with the surface.

His rambler led the way. Once the weight of the first root touched down, the river broke. The rambler poked its tendrils down to the riverbed as Kole gave the command for its passengers to ascend to the canopy. A handful of roots carried them up where they settled and hugged tightly to the branches.

Kole had his rambler go first. He held on to a pair of roots and steered the great tree into deeper waters. The rambler poised a few tendrils above the ice and stabbed them down repeatedly as it walked, creating a trench of flowing water in its wake. The crystal trees followed the cleared river in single file.

The further the rambler got, the higher the tide rose. Halfway up the roots. Higher and higher. Just below the base of the trunk now, an arm's reach from Kole's boots. Only when the water nipped at his toes did Kole join his companions in the canopy.

"How's it looking?" Kole asked as he slipped from the tendril and grabbed onto a thick branch.

"We're approaching the middle," Vienna said. "The river seems shallower here."

Indeed it was. The river came less than halfway up the rambler's trunk. No risk of full submersion. The crystal trees, however, stood severely shorter than Kole's prized rambler.

"Shikar!" Kole called to the Yamani, who had ridden the crystal tree at their tail. His voice barely carried to her as the broken ice freed the roaring waters. "It's too deep for them."

The warning set a smile over Shikar's face. "I do not fear the water. Let it try to tame me."

"She's going under?" Vienna said as the Yamani's grin dipped below the surface.

Admittedly, Kole knew little about the stone species, but the last time he'd been with the Yamani, they'd had no issue staying under for a long period of time. Shikar's kin had carried Kole's group through an underwater passage, which acted as a secret entrance to the dormant lava tubes beneath the volcano. Except, those waters had been still.

"She knows herself better than we do." Kole left it at that and turned his attention to his own rambler.

As Kole had thought, the army had dipped entirely beneath the surface. Their translucent forms blurred in the lens of the rushing water. At the center of the river, the current shook Kole's rambler. The canopy shuddered as the roots strained to keep anchored in the bed below. But Kole had crossed the river once before down south on their way to Zeal, and the rambler could do it again.

"Hold tight," Kole called to his companions. At his warning, the rambler curled its smaller branches upward forming protective cages around its riders. Vienna and the others clutched the wood bars while casting worried gazes down at the frozen river lashing the tree.

Kole welcomed the branches curving up around him. Now that he had security from slipping, he placed his hands on the thick bough beneath him and poured his energy into the rambler.

Since the roots had completely submerged, it left the massive trunk to carve out a safe path through the ice. Kole shared a shiver with the tree as the ice mauled away chunks of bark, exposing the smooth inner trunk. Gashes. Wounds that would ooze sap once they made land. Kole urged the rambler forward, though the tree needed little encouragement. The great rambler had a will that matched its size. The well of power and strength had seemed to double after the tree's long hibernation away from Kole.

The ice cracked and split as the tree threw its weight. Kole stared in awe, wondering if even the force of ocean waves could contend with his rambler. The stone trees progressed, too. Their sheer mass grounded them to the riverbed, unaffected by the undertow. Harsh waters they may be, now mastered by Kole's army of ramblers.

Soon, the trunk lifted out from the river as the ground sloped toward the shore. The roots emerged, thrashing arms pulverizing the glazed river to slush.

Kole's bones and joints felt brittle—frozen to the core just like his rambler. The sun shone bright, a meager attempt at warming them up against the nipping breeze. Once the great rambler graced the western edge of the Coroko River, its trunk slumped down to the earth with a quaking thump. The roots splayed out like a squashed spider.

The branches around Kole and his companions relaxed back to their natural form, freeing them from their cages.

Kole climbed down from the bough. "The rambler needs a rest." The root that coiled around his waist and gently set him on the ground had gone so cold, its icy touch burned through his clothes. Kole lifted his shirt to discover a red ring over his stomach.

The crystal trees marched from the river one at a time. Their stone structure appeared unaffected by the frigid temperatures. The water dripping from their branches made them sparkle. Wet trunks shone. If he'd never seen the crystal trees before, he would've believed them made of pure ice.

And there stood Shikar, one arm braced around her crystal tree. Her eyes burned bright, as if invigorated by the danger. The Yamani spotted Kole and pointed a stubby finger his way. "You doubted me."

"Never," Kole said through his laugh. "Never doubt a Yamani. That's one thing I've learned."

"Ah." She jumped from her tree, landing with a thud. "The same could be said about a shepherd."

"You know what Felix would've said?" Vienna came up beside Kole.

Kole pictured his curly headed friend gripping the canopy for dear life, eyes wide and probably wondering why he'd ever let himself be convinced to get on the rambler. "Get me off of this thing?"

"That's right." Vienna pursed her lips, holding back a laugh. "We'd never have been able to get him back on the rambler."

The tree shook its canopy like a wet wolf drying its fur. Droplets of ice fell, numbing Kole's face.

Caradin peeked out from the collar of Kole's shirt. The Soul must've sensed Kole's discomfort because the ferret scurried down his arm and jumped. Midair, the furry thing expanded into the familiar form of the moon-colored stag. An immediate wave of heat radiated from the Soul, who came in close to snuggle Kole's shoulder. Vienna and a reluctant Piper also edged in. Though they hadn't touched the river, water droplets deepened the fabric of their clothes from when the roots broke up the ice. It seemed they all could use some time to recover and warm up.

CHAPTER 24

Another abundant source of food would present itself when they reached the Azure River. Until then, they'd have to rely on hunting and foraging the land. The only major city anywhere close to their path was Cresthaven, where Obell had been sent to recruit Azmali's forces for the cause. Cresthaven lay at least a day's travel south from their direct path east to the coast. More time than Kole wanted to waste for one hot meal. No, they'd stay on course. Between his and Vienna's hunting skills, Kole felt confident they wouldn't starve.

The next few days went quickly. Flat lands meant seamless travel. Each day Kole awoke, the frigid temperature had softened. No more puffs of fog whenever he breathed. The bite in the air faded — still cold but comfortably so — and the snow had long melted. Though Ohr lay in the depths of winter, it felt more like the cusp of spring. Vara's influence at work.

Crossing the Azure proved easy. They'd stuffed their bellies once more on fish and restocked their waterskins with river water.

The further they got from Zeal, the lighter Kole felt, as if putting distance between him and the city made Felix's death and all the destruction seem less real. He still hadn't taken the time to process it. Kole hadn't seen it happen, and to him, it felt so recent, yet it had been nearly two months. He still looked over his shoulder, expecting to see Felix alongside his sister, bickering, teasing. The days were quieter than the last time Kole had traveled with Vienna. He found it hard to talk to her. What could he say? Asking about Felix seemed wrong somehow. Vienna took on a reserved demeanor as well. She sat next to Kole on the rambler most times, but she rarely spoke other than a few comments on the weather or the landmarks.

They had been so close before....

So he thought. Really it was Felix who held them together.

The rambler dug a small trench with the sweep of a root to mark the edge of their firepit. Kole tossed a few branches he had collected into the circle, then stepped back as Vienna got to work with her flint and starter.

"Obell could probably light it with the snap of his fingers." Kole leaned against one of the roots he'd shaped into a curved chair.

Piper sat across from him. "I've seen him do it."

More sparks flew. "Sorry to say, we have to do it the old-fashioned way. Unless you have some sort of power you haven't shared? Hmm?" Vienna pointed her starter at Piper.

"Nothing with fire."

On the fourth strike, the ember took. Vienna fanned the flame until the branches caught, then sat back. "So what exactly can you do, then—being a demigod and all? Besides heal mortal wounds, live forever, and telepathically communicate?" She listed them on her fingers.

"I can't mind-link with just anyone. We must have a connection. Blood."

Vienna leaned forward. "Can you do it with me? You healed me with your blood back in Zeal, after all."

Piper matched Vienna's position, forearms resting on her knees, and stared at her, seemingly taking up the invite. Kole waited silently. Both girls guarded their expressions well. They could have merely been staring at each other for all he knew.

Vienna's face suddenly reddened, and she looked away.

"What is it? Did it work?" Kole swung his head back and forth between the both of them.

Vienna gave a sheepish nod.

"Did what work?" Shikar neared the fire and plopped down to the earth, her teeth grinding on one of the pebbles in the side of her mouth like a wad of tobacco. The Yamani had been separating herself from the group each night when dusk summoned her Kayetan. Kole had noticed that Shikar ensured she kept the shadow a good distance from their company when giving the creature its nightly patrol instructions. Not that the shadow was dangerous. Quite the opposite. It traveled ahead searching for the best route and keeping a keen eye out for threats. No. Shikar kept the Kayetan away for Vienna's sake. Old wounds and all. Or in Vienna's case, *fresh* wounds.

"Piper is showing off her demigod abilities." Vienna kept her attention on her nails, picking at some invisible dirt. Kole remembered Felix having the same habit.

"And just what are those powers, exactly?" Vara chimed in. By her high-set brows, Kole clearly read her intrigue. "Forgive me. I had heard of Aterus' child, but I am quite unfamiliar with what that makes you, demigod. What traits do you share with the Souls? And what with the humans?"

Piper winced at the mention of her father's name. "I wish I had been blessed with more of my mother."

"Why is that?" Kole asked. "Your blood heals, you live ridiculously long—how old even are you? — *and* you can do sorcery. I'd kill to have any one of those."

"I don't really know my age," Piper answered. "I was born around the time the Souls were imprisoned. Haven't really thought to count."

Hundreds of years. Kole took a harder look at the auburn-haired girl sitting across the fire. No girl. Instead, a wise old woman in the skin of a teenager.

The Yamani grunted. "Many kill for what they don't have, without knowing the curse upon what they desire." Shikar's demeanor had gone bleak. "Long life breaks brittle minds. Even my kind needs to know when it's too much."

Her speech jogged Kole's memory. The Yamani were created from the earth and lived as long as they wished. Shikar herself must have centuries on Piper.

"It doesn't mean I can't die." A smirk crept on Piper's lips. "It's just no one has been a proper match."

"Orla," Vienna said.

Piper dipped her head, smile vanishing. Her eyes darkened as if an old memory resurfaced. "Orla. I think the only other person in Ohr who could've defeated her was you, Shikar. It took a Kayetan."

"Ah, but Felix had powers I did not," Shikar admitted. "His unfinished ritual altered many things. Things I have tried and failed to recreate."

Vienna fell quiet.

"And what of your mother?" Vara asked.

Piper spoke of Evangeline—things Kole had heard before. Their conversation fell mute on his ears. All his attention had slid to Vienna, who had gone back to her nervous nail-picking. He could say something to her. *Now? In front of everyone?* Kole scooted closer to her, his voice ready in his throat. And that was where it stayed. Hard as he tried—as much as he wished—he couldn't summon the courage to speak. Why did she always have that effect on him?

"Kole?" Piper's voice pulled him back to reality. He realized he'd been staring.

Kole cleared that infuriating lump in his throat. "What?"

All eyes around the fire, including Caradin's beady ferret face on his shoulder, glued to him. How long had they been watching? How long had *Vienna* been watching? No doubt she'd noticed his eyes on her. Kole snapped his face toward Piper, trying his best to ignore his burning cheeks.

"The canopies?" Piper pointed up at the top of the rambler. "Vienna is tired."

"Uh, yeah, of course." Kole rose from his seat and approached the trunk. He wanted to run to it. Get as far and as quickly away from the fire as possible, but he forced himself to appear calm and unbothered.

With his hand on the bark, Kole sent his will to the rambler. The branches above twisted and coiled, weaving themselves into four hammock-like shapes. Touching the trunk wasn't necessary. Not at his skill level. But he wanted an excuse to leave.

Vienna walked over. "Thank you."

"Sure." He had a root send her up.

"Goodnight," Vienna said on her ascent.

"Goodnight," Kole croaked. A ferret claw stroked his neck. "Knock it off." He shrugged. "You could've helped me out back there. You left me staring like an idiot."

Caradin squeaked. It sounded like an apology, but Kole didn't bother merging their thoughts to find out.

When Kole turned his eyes back to the fire, Vara and Shikar had stood.

"We should set off soon." The Violet Soul reached a palm out to Kole's shoulder. "You should bunk with me tonight. We have much to catch up on, Brother."

The ferret lifted his nose up to Kole and sniffed.

"Go on," Kole encouraged. "I don't need a self-warming scarf every night."

Caradin scurried down Kole's arm, cast him what could only be considered a pout, then leapt into Vara's waiting hand. The rambler took them up to the hammocks just as Shikar passed Kole.

A heavy hand patted Kole's back, forcing the air from his lungs in puffs. "See you in the morning, small one."

With Shikar off to bed too, only Piper sat at the fire. Her gaze trained on him, and she pointed at the spot across from her. A wordless command to sit.

Kole fought off an agitated growl, then went over, but refused to sit. "What?"

Piper folded her arms at his reluctance. "What was that about?"

"What was *what* about?"

"Don't play dumb, Kole." Piper flicked her gaze up to the canopy. "Vienna. You were staring."

Kole shrugged, trying to play it off, though his fears had been spot-on. It had been as blatant as he thought. Everyone had noticed. "I... zoned out. I have a lot on my mind."

"I'm sure you do." Piper didn't care to hide the double meaning in her tone. Kole ignored it, but his grinding jaw betrayed his annoyance. She must've picked up on it, because right when he turned to leave for bed, Piper said, "I mean that, you know. There is quite the burden on your back."

Tell me what I don't know. And yet, he hesitated.

"How do you see this ending? Or rather, how do you *want* this all to end?" Any previous trace of humor had vanished.

He turned back, eyeing her. "What I want versus how I see things ending have no overlap. It's a fantasy. One that, if I got my wish, it'd go against nature, as many have reminded me." Perfection never had and never would exist. All those deaths reversed... all the pain and suffering erased.... A fool's hope. No. Not a hope. It simply couldn't be done. It was a delusion he harbored.

"Then a realistic ending. If you could choose."

He thought for a moment. Was killing a god even realistic? Kole had lost sight of what things were and weren't possible. "I want Aterus gone. His influence has destroyed Ohr."

She nodded. A goal Kole knew they desperately shared. "And what about the other Souls?"

Now Kole felt as if he were being quizzed. "If Aterus is... gone — dead or banished somehow — there's still the issue of the imbalance of power. It means this could all happen again. Ascension is the only way. They leave. But you know all of this already. Why are you asking me?"

"I want your point of view. You are the key to all of this, after all. You should have a say. Besides, ascension is only one part of the end. They really have consumed you, haven't they?"

"What do you mean?"

"I ask you how you want things to end, and you think about the gods and Ohr. What about you, Kole? What do *you* want?"

"I want...." The question took him off guard. His mind wandered back to impossible wishes. But Piper wanted to know about his future, and his mind came up blank. "I haven't thought much about it," he admitted.

Piper waved her hand at the darkness. "We have the night."

Not really. Kole needed to get the rambler army off and marching soon. They needed to make ground tonight if they hoped to reach Rush on time. But it wouldn't hurt to play her little game for a while.

What did he want? He started with an easy one. "I want to live," he blurted. Easy, yes, but that wasn't in his power. "I want Ohr to survive. But I don't know what happens after. I think it's because those are so unrealistic to me right now, I can't see past it."

Piper tilted her head, then nodded for him to continue.

"At the beginning of all of this, after we took back Socren from Savairo, I wanted to return to Solpate. That's the only home I've ever known. But it's changed. The ramblers are gone. The orphans. My family and—" He stopped himself from saying Niko's name. That lump grew in his throat. He swallowed it down. "There is no home to return to. If I live, what awaits me? Nothing familiar. Everything feels hopeless." Now that he'd managed to form those first few thoughts, they flowed freely. "I've felt hopeless for so long, I'm not sure winning this war will be enough to make it pass. Too much death and grief have touched my life I... I can hardly remember what it's like to be truly happy. Carefree."

The last time he'd felt that had been the days leading up to when the Black Wall destroyed his camp.

"It's stupid."

"It's not." Her mouth pursed. "But it's not realistic, no. That pure bliss you speak of: those feelings are for children. None of us will ever have that again no matter how hard we search for it."

Kole wondered if there was a time when she'd searched for such things. What did a demigod want? What had her life been like with Aterus as a father? He opened his mouth to speak, but as if sensing his questions, Piper cut him off.

"What about Vienna?"

"What about her?"

"You can't be that dense, Kole."

"What do you want me to say? I don't know what she wants. You'd have to ask her."

"Do you see happiness with her?"

"What does it matter? Even if I do, I can't expect her to feel the same."

"If this is about your scars—"

"It's more than that," he snapped. "Her brother died for me. *Felix died for me.* That's all she'll ever see when she looks at me. I'd be surprised if she sticks around after all of this."

"I was with her while you were gone. Yes, she grieved — harder than anyone I've seen before. That loss tore her apart. And not once did she blame you." The firelight emphasized the deep shadows on Piper's face, which hinted at her true age. Despite the façade, Kole reminded himself that no mere teenager sat across from him. "Felix died for Vienna. For Ohr. For the cause. For a future he once hoped to see. If he hadn't, Ohr would have been lost that night. Vienna was right. I was no match for Orla." She looked away. It must've been tough for her to admit that. "Felix made his choice."

"You know, everyone keeps telling me that, but there's a big difference between a free choice and a forced one. A cornered one."

She went silent, eyes trailing from Kole to the firelight. Then, "Maybe you're right. But Felix is more than just his death. He would've wanted you and his sister to be happy. Holding onto the future helps us make it there. It's like that slingshot." She dipped her chin toward his belt. "You need to aim in order to hit your mark, otherwise you're blindly shooting."

Though Felix and Kole had parted on less-than-ideal terms, any ill will between them had been squashed when Felix's slingshot and pouch were passed to him. He rubbed his thumb over the embroidery hanging at his waist. Physical forgiveness. It was the best thing he had, for he'd never get the chance to apologize in person.

"All I'm saying is you might want to start looking beyond the war in front of you. It will help you live in the end. If that's what you say you want."

It was. With all of his being, he wanted to live. He hadn't chosen this path; it was forced upon him. He rolled the thought in his head as he peered at the demigod. They had similar paths. Piper had been forced into the bloodline that both blessed and cursed her. This war was as much hers as it was Kole's. And here she stood in the midst of it all, doing her part willingly, it seemed. There had to be more to her. Something under the façade that a life with Aterus must've hardened around her. "What is it that you want?"

She sat back, almost surprised by the reversal. Had no one asked her before? How could they? Few knew her true lineage.

"I want *balance*."

A simple answer. Not one Kole expected. But the way she said that word — the ire in her tone — made it feel deeper. Personal. A vendetta for revenge.

Whatever anger Kole glimpsed bubbling beneath the surface fizzled in the blink of his eye.

"We must succeed, Kole. I will see to that." With that, Piper stood, dipped her head, then followed the rest of their party to bed.

Kole understood her message. Wanting to live wasn't enough. He needed to hope for something more. Cling to it. Yet even though it made sense, one mountain of a problem stood in the way of seeing his future the way Piper urged. For the Souls to regain their full power — to ascend as they planned — they needed to be complete. Kole held a small sliver of each of their essences within him. Once they took it back from him — when they reclaimed their full godhood once again....

Well, no one could survive without a soul. Their completion would guarantee Kole's death. Why bother hoping? Why, when everyone said they were searching for a way to save him — to get around the flaw in their plan — but a solution had yet to surface?

Kole warmed his hands at the fire, letting the chill completely leave his body before he instructed his rambler to snuff it out. In one swoop, the tree dragged a root over the earth and buried the pit in a mound of dirt.

"Let's get moving, big guy," he said with a pat on the trunk.

While his companions rested above in their hammocks, Kole uprooted his army and marched the last leg to Rush.

CHAPTER 25

"The moon, the earth, the stars, the water, the air."

Kole stirred in his hammock. A knot in the branch dug into his back. The rambler must've sensed his discomfort because the wood turned beneath him and gifted him a smoother side. The fog of sleep clung to him and made it all too easy to fall back into slumber.

"Flesh, flowers, and taste. The smell of daybreak. The sound of sleeping tides."

The noise brought Kole back from the cusp of dreamland.

"Time. Space. Destruction."

Agitated now, Kole grumbled, hoping that would put a stop to whoever decided to recite poems on the edge of midnight.

"Time. Cold. Dark. Alone."

"Knock it off." Every muscle in Kole's body ached for sleep. He had half a mind to set a root on the culprit if they didn't get the hint.

"Alone."

A growl escaped Kole's lips, and he pressed up to his elbows. Heaviness weighed on his lids. It took more than he thought to pry them open, but when he got a glimpse around him, he found only dark empty space. No rambler. No star-filled night sky. No horizon or sign of his companions. Everything was just....

"Gone." That voice came again. And it came from... everywhere.

"Hello?" An odd sensation ran through Kole. Though the rambler was unseen, he felt the vibration of its steps as it marched over the invisible land. When he moved his hand, the bark scuffed his skin. He was still in the canopy. Stuck in the far boundaries of a dream.

But who did he hear?

"No! Not gone. Can't be gone," it howled. Then the rage settled, and the voice began its list again. "The moon, the earth, the stars, the water, the air."

"Who's there?" Kole said, louder this time.

"Flesh, flowers, and—"

"Hello?"

"Sleeping tides," it whispered as if something compelled the voice to continue but it didn't want to be noticed.

"Who are you?" Kole spun his head out of habit, though only darkness met him. "What are you?"

The sound of a deep breath hit Kole's ears. He turned toward it. Nothing.

"That's not the question we need answered." The voice finally acknowledged Kole's presence.

The answer clicked. "Braxus."

"Yes."

It didn't make sense. He never reached out to the Soul. Last Kole remembered he was driving his army of ramblers east, carrying not so much as a thought for the god. Yet their minds had connected. Had Kole fallen asleep? Even so, mind-links didn't just happen, they had to be made.

"How are you in my head?"

"*You* are in *my* head."

If that were true, maybe it was like sleepwalking: Kole's body had acted on its own.

"You must go before it returns." The way Braxus said it sent a chill through Kole.

"Before what returns?"

"The hand of death."

"What are you talking about?"

"The hand. It finds me. It suffocates. Squeezes."

These clues were reminiscent of the hints Kole had received from Braxus when they first spoke. But the Soul had never mentioned a hand. "What kind of hand?"

"All encompassing. It holds me for a time before it lets up, only to come back again."

All these ominous and useless clues. Kole needed answers. "Where are you, Braxus? There has to be something more you can tell me. Is the hand a person? Does someone have you? Maybe you are underground? On the moon?" Even as it left his mouth, Kole felt ridiculous. Clearly not the moon, but maybe something would spark the Yellow Soul's memory.

Kole tried a different angle. "Do you remember anything before the hand?"

"Yes! I do." The palpable excitement surged through Kole at the same time. "I remember the sound of the sea. But it's gone now."

The sea. Not the clear answer Kole had hoped for but something new to go on, nonetheless. The Tiot Sea. Unless.... Unless Braxus meant one of the many other seas or oceans the Black Wall had consumed long ago.

A deep roar echoed around Kole. Too deep to be a voice or an animal.

"It comes," Braxus said as if she stood down the reaper — the hand of death, as she named it. "You must go, Kole. Before it grabs you, too. I can't help you then."

Hand or whatever, it couldn't reach Kole. Not through a mind-link, could it? But pressure built around him like a snare tightening on a rabbit's leg. That sense of panic pushed Kole into flight mode. Lingering for a while longer might give him a better glimpse into Braxus' location. The hand of death could reveal something more to him that Braxus had missed. Every instinct urged him to flee — to wake himself up from his nightmare. He wished someone would shake him and drag him out of here so he'd be forced into the wise choice, but the unknown was too tempting.

Kole waited.

"Go!" Braxus urged.

That's when Kole felt the icy grip. Braxus' "hand of death" took Kole off guard. He had expected something to snag him. Instead, that growing pressure built below him, rising higher and higher. Something about the sensation struck a familiar nerve in Kole's head. He'd *felt* this before.

Movement below caught his eye. What he had thought was nothingness gave way to a faint image at his feet. It moved slowly, yet its true form evaded him. No shape to it. No outline to decipher. An unseen ghost.

The hand crept up Kole, forcing his mouth shut. He flailed at the sudden lack of oxygen. *It's just in my head. It's not here. It's not real.*

Yet it *felt* all too real.

His body switched into survival mode. His lungs ached for air. Heart quickened. Adrenaline gushed into his veins.

Get out. Get out!

Kole jerked up. His heart pounded against his ribcage. If his burned skin could still sweat, he'd be drenched head to toe.

A startled Vienna, who had been hunched over his hammock, drew back with a jolt. "Are you okay?" Worry glazed her downturned expression.

That darkness. That grip over his body lay fresh in his head. It burned into him. When he rubbed the sleep from his eyes, peeks of that ghostly image flashed through him again, printed on the darkness inside his lids.

"Fine," he grumbled, limbs shaking. His answer did nothing to sway her concern. "What are you doing?" After he said it, he regretted his snipped tone. He cleared his throat, hoping to play it off for morning voice, then tried again. "What is it?"

Vienna sat back and pointed to the horizon. "Rush."

Every time Kole blinked, the memory of his mind-link with Braxus pounced, sinking its teeth deep into his flesh, refusing to let him go. He shook his head and rattled it away, then followed Vienna's outstretched finger.

He should've been looking at the city, but the great body of blue enchanted him. He'd only ever seen the ocean drawn in black ink on maps. He knew the waters of the sea were blue. Something like the color of the sky perhaps. But the rich hue made his jaw drop. The waters really were that deep. Deeper than the rivers and lakes. Darker. The white foam cresting the rolling waves reminded Kole of low-hanging clouds. Like they had dropped from the heavens in hopes of riding the mighty waves. And the air. The wind had picked up in short gusts. A brackish scent tickled the nose.

Only after taking in the Tiot Sea did Kole drag his gaze back to the coastline. The city of Rush stood grand indeed, but in a less ostentatious way than Zeal had with its shiny spiral towers. The structures held sturdy by wood and stone. Blue and yellow flags dotted the cityscape, though they were too distant to make out any detail.

Great ships with bulging sails rolled along with the tides. More vessels bobbed at the docks, their masts thin and bare like naked trees in winter.

"This is where the army is?" Kole asked.

"No." Vienna tilted her head north. "*That* is where our army is."

Smokestacks rose halfway up to the clouds in the cliffs just outside Rush. Tents sat in neat rows. Too many to count. By the mass amount of housing, Kole's heart dared to hope it'd be enough.

Kole made his way down to the base of the trunk and took hold of a root for steering. The people of Socren knew about ramblers, though few had seen one. And the other gathered forces? They might've only heard about them in bedtime stories, thinking them a fairytale. It was best to keep perfect control over the ramblers as they closed in on the base.

Vara stayed poised on a bough in the canopy. After so long in her prison, Kole would've thought she'd have a greater reaction to a city or the land. She remained statuesque. Almost bored at the sight. Caradin, on the other hand, scurried down the trunk and hopped on Kole's shoulder. The ferret stood on its hind legs, nose sniffing the salt and smoke-scented air.

Their presence needed no introduction. Kole's trees no doubt drew heads. An audience formed on the edge of base when they were still a mile out. *Leo will already know we're here.* As he thought it, a hawk called on the wind. Kole spotted the fawn-colored bird circling overhead.

"Fiona," Kole murmured to himself. It amazed him how much pleasure that small bird stirred inside his heart. It gave him a slight sense of home, though he'd never really considered Socren as such. Still, it meant familiar faces. Friends. Allies.

Kole slowed his rambler at the base of the cliffs. The crystal trees followed suit. The army he brought needed no housing or accommodation save for a shepherd or two to look after them. He instructed his rambler to root. The land rumbled as his trees anchored deep into the rock.

Shikar stepped down from her tree and stomped the gravel with a foot. "This is more like it. No more softness underfoot."

"Are you a fan of the sea, Shikar?" Piper asked as she climbed down the rambler after Vara and Vienna.

"Only the cliffs," the Yamani said. "Water is well enough in small doses. But you'd never catch me on a boat. I'd sink it straight to the bottom." Shikar puffed her chest as if prideful of that fact.

"Remind me never to get on a ship with you," Kole said. He'd had trouble swimming as it was, nearly drowning in the current-less pond he'd released Issira from. Add waves and an undertow and he'd be swept away for sure.

When they'd all descended, Kole turned to the base. A crowd had gathered at their arrival. Wide-eyed faces gawked at the ramblers. Whispers and murmurs ran through the throng.

His uncertainty must've been printed clearly across his face because Vienna squeezed his shoulder.

"We'll find Leo quickly," she said, then glanced up to the hawk, who tilted into a nosedive for the back of the crowd. "He's close."

As a group, they began their climb up the slope. Kole instinctively reached to tug his hood down, only to remember he hadn't had one since he arrived in Zeal. His face would be on full display. Already people began to pull their eyes from the ramblers, and out of all six of his companions, they inevitably landed on him. At least his limbs were covered. Still, he found himself falling back to the middle of their formation. Vienna and Shikar seemed clued in on his motive, as they widened their strides and took up the front.

The intense heat around Kole's neck made him smirk. "There's no need to stay hidden like in Zeal," Kole said to the weasel, who had tucked his head further under his collar. "They know who you are. And if they don't, they will before it's all over. Go on." He held his hand out for Caradin to hop onto, then guided the furry creature to the floor.

Before the tiny claws could touch the ground, hooves formed. A silver light strained Kole's eyes as the Orange Soul shifted to his stag form. Gasps came from their audience, some in shock, others in excitement. Even a few hands clapped.

Kole placed a palm on the stag's back for comfort. More so for himself than the Soul. The grand transformation served as a fine distraction from Kole. Anything to get those stares off his burn scars.

"Get out the way, people!" A gruff voice shouted. The group of onlookers parted like a forked stream.

"Yeah, and don't you know it's rude to stare?" That second husky voice triggered a deep grin in Kole. He peered through the crowd. Two muscular teens shoved their way through the masses.

Then the last line parted, putting the twins on full display. Criz and Boogy. They looked tanner than the last time Kole had laid eyes on the pair. Changing from the liberation's underground hideout in Socren to the sunny coast would do that to anyone.

"It's about time you lot showed up," said Criz with a fake sternness.

Boogy abandoned all professional façade and bounded forward. "Vienna! Pipes!" He took them into a tight bearhug.

"Pip-er," Piper corrected halfheartedly, either winded from the embrace or secretly tolerating the nickname.

"I heard you're half Soul," Boogy said.

"That's—maybe we should talk about that later." Piper pulled from the hug.

"Don't worry, everyone already knows."

"Great," Piper muttered. She shared a glance with Kole, then cast a sour gaze over the people of the base.

"Boogy," Criz scolded when he caught up, "we're supposed to wait for Leo."

"Kole!" Boogy wrapped his arms around him. "I'm glad the Black Wall didn't eat you."

"Me too." Kole would've felt more comfortable if a bear had hugged him. The brute didn't know his own strength. His scarred skin pinched in the hold, making Kole wince, but a part of him never wanted the embrace to end. "Nice to see you, too," Kole croaked through the vice grip on his lungs.

"Where have you been? No wait—don't answer that. Leo will *debrief* you," Boogy emphasized the word as if he had recently been taught what it meant. When he finally released him, that dopey grin moved to Caradin. "I like your pet."

"Uh, thanks." Leave it to Boogy to mistake the glowing silver god for a pet. Caradin didn't seem to mind by the way he nuzzled the boy at the welcomed neck scratches.

Criz leaned in toward Kole, hands behind his back as if restraining himself from greeting Kole in the same casual way as his brother. Instead, he nodded toward Vara and whispered, "Another one of them gods, eh?"

"Yes, she is." Kole stared at the still leaned-in, expectant Criz, unsure what the gruff boy wanted from him.

Just when Kole thought to pitch forward in an awkward bow, Criz righted himself in a snap and yelled, "Okay, greetings are over now." Criz observed Shikar as he spoke. Awe flickered behind his eyes, as if he were tempted to break his own command. Instead, he bowed, which was probably meant for the group yet directed solely at the Yamani. "We will escort you to Leo."

"Clear a path!" Boogy moved to the crowd and waved his hands, then called over his shoulder, "Follow us."

The people had cleared a wide path straight toward the middle of camp. Not two steps through did the murmurs begin.

"It's the Souls," a whisper came from Kole's left.

Another echoed behind him. "The boy. Is he the key?"

Unfamiliar faces stared at him as if eager to get a glimpse or share a look. Everywhere Kole directed his gaze, he was met with another curious stranger. Did they expect him to wave? To greet them like a hero returning home from his ventures? Was he supposed to smile and give words of encouragement that promised their victory? That'd never be him. If anything, Kole felt more akin to a pariah.

The whispers multiplied and ran down the length of the crowd. One person knelt as Kole's group passed. Then another and another. Like a ripple in a still pond, those who had gathered lowered down and dipped their heads. Most were quiet. Some muttered prayers under their breath. But one thing was for certain. Every pair of eyes followed Kole and the others.

Whereas Criz and Boogy led the party with pride, Kole huddled closer to Caradin, wishing the glow from the stag was opulent enough for him to evade further attention. If the people wanted a show of power, they could find it in Caradin and Vara.

Once they had passed through the edge of the base, the crowd thinned to a bustle of activity. Those who had been too enthralled in their work to notice the ramblers' approach on the city and its passengers, carried on with their daily duties.

The mix of culture caught Kole's focus first. Some folk dressed in plain cotton garbs of greens and browns like Kole had back in his refugee days, while others donned more colorful embroidered pieces. Kole scanned the faces, hoping to find one he recognized, but the fast-paced work gave him no such prize.

The temporary base ran like a well-worked anthill. Certain roads seemed to be reserved for particular jobs: some solely for carts and others for pedestrian use. Criz and Boogy led them down the right side of the road while the other ran in the opposite direction like two passing streams. For a war camp, this place ran as smoothly as warm butter. No doubt Leo had played a part in that.

A ten-minute walk later, they came upon a large tent. Criz and Boogy moved to either side of the doorway and pulled the curtain back.

"Go on, then," Boogy said through his toothy smile.

Vienna went first.

One wordless pat to Caradin's rump and the stag shrank. The weasel skittered to Kole's shoulder then propped up on its hind legs.

Shikar had to crouch under the entryway. She flicked the fabric above her with annoyance as she moved through.

A part of Kole was reluctant to enter, for he knew what awaited on the other side. One journey had ended, and another would begin. Another step closer to saving Ohr. Another step closer to his inevitable sacrifice. His boots must've filled with lead because they dragged and protested those next few steps. Kole followed the group in.

It took a moment for his eyes to adjust in the dim light. His ears perked up at a strange gasp to his left. A pair of arms seized him.

CHAPTER 26

Kole stiffened against the hold, but when sobs and sniffles sounded in his ear, he let down his guard.

"You're alive!" Though a black film still lay upon Kole's vision, he made out the distinct short, spiky hair. If that hadn't given it away, it would've been the strong smell of burning metal.

Jax.

"I'm alive." Kole wrapped his arms around her petite frame and squeezed her back.

"I thought I'd killed you." The engineer pulled back and held him at arm's length, eyes puffy and bloodshot—too much to stem from crying alone. She must've been working long nights. More cannons? Another invention, perhaps. "I'm sorry I wasn't there to see you back through."

"You had a good apprentice." Kole was going to nod to Vienna, but he couldn't spot her in the crowded tent. Only now that his eyes trailed from Jax did he notice just how many people had packed in the room. Their incoherent talk filled the space.

"That I did." Jax squeezed his shoulders then released him. "But, Kole, you were gone so long. We all thought you were dead. Where have you been all this time?"

"I think that is something we would all like to know," boomed a voice.

The liberation leader leaned against the front of a circular table littered with maps, scrolls, compasses, and other trinkets unfamiliar to Kole. Leo's dark waves had grown down to his shoulders. Eyes so black poised on Kole. The scene gave Kole flashbacks of the first time he'd met the man. Felix had brought Kole into the abandoned mining tunnels beneath the Poleer Mountains, where the rebels had set up base. The moment he'd entered—oh, it felt so long ago—Leo had given him the same intense look along with a stern, unreadable expression.

Vienna stood by Leo's side. She had always been his right hand. A spark of light had returned to her face. She encouraged Kole with a nod.

"I've been behind the wall," Kole answered.

The whole tent seemed to stop breathing.

Kole scanned the crowd before he continued. A few faces stood out. Harlow and Lucca, camp leaders of the Solpate refugees, stood together on the far side of the tent. He'd last seen them briefly after the battle of Socren. They'd only ever looked at him like a child, yet now Kole sensed a mix of wonder and maybe fear in their faces as they watched. He also spotted the council from Zeal off in the corner. Councilwoman Tena sat in a chair at the table. Her face looked tired and the braided white hair down her shoulder seemed thinner, too, like she had aged a year in the month since he'd left.

Their presence meant the other attendees must be leaders or representatives of their own cities. Kole's arrival had interrupted some meeting.

The lump in his throat reappeared, but Kole shoved it down. "Time works differently there," he explained. "It was only hours for me. Not even a day." They all stared at his scars. No place to run. No mask to hide behind. "I returned as soon as I completed my mission." Kole gently grabbed the ferret and held him in his open palms before Leo. Caradin did a couple turns, beady eyes frantically shifting over every inch of the tent. "Caradin, the Orange Soul," Kole presented, then side stepped. "And the Violet Soul we brought back from behind the Black Wall."

"Vara," Leo said, "we have had an uncharacteristically warm week. You would not have anything to do with it, would you?"

The Violet Soul's mouth lifted on one side. "Perhaps."

"There is much I would like to discuss with you at a later time, if you would."

"You may have my audience upon your request," Vara confirmed.

Leo's mouth pursed, pleased, then he directed his attention back to Kole. "You have brought more than just the Souls with you." A statement rather than a question. "Ramblers?"

"An army." Kole hoped to come off more confident than he felt. "There are more on their way. We'll need shepherds."

"I can arrange that. They will be happy to practice their calling once more." Kole had almost forgotten Leo's perfect articulation. He spoke like a true leader. "Harlow, Lucca." The camp leaders stepped forward. "Gather your shepherds and have them relocate the ramblers to the north side, please. Set them in shifts to watch over the trees."

The two nodded and left the tent but not before Harlow could throw a wink at Kole.

Strange. Here Kole was at the heart of conversation while Harlow and Lucca were now the ones taking orders. Things had shifted indeed since he'd left Solpate.

"Have you heard from Russé and the others?" Kole asked. The rest of the crystal trees he'd sent off hadn't made it to Rush yet, so he knew Issira had yet to return. Kole had expected that. The Yamani she'd been sent to recruit were stubborn as the rocks they were made of. Kole could reach out and check in with Russé himself, but something inside him stalled.

Usually, Leo had perfect control over his expression, but he must've been surprised by the inquiry because his thick brows lifted. "The recruits from the southern coastline returned with him two nights ago."

The recruits returned with him? That phrasing caught in Kole's brain.

"I can have you taken to him."

Something was wrong. Terribly so. Russé would be here in this tent. No. He would've met Kole and his company at the edge of the base along with Criz and Boogy. Had he been injured? But that made no sense. The Souls could heal even mortal wounds.

"Please." Kole gritted his teeth to keep his voice from cracking. He wanted to leave the tent this very second.

"Criz. Boogy. Will you escort Kole to Russé's tent?"

"Yessir," they said together in their twin-like fashion. Criz and Boogy flanked Kole.

"I can have someone accompany you, if you wish," Leo offered, eyeing Vienna.

"No," Kole said. "I'm sure you two have a lot to catch up on."

With that, Leo dipped his head, and Criz and Boogy led Kole back out through the flaps of the tent. Leo's voice followed them out saying, "Forgive me, but I must debrief our new arrivals. We will pick up this meeting come tomorrow."

Others exited behind Kole, going their separate ways. He peered over his shoulder. Some traveled toward the smokestacks, others to the housing tents. Criz and Boogy had taken him the opposite way.

A special living site for the Souls, perhaps, so they could find some peace from those who would surely come to them with prayers, offerings, and guidance. Yet as they traveled, the crowd thinned. And so did the tents. Kole spotted a handful of people as they progressed, entering and exiting various tents. One made Kole stop dead in his tracks. A woman came out, apron covered in blood.

"Only a little further, blondie," Boogy said.

"Where are you taking me?" Then a cry came from one of the tents up the path.

"The infirmary." Criz nudged his elbow into his brother's thick stomach, to which Boogy came up and draped an arm over Kole's shoulders, gently leading him on.

"Don't worry, Kole, he's recovering nicely."

"What happened?" Kole asked under his breath.

It looked like Boogy meant to shrug, but his neck was so thick his shoulders had nowhere to go. "Leo's not sure. He was hoping you or one of the Souls could tell us."

Urgency quickened Kole's pace. *Who would dare attack a Soul?* Russé had been felled by a Kayetan once. His mentor had taken a claw straight through his back and out the front side of his chest. Kole had thought Russé a goner then, but the wound had healed in the span of a day or so. What had Leo said? Russé had been brought in two days ago? Which meant it had been at least that long. How far had the recruits carried him beforehand?

Finally, Criz stopped at a small path. They'd reached the end of the infirmary. The muscular boy held back the curtain to a tent on the right. That's when Boogy pulled away from Kole and nudged him on.

When Kole went to stoop inside, he heard Criz's hand slap on Boogy's chest. "Give him some privacy, bro."

"Aww, all right." Boogy said, clearly deflated. "We'll be just out here, then. Holler if you need."

The fabric fell closed at Kole's back, leaving the small room in dim light. A cot sat at its center and upon it, under a thin blanket, lay Russé. Asleep.

Kole stood there, feet too heavy to move. From this angle... in this light... no Soul lay in the room but an old man with sun-bleached gray hair and weather-worn, leathery skin, fighting for shallow breaths. The wheeze sounded of someone fated for death.

For all the time they'd spent together, Kole couldn't help but feel like he looked on a stranger. Yet the long nose and wild bushy brows resurrected old memories. Times when Kole had only known the man as a shepherd. A teacher. A tamer of the trees. Protector. Intimidating but safe. Safe but not honest.

Kole inched forward to the bedside and peered down. The blankets stood clean. No blood or bandages in sight.

"Russé," Kole whispered.

The Soul did not stir.

The wrinkles in the god's face had deepened. New ones had formed. Signs of aging in any human.

Kole reached out his hand. His fingers hovered over the god's cheek a moment before he allowed himself to feel the rough skin. Warm.

"Russé?" Kole tried again. "It's me."

A hand darted out from the sheets and grabbed Kole's wrist. He flinched at the sudden movement, then found the blue eyes had flashed open.

"Kole." Russé said the name with terror as if he had woken from a grave nightmare.

"I'm here." As easily as breathing, he fell back into his old role and lowered to the bed to sit by Russé's side. Kole used a soothing tone as he spoke and rubbed the old man's arms in circular motions. It had always calmed the young orphans in his refugee camp when they had bad dreams and hallucinations of their traumatic life back in Socren under the Warden's reign. Yet Kole had never done this to an adult—a god. He supposed it worked the same.

The fog over the Soul's brilliant blue eyes cleared little by little until he finally moved to sit up. Kole offered him his arm and propped him up against the headboard.

"You made it," Russé croaked.

Kole nodded.

The Green Soul studied him for a short time, eyes darting every which way as if inspecting him for injury.

Kole rolled his eyes. "I'm fine. You're the one in the bed."

"I'm just resting is all."

"That's what Leo said," Kole confirmed. "But it's not what he meant. What happened to you?"

"I overexerted myself."

Of course, he'd blow over it. Kole wasn't having it. He folded his arms and glared.

Russé's shoulders drooped forward. "I lent too much of my power."

It took a second for Kole to connect the pieces. When realization dawned, it came out in one breath. "The ramblers."

Russé's mouth rose to one side in sheepish admittance.

"*I* did this?"

"No." Russé put a wrinkled hand on the scars of Kole's forearm—clammy despite its time under the blanket. "You asked for the power to raise them. I'm the one who gave it to you. I did this to myself."

"You should've told me it was too much."

"It's just what we needed for this war. It drained me for a few days, but I'm recovering quickly." A smile stretched. "I'm prouder of what you've done, Kole. Raising a forest of ramblers isn't easy. No shepherd could do such a thing. I don't think I could've done it on my own. Not the crystal trees. They are not so easily swayed by my will."

"Because they are stone?"

The god nodded. "They started as trees but petrified to stone under Braxus' influence. It would take our combined power to awaken them."

And that was exactly what Kole possessed: a mix of the gods' powers.

"You have done well in my absence," Russé said. "Traveled through the bog, capturing and taming Caradin. Overthrew a cultess of Aterus' lost bloodline. Crossed the boundaries of fire and released Vara. Who knew my apprentice was so capable?" His eyes glittered with pride.

"It sounds grand when you say it like that. But it wasn't so easy. So many are dead."

"Victories are never given freely. Their prices can be steep."

So many were lost in the battle for Zeal, but Felix's sacrifice would forever be carved in Kole's heart. It felt like a piece of his soul had disappeared along with Felix. It did not bode well on Kole to dwell. Lingering too long on his friend's death might consume him. "There's still Braxus. I reached out to her, but I don't know where she lies."

"Show me." Russé moved his fingers to Kole's temple. Just as the god had shown images to Kole in the past through their connection, Kole touched the old man's forehead and relayed what riddled clues he possessed.

Russé leaned back in his cot, chin propped on his fist as he thought. "Every location has had to do with our true nature. Perhaps the very things we create bind us more potently."

"Within the earth. That's as much as we have guessed, but that could be anywhere. She could be a league beneath our feet for all we know."

Something passed over Russé's expression. "That's not true. It's not about what you saw, it's about what you felt."

"The hand of death." Kole used her words.

"It's not a hand at all."

"I guessed that much."

"If not a hand, then what?"

"If I knew that I wouldn't be asking you."

"The sensation was familiar to you," Russé encouraged.

Kole had to close his eyes to put himself back in that moment. "It didn't grab me; it crawled up from below. It covered my mouth and nose. Suffocating." His heart quickened at the memory as he relived the dream. He opened his mouth and sucked in air. The feeling of fresh air going down his windpipe triggered an answer. "Water. Drowning." He'd had the same sensation when he dove in the pond in search of Issira's soulstone. The water had attacked him — tried to drown him. "But it doesn't make sense. Water is Issira's creation. Why would Aterus imprison Braxus in water?"

"We must go about this differently, Kole. Water is another clue, not the solution. If the 'hand of death' truly is water, and it rose up, then —"

"The tide." It came clear as day. "She's hidden on the coast."

"Where darkness is thick and never waning."

Kole recalled Vienna's map and held the image in his mind's eye. He dragged up and down the edge of the Tiot Sea until one place held his focus. "The Linde Sea-Caves."

"Braxus created the land, but the moon was always her pride. Perhaps Aterus intended to torture her with a location like that. Never again to see her jewel in the sky."

The swell of high tide and release of low tide. That roaring. The permanent darkness. No signs of life. She must be deep within, indeed. Still, they could be wrong. A cave must be the answer, but many dotted the coastal cliffs.

"Shikar can help us," Kole said. "Her connection to stone might quicken our search."

"This will require Issira."

"She hasn't returned yet."

"She is close. A day or so out."

"We can't wait that long," Kole argued. "We should go now."

"The sea-caves are dangerous. They can fill up in a matter of minutes and entomb you. No, you will wait for Issira to return," Russé dismissed. "We can't risk everything when we are so close. It will give me time to recover, and you will sleep warm and well tonight."

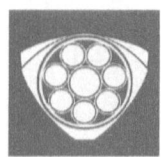

Kole lay in his cot, eyes fixed to the draped ceiling. He'd managed some sleep, but the restlessness in his body demanded attention.

The tent held a dozen beds, yet all were empty. The sounds of forging and building slipped through the seams of the canvas. If he wished, Kole could drown them out and find sleep again, but his mind played against him. Too many thoughts plagued him: faces that hurt to look upon haunted the still moment. He sat up in the dull light of the long room.

The glow of torches bobbed along the walls as people passed outside, their own minds fixed on whatever project they had to complete for the coming war. The camp never quieted. The workers slept in shifts. Whoever was assigned to these beds, along with Kole's party, had the night shift, it seemed. They'd probably come trudging in around dawn.

After Kole had left Russé's quarters, Criz and Boogy showed him where to get food and the bathing amenities. A large bowl of fish stew filled his belly. Shortly after, they'd brought him here. Piper and Vienna had been assigned to the same tent as Kole but had yet to show. It seemed they'd been given other tasks while Kole was meant to rest.

With sleep off the agenda, Kole kicked away the blankets, then moved to the entrance while pulling on the fresh clothes Criz and Boogy had brought him. They had included a wrap for his head. Kole looped it over his hair and draped it along his shoulders into a makeshift hood.

A pull of the tent flap and the muffled sounds sharpened: clangs of metal strokes, ordering shouts, and roaring fires. A waft of smoke dragged under Kole's nose. Night had fallen. The silver glow from the north told Kole the shepherds had relocated his crystal ramblers. But that's not what Kole sought as he crept from the tent. He turned down the adjacent road, one hand on the side of his hood to keep his face hidden.

People knew him here. Not only those who lived in the refugee camps alongside him throughout his childhood, but word had spread of the burned boy who had returned the Souls to Ohr. Kole had heard the whispers and caught the stares when he accompanied Criz and Boogy around the base. The scene at his arrival had not been because of the ramblers.

A dozen tents down, Kole found himself crossing the threshold between the living quarters and the forging zone. The jaws of winter had released its hold here, repelled by the ever-burning furnaces. Hot orange metals glowed from the open pavilions. Blacksmiths hammered away on swords and shields. And from the barrels, steam rose as the craftsmen quenched their blades. Some worked on more intricate pieces: small things Kole didn't recognize. No one noticed his presence—too consumed in their work.

As he passed between two tents, a familiar voice tickled his ear. Kole spotted two silhouettes in the shadow: one tall and lanky, the other with hair that flashed auburn in the dancing firelight.

"Why didn't you tell me?" The smooth male voice came to Kole's ears again.

Thomas. He was one of the original liberation members Kole had met back in Socren. The guy held a grudge against Kole for some unknown reason.

Thomas pushed his long black hair from his face, waiting for her answer.

Kole hugged the corner of the tent, allowing one eye far enough beyond the fabric to watch the scene unfold.

"Because it's none of your business," Piper snapped.

"None of my business? You are a demigod! You know what it was like to find that out from Leo? I thought we were friends." He reached for her hands, but she pulled away. "I thought Savairo had you. I thought you were dead."

"Savairo wanted Kole. I couldn't let that happen."

Had Thomas been in the tent with the other liberation members when they spoke with Leo earlier? Kole hadn't noticed. Thomas certainly knew of their arrival. Maybe his anger kept him away.

"Kole," Thomas said his name like a curse. "That's all I'm hearing about these days."

"He is pivotal to Ohr's survival."

"So Leo says." Thomas shook his head, dismissing the new topic. "You lied to me. You said you were from Rush. That the Black Wall got your parents at sea."

"We all lied," Piper said. "Can you honestly say you told me and the others the truth about your past?"

"I omitted things, but I never lied."

"Then you are a better person than me." The tone Piper used made the compliment sound sinister.

"I thought we were... friends." His hesitation made Kole doubt that was the word he intended to use.

By the lean of her hips, Piper had picked up on it, too. "And what gave you that impression? Did I say it? Did I do something?" She waited for Thomas to respond, but he only stared. "What you *thought* was merely a fantasy born in your mind."

Though fuzzy, the conversation sparked a memory of a moment or two back in the liberation's hideout, where he noticed Thomas fawning over Piper. At one point, he thought they were together, even if Piper had been cold in return. Thomas had comforted her on occasion, and he followed her around wherever she went.

"So you're with *him* now?"

"I'm not with—" Piper gripped the sides of her face with a growl. "Do you hear yourself, Thomas? A war is building around us, and you are stuck in your own head." She stepped back and rolled her shoulders, composing herself. "Yes, I lied to you. I lied to everyone. I had to keep myself safe. As for you—or us." She waved her hand between them. "Though I may look like your peer, I am centuries old. So many I have lost count. We have an alliance based on a mutual enemy. My *father*." She flicked a finger between the two of them. "Yes, we work well together. But there is nothing more between us. There will never be anything more—with anyone for that matter. Not that it's any of your business either." Piper opened her arms wide. "My line is an abomination. My mere existence plunges Ohr into disparity. If it's a crush you have, you need to deal with it or fix it on another because it is lost on me." Piper turned on her heel and stormed down the path.

Kole pulled back and stiffened behind the corner of the tent, breath held as to keep his presence hidden.

As Piper passed, her low voice hissed, "Enjoy the show?" She never stopped or turned back to acknowledge Kole, but her agitation pulsed in his head like a budding migraine.

He'd been quieter than the dead. How had she known of his presence? Maybe their shared connection through the Souls had something to do with it. Kole frowned at the thought of her knowing his whereabouts at any given moment.

Then her words came to him in his head, loud and crisp as if she whispered it into his ear, despite her retreating figure. *"I'm glad you're up. I was sent to retrieve you. Issira has returned."*

More stomps neared. Kole stayed put until Thomas had long gone, disappearing down the path.

"Keep up," Piper blasted in his head again. *"We've got ill news."*

Kole hurried after Piper. It took him jogging to make up the distance. Even when he caught up to her, her pace proved too fast for him. He found himself going in and out of a light run just to stay by her shoulder.

"What's going on?" Kole asked.

"Not exactly sure, but I have worked with Leo long enough to read him. He might look as composed as a statue, but he is panicking on the inside." Her sour gaze fell on him. "I was on the way to get you when I was... stopped."

Kole scratched his head, unsure how to respond.

"Do you think I was too harsh?" Piper said, referring to her talk with Thomas.

A shrug, then, "I don't really know much about that sort of thing." More like nothing at all. Kole had never confessed his feelings to anyone. Not that he had any to profess. Yet, as those thoughts passed over him, Vienna's freckled face came to him. Kole shook it away before it could root.

Piper side-eyed him. "Hmm."

They walked along in silence until the sounds of metalwork had faded and the tents grew bigger. A combination of torches and moonstone lit their way. Though Piper had only been in the camp for as long as Kole, she navigated the place like she'd built it herself.

Leo's tent came into view.

"It's different with you, Kole."

"Huh?"

"Thomas let himself build emotions based on lies. He formed connections that were never there. You have made a different mistake entirely by choosing blindness."

Kole tugged his hood back to get a good look at Piper. "It's none of your business. Isn't that what you told Thomas? Maybe you should follow your own advice."

Piper stood there for a moment, staring at him, before opening the curtain. Vienna stood by Leo's side, a troubled frown weighing down her expression.

CHAPTER 27

"Sorry to wake you," Leo greeted, "but now that everyone has arrived, it is pertinent we meet."

Kole dismissed the apology with a shake of his head. "I couldn't sleep anyway."

Vara hunched over a map that lay open on the table. A candle perched on one side kept it flat while a sprawled-out tube of a weasel secured the other. Caradin stretched and yawned, seemingly quite content.

Once Kole made it to the center of the rug, he spotted the blue silks of Issira's dress. Her pin-straight black hair shone as sleek as her garb. For someone who had just returned from traveling the length of Ohr, she looked ready for a grand ball.

"If your dreams are haunting you, I can be of help." Issira's melodic voice ran through the room like a silver flute.

"I'm fine," Kole lied. When she had last helped clear his mind, he had slept soundlessly and woke fully rested. Dreams weren't the problem this time, though; it was his own restlessness and the dread of a looming war, none of which the Soul could ease.

Shikar was there too, already leaned back in a chair, along with Criz and Boogy, who stood on either side of the entrance. Guard duty.

"We will get started once Obell returns with Russé." Leo gestured to the table for them all to sit. Everyone obliged.

"Obell is back?" Kole asked.

"We came in together." Issira pulled her short train aside and took her seat.

Kole rounded to the opposite side of the table from where Piper was heading. "Piper said you two had set out for different cities."

"We did." The Blue Soul's gleeful notes turned flat. "My venture was unsuccessful."

So the Yamani had not come. A part of Kole expected such. The Yamani had been cold to their presence at Grayfall from the beginning. With

Obell's release and the subsequent eruption of their volcano, much of the Yamani's city had been destroyed.

"Our numbers are few. Even fewer are happy with the Souls," said a solemn Shikar. "There are some who would come, but Mikal would never allow it."

Kole didn't blame them. They had a right to refuse to join the war on Aterus. And their stance on outsiders was made clear from the start. They probably still worked to clean up the aftermath of Kole's visit, which only strengthened their aversion to strangers. *At least we have Shikar.*

"All is not lost," said Leo as he pulled back a chair. "Obell convinced Azmali to send troops. Her army is settling in as we speak."

"Is she joining us?" Kole remembered the leader of Cresthaven. Tough and firm. They were right to assign Obell to her. Only fire could tame another flame like Azmali.

"We are conducting a more intimate meeting," said Leo. "The war effort is communicated to all leaders involved, but this is a separate matter, and as such, all discussion should remain with the people I have invited."

Everyone gave a silent nod just as Criz and Boogy opened the curtain for Obell and Russé. A wave of heat immediately filled the room as the Red Soul ducked in. With ease, he escorted Russé, who hobbled along, one arm twisted in his kin's while the other clutched his gnarled staff. An odd sight to see Russé moving as rickety as the age of his human disguise.

Obell's fiery eyes swept the table. When they crossed over Kole, if felt as though someone had swung a torch before his face. Yet all Kole could think about was how much more comfortable his journey from Zeal would've been if the god of fire had been present. *A portable furnace.*

"Looks like you had the worst luck of us all," Obell said to Vara as he helped Russé into the seat beside Kole. "What was it like?"

Kole pulled his eyes from the old man. Whenever he looked at Russé, guilt riddled his bones. *I did that to him. Me.*

"Torture," Vara said plainly. Her eyes never left the map, clearly unwilling to engage further with the subject.

"You can all get reacquainted later." Leo slipped a scroll from one of the many pockets of his jacket. "Criz. Boogy. If you would."

Boogy took a step toward the table before his brother caught him by the arm.

"He means outside, Boogy," said Criz.

Boogy's mouth sagged at the realization. "Why can't we listen?"

"'Cause we're standing guard," said Criz. "And your mouth is looser than a broken bow string."

"I don't mean to. It just happens."

"I know you don't. C'mon." Criz dragged his reluctant brother by the elbow. "We can play a game of 'what do you spy?'. Bet you'd like that."

The curtain closed, muffling the last of their conversation.

With their exit, Leo held the scroll over the candle's flame and burned the parchment. As the paper shriveled away, Leo spoke something in a language Kole had only heard from sorcerers' mouths. Some kind of protection spell? It must've been because the liberation leader spoke freely after he finished.

"As I said, the war strategy meeting with the leaders will come soon, but I need to get caught up with our efforts here before I can lay out any sort of plan." Leo motioned to the Souls one at a time. "Issira could not rally the Yamani. We have only received a small brigade from Hawthorne — their situation is more dire than I last heard years ago — and few numbers from the scattered villages off the southern coasts." Leo nodded to Obell. "Azmali has come, along with half her forces to see this through. That leaves us with the combined strength of Rush, and those who have traveled from Socren and Zeal."

Kole had expected more. Ohr's fate lay in the victor of the impending battle. Why would they not want to aid? Maybe they couldn't. Or a darker choice: perhaps they didn't want to. War meant death. And to fight against a god? One who had such a strong hold over the Black Wall and the other Souls?

"We are pleased to have the ramblers in our ranks. An unexpected addition that has put a bit of ease over the base." Leo sent a grateful nod Kole's way.

"And we have the Souls," Vienna added.

"And the Souls," Leo confirmed. "And that is what we are here to discuss. The plan for all of you. Kole has brought us the most important tool in felling Aterus. But one still remains. Braxus needs to be released. We cannot start an attack without all six."

Kole scooted forward in his seat. "I spoke with her. It's not much to go on, but Russé and I have a good guess. We think she's in the sea-caves of Linde."

"The sea-caves?" Piper leaned over the map, finger dragging to the place on the parchment.

An optimistic light shone in Leo's black eyes. "The caves are not far from here."

"The waters are ruthless," Piper said. "Sheer cliff faces."

"We were waiting for Issira," Russé said weakly beside Kole. "Controlling the tides will give us safe passage."

Piper dragged her finger from the Poleer Mountains to the edge of the caves. "Those caverns span a long way down the coast. It's not a singular place. They are underground mazes."

Shikar laid her fist proudly on the table. "If my people can navigate miles of lava tubes, I can manage a few caves."

"We can sense her soulstone when we are close enough," Issira said. "With the Yamani guiding us, we will find our way."

Leo swept the ash from his scroll off the table. "Then that is settled. Kole will set out with a small party at dawn. Hopefully we can expect you back within two days. Onto other matters." The wooden chair groaned as Leo leaned forward in his seat. "I need to present the leaders of Ohr with an attack plan. My knowledge of Aterus only goes so far. I know not where he resides or what power he possesses to combat our armies." His chin turned to Piper. "Perhaps you do?"

"He has no army to match the one we've gathered. He doesn't need one." Piper hovered over the map. "Humans are his creation. He can manipulate them as easily as Russé bids his trees or Issira summons water."

"Like he did with me?" Kole asked. It made sense. Aterus had offered him a deal to switch sides. A stronger force must have been at play to make him agree. Maybe he didn't bare all the blame.

Pity crossed her eyes. "No, Kole. He didn't need to use his influence on you. Words were enough."

Kole swallowed hard. A lie. It had to be. But the more he tried to deny it, the stronger the truth pushed back. He had been desperate when he made his deal with the Gray Soul. Not even he could hide from that fact.

No one looked at him. Either sparing him further embarrassment or disappointed at his previous betrayal, Kole couldn't tell.

Russé placed a hand on Kole's shoulder and gave it a squeeze as if to say, "You are not to blame."

Piper pointed a finger just southwest of the Linde Caves. "The house is here. Where I lived as a child."

"House?" Leo asked.

"My mother insisted on living quaint," she explained. "But I doubt he'd be in there now. He knows we have an army. He knows where we are and that we intend to strike soon. He knows this because *I* knew when I helped Kole rid himself of my father's presence on our journey to release Vara." Piper nodded at the Violet Soul.

"Your minds leaked information," Vara said.

Piper's silence confirmed it.

"He doesn't know of the ramblers," Kole offered. "I awakened them after our connection was broken."

"Perhaps." Piper chewed her lip the way Kole always did when his mind searched for answers. "All this time, he's been playing well within his strength. Now that the pact with Kole is broken, he'll be using every bit of his power. His connection to the black flames are unparalleled. All he has to do is release his hold and Ohr will be engulfed."

"We have five Souls — six soon — that has to count for something," said Vienna. Her faith in the Souls had always been more potent than Kole's.

"Six fragmented Souls," Kole corrected. "They only have so much power in their current state."

"Still, I've seen what they can do." Vienna turned to Issira. "You brought my brother back from the brink of death after he'd gone through the Kayetan ritual. And Obell," her head whipped around to the Red Soul, "You roused a dormant volcano to save us from the cursed Yamani. Those aren't feats of a sorcerer. They are godly acts."

"Power that we have accumulated over the course of our imprisonment." Russé leaned heavily into the armrest to keep himself upright. "Powers that come easy to us in our full forms but not in this state."

"Russé used his reservoir to save me at the beginning of all of this." Kole scanned the scars of his body. Even then, that power had only stretched so far. "Issira used hers on Felix. Obell on the volcano...."

Obell grunted. "The volcano did not take as much as you think. I still have enough."

"That leaves Caradin, Vara, and Braxus with full wells," said Leo. "Once we release her, of course."

"Is that enough?" Vienna asked.

"But Aterus isn't at full strength either, is he?" Kole's attention landed on Piper. "His Soul is also fragmented. A piece of him is in Piper."

At that, everyone in the tent shifted to look at her.

Leo's ever-stoic expression morphed to shock. "It is true?"

"I meant to tell you sooner, Leo." Piper balled her fists. "But it doesn't mean my father is any less capable. I suspect he's drawing from another source of power. Extracting it from his humans."

Leo lay quiet. Even the Souls were speechless. *Just as shocked as the rest of us.* It was moments like that when Kole saw them in a more humbling light. Not all-knowing, ever-existing beings as relayed to Kole as a child.

"This is news, indeed," Leo said. "Similar to what my brother did with his Red Cloaks, I presume?"

Piper nodded.

Kole had thought the same when Piper first told him.

"It's not just sorcerers," Piper added. "Maybe in the beginning, but so many generations have come and gone. Mixed. Some blood is more diluted than others. While he can take vast amounts from sorcerers like you, he can siphon from anyone. Untraceable energy too small to manifest into magical abilities. Either way, it keeps him strong. But it's only a theory," Piper clarified.

Leo absentmindedly fiddled with his pockets. "One that I must look into before we march so many to his doorstep."

A shiver wormed up and down Kole's skin. He'd seen Leo's brother, the former warden of Socren, kill a band of sorcerers in an instant. One simple wave of Savairo's hand had sent the Red Cloaks to their death, just to grant the warden enough power to escape. Could Aterus do the same to them? The image of thousands of bodies piled at Aterus' feet burrowed into Kole's thoughts.

"There is a way to weaken him." Piper broke the silence. "My mother."

"Evangeline?" Issira said mournfully as if recounting a fond memory. It dawned on Kole that the Blue Soul had once helped Aterus conceal his relationship to the human before things got complicated with the pregnancy.

"She is the source of his happiness. She is everything to him." Piper's tone conveyed that her father's truth was also her own.

"What are you proposing, exactly?" Leo asked.

The muscles of Piper's jaw rippled as she clenched and unclenched her teeth. "If we are to overpower him, he needs to be distracted—weak. If I can get to my mother, I can...." She pulled her hands from the table and clasped them together.

"Kill her," Kole finished for her.

Vienna gasped. Horror-filled eyes slowly turned from Kole to Piper. "But... it's your mother. You can't—"

"My mother is already dead," Piper said through clenched teeth. "She has been in and out of a coma for as long as I can remember. Her heart beats simply because Aterus wills it, but that does not mean she is alive. She is a warm corpse. Death would be a mercy."

Vienna closed her mouth, but the horror remained clear on her face.

"Aterus will never allow you to get close to her now," Russé said with a cough. "Not after you've shown your loyalties to us."

"It will be difficult." Piper nodded. "If we can pull his attention long enough and I go alone...."

Obell clapped his hands together. "A distraction for the distraction. It'll have to be something big to draw him." A grin spread. The curve of his canines reminded Kole of a wildcat. "Something foolish on our end. The thing he wants most, I'd say."

"You want us to bow down to him?" Vara asked.

"No!" Caradin squealed, raced across the map, claws puncturing holes into the parchment, then jumped into Kole's arms.

"It's okay." Kole held the trembling weasel close to his chest. "I won't let you get trapped again."

"It's nothing more than a ruse, Caradin." Obell rolled his blazing eyes. "And no, Vara. Not bow down. *That* would spark his suspicions." His thumb trailed over his mouth as he thought. Kole knew the exact moment Obell's idea came to him because the room boiled. "No. We give him an audience. A chance to convince us. For us to listen."

"Aterus does love to talk," Issira added. "When I worked with him, all he wanted was a chance to change our minds."

"The timing needs to be perfect," Leo said.

"I can mind-link with Kole to get the timing right." Piper peered at Kole. "If that's okay with you, of course."

Kole nodded. "Whatever needs to be done." He held the weasel closer.

Every breath in the room sounded as loud as thunderclouds. The war was no longer a thought—a problem to worry about later. No. It was here. It was real. And Kole wondered as he scanned the room, how many of them would still be around in the coming days—himself included.

"Our army will wait to strike on the chance this fails." Leo rubbed his temples. "There will be some who will oppose, but I am sure I can get the leaders to follow if this is the will of the Souls."

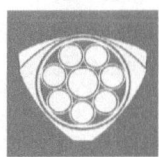

Criz and Boogy had offered to escort Kole and Vienna back to their sleeping quarters, but Leo sent them to collect the counsel for the battle strategy meeting. Admittedly, neither Kole nor Vienna knew the layout of the camp well enough to go straight back, so they wandered along the paths until something sparked their memory.

"Did you manage to get some sleep?" Vienna shortened her stride to match his.

"A bit. The cot is better on my scars than bark, but there's something about the rambler that's comforting."

"It's the sway in their walk."

"Is that so?" Kole pulled his coat close, banishing the cold from nipping the skin at his neck.

"It reminds me of riding in the back of a wagon. The wheels rolling over rocks and chunks of grass. The bobbing can lull even a fussy child to sleep."

Kole hid his smile under his hood. Vienna thought using the fabric was unnecessary. She'd told him before that he didn't need to hide his scars. Still, it made him feel safe. Progress was slow when it came to accepting his maimed body, but it would be a long while yet—if ever—before he could genuinely say that he held no resentment for his transformation.

"I missed you earlier. Well, everyone really." He backtracked when his brain registered the words that had slipped out. "The tent was empty. Everyone had something to do but me."

"You don't always need to be at the front of things. Sometimes you can relax, you know. Let your friends take the lead."

"I guess I've been on edge lately."

"It's in the air. Leo may not look it, but he is close to breaking. I'm glad the Souls showed up when they did." Vienna stopped at the corner.

They had left the more formal-looking tents and come upon the open pavilions of the blacksmiths. Finally, something familiar.

"We're close. I remember coming this way earlier." Kole squinted through the orange glow of torches. "Just not sure which way."

"Follow the edge," Vienna said, steering him right.

A dozen steps of silence. Vienna's hand brushed against Kole's as they walked by a forge, and a jolt surged through his body. He pulled away, realizing she had done the same.

"Sorry." She tucked her hands in her pockets. "I think my body is steering me toward warmth."

"It's okay," Kole mumbled and did the same. But his fingers wanted nothing more than to reach out and hold her hand in his. His mouth dried at the thought. "You don't like the plan, do you?" Kole blurted. Anything to keep his head on straight. "I saw the way you looked at Piper." The moment her mouth drooped into a frown, he regretted bringing it up.

"I never understood her. Now I know why." As she spoke, she closed the distance between them little by little. "I can't imagine growing up half-soul. Or with Aterus as a father. A blessing and a curse all at once. But her mother... I can't fathom ever getting to a point where I could go through with something like that."

"I don't remember my mother to know that sort of bond. I suppose it's like killing your best friend?"

"Something like that. It feels like betrayal."

"Piper said Evangeline has been suffering for years. Who knows how long that really is in Piper's perception. And Aterus is destroying the world in her name. There's a lot of conflicting emotions there, I'd bet."

"It makes sense in my head. But to actually do it... I could never bring my hand to fall."

Kole thought for a moment. He put himself in that scenario, except the person he cared about most was Vienna. Could he do it? Could he murder Vienna to secure Ohr's victory? A long peek over to her sealed his decision. No. He'd never. Even if she were in pain and begging for it to end. He felt for Piper. Though the demigod was a master at hiding her true feelings, she was surely a tangled mess on the inside.

"What are you going to do when this is all over?" Kole asked.

Vienna had moved closer again, the fabric of her sleeve brushing against his own. "I'm going to give Felix a proper sendoff next to my parents' graves. After that—well—I'm sure there won't be time for leisure. We can't predict what state Ohr will be in, but I imagine Leo will need a lot of help getting things back in order. I'll stay by his side as long as he needs me." She eyed him. "What about you?"

"I haven't given it much thought." An obvious lie, but he hoped she looked past it. He had thought on it quite a bit since Piper had spoken with him around the fire. Only, he couldn't think of a true answer other than to live to that point.

"There's no need to hide in Solpate anymore with Savairo gone."

"It's not really home, anyway."

Vienna dipped her head. Her brows furrowed.

"What's wrong?"

"It's just... I figured that you'd stay with me."

The warm firelight of the pavilions cast soft shadows across her freckles. A golden curl had come loose from her braid. Kole wished to reach out and tuck it behind her ear. His fingers twitched at the thought. He set his jaw with a breath, then pulled his hand from his pocket. The hair must've tickled her cheek, because she reached up and pushed it back before Kole's hand passed his belt. He crossed his arms to hide his intention. Thankfully she didn't seem to notice.

"I guess you were closest to Felix," Vienna said. The light in her green eyes dimmed. "I understand if you'd need some distance."

"No, it's not that I—"

"Is that Piper?" Vienna pointed to a form stomping from a tent. Only one person had hair that shade of red.

Even from this distance Kole could tell Piper was fuming. "We found our sleeping quarters."

By the time Kole and Vienna rushed to the tent, Piper was long gone. What had made her so angry? He wanted to go after her, but he knew he'd get lost. Where were Criz and Boogy when he needed them? Maybe her mother was on her mind. A mission like that could swing anyone to anger at the bat of an eye.

Before Kole could pull back the curtain, it ripped open. Russé's abnormally pale face greeted him.

"Oh, there you are." Russé staggered back, clearly not expecting to see Vienna or Kole at the entrance.

"Where are you going? You should be resting." Kole grabbed the old man's arm and steadied him. "Did they transfer you to our tent?"

"I needed to find you." It seemed the short walk had wiped the breath out of him. Vienna took up the Soul's other arm, and they both escorted him to a cot.

"No need to find me anymore." Kole helped lower Russé onto the bed, then propped the pillow behind the Soul's back to rest against. When he had last spoken with Russé, the Soul insisted he was on the mend—maybe a day or so left to recover—but the energy Kole had forced out of him had taken a much greater toll than any one of them had thought. The poor thing looked absolutely delirious. "We saw Piper leave a second ago. Did she talk to you? Is everything all right?"

"No. It's not. I need to tell you—" A long gasping breath. "I need to tell you." Russé 's tone reeked of desperation.

"Tell me what? Is it about Aterus? The war?" Kole locked eyes with Vienna, who shook her head, just as confused.

"No, no, no...." Russé's head rolled back to the cushion. Quick, shallow breaths lifted the old man's chest. "It's not fair, Kole." His face contorted. An expression Kole would've recognized on anyone else, but on a Soul, it looked unnatural. Terrifying.

"What's not fair? Russé, you have to talk to me."

A thick sob escaped Russé's open frown. Drool slipped from the side of his mouth.

"I'm going to get some help." Vienna reached over and squeezed Kole's arm, then rushed from the tent.

Once Vienna had left, Kole closed his eyes and reached out to Piper's mind with a vicious swipe. "*I saw you leave Russé. What did you do to him?*"

Her response came quickly. "*Why don't you ask him? His state is his own guilt and shame surfacing.*" With that, she cut off their connection.

"Russé? What were you and Piper talking about?"

Through his sobs, the Soul extended a hand toward another bed, where two books sat. One Kole recognized; the other looked more sinister with its blood-colored leather and black script on the cover. Kole grabbed them. The first was his old camp leader's journal. Niko had swiped it from Goren before the Black Wall came that night. Kole already knew its contents: stuff about the Souls and how Goren used Kole as a sacrifice to release Russé from his prison within the great red tree. But the pages were encoded. Only through earnest effort did they decipher it.

The other book, Kole had never seen, but holding it in his hand sent a chill up his arm and into his chest, where it pooled around his heart. His pulse skipped and faltered. In his hand, the book thumped in time with his blood. And it warmed as if it sucked something out of Kole's body, quenching an insatiable thirst. Kole threw it down next to Russé. That chill lingered in his ribcage, as if the book still had some hold on him.

"What is that?"

The tears had slowed now. Russé let his head fall to the side. His eyes lingered on Kole, yet distant as if he looked through him. "Savairo's grimoire. Spells and rituals."

Kole flexed his hand. The numbness faded. "What are you doing with it?"

"Leo lent it to me. I was looking for a way out."

"What do you mean?" Kole wanted to grab the old man by the shoulders and shake some sense into him. "Stop being so vague and tell me what's going on." He found his voice had grown harsh.

"I wanted to uphold my promise to you. I wanted to find a way to let you live. But it's no use. If it had been different, I could've done it. Had I known what was happening. But I was too late." Russé's shaking hand grabbed Kole by the shoulder. "I killed you, Kole. And I'll have to do it again before this is all over."

CHAPTER 28

"The book. The book." Russé grabbed the grimoire and flipped open the pages. The moment his flesh touched the spine, a wave of goosebumps ran up the old man's arms, hairs raising on end.

Maybe this thing is what's hindering Russé's recovery. Kole scooted back, ensuring the book would not touch him again. "I don't think you should be touching it. Russé?"

He ignored Kole, thumbing through the contents until a page in the back half made him stop. A crazed light seemed to radiate from Russé's blue eyes. "Blood sorcery can transfer a soul. Look here." Russé flipped the book around and shoved the page into Kole's face.

Kole jumped back. He dared not touch it. Odd rust-colored symbols painted the page. Neat script, but Kole could not read it. Blood magic runes, if Kole had to guess. Yet something drew his gaze to the writing. He found his eyes glued to it. Try as he might, he couldn't pull away. Slowly, he leaned in for a better look. His mind screamed at him to stop, but his body ignored the plea. The tip of his finger brushed the page.

An image of blood and gore flashed in his eyes. Bodies broken on a wooden table. Screams of anguish echoed, crying out from the past. Pleas to live. Corpses piling up, drained of blood.

Then Russé's voice came over Kole. "The spirit can be transferred from body to body. It can be twisted and reformed with the right influence."

The scene in Kole's head shifted. Savairo was there. A spitting image of Leo save for a more prominent muscular build. And those eyes, even in this vision, held a foul hatred.

Savairo stood over the naked body of a woman. A small ball of light floated away from her mouth. Savairo reached out. His hands dripped blood, covered in the warm fluid from fingertip to elbow. The sorcerer cupped the light in his hands, muttered a spell, then let it loose, watching until it faded away.

This time, Russé's voice morphed into a lower octave. The deep register sunk down into Kole's bones. Savairo now spoke. "I have failed to bring a lost soul back to a cold corpse."

Savairo screamed. The veins of his neck and forehead popped to the surface, angry and purple. With blood-covered fists held to the ceiling of his dungeon, he fell to his knees.

That voice echoed again. "Once gone to the ether, a spirit cannot return."

The book snapped closed, jolting Kole. In an instant, the vision of the blood sorcerer disappeared, replaced with the sight of a worn-down Russé hunched on the cot. Kole blinked a few times and pinched his forearm to ensure the dream had ended.

"It cannot be done." Russé's blue eyes brimmed with tears. "I thought Goren might have a clue in his journal. He dabbled in dark magic, but he was not as practiced as Savairo." He put the grimoire down and tapped the cover of Goren's journal. "All I gathered from Goren was the steps of his spell to release me. What he did to you. How it all played out. I was wrong about you acting as a road. You give that to my kin — the other Souls you've released — but for the first, it was a full sacrifice."

Kole sat there, frozen. Every word floated to his ears but danced there as if unwilling to enter. No. Not unwilling. Kole kept them there — kept them at bay. He didn't want them, for if he denied them, he'd never have to face the truth. But Russé wouldn't allow Kole that comfort.

"It cannot be undone." Russé said it clearly. "I cannot save you."

Kole held his lower lip firm. Swallowed. "I am going to die."

"It was doomed from the beginning. I always had a hunch, but I had to know for certain."

Only when Russé grabbed Kole's arm did he notice he'd stood from the cot. The Soul pulled at him.

"There's more. You need to know." The color in Russé face drained. "Goren's ritual killed that child out in Solpate. That boy died. His soul is gone. You are not that boy. You have a spirit, but it's a conglomerate of me and my kin. Pieces of us. *You are not that boy,*" Russé said again. "You never were. You just inhabit his body."

"My body?" Kole pulled up his sleeve and stroked his skin. Hands went to his face and skimmed the corded scars of his burns. *This body is not mine?*

"Even if there was a way to get that child's spirit back and return it to this body, it wouldn't be you who awoke. You wouldn't be here at all."

It couldn't be. Kole knew himself. He was someone. He was *him*. His own person. Sure, he held pieces of the gods within him, but he was still a teen. Just a kid. *Kole.*

"I thought the memories of your past were blocked from you because of our interference." Russé shook his head as he persuaded Kole back to the edge of the cot with a gentle pull.

That had been Russé's first guess. Kole remembered. The old man had said he thought once all his kin were released, those memories would come back to Kole. Those five years he'd spent in Socren with his mother and father. Those years he could never conjure up, unlike the other orphans in the refugee camp. He had listened to their stories hoping one day his own would return to him. But all he remembered was the forest. Nothing before Russé's release.

"They are not there because they were never yours."

A lie. Yet the words struck deep. It scared him. Kole tugged free of Russé's hold and clutched his temples. If he could only recall *one* thing: a face, a smell, a sound from before. Then he could deny Russé's theory. But he had been trying to conjure up something that lay out of reach for ten years. This moment proved no different. He hoped to pull jewels out of an empty jar.

"It's not there, Kole," Russé said lightly, gently, as if he knew exactly what Kole had intended.

Then what was he if not that boy? A mesh of the Souls? Was his anger just an extension of Obell? Did his compassion come from Caradin? There had to be more. Otherwise, Kole was nothing more than....

Hollow. A shell. A void. Not a real person but a puppet in every way. And the puppeteer had driven his every move whether Kole realized it or not.

Not a real person, just a tool to free the Souls. A hollow key.

"When it comes time for us to ascend...."

Kole already knew the answer. "I'm a corpse."

Silence. It thickened.

Russé's voice barley came to a whisper. "It's still your choice."

Those four words bubbled the marrow of Kole's bones. "A choice?" Kole snapped up from the cot and turned on Russé. A feral rage awoke as he seethed. "I have no choice. Whether you meant to create me or not, I live for a single purpose. My fate was determined the moment you left your prison. I live to die."

"If we don't ascend—"

"If you don't ascend, Aterus can't be controlled. The Black Wall will endure. And it will be me who allows that." Spittle flew as he spoke.

Nothing could reel in his anger. Not the smiling face of Vienna or the thought of Felix or Niko. "What choice do you think I have? Truly. To deny it would turn me into a mirror of Aterus. Selfish. Evil. All would resent me. Guilt would consume me. I would bring doom to Ohr. So no, Russé, I have no choice. I have borrowed time in a borrowed body and a sacrifice to make."

"Don't say that." Russé reached his hands to him, but Kole turned on his heel for the door. "Kole, wait."

He heard the old man climb from the bed and follow, but Kole didn't stop. Not even when the thump of Russé falling to the floor met his ears.

"Kole!"

Kole pushed open the curtain to see Vienna's huffing red face. Two healers hurried behind her.

"Is everything okay?" Vienna's eyes moved from Kole to the scene over his shoulder. "What's—Russé?" She cast Kole a look of concern before pushing past him.

Kole strode into the darkness and welcomed the cold on his skin for once. He hoped the icy wind would cool his blood. Though his feet moved along the road, Kole kept his head down, unaware of his destination. He needed out. Needed time.

The dark shadow to the east called to him. His feet brought him out of the camp and up the steep incline. His legs burned, urging for rest. Kole pushed on. If he was to feel something, it might as well be pain.

The crest of the cliff came fast. The clouds split and moonlight doused Kole head on. The great expanse of inky black waters stretched out to the shrouded horizon. The ocean seemed to bleed into the sky. He thought his first sight of the Tiot would bring euphoria. Instead, it left a deep cut of longing. How much had he still not seen of Ohr? This was it. War hung in the air. The end was here, and he wasn't ready for it. He wanted to live to be a man. He wanted to fall in love. Grow old. All stolen from him.

"Was there ever any hope?" Kole said into the air as if the sea could answer back. "I don't understand. I did everything I was supposed to." It felt as if he'd fallen from the highest peak of a mountain with nothing to grab hold of. Waiting. Waiting for the inevitable impact.

Pressure built in Kole's head. Caradin was reaching out to him. Word must've gotten out about his talk with Russé. Kole could feel the concern radiating from Caradin, but he pushed the god away. Surely, they were looking for him. Perhaps the entire camp would rouse to find him. They couldn't lose their sacrificial lamb. He wondered how much freewill he actually had. If he did refuse his mission, would they detain him? Force him to proceed with the act?

A sense of shame immediately crawled through him, and he shook away the thought. Russé had said he had a choice. One that Kole would never make, but it was comforting that his old mentor would allow the illusion of freedom.

Instead of waiting for a search party to find him, Kole said his goodbye to the Tiot Sea and headed back toward the war camp. At least that was one more thing he could cross off his list of things to see.

When he returned to camp, Criz and Boogy had posted up on the outskirts. They nodded to him, then led him back to the tent. They must've been given some sort of order because they were uncharacteristically quiet. Solemn expressions fixed on their faces as they held open the entrance.

Russé was gone. Instead, an anxious Vienna paced before the foot of the beds. Her face lit as he entered. She ran up and flung her arms around him. "I was so worried." Face pressed into the nook of Kole's shoulder, she said, "Russé told me everything."

He all but collapsed into her embrace. Whatever dam had been holding back his tears finally ruptured while in her arms. He sobbed.

Vienna rubbed his back. "It's going to be okay, Kole."

She let him cry.

When Kole was just a refugee in Solpate Forest, he'd imagined all the places he'd visit. Goren had shown him and the other orphans the great sites of Ohr—told them stories of the past. Looking back now on his journey, he'd gotten to see almost every place on the map. He could mark off the Tiot Sea from that now, too.

There were some things that would forever be out of his reach. Kole held her tight, never wanting the moment to end. Those dreams would have to die. His countdown had begun.

When the initial wave passed, Kole took a few deep breaths to calm himself.

"It's going to be okay." Vienna pulled him to arm's length. "It will."

He didn't bother arguing and nodded, numb. The tips of his fingers lay heavy on Vienna's bare arms, yet he felt nothing. His heart didn't flutter like it normally did when he stood this close to her.

"You need sleep."

Though stuck in a haze, Kole knew she was right. He let her lead him to his cot. Only now did he catch a glimpse of another person standing in the tent.

Piper stared at him from just inside the entrance. Had she been there the whole time? In any other instance, Kole might've been self-conscious about her seeing him in such a state, but his nerves were too shot to care. Still, he felt her eyes on him while Vienna set him down on the mattress and pulled the blanket to his chin.

"I'll be right next to you." Vienna patted the neighboring bed. "Just sleep."

Kole's swollen lids made it all too easy to comply. Vienna and Piper's voices lingered in the background before finally carrying him to sleep.

CHAPTER 29

Kole had reached out to Braxus one last time before leaving. It had failed. He hadn't even managed to enter her mind this time, just pounded at the door, waiting for an answer that never came. Kole blamed it on his pent-up emotions—resentment even. His brain must have known that releasing the last god took one step closer to death. It worked against him. Sabotaging. Still, what more had he hoped? That this time she'd leave him exact coordinates?

The bitter chill of fresh morning fizzled away as Kole rode atop Caradin's stag form. The sun hung overhead. He'd been so wrapped up in his own thoughts that he'd hardly noticed they'd reached the southern-most point of the caves.

Horse hooves pounded hard against the rocky terrain on either side of Kole: Issira on one side, riding with Russé, who's weak body needed an arm wrapped around his waist to keep mounted, and Piper on the other. Obell and Vara had stayed behind to ensure the council would agree to Leo's battle strategies.

Vienna's warmth radiated through the blanket tucked around Kole. A hint of honey hit his nose as the loose pieces of her braid tickled his cheek.

It may have been quicker to travel by rambler, but both Kole and Russé were too weak to command them. Leo had offered his fastest horses. They certainly lived up to their reputation.

Piper pulled on her reins, cutting the group off. "We should start searching from here. Comb the cliffs as thoroughly as possible. Where is the Yamani?"

No horse could carry the weight of the stone woman, so she had decided to travel on foot. Faint thumps came up from the bottom of the hill. The obsidian body of Shikar glinted in the high-noon sun as she crested the peak. Kole fully expected her to huff and puff, yet the Yamani stood tall, unphased.

"No stopping." Though she hid it well, Shikar's voice came breathy. "The horses can take it."

"The first caves are below," Piper said. Her horse danced as if twitching to continue. A sudden break did their muscles no good. "Unless we intend to backtrack, we need to start sweeping the area from the south."

Shikar grunted. Displeased or not, the Yamani's grumbles all sounded the same. She stomped her feet on the rocks and closed her eyes as if meditating. The stance lasted a second before Shikar shook her head. "Not here. We keep moving."

Piper frowned. "Are you—" A fierce glance from the Yamani made Piper drop her concerns.

"How does it work?" Kole asked. Those yellow eyes swerved to him.

"I come from the earth. I can sense the materials below for miles," Shikar said.

"You'll feel Braxus' soulstone?"

"No. Soulstones may look like gems, but they are not of rock or earth. I feel the power they leak into the earth around them."

"Like Obell's did in the volcano." It made sense. The Yamani had lived in tandem with the stone for centuries. Shikar would be all too familiar with the energy.

"A poison," Shikar growled.

Kole didn't blame her for her anger. The tension between the Yamani and the Red Soul was probably the reason Obell stayed behind. The fire god had attempted to make a species like Aterus' humans; thus, the Yamani came to be. But Obell had been careless, seeking to rival Aterus rather than perfecting his creations. The Yamani had been made with a defect. Their offspring were cursed, succumbing to a feral bloodlust as they aged. Kole had encountered the monsters when they had traveled to the Yamani home near the volcano. He could never forget those dripping teeth. Those red eyes....

The Red Soul's transgressions against Shikar's kind were probably why she left her Kayetan behind as well. To keep an eye on her enemy.

"Let's be on with it, then," Piper called from ahead.

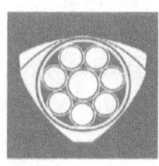

- 187 -

They searched for miles to no avail. Shikar had taken the lead and kept pushing them north. No sign of Braxus. When the sun bottomed out on the western horizon, worry bubbled in Kole's blood.

"She isn't here," Kole said loud enough for only Vienna to hear.

Vienna leaned forward and whispered back, "She is, Kole. Don't doubt yourself."

"It was a guess, and I was wrong." He'd steered them in the wrong direction, wasting precious time. Braxus could be in the heart of one of the peaks of Poleer for all he knew.

"The clues line up. It's the caves. Have some faith." Vienna's squeeze to his arm did little to comfort him.

Faith. Is that what I need? No, he needed a miracle. One the gods couldn't grant. Having a little faith or not would've led him to his same inevitable fate. He was stuck to it.

Caradin halted so abruptly Kole's nose bumped into the stag's neck. He glanced up, annoyed.

Shikar had paused to check the land. What had previously taken a second or two all afternoon now lasted a minute. When the Yamani opened her eyes, she tilted her head, saying, "I sense something."

"The soulstone?" Kole asked.

"Possibly. But the source is faint and widespread." Something about the Yamani's expression set a bitter taste on Kole's tongue.

"What does that mean?" Piper looked to the Souls for answers. "Faint?"

"Maybe Braxus is weak," Issira offered. Her usually calming sing-song voice struck sour on Kole. "We won't know until we find her."

Russé's hunched form perked up on his saddle. "It means we look. Take us there, please, Shikar."

Hesitance marked even the smallest movements from the Yamani. Something was off. Something that struck a fear in Shikar. Yet somehow, only Kole seemed to notice.

"See, what did I say?" Vienna said as they turned to the cliff face. "A little faith in yourself."

They dismounted once they reached the sheer drop of the cliff face. Kole had Caradin grow his wings to carry them two at a time. Shikar, though, slid down the rocks on her own. She landed like a crashing boulder on the ledge far below, shaking the cliff to its core.

Perched at the lip of an outcropping, Kole studied the side of the exposed sea cliff. The sight made him draw his breath. Black holes riddled the rock face. Dozens and dozens of caves drilled inward. The further he allowed his eyes to go, the deeper his stomach dropped. Too many to search. He wondered if Shikar's senses were up for the challenge, especially if Braxus' call was as faint as she said.

Russé was the last one down. The stag carefully knelt so the old man could slide off with ease. Kole questioned why Russé had even come in his state. He could barely keep himself upright. A quick once over and Kole spotted the corner of the grimoire peeking over the seam of Russé's coat pocket. *Still holding on to the thing.* No wonder he hadn't recovered. Russé probably insisted on coming along to keep an eye on him. Kole could barely bring himself to look at the god, much less speak to him.

"Which one, Shikar?" Kole pulled his borrowed coat to his chin to alleviate the constant pummel of ocean wind.

"Any entrance will do. They all connect at some point." The Yamani marched into the wide mouth of rock, the last light of sunset glinting off her faceted back.

One by one, they followed. Kole hung back.

Long, jagged stalactites jutted from the rock in unkempt rows overhead. He couldn't help but feel like they were walking straight into the maw of an eager beast.

"Come on, Caradin." Kole stroked the down feathers. "You can't fit like that."

The wings vanished, and the animal shrunk. Tiny claws climbed up Kole's pant leg. The weasel took his usual spot, looped around the crevice of Kole's neck. Before the group got too far ahead, he hurried in, the sun fading from his back.

The caves ran deep, twisting and turning like ant tunnels. It seemed odd. Kole had thought caves had been carved out of the stone by the constant lash of waves, yet even at high tide, the highest break of water couldn't stretch to this height. How then, was this created? Kole had a feeling they were missing a major piece to this puzzle.

Shikar led them downward. It made sense. If Kole's visions were correct, the overwhelming grip on Braxus was due to suffocation. They needed to descend to sea level.

Soon, darkness overwhelmed them. The last swerve they made had banished any lingering light of day. Kole's boot caught on uneven ground, and he landed right into Issira's back. He only knew because of the feel of silk on his face. He mumbled an apology as she righted him.

"Not everyone can see through the pitch," Issira said in a tone a little too cheerful for the caves. A blue glow appeared in the water goddess' hand. Water pulled from the sides of the wet stone in droplets and floated to her open palm, where it formed a sphere. The sudden light gave a wash of clarity to their surroundings.

Rock and more rock. Kole didn't know what else he had expected.

"Are you sure you know where we're going?" Piper's voice echoed down the path ahead.

A grunt came from the Yamani. That one *definitely* held some anger. Kole was getting better at reading the woman.

They pushed further.

Down here, the scent of brine and old earth assaulted Kole's senses. He could taste it on his tongue, feel the thickness in his lungs. The sensation made him cough. Vienna offered him her waterskin. He drank, but it only chased away the grip on his throat until he took his next breath.

Puddles littered the cave floor. Despite Issira's light, Kole stepped ankle deep into a pool of water. It seeped through the leather and soaked his sock to the skin. Just what he needed. His sloshing steps filled the air for a moment before Issira took notice. With a curl of her finger, she beckoned the water away, and it joined in a small stream to her orb.

Shikar stopped them where the tunnel pronged off in three different ways. "It's here." The Yamani placed a hand to the wall, then pointed down the center path. "This is where it starts. Her presence gets stronger down there."

"Be on your guard," Russé warned. "We don't know what her powers have leaked into this place."

Like how the trees of Solpate turned into ramblers from Russé's presence in the forest, and the murderous water that tried to drown Kole when he went to free Issira, all the Souls' prisons were guarded. Not that the Souls meant it, but their auras changed the nature around them. Braxus' defense would have something to do with the earth, which set Kole on edge since they were surrounded.

Shikar led them on.

The Souls followed, then Piper. Vienna lingered, as if waiting for Kole to make a move. She gave an encouraging smile, then grabbed his elbow and pulled him along.

Kole dreaded stepping into that tunnel.

And for good reason. The moment he stepped through, the earth shook.

Dust and rocks poured down. The deafening roar of collapse shoved Kole off his feet. He shielded his face and braced himself against the wall as a gust of wind hit him. He clung there until the tremor passed.

"Is everyone okay?" Shikar called through the haze of filth. The light taps of settling and rolling rocks in the aftermath sounded like beats of an erratic drum.

"Kole?" Russé's cried in a panic.

"Fine." Kole pushed off the wall and steadied himself. A small tongue licked his cheek. The weasel moved to Kole's shoulder and shook off the dust. "We're fine."

"Not exactly." Vienna pointed behind Kole.

The archway Kole had stepped through a matter of seconds ago now lay piled high with chunks of stone.

The way back was shut.

CHAPTER 30

Forward was the only way out now. Once they released Braxus, she could carve a path straight out of the cliff. All they had to do was make it to the soulstone.

From here on, the caves tightened. The group walked single file, but the Yamani's body scraped against the walls and ceiling. If the path shrank any more, Kole feared the stone woman might cork herself in.

Paths upon paths led on; twists and turns, forked choices at every bend. A labyrinth: one only Shikar could lead them through. Even with her senses, she lingered at each crossway as if choosing with trepidation.

Kole walked near the back, counting the taps of Russé's staff that clicked on the cave floor with each step. Lost in numbers, he hardly recognized the slight tickle on the back of his neck as they came upon the next four-pronged path. While the group paused for a moment for Shikar to figure out their next move, Kole reached around the weasel and scratched the irritation.

The itch strengthened at his touch.

That's when he realized the sensation had come from within. Someone was trying to contact him, ever so subtly. Did Braxus feel him nearby? Maybe she could guide them. Kole opened his mind to her. *"Braxus? Where are you?"*

No words answered. Only a feeling. An urge in his muscles to go left.

When Shikar stepped for the right-most tunnel, Kole stayed back. "I think we should go left."

The whole group turned to him.

"I have a feeling. I think it's Braxus." Kole swayed side to side as they swiveled their heads back to Shikar, who touched the wall again.

"I don't feel the energy that way. This tunnel leads down to the source." Shikar jabbed a gleaming obsidian finger toward the darkness of her tunnel. "We go right."

"She's speaking to you?" Russé wheezed.

Kole shrugged. "Not exactly. I guess it's more of an urge."

Russé's blue eyes shone more vividly in Issira's light. A puzzle worked behind the old Soul's gaze. "Do they intersect, Shikar? The left and right tunnels?"

Another brief pause, then, "No. The left loops back the way we came."

"Are you sure it's Braxus?" Russé said.

Anytime the Soul had reached out it had been through a dream-like vision, or she had spoken directly to him. He'd never felt this before. Maybe it was just his own instincts. Or the caves were messing with him somehow. This place *was* home to a soulstone, after all. "I... guess I can't be sure."

Without further discussion, Shikar set down her path. Russé moved back to walk alongside Kole. Probably to keep an eye on him. *Just like old times.* The dim light hid his deepening frown.

Left. The urge came again as Kole stepped through the arch. "Well, we're going right," he said under his breath.

Not two-dozen paces in, a vibration soaked through the soles of Kole's boots. So light, Kole thought he was imagining it. The buzz climbed up his ankles, then his legs until it reached his jaw and chattered his teeth.

"Does anyone else feel that? That buzz?" he asked. More wide eyes looked back at him. "Something's wrong."

"Maybe we should listen to Kole. He's the one connected to Braxus," Vienna said.

Russé laid a hand on Kole's shoulder. "What is it?"

"I don't—"

A tremor cut him off. Like last time, Kole dove for the wall to take cover. He expected pebbles to rain down again and the entrance to collapse. But it never did. The quake seemed more distant this time. Quieter. Yet second by second, the roar of destruction grew.

"Go back." Shikar took two slow steps in retreat, her face turned down the depth of the cave. Then she spun and lurched toward them. "It's collapsing. Run!"

The panic in her face sparked a boost of wild adrenaline in Kole's veins. He scrambled from the wall, his feet tripping over each other. A hand yanked him up before he could hit the floor.

Once he'd steadied, Piper pushed him on. "Get a grip, Kole."

Being in the back of their group meant he was now the front of their escape. Not the best choice to have the slowest runner leading a retreat. He pushed his legs hard, but the taut scars limited his stride.

The fuzzy scarf at Kole's neck scampered down his shirt, those frantic claws piercing the cloth and catching his skin. The weasel had stopped at Kole's thigh. Between his next stride, the animal enlarged. Kole's feet lifted from the ground as Caradin reshaped into a wolf beneath him. The sudden transformation sent Kole reeling backward, but the wolf bucked and repositioned his rider.

Kole wrapped his arms around the canine's neck and tucked his knees up so his feet wouldn't tangle with Caradin's. Atop the Soul, Kole split from the pack to the edge of Issira's light. He looked over his shoulder. His companions fell behind now, struggling to keep up. But the sight at their backs made Kole's heart thump.

The cave walls rippled. The stone of the tunnel slammed together, closing like a zipper behind them. If one of them faltered.... Kole wasn't sure how even a Soul could survive it.

"Hurry," Kole screamed.

Russé fell behind. No matter the Soul's pride, he clearly hadn't recovered enough. Kole doubted the old man had enough energy to use his powers. Shikar scooped Russé into her arms and raced for the exit.

"Left," Kole commanded the wolf once they reached the archway. "Take the left tunnel."

Caradin made a hairpin turn, cutting off Kole's sight on the group, and leapt for the far cave.

One by one, his companions exited: Piper, then Vienna and Issira. They joined Kole and the wolf in the alcove.

A second went by.

Two.

Three.

Or had it been a minute?

Where was Shikar and Russé? They hadn't been that far behind.

The grind of stone was upon them. Kole covered his ears at the cacophony just as the tunnel entrance smashed together like sliding doors. A cloud of dust fogged the alcove.

Then all went silent.

"Russé?" Kole hurled himself off the wolf and ran to the archway that now stood as a solid wall—no sign it had been anything other. "Shikar?" He pounded his fist on the rock.

No answer.

"Please, no." The back of Kole's throat swelled.

The cave had taken them. Entombed them.

"They're not... they can't be...." Vienna's voice echoed through the alcove.

Then, a scrape from the other side. A muffled voice.

Hope stirred. "Bring the light," Kole demanded.

Issira neared. The illumination gave no hints to a door or a way to reopen the path.

"Russé? Shikar? Can you hear me?"

Another muffled sound. Too deep in the stone to make out. If they couldn't speak directly, Kole would use another way. He opened his mind to Russé. A breath of relief caught in his throat when he discovered the old man's door remained in his head. That had to mean Russé was at least alive.

"Russé? Are you okay?"

"I'm alive. Shikar is injured. She used her body to protect me. We are surrounded by stone."

"They're alive," Kole said, before continuing his conversation with Russé. "We're going to get you out."

"No. You need to go on before the tunnels change again. I think this is Braxus' influence. Whatever urge she sent you, you need to follow it, now. I think she's trying to guide you through a safe path."

"I'm not going to leave you here."

"Shikar has assured me she can break down the barrier. She just needs time."

"Russé –"

"Listen to me. The sooner you find Braxus, the sooner we'll all be out of danger. So go. You know the way."

Kole let his hand drop to his side. "He wants us to leave them."

"Then we leave," said Issira.

"You're not serious." Vienna shoved a hand at the closed tunnel. "They're buried alive."

"Shikar is going to dig them out," Kole recited.

"Can she do that? It's solid stone!"

Kole gave a guilty shrug.

Issira lowered her light and moved for the left path. "The Yamani knows her strengths better than us."

"Piper?" Kole hoped she'd have another idea.

"We go now before this happens again." The demigod held no remorse in her tone. "We need to be fast. We don't know what's triggering the tunnels. It could be random, or it could sense us. Let's hope for the former. It gives us a better chance."

With that, Issira headed for the tunnel, Piper on her heels. Caradin sat at the entrance and whined, waiting for Vienna and Kole to follow.

Vienna touched the wall one last time. "This doesn't feel right."

He grabbed her wrist and gently tugged her away. "None of this does. But they're right about one thing," Kole said as another hum of vibration crawled up his ankles, "we need to keep moving."

Caradin licked at their legs as they passed. His cold nose pressed on the back of their knees, encouraging them to catch up to the other two. Soon the blue light draped them. Even though they'd caught up to their companions, Kole still held onto Vienna's wrist. If there was going to be another cave in, she'd be on the wolf with him this time. But then her muscles twisted in his grip. Kole guessed his hold probably felt more like a shackle than a line of safety, so he released.

A shock of surprise pounced through his nerves when instead of pulling away, her fingers laced through his. Even in the cold cavern, heat pooled in his cheeks. He risked a glance her way. Maybe it was the lighting, but he could've sworn the same blush darkened beneath her freckles. It took every fiber of courage in his body to squeeze her hand.

She returned the pressure.

Focus. The tunnels are trying to kill us. You can't be thinking about stuff like that. Despite scolding himself, his heart continued to flutter. It pounded so heavy against his chest he feared the whole party would notice. Slow, controlled breaths did nothing to settle him, so he kept his eyes down as stealing a sideways glance would further distract him.

Piper halted at the front. "Shikar said it looped around, but...." She cocked her head. "It leads down."

Kole only now realized the hum in his feet had faded. Had more stone moved? This tunnel? Fingers still intertwined in Vienna's, Kole peered over Piper's shoulder.

The scrape of sliding rock startled them all. Movement at Kole's feet stole his attention. The others must've noticed it too, because hands grabbed hold of his shoulders as if ready to drag him back and run.

"Wait." The ground at Kole's feet had changed shape. "It's a step." He wiggled free from the tense hands and stepped down.

The bare slope beneath the platform jutted out into another step as if luring him down the path. The caves wanted him to go this way. *Braxus* wanted it.

"A staircase," Piper said flatly. "Feels like a trap."

"You have a better idea?" Kole descended another two steps. Each time, the cave floor reformed and lifted to meet his boots.

"It's a lot harder to run uphill if we need to bail again," Piper grumbled.

"A good point," Issira said. "Caradin, see to it you stay with Vienna and Kole should they need your assistance."

The wolf nipped the hem of Vienna's sleeve, brought her to the front next to Kole, then pushed past their legs to take the lead.

"One thing is for sure," Issira went on. "By the behavior of the steps, the cave system isn't random. The earth knows we're here."

"That means it *did* try to kill us. Great," Vienna said behind Kole.

"I'd take this over the volcano," Kole noted. "At least this place gives me a warning. And there's nothing to fight."

The staircase curved to the left. Water trickled from the cracks in the walls, collecting at their feet in small puddles.

"I'd take my chances with fighting," Vienna said. "At least I know I have good odds of winning then. Collapsing caves? If we're too slow, we'll end up like Russé. Except we won't have a Yamani to dig us out."

"I hate this place." That was all Piper needed to say to both agree with Vienna and share her disdain for their current situation.

Before long, Caradin stopped.

They had come up on a dark body of water. Issira's glow bounced off the flooded path. Kole knelt beside the canine. Their reflections shifted in ripples. Something about his own appearance made him linger. He couldn't remember the last time he looked into a mirror. His features looked sharper than he remembered. Bags weighed under his eyes from restless nights. And his scars. This was the first time he gazed at them without wincing. They hadn't healed any more. The thick, corded texture was still prominent, but something about them now made them feel... less. Maybe the poor lighting helped hide the severity, but in that moment, he didn't feel bothered.

Kole slid his hand into the abyss. More steps. He stretched as far as he could without falling in. "It's deep." His fingers returned numb and pale.

"Unless Caradin can turn himself into a raft, I think you're up," Piper signaled to Issira.

Kole and Vienna hugged the side of the cave, allowing the Blue Soul to pass. One hand still holding the globe of water, she used her other to summon the flood. Instead of siphoning it away like Kole had seen her do before, the Soul parted the brine. An arch formed in the liquid, lifting all the way to the ceiling until the path ahead grew wide enough for them to walk through.

With the water out of the way, Issira urged them in. "It will hold," she said, as if those words alone would squelch all their fears.

Yet all Kole could think about was the pond where he'd found Issira's soulstone. That sentient water had pulled him to the depths and almost drowned him. The memory played on repeat as he took a shaky breath and entered. If the water came crashing down, killer or not, he was a goner. Nothing other than shallow streams and creeks cut through Solpate Forest. He'd never learned how to swim.

The stair ended three steps down then leveled out into another long path. His shoes slipped on the slick buildup of grime and algae on the stone floor. He wondered if anyone had ventured here before. Was anyone dumb enough to explore a place like this? *Yet here I am.*

The walk turned quiet again. Partly because their voices down here gave off a wobbly, all-encompassing sound, but the true reason came from the water. Shadows flitted inside. Even above them. Kole kept telling himself they had to be fish — some sort of sea life — but they passed too quickly to see clearly.

Deep. Deep. Go deep.

That same instinct came to him again. "I think we need to go down," he said.

"Do you see a path?" Piper asked.

Kole squinted into the water ahead. Nothing appeared beyond the stretch of Issira's light. "I guess n—"

The ground gave way beneath Kole's step. He plunged deep into glacial waters. Salt flushed up his nose and seeped into his mouth. He gagged and wildly flailed his arms in an attempt to find the surface. A yank to his collar pulled him upward. Air hit his face. The smell of wet dog filled his nostrils as Caradin dragged him back to land.

The arctic temperature kept him on high alert. He hacked up brine, huffing in between.

"Are you all right?" Vienna lifted his chin to inspect him.

"Fine. Just need a second." One moment, his clothes clung to him, waterlogged, and the next, droplets pulled free and added to the tunnel, leaving Kole feeling sunbaked. At least on the outside. His ears still sloshed. Kole sat up. "I guess that's what 'go deep' means." Even now, when Kole knew where the hole lay, the water's reflection hid its secret well.

Issira leaned over and set her orb on the surface. It sank. Though darkness flushed over the group, the sphere lit up the depths of the cavity leading down.

A minute went by and still it sank. Issira called it back.

"It runs too deep. I can clear it, but the fall would be fatal." Kole hated the way her melodic voice sounded when she spoke of serious matters.

Caradin nudged a cold nose to Kole's arm. "No, buddy. The hole is too small for you to fly us down." The wolf whined.

Piper put her toes on the rim of the hole. "We'll have to dive."

"If you haven't noticed, I can't exactly swim." The water had stilled back to its glass-like state. Despite his freshly dried clothes, his skin still retained goosebumps. He rubbed his arms and flexed his toes, but he knew it'd be a good while until his blood thawed.

A lopsided frown stretched over Piper's face. Then the sides raised into a smile. "You can create a current, can't you, Issira?"

"I can."

"Then all you'll have to do is hold your breath, Kole," Piper said.

"I'm not going back in there."

"Why? Because it's cold?" Piper mocked. "Obell isn't here to make you bath water. You'll have to get uncomfortable, I'm afraid."

Kole wanted to protest, but even Vienna had rolled up her sleeves and worked on tightening the laces of her boots in preparation. "What else is new?" he muttered as he lugged his rigid limbs to stand. "Can you tell where it leads at least?"

Issira held a palm over the water. Her skin glowed blue as she worked. Her fingers danced as if controlling some invisible stringed puppet, likely prodding the hidden places of the hole with her water. "The tunnel goes deep," she said, eyes closed. "The water opens to a larger cavern. It seems the floor ascends from there. Up until my reach fades." Issira swiped the dirt off her silken bell sleeves. "That must be dry land." She circled her hand above the hole.

The water moved at her command, swirling at Kole's feet. The surface spun faster and faster until the middle pulled down, forming an underwater twister.

No chance he'd be able to see in that. Not that he'd have to do much of anything. Kole worried more about holding his breath long enough.

"I'll keep the current going from here." Issira stepped back from the hole, still swirling her wrist. "Whenever you're ready."

"I'll go first." Piper barely got the words out before she swan-dived into the darkness. Kole hadn't even heard her take a breath. A subtle splash flicked up to Kole's pant leg and she was gone.

Vienna crept to the edge.

"Be safe," Kole blurted out.

A small smile pressed her lips. She took in a few slow, deep breaths, body relaxing with each exhale, then after the last one, she slipped in headfirst. The water stole her away.

"I can feel the blood within you race." The Soul's stormy eyes landed on Kole. "You are perfectly safe. I promise." She scratched the wolf with her free hand. "Go with him, will you, Brother?"

Caradin's nose retracted. The silver coat pulled back into his body as scales poked up and laid themselves flat over his elongating form. A giant eel. The beady eyes still held a sense of Caradin, but the jutting fish jaw and slimy skin were wildly different from any feature the Soul had donned before. Not Kole's favorite, though he still wrapped his hands around his companion. The body was warm and velvety, at least, something he didn't expect of the slimy looking skin.

"Let's get this over with." Kole copied Vienna's approach and slowed his breath. His heartbeat followed suit. If he could calm his nerves, he'd manage to hold his air a little longer. One last inhale. He expanded his lungs until they pressed against his ribcage, then let himself fall into the pitch.

The bitter temperature shocked him once again. On impact, the air he'd saved in his chest punched out of him in a giant bubble. Water swirled up his nose as the current dragged him down. Instinctually, his body wanted to gasp and refill what was lost, but Kole clamped his mouth shut.

Spinning. Spinning. Up was down. Down was up.

Caradin slipped in his hands. The slick scales and harsh water came as a disastrous combination. Kole pulled the eel into a bear hug. The fish's body wriggled in his hold, but his new grip kept him from slipping.

Seconds passed.

A fire started in Kole's chest. He focused on anything else; the dry land at the end of the tunnel, the satisfying feeling when Issira removed the water from his clothes. Yet the burn grew.

Kole could only handle a moment longer. He was in Issira's killer lake all over again, resisting suffocation, except *this* water was supposedly helping.

Just when a faintness overcame his head, the slap of air hit his face. He'd never been so grateful to lay on the hard edges of a cave floor.

"See, that wasn't so bad, now, was it?" Piper's voice barely rose above Kole's gasping breaths.

He coughed, then shook the water from his hair. "Yeah, not so bad."

He laid the sarcasm on thick. Kole released Caradin and collapsed to his back. The cold had seeped into his bones. They felt so brittle Kole thought if he moved too soon, they'd shatter like ice.

Vienna hunched over him. "You didn't swallow any, did you?"

"Just what went up my nose."

Like an angel draped in blue light, Issira floated up from the water. The droplets in her hair drifted away in a glittery crown, adding to the divine ease of her grace. The difference in the god's exit and Kole's soggy crawl to freedom was laughable. She did her thing and dried them off with a flourish of her hand.

A soft tongue licked Kole's cheek. Caradin had reverted to a wolf. The canine's nose nudged him to stand. With Vienna's offered hand and the wolf's encouragement, Kole lugged himself back to his feet. Only now did he notice Issira's blue light had gone. Yet he could see quite clearly.

Every nook and cranny of the cave lit up with a brilliance of yellow. The rocks here were not of molded earth or stone; they were crystalline in shape. The kind of precious stones people mined for fine jewelry. Their colors ranged from rich honey to the delicate vibrancy of sunflower petals.

Kole's companions must've shared his awe because no one said a word. They all walked deeper into the bejeweled cavern.

A vibration shifted the air. This time, it came from all around Kole, and by the panicked look of Vienna and Piper, they felt it too.

Kole grabbed Vienna's hand, ready to flee at Braxus' signal. It never came.

The cave walls began to move.

"What's happening?" Vienna squeezed Kole's hand tighter.

The gems all around them shifted — rotated. Some moved in line with one another, following some unknown predicted road, while other jewels spun or sank into the stone only to reappear in a different place.

Then, the place settled. Sounds of shifting earth came from somewhere far off. That's when he recognized a sort of pattern in the seemingly random design.

"It's the cave system. Look." Muscles still stiff, Kole limped up to the tunnel wall and traced a hand over a line of pale stones. "This is a tunnel." A darker gem had jutted out at the end of the snaking line. *A blockage?*

"What are you talking about?" Piper asked.

"There's another over here." Kole turned to where Vienna had found another streak of common-colored stones. She followed the line until the end, except the block of her tunnel held something different.

Green.

Kole hurried over.

"So it's a map?" Piper asked.

They all gathered around Vienna's discovery.

"Why is it green?"

Kole stared at the miscolored gem. Something shifted in the center. He drew in until he saw....

A face.

Russé's face.

Kole pulled back. "It's Russé. Him and Shikar." He backed up to get a better view of the entire wall. "It's where they are trapped."

"No kidding," was all Piper said as she took her own look.

"Then that is us." Issira's trill bounced off the glittering scene. Her finger pointed to the apex of the tunnel, where a faint glow of cobalt filled a stone. Something odd sat next to it.

Kole jogged over, knees throbbing as they rewarmed.

A black stone had wedged itself next to the blue one, and Kole knew exactly what it meant.

"You and me." Kole had meant to say it to himself, but his voice carried in the underground space.

The hollow key. The hollow stone. A void. Nothingness.

"If these things are a map of the tunnels, then we should be able to find a way to Braxus," Piper said.

"This *is* Braxus," Issira chimed in. Her eyes took on a serene glow. "This whole cavern is her — her creation."

"They're all soulstones?" Vienna asked.

"No." Kole had been around these things too many times to be fooled. "Only one."

"Braxus is the Yellow Soul," Vienna's voice came breathy as if confirming to herself. She spun in a circle, eyes to the ceiling. The amber light played in her hair, making it look like strings of gold. "But they're *all* yellow. It could be any one of them. How are we going to find out which is her? You can't spread your blood over them all."

Kole chuckled at that. "Yeah, probably not a good idea." He sure hoped he wouldn't have to spill that much today.

The cave went further, curving away from them. Kole wandered down the cavern while the others continued their own investigations. A quick press in his mind told him Braxus was still blocked from him. Inconvenient, especially when they stood in her chamber. It could shorten their journey if the Soul simply reached out now.

Rounding the turn, Kole's feet planted themselves like iron weights. "Over here," he called over his shoulder.

A pedestal of stone stood low on the floor. Though Kole couldn't see what sat in the bottom of the basin, he could surely guess from the pulsing light reaching up to the lip. On one hand, Kole felt a sense of relief. This had turned out to be much easier than he'd thought. Yet on the other, he knew he'd have to conduct the ritual in a matter of moments. No matter how many times he put himself through it, it wasn't something he could get used to. At least he had Issira with him if anything should go astray.

"We should make haste," Issira said. "The water level is rising."

"That doesn't make sense. High tide doesn't come until midmorning," Vienna said.

"Does any of this ever make sense?" Piper quipped back. "Let's just get this over with so you two don't drown, please."

The Blue Soul could protect them from the water, but her reach only went so far. He doubted she had the strength to draw back the entire tide from the cliffs.

Kole pulled out his blade as he marched to the basin. The lip came up to his knee. A small puddle of water still stood in the bottom, half covering a chunk of pale stone. The color wasn't as saturated as the cave walls — more like the hue of old, dried hay — and the surface held a cloudy haze. It reminded Kole of the sick farm fields of Socren.

With the sharp edge of his dagger poised on the meaty part of his thumb, Kole pressed. He hissed as the cold steel slit his flesh. He rubbed the surrounding spot, luring the blood out, then reached inside the bowl.

"Be careful," Vienna said. He didn't have to look back to know the crease on her forehead sunk deep between her brows the way it always did when worry claimed her.

Careful wasn't a part of this game. Kole's life lay in the hands of Braxus, now. Should she be gracious, he would wake up in a moment, unscathed.

Kole bent and reached for the soulstone. The moment his flesh touched pallid rock, his skin prickled, and he knew he had fallen into a trap.

CHAPTER 31

Pain shot through him like a tree struck by a bolt of lightning. Every nerve, every vein, every morsel of skin, trembled at the energy. Cold and searing all at once.

Kole cried out.

He heard the voices of his companions around him—felt their hands shaking him—but the pain forbade any sort of freedom.

A presence slid through his head, caressing his memories and thoughts. A fog of anger tailed behind it as it looped through Kole.

"You're not Braxus." Kole managed to clear the words through the pain.

"I am not," came Aterus. *"You betrayed our deal. It's only right I pay you back. I will be generous."*

The bolt hit him harder. Kole's vision went white. His heart threatened to burst. If Aterus kept this up much longer, Kole knew his body would give out.

The intensity dialed back, and Kole gasped for air. Breathes came quick and shallow. *"If you're looking for help, I won't give it to you,"* Kole said. *"You lied to me."*

"You are a pawn, Kole. Nothing more," Aterus snapped. *"Whoever claims you is the victor. I will have you. Even if it's not by choice."*

"Never."

Another jolt sped through him. Kole's insides shuddered. It felt as if each of his organs lay in the grip of squeezing hands. Ruthless. Bloodthirsty.

"I am no one's!" Kole roared. When the pain subsided, he realized he'd said it aloud, too. *"I will not be used by you or anyone. I will not be a pawn."*

"Tell me, has Russé read the grimoire?"

Kole swallowed, rage building. The shakes of his comrades barely registered now. There was no way out of Aterus' hold. Not unless the Gray Soul himself released him.

"Then you know you can't be saved. Why choose their side when the outcome is the same for you?"

More head games. He wouldn't entertain Aterus any longer. *"Where is Braxus? What have you done to her?"*

"I have relocated her. You move too slow, Kole. I have been waiting on you for weeks."

A fake. The stone in the basin was a fake. But—wait—what had he said? Weeks? *Waiting for weeks.* The timeline didn't add up. If Aterus was telling the truth, that would mean the Soul took Braxus before Kole had even crossed the Black Wall.

Then it clicked. *"You took her after we made our deal."*

"I had to have collateral. Trust is hard to come by these days."

"Then the visions... I was never talking to Braxus. It was you all along. You lured me here. Why?"

First, Aterus had imitated his dead friend, now Braxus. Kole scolded himself for ever laying his hope in the Gray Soul.

"My plans have changed. If you will not obey, then I reset the game and wait for the next key to be made. Pray your death comes swiftly."

Before Kole could process Aterus' words, the Soul set his anger on him. This time, Aterus didn't hold back. The killing blow. All Kole knew was light and pain. Aterus' hatred twisted through him, clawing at his insides, down to his very spirit.

This was the end for him.

Then.

A light touch encased Kole's hand. It tugged. His fingers unfurled and the tink of clattering stone filled the cave.

The connection with Aterus severed.

Kole's knees wobbled, and he collapsed into waiting arms. His eyes flicked wildly back and forth, taking in the golden cavern once more. His skin felt everything and nothing all at once. The hands on him were too much. But they squeezed tighter as he squirmed to break free.

"It's okay. I have you," Vienna hushed. "You're safe."

The sound of her voice set on him like warm summer rain. It doused the panic and soothed the lingering quiver in his shocked nerves. From the heat of her breath on the back of his neck and the sweet scent of her hair, to the feel of her own heart pulsing in time with his, she was his ultimate remedy. He believed her words. Aterus was gone. Kole couldn't imagine anywhere safer than in her arms.

"He took her," Kole croaked. "He took her the moment I made the deal with him."

Piper, Issira, and even the wolf held their jaws firmer.

"Aterus fed me those visions," Kole rambled on. "He relocated her. She could be anywhere. And I have no—"

"It's a ploy," Piper cut in. "He's desperate now. To him, the safest place now is in his own hands. He'll have Braxus' soulstone with him."

"Then why the show? Why would he lead us here?" Vienna loosened her hold around Kole now that he had calmed, but he let himself stay there, propped up against her chest. "To get Kole alone?"

"Not alone. He knows the Souls wouldn't allow that. Kole triggered a different ritual when he put his blood on the false stone. If he had done it any other way, we wouldn't have fallen for it." Piper walked off where the stone now lay after Issira had her water knock it from Kole's hands. The sallow thing had lost its ethereal glow. Piper nudged it with her boot. "He's gone."

"He was killing me." Kole shook the fog of his head away. "Said he was going to restart the game. Wait for the next key."

Issira dipped her head at that. "Aterus means to banish us once again. Send us back to our prisons."

"Can he do that?" Vienna asked.

"He did it once," Kole said. "Who's to say he can't do it again?"

"If he kills you," Issira began, "the fragmented pieces of us within you will be freed. At that point, they are up for the taking. Aterus needs only to get his hands on you to siphon the life out of you."

Piper kicked the stone into one of the shallow pools littered across the cave floors. "I guess this was his attempt."

"If that happens," Issira continued, "then it is as Aterus said: the game is reset. We can once again be locked away from Ohr." Issira patted the whining wolf, snuggled at her side.

"We can't let that happen," Vienna said fiercely. "Even if by some miracle Leo should unite all humans and Yamani on the continent, we can't rival the powers of a Soul."

"You, Caradin, Russé... the others...." Kole found the strength to peel himself from Vienna. He sat up, yet his body ached, warning him against standing so soon. "You need your unbroken souls to defeat him." His hand absentmindedly found the pendant at his neck. Fingers stroked the bumps of the colored gems.

"To *undeniably* defeat him, yes." Pity laced her voice. "Russé believes there is hope for another way."

"It's a dead end." Kole pushed to his feet. Wobbly. He latched onto Vienna's offered arm to steady himself. "There is no other way."

A hum sprouted under Kole's feet. The glow of the cave flickered as the stones moved and rearranged into another random configuration. The caves shuffled again. Aterus may have removed Braxus from this place, but her presence lingered. The tunnels would remain fixed otherwise. Not to mention Kole's 'instincts' like the one currently baring its head, telling him to move. "Let's find Russé and Shikar and get out of this place before it swallows us whole."

"Looks like Russé is on his way out." Piper held a finger up. The green stone had moved from the previous spot to the edge of the makeshift jeweled map.

One less thing to worry about. Shikar's state, however, preyed on Kole's mind. She had taken the brunt of the collapse on her literal shoulders to protect Russé. The stone woman had once bragged her body had the durability of a diamond. But even a diamond could only take so much stress before it shattered. Kole hoped the Yamani's talk of resilience wasn't an exaggeration.

The watery entrance they had used a moment ago had disappeared, but Kole's intuition—now confident it came from Braxus—sent him in another direction. A new tunnel had opened. Steep but, more importantly, dry. Kole refused to dive into another one of Issira's whirlpools.

Now that Kole and his group knew what to expect, the journey out proved quick and simple. Caradin replaced his padded feet with claws and carried Kole when he could not make the climb on his own. Soon, the fresh breeze of the Tiot swirled in the air, signaling their success.

Kole trudged to the mouth of the cave to take in the dark scene. The moon and stars sparkled off the restless waves as they peeked through the cover of clouds. The openness felt nice around his body after hours spent in the cramped spaces of the tunnels. Breaths came easier, like a hand had finally been pried from his throat.

"Kole!"

He lifted his eyes to where his name echoed somewhere far above. Russé was on hands and knees, peering over the bluff. The large form of Shikar stood behind him.

Caradin flew Kole and his companions to the top, where Russé had started a fire.

"You made it out." Kole took the pair in. Up close, he noted several new scrapes and bruises across the old man's thin skin. On the whole, Russé appeared no worse off than when they left him. The bags under his eyes remained in shadow, and a jaded fatigue lived in his gaze.

"It will take more than a few rocks to fell me," Shikar said with a wide grin. She made a show of flexing her stone arms before patting Kole rough on the head. "I'm offended if you expected any different, little one."

Kole matched her smile.

"And where is Braxus?" Shikar asked.

His mouth drew a hard line. "She's not here."

"Not here?" Shikar swung her head to the rest of the group. "What do you mean?"

"Aterus has taken her," Issira said, locking eyes with Russé. "She will be with him."

The old man dipped his head. His stoic façade faltered, allowing Kole to glimpse the utter disappointment of his mentor.

"He set a trap," Piper added.

After explaining their time in the caves, Issira helped Russé to a seat on a boulder by the fire.

"I never expected it to go without a hitch, but this...." Russé jabbed his staff into the gravel. "We can't allow things to go backward. Not when we've come so far."

Kole neared the fire and held his hands to the heat.

Piper plopped down and crossed her legs. "He will have abandoned the cottage with Braxus and my mother. That place has no defenses. He's going to make his final stand."

"Where?" Vienna took the question from Kole's mouth.

"There's a place on the north peak of the gulf. Not far from Rush. He'd take me and my mother there on occasion when we visited the sea in the summers. There's a structure there."

"A base?" Kole rubbed his warmed hands over his arms, hoping to fend off the chill.

"Of sorts. More of a ruin."

"How can you be sure?" Vienna pressed.

Piper tilted her head back and let out a laugh. "I can't. Unless I reach out to my mother. She will be where he is. That is the only certainty in this world."

Vienna and the Souls looked at her expectantly.

"Hell no. Not now." Piper kicked at one of the burning logs, sending a flurry of embers flying into the smoke. "He'd know. If he catches me again, it's over. He'll shut me down."

Like a puppet. Kole had been on the wrong side of the Souls many times before. Anyone who got inside another's mind had the potential to use them.

"We'll do it when you offer him the Souls' council," Kole said to Russé. "He'll lend his full attention to you. Piper can connect with her mother then. Find out where he's set up, then when we take Leo's army out to face him — while you listen to his proposition — we'll go looking for Braxus and Evangeline."

"I cannot think of a better plan, "said Russé.

The Soul's statement gave Kole a brief sense of pride. His old self would've beamed at that sort of praise from his mentor.

Kole followed suit while the others pulled out their bed rolls and munched on bread they had taken from the war camp. After their bellies had their fill, the group settled down for the last few hours before dawn. Kole, however, knew he'd never wind down enough to sleep, so he grabbed his slingshot and moved along the ridge.

The crunch of footsteps followed him. The silver wolf trailed after Kole.

He held up a hand. "No, Caradin. Not this time." The wolf gave a high-pitched whimper in protest, but Kole held firm. "I won't be far. You can watch from here if it helps, but I need some space."

The canine lay down, rested his head on his paws, and set those wide eyes on Kole.

"I won't be long, promise," he reassured, then continued down the slope until the firelight had shrunk to a speck over his shoulder and he could just make out the silver silhouette of the wolf.

Kole loosened the drawstring pouch at his hip with a finger and fondled the metal pellets within. They rattled like bells at his touch.

He pulled one out and rolled it in his palm while his other prepared the slingshot. The tattered cloth still clung tightly to the handle, where Vienna had adjusted it to better form to the limited mobility of his scarred hand.

The rocks would be his targets.

Each step ran through his head like a checklist. He planted his feet as he set the pellet in the pocket of the string. Arm extended, he braced, and his right hand pulled back to his chin. For some reason, he could picture Felix at his side. That head of brown curls and that toothy, vulpine smile encouraging Kole.

He imagined what his late friend would say in this moment.

"Whatcha waitin' for, blondie? Shoot already." That city twang calmed Kole.

He took in a breath and released.

The metal ball hit dead center of the boulder, taking off a thick chunk of rock along with it.

Felix let out a whistle. "I reckon yer almost as good as the master now, mate."

He wished more than anything he could see his friend again. The fact that Kole hadn't been there when Felix needed him most twisted the already festering wound.

"You've gotten quite good." This voice hadn't come from Kole's imagination.

He turned.

Vienna watched him from the ridge. "Those bow skills of yours transferred over nicely."

Kole fiddled with the handle of the slingshot. "It's more or less the same."

"I remember when you had a hard time hitting a frying pan." She smirked.

Kole laughed at the memory. His poor aim had been more about relearning old skills with his scars. It had been frustrating at first to see himself struggle with things that had come so easily before. But he'd had a good teacher in Vienna and Felix. Oh, if he could relive those days.

"I think it's time you tried something more in line with your skills." Vienna bent down and grabbed a handful of rocks. Tucked in her arm, she carried them down to Kole. "How about moving targets?"

"I could use the practice." Kole reloaded the slingshot and readied himself. *Wide stance. Soft knees.* He drew back the string.

A rock the size of her palm rotated in her grasp. "Tell me when you're ready." Anticipation hung in her gaze.

One deep breath. "Now," he commanded.

Vienna chucked the stone high into the air, where the night concealed it. He followed the target with his weapon. Before he knew it, the rock had already begun his descent. Not much time left. Kole let the pellet fly.

A sharp crack and a burst of dust told him he'd hit his mark.

Vienna went to retrieve the target. "Clipped the top." She brought it over to him. "You hesitated too long."

He took it from her and thumbed where his hit had blown off a small portion of rock. It had nearly missed. He hoped he'd never have to aim for something that small, but he was determined to improve.

"Again?"

He nodded and returned the target to her. Kole's body lit up with a spark of heat as her hand brushed against his. *It's target practice,* he scolded himself. *Stay focused.*

Reset in her position, Kole lifted his slingshot.

"Predict its path," Vienna encouraged. "Aim where it *will* be."

Kole chewed his lip. "Now."

The rock sailed high. Kole waited for the thing to reach its peak, where it would slow down for a fleeting second and hang there, caught in the fight against gravity, before plummeting back down. That was when he made his move.

Aim where it will be.

He sent his pellet to the space below the twirling pebble. By the time the silver ball made the journey, the rock dipped down straight into the line of his trajectory.

Pieces of rock showered down.

"Fast learner." Vienna smiled. "Felix would've been proud."

Kole swelled with pride. Coming from her, it meant everything. "I have to live up to him if I'm going to use his weapon."

Her head tilted as if she were taking him in head to toe.

His heart shrank a bit under her gaze. Old insecurities panned to the surface, yet he fought the urge to turn away and hide his face. If he couldn't be himself around her, there was no hope for anyone.

"What?" he asked.

"I—um—" Vienna shook her head. "It's just, I've been thinking about what Russé discovered the other night in Savairo's grimoire."

The reminder cast a glum shadow over him. He twirled the slingshot in his hand. "What about it?"

"I don't believe it." Vienna closed the distance between them.

Her statement surprised him. "What do you mean? There's nothing to contest."

"You don't believe that do you? Deep down?" Her eyes glistened in the moonlight. They searched his face—shifted with the slightest movement of his expression. "You can't believe that there is no Kole inside you."

The way her jaw set... the hope in her gaze. Kole knew what she wanted to hear, yet he could not give it to her because it was not real.

"Russé said—"

"Forget what Russé said," she whispered harsh and quick. The shake in her voice grew. "Forget what he found. Forget those words in that wretched book." She shoved a finger into Kole's chest. "You can't believe it, Kole. Do you hear me? You can't."

Kole stood there, frozen, jaw slacked. He'd been on the other side of her anger once before, but this was different.

Not anger at all. *Desperation.*

He'd often thought about his fate—wallowed in self-pity. Yet for some reason, he selfishly never thought about how it would affect anyone else. His friends... maybe even the Souls.

Tears brimmed her eyes. Vienna's shoulders slumped forward. "I can't lose you, too."

Kole closed the gap between them and wrapped her up in his arms. She fell into him just as *he* had back in the caves. Trembled breaths came as she calmed herself. Kole rubbed her back until she settled. They lingered there in that embrace, but it would never be long enough for him. Being this close to her sent electricity through every nerve in his body. It made him feel alive. Made him feel like he could be happy beyond an eternity.

Finally, she pulled away.

He wanted to say something encouraging, but no light waited at the end of his tunnel. He refused to lie. And she wouldn't be placated with such things, either. So he said the only thing that came to his mind. "I'm sorry."

It took a moment for her to respond. "So, you do believe it, then."

"I don't want to. Of course, I wish there was another way. But you heard Russé. I'm a conglomerate of them."

"Not another way." Vienna grabbed his hands. Her touch made him swallow. "Another truth. You are not the Souls, Kole. You have them inside you, and they may be the base of you, but you are not solely them. I believe that."

At his silence, she continued. "You can't tell me they have chosen everything for you; likes, dislikes, experiences. It may have started that way, but you have lived ten years. Growing, changing."

"I mean, maybe. But I have no soul of my own," he reminded her. "No one can live without one."

By the drop in her face, he could tell it wasn't the answer she wanted to hear. "I'm not going to lie down and let it happen. I'm going to fight for you until the end. And you should too."

Kole knew he should say something. His brain raced to find the words, but the moment ended before he could string together anything coherent.

"I should get some sleep." Vienna gave his hands one last stroke before pulling away.

Kole watched her climb the ridge back toward the fire.

Russé's words rounded over and over in Kole's head. "*A conglomerate of the Souls.*" *Is that really all I am?* Vienna didn't think so.

Were his skills as a shepherd merely inherited from Russé? If that were true, then his victory in the shepherd's trials were wrongly won. It meant Kole had cheated. The runner-up, Daya, should've been the apprentice that year. Would Kole have even had a chance at the trial without Russé's spirit in him?

He did have a knack for handling the ramblers now and possessed an innate head start no one else had among the refugees. Even so, many aspects, like the art of calming the great ramblers, he'd needed many hours of practice to make the smallest progress. He struggled in that area like the rest of the shepherds.

Kole moved to the edge of the cliff and sat, letting his feet swing freely over the side. A clump of vine-like plants draped over the ledge like flowering waterfalls. The blooms held a velvet sheen in the pale moonlight. Their blossoms lifted their heads to the east, as if anticipating the coming sunrise. Frost crowned the leaves, yet still the little things endured.

Kole plucked a few and held them close. What he once thought were plain white petals held a colorful secret at the base of the blossom. Black spots dappled the innermost part, fading away to the pristine, rounded tips. He looked to the next in the bunch. Not a single discoloration anywhere on the flower. It always amazed Kole how plants of the same species could look so different.

The muscles in his face resisted his attempt to smile. Something shifted inside Kole as he examined the delicate flowers. What *had* made the blossoms so different? They had both stemmed from the same vine, and yet....

They'd grown. Developed. All from a single seed. *Or a handful of seeds.*

Is that what Vienna meant?

What if the same could be said of *him*. The fragmented pieces of each Soul were his roots. They started that way when Goren had sacrificed the child to free Russé those long years ago. That was his *nature*. But oh, how he had grown since then. He had experienced joy and friendship. Death and disappointment. Love. Pain. No one could deny Kole's experiences. His roots had spread deep, and he'd blossomed like the flowers clutched in his fist. Still of the origin but unique from it at the same time because of the life he'd lived since.

Kole was more than a collection of others. He was his own person. He may not have his own spirit, but there was something inside him worth fighting for — worth living for.

Vienna believed it. He had to believe it, too.

Something in him stirred.

Kole checked the slope. Vienna's distant silhouette closed in on camp. He hurried to his feet and ran to her.

"Vienna! Wait." His legs had never moved so quickly, racing faster than his heart. He knew what he wanted to do, but would his newfound courage falter once he stood before her?

She turned around.

The adrenaline in his blood stream pushed aside any discomfort in his legs. It powered him up that hill and to stand before her.

A mixture of surprise and worry spread across her face. "What's wrong?"

The dead sprint caught up to him the moment he opened his mouth. "I... I have to tell you...."

She waited while he struggled to compose himself. That heart of his fluttered faster as he took another step closer to her. Only an arm's reach away.

"What is it, Kole?" Those perfect lines in her forehead creased.

"I want to live. I want to fight."

Her eyes softened. "I'm glad to hear you say that."

"That's not all. Vienna, I—" Why was it so difficult? The words played in his head, all he had to do was form the sounds.

Kole *wanted* to live. If that option revealed itself, he'd take it like a starved animal. But the chances of that happening... well, he didn't exactly have a plan. If death really was his fate, he'd regret never confessing to her. Kole harnessed the nerves that weakened his knees and forced it to aid his voice.

"I've been through the Black Wall and back. I've touched those flames. I've even faced Aterus himself." He took a deep breath then gingerly laced his fingers between hers. She stared at him, never pulling away. "But nothing terrifies me more than you."

The side of her mouth curled up into a smile, and she laughed.

Only then it registered how the words came out. A sheepish smile tugged at his lips, and he huffed his own laugh. "That's not what I meant. I can start again."

She pulled a hand from his. In that instant, Kole knew he'd messed up. His stomach became a cannon ball, sinking down.

But then, a finger curled under his chin and lifted it up. She raised his head until his eyes found hers. Green. Soft. No resentment. No embarrassment. Kole could've sworn he saw his own emotions reflected in her gaze.

"I know what you meant," Vienna said softly. A small laugh, then, "You scare me, too."

Her finger drew across his jaw where the thickest cord of scar tissue ran down the length of his neck. His breath caught. No one had ever touched him like that before. Explorative. Loving. He barely tolerated people viewing his face, let alone allowed them to get close enough to feel the ghastly wounds.

Vienna was the exception.

Kole leaned his cheek into her hand, relishing the warmth—the feel of her skin on his. A lightness embraced his body as if he had wandered off into some fantastical dream. Riding on a burst of bravery, Kole leaned in.

She followed.

Their noses brushed.

Kole could hardly breathe, so he rested his forehead against hers. It was all too much. He closed his eyes and listened to her quickened breaths. It grounded him—granted him a peace he had never known before.

The surroundings faded. No chill remained in the winter air. His body ran so hot, it could've been the peak of a summer drought. The very sea quieted its crashing waves as if observing in anticipation.

Kole opened his eyes.

Vienna still rested against him, eyes closed, lips slightly parted. He'd loved those freckles since the first time he laid eyes on her in Solpate. He had come this far. He might never get the chance again. Kole tilted his head to the side and closed the space.

He kissed her.

The moment their lips met, Kole's body exploded with a fire that could rival the temperature of the Black Wall. When Vienna pressed against him, matching his movements, all his worries burned away.

They stayed there, locked together in pure bliss. Time loosened its hold on the moment. Euphoria had ensnared him.

Soon, Kole's lungs ached, urging for a breath. When he pulled away, she looped her arm around his neck, laced her fingers into his short hair, then brought him back to her.

Another explosion. He swore if he moved an inch, his legs would fail him and send him collapsing to the earth.

Finally, they parted, chests heaving.

Her hands slid to his chest, where she nestled in, tucking her head down in the nook of his neck.

Kole traced his fingers along her back as they stood there, relying on the other to keep them standing. His lungs managed to get control of his breath, but his pulse ran wild.

"I've wanted to do that for a while now," she admitted, voice muffled in his nape.

"Really?"

Vienna drew back. Those green eyes locked onto his. That's all it took for his head to swim again. "Yes."

"I thought... for the longest time, I...." He couldn't get himself to say it.

There was no hiding from Vienna. She lifted her head and her expression hardened. "Your scars?"

He nodded.

"Their presence or absence... they have nothing to do with how I feel." She stroked the hair behind Kole's ear, and he instinctually leaned into it. "Please know that."

"I do."

"Good." Her smile could outshine the sun. "We should head back." After a tender kiss to his neck, Vienna slipped her hand into his and they walked back to the fire.

Kole's body deflated. He wished the moment could've stretched out for eternity, but he knew better.

A war loomed: the last stand against Aterus.

But first, sleep and a new dawn.

CHAPTER 32

Morning sun blasted Kole's eyes as he turned in his bedroll. He pulled the blanket over his head to block it out. He'd had a wonderful dream where he and Vienna had kissed, and he didn't want to lose the feeling, so he clenched his lids, hoping to fall back into the moment.

His stomach had other plans. It growled as the scent of meat permeated the fabric. Hunger refused to let him return to dreamland. He stretched in the warmth of his bed, then sat up and ruffled his hair.

"Finally." Piper sat across the fire, digging into a bowl of stew. "Everyone is packed and ready to go besides you. 'Let the boy rest,'" she mocked, before taking another spoonful. "I've never seen you sleep so soundly. Yesterday must've been *exhausting* for you."

He narrowed his eyes at her. Something in her tone gave off a hint of sarcasm, but the lingering haze of sleep dulled his senses.

A stir came at his side. Caradin lay belly up beside him. The wolf rolled from his slumber and yawned.

"Looks like I wasn't the last." Kole scratched Caradin's chin to the animal's delight.

"Midmorning nap." Piper took a sip of broth. "He's the one who got the rabbit. Well, he and Vienna."

Vienna. Last night's memory came rushing back. It hadn't been a dream at all. He remembered falling asleep next to her, hands intertwined. With Piper's attention still on him, Kole quickly swept it from his thoughts. He touched his cheek. Warm. He hoped he hadn't blushed at the mention of Vienna's name. If Piper knew, she'd tease him. Probably revel in the fact that she'd been right.

"Good morning." Vienna smiled at them both, then brought Kole a bowl of stew. "Hungry?"

"Yeah." Kole took it and swirled the spoon around as Vienna sat on the other side of Caradin.

All the while, Piper stared, eyes trailing back and forth between the two with a sly smile set on her mouth. "We were just talking about you," Piper said.

"Oh?" Vienna gave a few pats to Caradin as he wandered off toward the near-empty cauldron of stew. "What about?"

"Kole was just telling me how you're a good teacher."

Kole choked on a potato and coughed. "What?"

"You said she was helping you practice your aim with the slingshot last night."

"Moving targets," Vienna said. "He's pretty good."

Piper's brows lifted. "I'm sure he is."

Kole pressed his mind across the fire. "*I get it, Piper, you saw us. So what? Let it go.*"

"*But it's so fun to see you squirm,*" she answered in his head, then laughed aloud, pulling Vienna's attention.

"What's so funny?"

"Nothing," Kole assured her. "She's just being her usual unpleasant self."

Caradin had sidled up next to Piper, who still held an amused look on her face. The wolf sneezed, sending a splatter of liquid all over Piper and into her bowl. The shocked, wide-eyed expression on the demigod gave Kole a bit of satisfaction.

"Really?"

"That's a good wolf," Kole said. Caradin wagged his tail, mouth open and panting as if proud of his work.

"*Fine. I get it. I'll leave it alone.*" Piper's words echoed in his thoughts. She set down her bowl and wiped her face on her sleeve. "*But I did predict it, didn't I?*"

"Uh." Vienna peered between the two. "Russé had me come get you up and ready. We need to move. There's been a message from Leo." Right as she finished, the cry of a hawk filled the sky. A brown flutter of wings flapped at Vienna's outstretched arm and Fiona, Leo's longtime messenger, landed on her wrist. It still amazed Kole how docile the bird of prey was with her. Those sharp, curved talons wrapped calm and gentle around her forearm. No doubt a simple squeeze or careless twitch could have opened flesh easy as a knife.

They were only a day's ride away from the war camp, yet Leo had sent Fiona. It had to be important. "What happened?"

"Kayetans." In the past, that name on any lips held a heft of anger. Now Vienna said it with a more neutral tone. Her brother and Shikar were most certainly the cause of that softening.

Kole felt the same. The more he knew about the shadows, the more he understood they were misjudged creatures. Not inherently evil, like he'd once thought. They did the bidding of their masters. "Kayetans at the war camp? But whose?"

"Whose do you think?" Piper dumped the contaminated stew from her bowl, then set it aside.

Aterus. The answer came so obvious, he felt dumb for asking. "He made new Kayetans?"

Piper shrugged. "Or old ones."

Kole whipped around to Vienna. "They attacked the camp?"

"No, that's the thing. Leo wrote that they showed up the night after we left. They took post a half mile outside of the base, just standing there."

The moment we entered the caves. Aterus had been one step ahead the whole time. The Soul knew where they massed their army and waited for Kole and his group to seek out Braxus to act. "He's watching us. Waiting for our next move."

Both girls nodded.

"Now we know he has Kayetans at his command," Piper said.

"We can handle that." Caradin whined when Vienna smoothed Fiona's feathers as if jealous of the affection. "But we need to get back soon."

"Where are Shikar and the Souls?"

A splash of water rained down on the fire, extinguishing it with a hiss. "Retrieving the horses," Issira said, holding the reins of two bay steeds.

Russé guided one more behind her. "I trust you slept well?" His eyes wouldn't lift to meet Kole's gaze.

"Let's get on with it then," said Shikar. "I'm the one who has to run it."

Kole had hoped to get a moment alone with Vienna, but within minutes, they were atop their mounts heading south back to the war base with Fiona hovering high overhead.

This time, Vienna held him more freely. Her arms gripped tightly around his waist, bracing against the bounce of the stag's light gait, and her chin perched on his shoulder. The warmth of her cheek pressed against the side of his face. It made the grueling ride more than tolerable. In fact, Kole often got lost in his own thoughts, thinking about their kiss last night. When Vienna would adjust in her seat, it would bring Kole back to reality, and he'd find they'd gone miles since he'd last checked in.

Every now and then, she'd speak with him, and that buzz in his head would heighten at her voice. Kole was grateful he rode atop Caradin. If he had to steer his own horse, they'd be struggling to stay on course.

Smokestacks rose in the distance. Fiona flew off toward them to announce their return. Leo would surely want to see them, especially when they returned without a new god in tow.

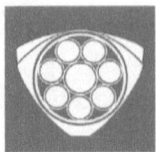

Leo's grand tent was filled to the brim. Wooden leaves had been added to the round table to provide adequate space, yet chairs were scarce, so the surrounding leaders stood.

Everyone had gathered for the emergency meeting. Solpate's refugee camp leaders, Harlow, who looked more like a bear, Lucca, with her eccentric, nest-like hair, and Darian. Kole ignored the balding man. Unpleasant as ever. Even after everything, the man still turned condescending eyes Kole's way. It seemed the man would never get over a boy being more important than him.

Others Kole had met along his journey also attended. The hardened leader of Cresthaven, Azmali, looked more like a warrior, with a great spear strapped to her back and scaled helmet tucked under her arm. Her stern expression set on Leo.

Tena had been wheeled in by her surviving council of Zeal. Despite the tension in the pavilion, Jax held a smile for him. The engineer had waved to Kole when she first spotted him but clasped her hands dutifully after garnering a few disgruntled gazes.

More leaders from the coast stood around the oval table. It troubled Kole that Shikar acted as the only representative from Grayfall. The Yamani had suffered a great loss, but Kole had hoped they'd changed their minds. The stone creatures were invaluable with their superhuman strength and unmatched wisdom.

Sharing the small space with gods sent a wave of awe throughout the tent. As the attendees had entered, most paid their respects to the Souls. Some brought gifts, others knelt or bowed, offering prayers and thanks. Probably the reason Russé had been so adamant on traveling inconspicuously since leaving Solpate. Kole understood the people's wonder, but a meeting on the brink of war was not the place.

Kole stood off in the corner, out of the way, yet somehow, people kept finding him and staring. Not somehow. His scars drew their interest, almost as much as the gods. Many had met him before, even if they hadn't realized exactly who he was and what his mission entailed. Word had long gotten out about the boy who'd touched the Black Wall, and this was their chance to witness him.

His hood lay idly on his back. He had no intention of hiding anymore. Maybe his scars could instill courage instead of fear.

"Our enemy has the last soulstone," Leo began. "The plans are the same, but timing is key. We must wait to strike until Braxus is released. There is no way to take down Aterus without her."

Azmali placed her helmet on the table. "The Gray Soul knows our goal. He already has Kayetans watching our army at nightfall. How do we expect to retrieve it when he knows our every move?"

"We will draw him out," Russé said from his seat. His staff was propped up against his legs. "What he wants most is an audience with us, and that's what we will grant him."

"And leave the soldiers behind?" Azmali pressed.

"We bring them with us," Leo answered.

Tena shifted forward in her wheelchair. "Will Aterus allow that?"

Kole leaned against Fiona's perch. The ferret around his neck clicked his teeth at the hawk anytime Kole so much as glanced its way.

Obell spoke next. "If we leave the army behind, it will draw his suspicions. Aterus expects aggression. Anything less will clue him in on our true purpose."

"We act like this is our last stand, because it will be if things should fail." Leo found Piper in the crowd and nodded to her. "Piper, Aterus' daughter, the demigod," he announced.

Her auburn hair had been braided back, making the sharp features of her face appear harsher. That along with the overhead lighting gave her an undeniable resemblance to the Gray Soul that Kole had never registered before. It made him shiver as she approached Leo's side. Vienna stepped back, giving her more space.

Whispers filled the tent. They silenced as she cast her eyes around the room. "If we don't succeed in releasing Braxus, there is one other way to weaken Aterus to a point he could be subdued without the full force of the gods. Our fallback plan. This is where the timing that Leo mentioned comes in." Piper folded her hands over her stomach. Though the position appeared calm, from Kole's angle, he could see her thumbs rubbing her palms. "The window will be small."

"I will be in contact directly with Piper," said Leo. "Our armies will strike on my command."

That caught Kole off guard. Direct contact meant a mind-link. He never thought the straight-and-narrow liberation leader would give in to using blood magic himself. The neutral faces around the tent meant no one else seemed surprised by the mention of blood magic. Dark measures for what may be the last days for everyone standing in the room. But desperation seemed to shift the light on the horrid tactic.

The rest of the discussion consisted of a review of numbers of each city's forces, weapons at their disposal, and special equipment, mostly of Jax's creation. Talk of moonstone cannons Kole was used to, but Jax also presented smaller handheld weapons like he'd seen the cultists use back in Zeal.

Once the meeting ended, Leo dismissed the leaders to prepare their soldiers for departure. Azmali didn't stay to pay her respects to the Souls, though most of the others bowed and muttered prayers asking for protection or blessings. Things Kole knew the gods could not grant.

Jax pushed her way through the stream of people to the corner where Kole stood.

"I was hoping I'd get a chance to talk before the battle." Even a meeting with the gods couldn't get her to comb her hair. Grease stained her tweed vest, and she smelled of metal and fire.

"You've been busy." Kole pointed to the hand-cannon she'd presented to the tent earlier, which now sat holstered at her hip.

"You're telling me. I got these babies coming out by the dozens. Made my own molds for the parts." She pressed her mouth together, catching herself. If no one stopped her, Jax could go on for hours about her inventions. "Anyway, I had more ammunition made for you." She held out a bag. Dirt had buried deep in her fingernails. "Moonstone pellets for your slingshot. Leo enchanted them himself."

Kole took the gift. A tug at the drawstring loosened the mouth of the fabric enough for an aura of creamy light to seep through.

"Figured with the Kayetans showing up they might be useful."

Kole tied the bag on his belt next to Felix's embroidered one. "Thank you, Jax."

"Jax," Leo called.

The room had cleared out save for the Souls and the liberation. The engineer nodded to Kole and whispered, "See you around, then," before taking her leave.

He wished to talk with her more. They hadn't known each other long, but she was the only person from Zeal's council he placed his full trust in. After all, she had been the one to get him across the black flames.

With room to breathe, Kole left the cover of the corner for Vienna's side. She gave him a welcoming smile at his approach. Criz and Boogy had entered from their posts outside, and so had Thomas, who still refused to even look Kole's way.

"Now it is time to put this plan into play," Leo said to the dwindled-down group. His black eyes narrowed on Obell, who stood at the opposite end of the long table. "Set the meeting."

Caradin slipped from Kole's neck and scampered over the tabletop to the Red Soul. The rest of the gods formed a circle, hands on one another's shoulders. Criz had offered to help Russé, but the old man waved him away, using the aid of his staff instead.

Each Soul closed their eyes. After a moment, their skin began to glow in their respective colors. Kole's hand went to his pendant. Though his mind was free from the conversation, he could feel the moment they reached Aterus by the sickly rush of nausea frothing in his stomach. Voices came in his head, muffled, like the Souls were talking from the other side of a wall. It made his brain throb.

Vienna must've noticed his discomfort because her hand found his back. The soft strokes did nothing for the pain, but it felt nice to know he didn't have to face it alone.

"Now, Piper," Leo commanded.

Piper slipped into a chair and propped her elbows on the table. Head down, she worked.

Kole, Leo, and the liberation watched on through the silent tent. Waiting.

Piper's head snapped up. "I've got it." A hint of disgust shaded her tone.

Not a minute later, the glow coming off the Souls' skin faded, and the gods fell out of their trance.

"It has been set," Obell said.

"He is not without caution," Vara said. "I don't think this will go as smoothly as we hope."

Russé hobbled over to the Violet Soul, "It is our best option, dear sister."

"You know what he will want. It's the only thing that will convince him." Vara moved her dual-colored eyes to Kole. "You shall come with us, or he will see through our ruse."

"He can't." Piper leaned back, head tilted wearily on the headrest. "The soulstone isn't with him."

"He's already rehidden it?" Kole asked.

"It's with my mother," she said flatly.

That explained Piper's previous disgust. Using her mother's comatose body to keep the soulstone crossed a line.

Vara clasped her hands together. "That's why he wants Kole with us. To ensure Braxus remains untouched."

"He needs to free Braxus," Piper argued. "It's our only chance. We have to stop playing to his whims."

Leo held up a hand. The room went still. "There is a way for Kole to do both." He held out his hand expectantly. "Russé."

The old man hobbled over, reached into the fold of his coat, and produced the claret book. No wonder Russé looked painfully pallid. The vile thing still leeched off him.

It passed from Soul's hand to sorcerer and with it the burden of its power. Russé stood instantly straighter, while a crushing weight seemed to press down on Leo's shoulders once the leather caressed new skin.

"There is a spell in here that could help us." The pages flipped in Leo's fingers.

The scent coming off the book made Kole recoil. Decay and something sour wafted from the parchment. Kole fought against the urge to plug his nose.

"Umbra's shroud." Leo had landed on a page deep in the grimoire. "It is a spell of concealment, but I think I can adjust it."

Obell stepped behind Leo and peered over his shoulder. "What is your plan, young sorcerer?"

"He plans to trick Aterus." Piper shook her head. "He'll see through it."

The frown on Leo's face deepened. "Not if I use enough blood."

A shiver played along Kole's spine. The first time he'd met the liberation leader, the sorcerer had been disgusted by his brother's use of blood magic. Leo had sworn off the use—the very idea of it. Now it all came back around.

Desperation brings morality to its knees.

Kole himself had flinched from the thought of the foul craft. Yet many of his victories and narrow escapes these last few months had been secured through blood. Even Vienna. His eyes moved to his hand wrapped in hers. If she hadn't been fed Piper's blood back in the battle with the cultist, Kole would be standing alone.

"He'll sense Kole," Piper warned.

Leo cast his black gaze to Kole. "Not if I mix the both of them."

"What are we talking about?" Kole asked. The distance in the sorcerer's eyes made Kole turn.

No. Leo hadn't been looking at Kole but something over his shoulder.

Some*one* over his shoulder.

Thomas.

CHAPTER 33

"You don't have to go through with this," Vienna said as she fixed a circle of rope through her belt alongside her daggers. Leo had appointed one of his blacksmiths to bring a variety of weapons and armor to their sleeping quarters. Vienna had taken bits and pieces but overlooked some of the grander items for a simple sword. Everything had been tipped in sunstone since the Kayetan sightings. She chose a leather vest that tied up at the side for her armor. Fitting for her. It would allow her full movement. She'd set aside a similar piece for him.

Kole sat on the edge of his cot with Felix's pouch of ammunition poised in his hands. He thumbed the intricate embroidery of the Kayetan claw shaking the red hand. Grief clenched his heart. If his friend were alive, he'd be on some sort of rant, trying to lift the mood, despite war clinging to the air.

"Kole? Did you hear me?" The bed sunk as she lowered next to him.

"I did." Kole put the pouch back on his hip. "I'm not scared. I just never thought I'd be doing this willingly." Force-fed was one thing. Piper had saved him from certain death with the healing powers of blood before. It was more knowing it was about to happen. Anticipating the grotesque tang. The sprouting pain.

"I'll be with you." Vienna rested her head on his shoulder.

That same electricity zapped Kole's nerves. His heart skipped and played in his chest. It didn't matter that she had been this close before; it felt like the first time she'd touched him. He wondered if she felt that same energy flittering between them — if he made her body melt like she did to him.

A throat cleared near the entrance.

Vienna gave his neck a quick kiss before pulling away. That spot lit up like a bonfire.

"Leo says you can come back now." Criz stood at the opened curtain, eyes up to the ceiling, while his twin jumped up and down behind him with a goofy grin plastered on his face.

"Yes, we're ready," Vienna called.

"Ready as I can be."

Criz and Boogy led them back to Leo's tent. All the while, Boogy kept sneaking glances back at Kole and Vienna, then giggling like an elated toddler. Criz elbowed his brother every so often to refocus him, though it never lasted long.

The twins took a spot on either side of the curtain and pulled it back, releasing a cloud of smoke from inside.

Kole and Vienna waved their hands to clear the fumes. It tickled Kole's throat, giving him a small spate of coughs. Once the air had cleared, the room revealed its quick transformation from war council room to laboratory. The fabric swung shut behind them, leaving the room in low candlelight.

Strange ingredients littered the table, and the tent held a putrid odor. Leo had pulled two chairs to the center of the room, one of which already held an occupant: Thomas. His long black hair dangled in his face, despite his efforts to push it behind his ear. As Kole and Vienna entered, he swung his head to them, scowled, then, turned his attention back to his arm, which was propped over a bowl in his lap.

"Good. You are here." Leo motioned for Kole to sit in the chair opposite Thomas. "I have already begun."

Piper came through the tent as Kole took his seat. "I found a rat." The wriggling creature squealed between the pinch of her two fingers.

"I am sure it will do." Leo hurried her over and had her place the rat in a bowl before he slipped a lid over it. Tiny claws scraped the clay from within.

"I think it calls for something more substantial," Piper said. She lifted her eyes from the open grimoire for a moment to glance at Kole and Vienna. The best greeting they were going to get. "Human, probably."

Leo glared at her. "The rat will do," he insisted.

"It won't be as potent."

"We will make up potency in other ways."

"You wouldn't really suggest a human sacrifice, would you, Piper?" Vienna asked from the back of Kole's chair.

"I wouldn't put anything past her," Thomas mumbled.

Piper huffed, crossing her arms. "I'm not saying to grab someone from camp kicking and screaming and murder them. There are ways we could get around it that are more humane." She shrugged. "Find someone on their deathbed. Call it an act of mercy."

"That is still too far for me," Leo said darkly as he finished grinding powders on the table. When Piper opened her mouth to speak, Leo put up a hand. "Even if you were to do the killing."

At that she rolled her eyes. "That's always been your weakness, Leo. Not willing to fight blood with blood."

"I apologize I do not live up to the standards my brother set. And yet, he is dead, and I am not. By your hand, I might add."

"Well, I'm not sorry for that. And it just proves I'm capable of doing your dirty work. Should you request it."

Leo set aside his powdered concoction and tapped the side of the pot. "Now, if you will."

Piper snagged the terrified rat from the bowl. A small pop, like the crack of a knuckle, came from between her hands as she snapped the neck. Kole winced. Those little legs flinched a few times before finally going limp. She laid the dead rat on the table.

"Oh, don't be so squeamish. These vermin were killed by the dozens on the daily back in Socren. Little nuisances. Disease bearers." Piper leaned onto the table to read the page Leo had propped open in the grimoire. "A more merciful death than being bludgeoned by a broomstick."

"The ever-merciful Piper," Thomas grunted. "I'm sure that's how we'll all remember you."

The room stayed silent at that. Kole had never gone out of his way to kill anything that did not seek to slaughter him first or that had not ended up as supper. That Piper had implied she'd be willing to bring them a human sacrifice sent a wave of nausea straight to Kole's stomach. His eyes met Thomas', and he seemed equally bothered. Or maybe that grimace was just Thomas' natural expression. Kole didn't know the boy well enough to be certain.

A strange language came from Leo's lips. Kole had heard him speak it before when casting spells, but the cadence felt off—different from the others. The open vowels and hiss-like lingering on some of the sounds made Kole's spine rigid.

Their resemblance was uncanny. Leo and Savairo. Brothers. As Kole gazed upon Leo, he could envision Savairo hunched over a table reciting the same string of words while his victim wailed for mercy. All that blood and pain. Had blood magic sucked Savairo down a dark path? Or had the evil been sleeping in the depths of the warden's soul since birth, waiting for its time to emerge? Kole clenched his jaw. Either way, he hated seeing Leo use it. He hoped the liberation leader had a stronger will than his late brother.

The rat's blood mixed with the powder to create a paste. Leo piled it in his hand and moved to Kole and Thomas, still whispering the incantation. He pinched a bit of the substance off and wiped it with his thumb across Thomas' forehead and neck.

"Remove your shirt," Piper instructed. "Both of you."

Thomas reluctantly complied. Once his chest was bare, Leo smeared the paste over his heart. Then, Leo turned to Kole.

Kole shrugged off his coat. His fingers stalled at the bottom of his tunic. His hesitance originated less from his scars and more from being half-naked in front of the whole room. His own body was a far cry from Thomas' statuesque build. He cared what Vienna might think. And yet, she'd seen him like that before when she'd pulled him from Issira's pond a long while ago. Kole tugged his shirt off.

The paste came warm on his forehead: fresh death. Once Leo had marked him in the same fashion, he scraped the remaining gunk into a bowl and returned with a knife in hand. A delicate blade. Surgical. Kole knew what came next.

"The bowls, Piper." Piper offered the sorcerer two wooden vessels, but Leo waved her away. "One to Thomas, give the other to Vienna."

"Me?" Vienna clutched the bowl that had been shoved at her chest.

"I need you to collect from Kole. I am sure he would prefer your company to mine." Leo grabbed Kole's arm and gently turned it over to the soft side. "Ready?"

Kole bit down on his lip and clenched his toes for the cut. "Do it."

The incision hurt no less despite his preparation. Once the flesh parted, Kole looked away. Warmth trickled down his arm. He heard Leo move for Thomas.

"Not long now." Vienna's soothing voice calmed him. Either that or the blood loss.

A moment later, Leo stopped the bleeding and dressed the wound while Piper and Vienna brought the boys' blood back to the table.

"I hate this shit," Thomas mumbled. "Never thought I'd be trading blood with you."

Kole peeked up. "Trading?"

"What do you think this whole thing is?" Thomas flexed against his bandages and pulled his shirt back on. "We're trading our auras. Mixing, masking—whatever. I'm your decoy. I get to be Kole for the day." A devious smile. "And you get to be me."

A horrifying thought. "How does it work exactly?" Kole tried to slip his own shirt back on, but his left arm was too weak to move above his head.

Then, Leo turned back to them with two cups, one offered to Kole, the other to Thomas. "Drink."

Kole grabbed his and peered at the thick, black-colored liquid. His throat closed on sight.

"Guess we'll find out together." Thomas lifted his cup in a makeshift toast, then threw it back.

Kole waited a moment, watching as Thomas chugged. When nothing immediate happened, he sniffed his own. Blood and dirt. He pressed his lips to the rim and tilted it back.

Bitter metal hit his tongue. It stung a place far back in his jaw. The thick liquid rolled over his tongue and collected at the back of his throat. He forced a swallow. He gagged and pushed the cup away.

"All of it," Leo instructed. "Or it may not be convincing." Meanwhile, Thomas had begun a coughing fit. "Keep his head back, Piper. It needs to stay in him."

"You can do it," Vienna's encouraging voice came to his ear.

"It's vile."

"I know." Her voice came out deep. She clearly did not envy him.

He felt the precise moment the heavy stuff landed in his stomach. It churned. If he didn't take the rest now, he might not bring himself to do it at all. Kole pinched his nose, closed his eyes, then threw back the last of the blood mixture. Swallow after swallow. Stopping up his nose helped get it down, but the moment he released, the full taste claimed his senses.

Like Thomas, Kole coughed. His body wanted it out.

"Here." Vienna had tipped another glass to his mouth. Cool water hit his tongue. It diluted the foul taste, but the extra liquid filled his belly. The slosh made him more uneasy. At least with the taste mostly gone, he could focus on keeping the stuff down.

The spell wasn't over yet. Leo held the grimoire, a cloth set between the book and his skin, and he recited the page.

A warmth budded within Kole. It spread to his limbs, his eyes, his brain. An uncomfortable heat. Feverish. He longed to sweat, though his burned skin wouldn't allow it. Instead, he panted like a tired dog.

Kole's eyes locked with Thomas'. The teen's face held a sheen. They stared.

The tent disappeared. Vienna no longer stood by Kole's side. Leo, Piper — gone. Only Thomas.

A pressure built around Kole's chest. Something rolling within like a chick ready to break from its shell.

Then it burst.

He felt a ray of energy shoot out to Thomas just as another source of energy hit him back.

Trading auras. That's what Thomas had said.

But he didn't want to trade. He already felt like a patchwork quilt, with the Souls residing within him. Now he gave more of himself.

As suddenly as they had started, the rays withered away, and the room came spinning back.

"What happened?" Kole patted his chest and arms, checking himself. He'd never been so relieved to see those red scars. For a second there, he thought their bodies had swapped.

"It is done." Leo careened his head between the two of them. "And without injury, I should say." Something about his tone worried Kole. An excitement lay in the back of his voice, as if giddy in his success.

Kole found Vienna still at his side, but her body seemed tense. "What's wrong?" He touched his face. Corded skin. The flesh under one eye slightly drooped. Normal. "Do I look different?"

"No, it's not that. You just...." She took a step closer. "I know it's you. You just feel different is all. A bit like Thomas."

If he felt like Thomas, then Thomas surely felt like him.

"It's a bit strange," Vienna said as she looked across the room where Thomas sat.

Kole looked hopefully to Leo. "How long will it last?"

But the Sorcerer only shrugged. "The spell was adjusted from the original text. It could last the full day or less. Criz. Boogy." The twins poked their heads in. "Tell Russé we are ready."

"Sure thing, boss," they said in tandem then slipped out.

Kole's stomach bubbled. Even now it felt like he could vomit at the subtlest of movements. So, he lay back and closed his eyes until new sounds rustled at the entrance.

"It's done?"

Kole opened one eye to find Russé hobbling over with his staff. The old man inspected him. "He feels different just standing next to him."

"I felt that, too," said Vienna.

Russé crouched down to eye level. "How do you feel?"

"Like shit," Kole croaked.

The answer made the Soul's mouth thin. "That's to be expected, I fear. But the true test...." Russé touched Kole's temple. The cold fingers shocked him. A pressure rose in Kole's head as Russé skimmed the edges of his mind. "He feels unfamiliar even to me."

"And Thomas?" Leo gestured to the other chair.

The Green Soul moved across the room to Thomas and did the same check. "I feel Kole in him. But it's faint. We need to make it stronger if we are going to fool Aterus. Even with our distraction."

Leo went back to the book, careful to only touch it with a barrier of cloth. "The more blood we transfer, the better the concealment."

"No more," Kole groaned. "I'm going to be sick."

Piper swiped her long braid from her shoulder. "Blood builds. It runs slower through the system. We can have them finish the leftover solution to make it stronger."

"A daily dose," Leo confirmed. "I will bring it along. We can only hope it works. I have nothing else."

CHAPTER 34

The armies had marched out from the war camp and made it halfway to Aterus' lair, where they settled for the night. Kayetans once again surrounded the army while they slept. Aterus' way of telling them he knew exactly where they were and when they were to arrive. Once dawn had come, the Kayetans fled, but Kole still felt watched.

Midmorning, while the army marched on, the sudden sound of a horn droned from the back of the formation—the long note of warning the refugees used when they spotted danger.

Kole flipped around, as did the rest of his companions. The soldiers halted. Tension rose despite the leaders calling for attention.

An attack. Aterus has made his move. Those were Kole's first thoughts, and he'd bet that same string ran through the troops as well.

Panicked voices whispered through the crowd despite their orders. It took a moment for the word to ripple up to the front where Kole stood.

"Kayetans spotted."

He heard it as clearly as the blue sky hanging overhead.

Vienna squeezed his arm the moment she heard it. "Can't be."

"Another Idris?" Kole's hand went for the sunstone pellets at his waist.

"An army of day-walking Kayetans? No. Not even Aterus." But her voice faltered at the end, as if unconvinced herself.

A screech came from above as Leo's tawny hawk dove for its master. A quick second with the creature, then Leo lifted the bird, giving it flight once more. He raced to the edge of the formation and looked down on the valley.

"They are not Kayetans." Shikar's voice boomed so loudly that half the army probably heard her. Softer now, she said, "My kin have come."

Talk of Kayetans faded, replaced with the Yamani name on the soldiers' lips. An awe layered their tone, but some still held a sense of fear.

"Mikal?" Kole followed the stone woman to the edge, where Leo stood. "He came?" Shikar was a beam of sunshine compared to the abrasive leader of Grayfall.

Once they caught up to Leo, Kole spotted the dark forms of the stone people stalled about a mile off. To him, they looked nothing like a Kayetan, but the shepherd that had first noticed them had never seen a Yamani. Kole had only heard of them before he first met Shikar. Their kind was scarce—almost a legend at this point. From this far up, Kole guessed near twenty had come. They stood there, halted as if waiting, yet Mikal, who Kole assumed headed the front line, made no move to split from his people.

"He will not come," Shikar said to Leo. "He will not meet you."

"They have come to watch, then," said Leo.

"To monitor."

Kole stared at the Yamani below. "They're not going to fight? Even after coming all this way?" He understood the stone people to be a proud race—a protective race. They cared first and foremost for their own kind. If not for Shikar's presence and persuasion, Mikal made it clear he would've refused to help Kole on his quest to find Obell within their volcano. They wanted to banish Kole and his group from the lands entirely.

"It is a miracle they left the volcano at all," said Shikar. Her tone held a mix of pride and resentment, which further confused Kole. "They intend to watch the outcome. It would take a miracle to join humans in battle."

Kole shook his head. "It doesn't make sense."

Shikar shifted her chin down to look Kole directly in the eyes. "Not to a human."

"She is right. No one owes us forces in this fight. The Yamani included. They will act as they see fit for their kind. We continue on with our plans." With that, Leo strode back to the front lines and rallied the army back into focus.

Kole lingered. "The fate of Ohr resides in this battle."

"It is not for you to understand, little one. To a Yamani, Yamani come first."

"Not to you," Kole offered.

"I am no more Yamani in their eyes than you."

Kole looked up at her, but she'd already turned and left.

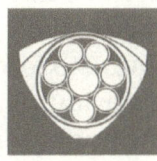

Another two portions of blood left Russé and Leo satisfied with the spell's transformation. Thomas had been just as reluctant to take the vile stuff as Kole. As noon approached, a spire of stone revealed itself on the distant cliff.

"That's the place," Piper confirmed. "I can feel him watching us."

"Then we part ways from here," Leo said.

The crowd slowed to a stop while Kole and his group prepared to depart. Scarves had been given to Kole and Thomas to hide their faces and bodies. Though, if prodded, their auras might feel like the other, the differences in appearance remained stark.

Once Kole had covered himself, Russé came over to him. "Don't linger. Get in, release Braxus, then come back to us." A strain hung in the old man's expression, as if he wanted to say something more.

The rest of the Souls gave Kole a curt nod, then moved to the front of the formation. Caradin, though, back to his grand stag form, came to Kole's side. That warm nose tapped his chest until Kole gave in and hugged his massive head.

"It's not goodbye," Kole said. "Just good luck. We'll both need it."

The stag huffed a warm breath that tousled Kole's hair.

It took Piper waving him on to break them up, but not before he gave the beast one final pat.

Vienna and Kole hurriedly followed Piper to the side of the army. At first, the plan had been for Kole and Piper to go alone, but Vienna had none of that. She argued with Piper until the demigod finally relented. The smaller the better. That's' what Piper had said. Not even Shikar or the twins would come. They needed to get in and out undetected.

"You're sure you know where we're going?" Vienna asked as they slipped away from the army and down the slope through the tall grasses.

Piper shot a stern look behind her. "I know where my mother is."

One final look back made Kole wish he had a rambler or Caradin at his side. He felt naked without them. Powerless. He was glad Vienna came. He needed one person he trusted completely.

The armies assembled as they snuck off, readying for war. Greater numbers than Kole had hoped for. Not only soldiers but dozens of ramblers and a handful of surviving shepherds. Every giant tree had a group of crystal trees in tow. Jax's cannons sat in the back in a great line with a wheeler tacked to the front of each for towing. Kole could easily spot the refugees from his home by their mounts. The great stags with wooden antlers and skin of vines stood out against the steel of Zeal's forces. Then there was Azmali's army. Their scaled armor shifted from blue to purple like oil slicks in the bright sun. Tall spears lined their backs.

Beyond that, the beauty of the stone Yamani lingered a mile back. Every time Leo's forces moved, or halted, so did they, maintaining their distance. *Spectators to our deaths.*

A touch to his elbow pulled him back.

Piper led them through the field to the side of the spire. Bricks towered four or five stories high. Bigger than most of the buildings Kole had seen in Socren but plain compared to the masterpieces in Zeal. It didn't feel like much of a lair to Kole. More like a grand mansion. And it looked... pleasant.

"Not what you expected?" Piper must've read the cues on Kole's expression. "It's a summer house he built for Evangeline. She liked the look of brick and an ocean view."

"I thought you said it was a ruin," said Kole.

"It was when I left it. Seems he's been busy."

As they rounded the building, they came upon a wooden door. Piper pushed it open.

"Not even locked?" Vienna stood her ground while Piper waved them inside. "It seems like a setup."

"You clearly don't know my father." Piper walked right into the dark corridor, only the stream of the sun lighting the way. "You forget he's a Soul and what that means. He created humans. He doesn't fear them. It's like you fearing a sandcastle. You made it. You can easily destroy it with a kick."

Kole moved to the arch, peered in, and listened. Silence. The small stream of light poured onto the steps of a spiral staircase. Trap or not, their window of opportunity only lasted as long as Russé and the Souls could distract Aterus. Either that or until Aterus saw through Leo's spell on Thomas. Kole moved inside.

"Are you coming? Or is it just me and Kole from here?" Piper asked. "You can always play the lookout if—"

"I'm coming." Vienna pushed past her and marched up the stone stairs.

By the time they passed the second floor, Kole's lungs were working on overdrive. He paused at a window that looked east. The sea lazily lapped at the beach below.

"We can't stop," Piper said.

"And I can't pass out," Kole snapped. If he overheated, he'd faint. Who knows how long it'd take him to come to. The last dose of Thomas' blood weighing down his stomach didn't help the matter, and neither did his leather vest. He pulled on the laced sides, but it offered no relief. A few long breaths to cool down, then he was ready to continue. "How much farther?"

"Top floor. We're halfway." A dark glint of humor lay in her eyes. "I can always carry you."

"Just lead the way."

Muscles screamed at him those last few steps. The stairs spit them out into a long hallway lined with doors. Sunlight cast long rays down the wood floor from the open window at the far end. Still no sign of Aterus or otherwise.

Kole paused. "It feels weird being so quiet. Empty."

"Hopefully it means the plan is working," Vienna said.

Piper strode down the hall, halting at the last door that lay ajar. When they caught up to her, she pushed it open.

The hinge whined.

A large room spanned out before them. Far off in the corner roared a warm fire that heated up the entire space. A rich blue rug, albeit dusty, sat at the center beneath a grand bed with intricate wooden posts. And on it lay a woman Kole had heard many stories about: Evangeline.

Piper rushed to the bedside while Vienna circled the room, but Kole couldn't bring himself to enter. He watched the woman from the door. Even from this distance, he spotted peeks of Piper's vibrant red hair beneath Evangeline's grays. The way her chest rose and fell made it seem like she was stuck in a deep sleep. Yet something about her position — too perfect, with her hands atop her chest and her hair brushed to the side — made her seem placed. *Like a viewing.*

"It's started." Vienna stood at the edge of the western window. "I can see him."

Him. She meant Aterus. Kole quickly forgot how much of a recluse the Gray Soul was. All this pain and torment at his hands, yet he never showed his face. This was a first. Vienna must be dying to see who was responsible for creating the fires that killed her brother.

"The soulstone," Kole called from the door. "Where is it?"

Piper rounded the bed as she gazed on her mother. The comforter sagged when she sat on the edge. Her hand reached for her mother's face but stopped. "My father has a sick mind."

Something about her voice made his skin ripple as if thousands of ants crawled beneath the surface. He moved into the room. "What is it?"

Vienna, too, swung her attention to the demigod, her hand tense on the hilt of her sword.

At the foot of the bed, Kole's eyes found what triggered Piper's horror. A perfect yellow topaz lay on Evangeline's forehead. Not lay. That would be too gentle. Inserted. The soulstone had been inserted — jabbed — into the old woman's head. A line of dried blood that looked as though it had been wiped away shown faintly on her temple.

"I think he's tried to merge them." From the shake in Piper's voice, Kole could tell she held back a sob.

Kole rushed over. "Why?"

"Maybe he figured out a way to harness the soulstone to prolong her life. It's the only thing I can think of." Piper touched the wounded skin around the stone. Nudged the topaz, but it stuck firm.

"Can we remove it?" Kole lowered to the other side of Piper's mother. His weight on the bed made her arm slip from her chest.

"It might tip him off." He'd never seen Piper in such a way. Unsure. Timid. The demigod had always seemed to be a step ahead. The change wavered Kole's confidence in the mission.

"And if I try to release Braxus with the stone still in her?"

"Is that possible?" Vienna asked.

Piper's silence told them everything. Kole shared a look with Vienna.

"Piper, I...." Vienna moved behind the demigod, but her hand hovered above her back as if hesitant to comfort her.

"I knew it would come to this." Piper stroked her mother's face. "I've known for a long while now." Her amber eyes tore from Evangeline and found Kole. A fierce spark ignited behind her sullen gaze. "The timing will be key, Kole. You can't take long, understand? Get in there and release Braxus. We'll have a handful of minutes at most from the time you enter until Aterus returns. By then, we need to be well out of here."

A quick release. *Yeah, no problem.* He only had to die and drag the god's essence back to their realm of existence. All while hoping Braxus didn't suck the life out of him in a desperate attempt at freedom.

"Vienna, keep watch." Piper instructed. "Tell me the second things change down there."

After giving Kole an encouraging nod, Vienna swept back to her station at the window.

Kole pulled the dagger from his belt, but his brain was a cyclone of nerves. Going in like this put him at a disadvantage from the start. Piper grabbed the blade from him. He winced, thinking she was going to make the cut for him. Instead, she made her own on her palm and placed it over her mother's mouth.

"I'm hoping he's only in tune with her health." She balled her hand into a fist and let her blood drip into Evangeline's parted lips. "I can keep her from fading. If nothing else, it'll give you more time."

Kole took the weapon back from her and readied himself. He'd done this five times before. One more time. *The last time.* The thought brought both relief and pain. His journey would be over soon. Whatever tangled fate lay in reach now.

One last cut. One last blood sacrifice. Kole began the ritual. A small prick was enough. He tossed his dagger aside and pressed his bloody thumb on the amber soulstone.

A flash of brilliance blinded him. Deep cracks shook his eardrums. It sounded as if the earth had opened its maw beneath the spire, ready to swallow it whole.

The darkness enveloped him.

"Braxus," Kole called into the ether. "I've come to release you."

Her voice came quick with panic. "No need to explain, Kole. I know the deal. I know the stakes. I've seen him—" Her fear linked with Kole, and it made him shudder. "I saw his plans when he put me in the woman."

"His plans? How?"

"Aterus hides nothing from Evangeline. She hears everything. They replay in her broken mind over and over. She can't fully understand them anymore, but what I've seen.... He's going to take their power."

The blank space in Kole's head filled with an image. Five figures stood before Aterus, locked in conversation. A heated debate. But the words were muffled. The figures, though blurred, Kole could make out as Russé and the other Souls.

The only crisp image lay at Aterus' waist, where one of his hands was tucked into a pocket. At his curiosity, the vision zoomed in through the fabric to see Aterus palming something. Five somethings.

Stones.

"Evangeline knows everything. She's warned me, but I couldn't reach you. You can't let my kin go to him."

Newfound terror birthed. All this time they thought they were getting the jump on Aterus—that they'd laid the perfect trap. Apparently, the Gray Soul had his own.

"They're already there," Kole confessed.

CHAPTER 35

With Kole well on his way, Leo summoned Thomas to his side and led him to the Souls. "Stay quiet. Keep the hood low and keep your eyes down."

"Be invisible. Understood," Thomas said. Leo detected a hint of snark but let it go. He knew the boy held ill feelings toward Kole for some reason, but now was not the time to discuss it.

"If Aterus should notice you as a decoy, we will be the front line of this war." At that, Thomas stood a bit taller. "Stay focused, but do not act unless I give you the go ahead. We will play this fraud as long as we can."

Russé turned to them as they approached. "We are ready."

"As are we."

Leo kept a hand on Thomas' shoulder as they walked into the depths of the field. The Souls led. Position was crucial. Kole was the most important key in all this turmoil. They'd have him at the back, behind the wall of gods and the sorcerer, so the same would be done with Thomas as a fill in.

He never thought he'd be here at the heels of the gods. Months ago, Leo had been leading a resistance against his brother, a weak and dying one, at that. Aterus was a foe on another level entirely.

The truth awoke a fear within him that he'd never known before: if they failed here, Ohr would fall.

Once in place, Russé and the others stepped forward, forming a semi-circle. Leo made sure to stay far back from the group and nudged Thomas behind him.

"We have come as your audience, Brother." Russé wriggled his staff into the soil and leaned his weight into it. From the moment Leo laid eyes on the Green Soul's form back in Socren, he knew it to be a façade. Too much power lay in Risil's presence.

Leo scanned the tall grass. It swayed in the quiet wind. A scene of beauty with the scent of ocean salt in the air, and the drowsy lap of waves concealed behind the cliffs. Fog trailed from Leo's nose with each breath, though the cold couldn't touch him. The suspense—the thick unease—kept his blood running hot.

A figure appeared on the hill. A tall man with salt-and-pepper hair descended toward them in plain gray clothes. Leo remembered that face. He'd seen Aterus before in passing. Often the Gray Soul had called on Leo's brother, Savairo, when they were teens and well into adulthood. Always experimenting and fiddling with blood magic. Breeding Kayetans.

Aterus held his arms wide. "Brothers. Sisters." The god didn't so much as glance Leo's way. "It feels like a millennium since we last spoke." Even from a distance, Leo spotted the twinkle in Aterus' eyes.

Obell stepped up. The temperature spiked at his growl. "You little—"

The Blue Soul placed her hand on the fire god's chest. The faint glow coming off her skin instantly cooled his temper. "We have agreed to listen to your terms, Aterus," Issira said after Obell had calmed and stepped back into formation.

"That is, as long as they are agreeable," Vara added. "Ohr and its creatures shall have their freedoms."

"They will be freer without the rule of squabbling siblings," Aterus said.

"Isn't that what our ascension granted them?" Russé twisted his staff in the grass. "If that is your thought, why not keep the former offer?"

Aterus' eyes turned to slits. "You know want I want."

"Power," Issira boomed. "That's all you've ever wanted. Power without limitations."

The Gray Soul slowly shifted his gaze to her. "I remember a time when you wanted the same, dear sister."

Meeker now, Issira said, "That time has long passed."

"Well, it hasn't for me. My love for the humans isn't so fickle."

"Enough," Russé wheezed. He clung to his staff as he coughed. "Lay out your wishes plainly."

Aterus cocked his head, a new interest in the weakened god. "You look unwell, Risil. Or should I call you Russé now?" The poison in his voice would've made anyone glare, but Russé merely stared, unphased. "I'm sure Kole has already relayed my offer." A quick glance Thomas' way.

Leo tightened his hold on the boy. Only now did he notice that Thomas had clammed up. Not so much as a whisper of a breath from the kid. Leo didn't blame him, but he hoped Thomas could hold it together long enough.

"Humanity has suffered from a crowded reign," Aterus began. "Seven was meant for balance, but it has only brought destruction."

"Destruction you brought on yourself." Obell broke from Issira's hold and raged toward Aterus. "It was your interference with humans that caused the plague. It was your resistance to ascension that brought the Black Wall. Don't try to pin this on anyone but yourself."

The great stag dipped his antlers as if ready to charge.

Aterus merely stood there, chin held high. "And here I thought this meeting was about listening."

"It would do you well to listen yourself," Obell fired back.

"Obell," Russé said faintly, shaking his head when the fire god looked his way. "Stand down."

The heat radiating off the Red Soul dissipated, and he stepped back, a sneer plastered across his face. Leo found it intriguing that Russé, even in his weakened state, continued to act as leader. Though Leo had never heard them discuss it, the Souls allowed him that position quite readily.

"Patience has never been your strength." Aterus' stance relaxed as if disappointed at Obell's withdrawal. "That fault played a hand in your Yamani, didn't it? How are they doing?" His smirk was intentional. Bait.

Russé cut in before Obell could ensnare himself. "You came here to speak, so speak. If we are willing to find a common solution for the good of Ohr, then we will consider your proposition."

Aterus kept his hands tucked deeply in his pockets while eyeing his kin. Something about the look in those eyes made the god appear more like a snake than a man.

"The deal is simple. Gift me your power and ascend. Ascension is what you wanted when last we spoke, and I know that goal hasn't changed. I gift you the promise that Ohr will be taken care of under my watch."

"*One* cannot rule with fairness. Solitude is the root of biases," said Issira. "The balance of seven—"

"The balance?" Aterus sneered. "Balance, as you call it, means nothing can flourish. My humans grow and develop too fast to wait on seven gods squabbling over what comes next. Ohr needs one authority."

"You only think of your humans." Vara's voice came as calm as a still winter night. "They are not the only living creatures to consider. The plants and animals, the earth, the Yamani." She sent a sympathetic glance Obell's way. "You think you can give them all the same care as your creations?"

"Of course. Humans need all of them to survive." Aterus shrugged. "As for the Yamani, depending on how badly our *dear brother* has cursed them," he drew out the endearment, "I can only promise to look into it. But they may need to be exterminated."

Leo felt the tension rise. Hands on Thomas, he drew back, knowing the matter wouldn't stay civil when the muscles beneath Obell's rich skin rippled.

Russé must've felt it too because he shifted his staff and thrust it between the two as a warning to contain themselves.

Obell flicked the staff away like a twig and lunged for Aterus. His massive hands wrapped around the Gray god's neck, but Aterus only grinned at the attack.

That smile set off an alarm in Leo. Bait. The whole thing was a ploy. For what, Leo had no clue, but he recognized this as the first step.

Then, that hand. The hand Aterus had held in his pocket slipped out.

"Russé!" Leo called in warning.

Too late.

Aterus slammed his fist into Obell's neck. The god released his hold and staggered back. A red crystal the size of a finger protruded from the skin. Obell fiddled with the stone—pinched and pulled—but it stuck firm.

The crystal brightened with a crimson, pulsing glow. Each throb ignited Obell's veins in the same color. The Soul swayed like a drunkard. It only took a few seconds for him to fall to his knees as the crystal leeched away the Soul's strength. "What have you done?" Obell whispered.

"The only thing that can be done," Aterus said.

Leo locked eyes with Russé, who mouthed, "Run." He took Thomas by the shoulder and spun. Not three steps in, a rigidness grew in his body. He halted there, mid-stride, with Thomas in tow.

"I don't think so," Aterus said.

After he spoke, Leo's limbs moved on their own. He urged them to run back to the safety of the army, but instead, they made him pivot back to the scene and stand witness. From the corner of his vision, Thomas was held in the same manner. The hood still draped over the boy's face, but his mouth set agape in horror.

"I'll be needing Kole soon enough."

Russé shook his staff at Aterus. "We came here for civility."

"Oh, Russé." Aterus set his sights on the old man as the others went to Obell's side, who remained unresponsive. "Always the diplomat. But you've softened after your time spent with my humans, haven't you?"

He tsked and gripped the middle of Russé's staff. The tip of the gnarled wood coiled around Aterus' wrist and squeezed. "I appreciate the attempt, but you have run your reserves dry with your constant efforts to preserve dear Kole."

With his fingers curled around the wood, Aterus twisted his arm and snapped the staff in two. The piece shackled around his wrist grew limp and fell to the grass.

"You should've let him die when he released you. And again, when he touched the Black Wall. You could have taken back your fragment and become whole alongside me. So many chances, and yet you chose to remain weak. I guess you enjoy being half a god. For that, I have a gift."

Russé held his palms to the ground. The tall grass tangled around Aterus' boots, but one step and the Gray Soul pulled free.

A green crystal lay in Aterus grasp. "This one is for you." A swift arc of his hand and the stone pierced Russé's chest.

The crystal lit up and sapped what little energy Russe still possessed. Once Aterus removed his grip, the Soul collapsed to the ground.

Leo swiveled his eyes to Thomas, who caught his stare. "Kole," he breathed so quietly through his frozen lips he thought it may be lost in the wind. "Can you feel him?"

"No," Thomas said. He muttered something else, but all Leo could catch was the word "blocked."

Despite the foreign hold on his body, Leo trembled. *Souls save us.*

CHAPTER 36

"We must stop Aterus before he takes them all. There will be no hope if we are too late. Hurry," Braxus pleaded.

Whatever those stones were for, they were bad news. Kole released the hold on his body and let Braxus take control. He felt her presence move through him and unweave her fragmented soul from his as the life left him. A rushed job. He hoped his death this time would be short. Returning to a slightly cooled body always left him with a ghastly feeling, like he had entered a borrowed corpse.

While Kole floated there in the void between the living and dead, his thoughts whirled around those stones. Aterus had talked about resetting the game. He could be acting on his threat this very moment. But the Gray Soul had been so keen on flipping his kin to his side before. If that goal had truly been abandoned, it meant the Souls were in grave peril, since their plan relied on biding time.

A force wrapped around him and dragged him back to the warmth. Kole slammed back into his body. Soft fabric lay beneath his cheek. He opened his eyes and gasped for air. A white pillow snuggled his head. He'd collapsed at Evangeline's side during the ritual. The tingle in his limbs ran rampant. He moved against it, testing his muscles. Each effort triggered a fresh wave of pin pricks, but it pleased him to find his blood just as warm as he'd left it. Though his mind had felt like it wandered for hours, he couldn't have been out longer than a few minutes.

"He's back." Vienna's voice gave him new strength. He rolled over to see that face of freckles staring down at him.

"I'm fine," he grumbled. Then Braxus' words rushed back to him. "Russé. He's—"

"Aterus took him out," Vienna offered. "I don't know what's happening, but it's all-out chaos between Caradin, Vara, and Issira. They are fending off Aterus alone."

"Not alone."

Kole sat up and snapped his head to the new face in the room.

Braxus stood at the foot of the bed. The first thing that caught his attention was her clothes. No fabric moved like that. A swirl of golden light played over her dark skin. With a bald head and plump cheeks, she reminded Kole of how Goren had described angels.

"I thank you for releasing me, but our greeting must be cut short. My kin need me." Braxus moved to the open window in one graceful sweep. Her chin moved over her shoulder, though she did not look at them. "It is perverted what you must do. I do not envy you, Piper. I will give you as much time as I can."

Before Kole could register the Yellow Soul's meaning, she leapt from the window. He pushed up to stop her, but Vienna held him back. "No, Kole. I need to get you out of here."

The quick resurrection made him feel like he'd been roused from the depths of a REM dream. A fuzzy haze of confusion curled around his brain as Vienna pulled him to his feet. He limped along with her, unsure where they were headed. When he noticed it was only the two of them heading to the door, Kole pulled against her.

"Piper." He swallowed against his dry throat.

"She needs to stay." Vienna slipped her arm around his waist and half dragged, half carried him into the hall.

A quick snap of his head granted him one last glimpse of the scene. Piper had thrown her body over her mother, her back heaving up and down.

"She's crying."

Vienna had moved him to the staircase. "I know. C'mon. We have to go."

They took the steps one at a time until Kole's body caught up with him and he could move on his own. And as his muscles began to move freely at his command, the confusion subsided and reality sunk in.

"She's really going to do it?"

Vienna had let go of everything but his hand, though she still took the lead, flying down the stairs two at a time. They passed the second floor.

"The only person who could is Piper."

CHAPTER 37

Kole's and Vienna's footsteps fell into the background as they exited the fourth-floor hallway. Piper pressed her face into her mother's stomach. Her tears soaked the fabric of Evangeline's white nightgown.

She pried herself up and looked down. The dull yellow stone jammed in her mother's forehead had lost its glow once Braxus broke from her prison. Other than the shard, her mother looked peaceful. Forever held in her endless coma. Most of her mother's hair had whitened, but a few red strands peeked through. Paper-thin skin emphasized the skeletal features of her face. Sullen and empty where it had been full some hundred years ago.

Piper stroked the caved-in cheek. The skin was so delicate, she feared too much pressure would tear it.

A living corpse. If she could just keep telling herself that, the next step might come easier.

The longer she waited, the worse the outcome. Braxus and the others could only do so much to hold off Aterus.

Her hand moved to her belt and slipped her dagger out. She clenched the hilt, knowing what she had to do. Yet now that the time had come, her will deserted her.

"I'm sorry."

Piper raised it high. Fingers trembled.

"I love you," she whispered. Her arms shook, tense and ready.

But her fingers betrayed her.

She slumped and let the weapon fall harmlessly onto the blanket.

Piper. The demigod. Daughter of Souls. She had killed before and knew she'd do it again and again if necessary. But here—with her mother—she had met a wall. Too weak to do what was right.

"Piper."

Her head jerked up at the name.

Evangeline's eyelids had cracked open. No matter how many years passed, the brightness of those honey-colored irises never dulled.

"Mother?" She was awake. Now. Of all times. "How did you...?"

Those thin lips parted. "I heard the anguish in your heart, my sweet girl." Evangeline lifted a weary hand toward Piper's face, but it dropped back to her side before it could touch her.

Piper grabbed it and squeezed. "I can't do it."

"You must." Her chest heaved in a labored gasp for air. "I can't do it myself."

Piper shook her head. Welled-up tears poured down her cheeks. "It's too much."

"I know, Piper. I know," she soothed.

A deep breath granted Piper a grip of clarity. "There isn't much time."

One side of Evangeline's mouth lifted into a smile. "And yet we have had so much time. More than anyone could ever dream of getting."

Piper brought her mother's hand to her cheek. The fingers brushed back and forth, though Piper knew if she released, the frail arm would fall to the bed again. So she kept it there.

"Do you remember our times on the beach?" Evangeline asked.

"Of course."

"You would build sandcastles when you were young, and we'd wait for the tide to come in and wash it away."

Piper nodded. She always loved how her mother would decorate her castle with shells and sea glass. It made the thing sparkle in the sun.

"Your father was the one who taught you how to build them so high," she said with a distant longing.

"Aterus?" Her father had been close to her at one point, but the memories were so far back, none of them came to her when beckoned.

"I love you, Pipes. And I love your father, too, but my life has driven him to madness. I should've realized it when I first got to know him, but I was a young, enchanted fool." The speech winded her. She took a moment to recover before she continued. "Aterus is a Soul, not a man. He is not capable of love as we are. Not in the same way. His feelings are driven by a need. Control. Humans...." She coughed.

Piper held her hand tighter. It had been a long while since seeing her mother so awake. Usually, when her coma subsided every few years, she'd be tormented with amnesia for a time.

"Humans," she said, "whether he meant to make us this way or not, love with a selfless passion. Unconditional. Aterus can never love like that because that kind of love stems from knowing there is an end. An end we must all face. A love only mortals can behold."

Any sort of love was out of reach for her father. There may have been moments of kindness in his past, but they were all driven out by his greed.

"Piper." Evangeline's voice called her back from her thoughts. "You are half of me. You are capable of love and pain he can't understand. Because of that, this burden is tasked to you. He will not let me go." She crawled her fingers to Piper's dagger and handed it over. "I am so very sorry it falls to you."

Piper took the blade in her hands.

"Before it's too late." Those brown eyes held a glint of sympathy, but she gave an encouraging smile.

Evangeline nodded as Piper wrapped her fingers around the hilt and poised the tip of the knife over her mother's heart. That face. She'd never again see it. Never again hear the voice call out to her.

All she had to do was press and the moment would end. Her mother would leave this dreadful existence. She'd be free.

Piper's whole body trembled with such ferocity the blade moved from heart to stomach and back again. She focused on her target, but her mother's soft eyes on her made it difficult.

"I can't," she cried as sweat built in her icy palms, loosening her hold. "I can't do it."

"You can." With a wheeze of strain, Evangeline placed her hands over Piper's to steady them. They trained the dagger over her heart. Stilled it. "We will do it together."

Piper's gaze flicked from her mother's face down to the knife.

"Come on, angel. It's okay."

That tone. Piper closed her eyes. Her mother reserved that specific pitch for when Piper had been scared. An old memory of the beach floated to the surface. From a time before she enjoyed the water. The waves had terrified her with their violent roars as they crashed on the cliffs. Evangeline had used that tone then. Her voice could chase off the worst nightmares.

"Come on, Pipes. My darling." Evangeline lifted her chest toward the steel, and it poked through the fabric of the nightgown.

Piper opened her eyes with a new focus. The misery would end here. Not just for her mother, but for Ohr.

"I love you," Piper whispered through her sobs.

"And I love you. More than anyone could ever love another." A flash of sorrow passed over Evangeline's eyes. But Piper sensed it wasn't for the incoming agony of steel, but rather grief for them to be parted.

Be free.

A roar kindled in Piper's throat and burst forth. A cry of pain. A cry for love. It gave her the last strength she needed to break through her mental wall.

The last thing she saw was a serene smile on her mother's face as she plunged the dagger through her heart.

CHAPTER 38

The battle ensued before Leo. His body kept firmly in place and out of his control by Aterus' strange hold. All he could do was stare in horror at the Souls dashing across the field.

Russé lay motionless on the ground with a green shard impaled in his chest. A few yards from him knelt Obell, his own red stone protruding from the side of his neck. Both incapacitated.

Issira, Vara, and Caradin moved in unison, circling around Aterus, who spun to keep them in view.

"You can't outmatch me. It would take all our kin to even try." Aterus fiddled with the colored stones between his fingers. "Join our brothers. I can give you peace."

"You think prison brings peace?" Vara scoffed. "I wish you a millennium of the same torment you put us through."

The Gray Soul's focus landed on the silver stag. He bolted for the beast.

Caradin dipped his deadly antlers toward his adversary and charged. The crown of horns came right for Aterus. At the last moment, Aterus ducked and fell to his knees, sliding beneath the stag's head. Crystal ready, Aterus went for the animal's belly.

Before the stone could touch the fur, a funnel of water hit Aterus' hand. One of the crystals slipped from his grasp and went spiraling into the air, glinting blue in the sunlight. It landed out of Leo's view somewhere in the tall grass.

The Souls knew this was their time to act. Caradin reared, punching his hooves at Aterus' face as a distraction while Vara swooped in to search for the trinket. Meanwhile, Issira, who had siphoned the moisture from the ground, put up a dome of water to shield her sister as she searched.

Aterus' grabbed one of the stag's legs mid-air and pulled the rearing animal to all fours. The stag slammed down, hooves sinking into the earth on impact. Caradin pulled at his feet, but they seemed too far in the dirt. Stuck. Aterus lunged. But the Soul was too quick. As the orange shard sailed for his flesh, Caradin shrank, leaving Aterus' swing sailing wildly through empty air.

Leo gasped in relief as a small sparrow flitted into the sky.

All at once, Vara popped up with the blue shard in hand and Issira transformed her shield of water into a jet. It shot for Aterus, but he didn't shy away. The blast struck him hard in the chest, pushing him closer to where Leo and Thomas stood, rigid as statues.

"You are one stone down," Issira said as she took her blue shard from Vara. They both closed in on Aterus as Caradin flew out of reach.

The god laughed and climbed to his feet. He backed up as they descended on him. Though Leo only had view of the back of the Gray Soul's head, he knew he held a smile for his kin.

So close now. If Leo could only move his arm, he'd have Aterus in a choke hold long enough for the Souls to subdue him.

Aterus waved a hand at his fallen kin in the grass. "You seem to think we are even, dear sister." Another breathy laugh. "But I don't need you all down for this."

A flash of darkness whirled in Leo's vision as Aterus spun and moved for Thomas. Not a second later, a guttural groan came from the boy like he'd been punched in the stomach. Aterus' hand moved from Thomas' abdomen, revealing another stone Leo hadn't spotted before.

Black.

It sat a good two inches deep into the boys' flesh. Tears streamed from the corner of Thomas' eyes, but his silent cry of pain never found its voice.

"No," Leo's shout came out as a whisper.

Aterus' face held a smug sneer as blood seeped from the wound. "No matter what you chose, your fate was always to die. By my hand or theirs. You are the key, Kole. To be used and disposed of. That is your purpose." The Soul twisted the stone.

Thomas buckled. Though his body remained upright in Aterus' hold, the boy's muscles relaxed, and the light in his eyes dimmed.

Thomas was merely meant to be a decoy. To delay Aterus' plans. Leo knew the swap would put the boy in danger. Even Thomas knew the risks when he agreed to the trick. Death was on the table. But not like this. Held and helpless. No chance to defend.

Seconds ticked by. That sneer on Aterus' face dropped into a frown. The god ripped back the hood, revealing his victim's identity. The confusion in Aterus' eyes morphed to anger before finally settling into terror.

"It was you. You switched their blood." The Gray Soul moved his rage to Leo.

A sting hit Leo's cheek as the god backhanded him. The hold over his body dissipated on strike — too sudden for Leo to find balance — and he fell to the ground.

"Kole. Where is he?"

Leo spat the blood from his mouth. Even if he wanted to answer, his lip had numbed from the blow. He looked up at the panicking god.

"Kole is releasing Braxus." Issira's melodic voice trilled like a flute.

Aterus whirled. His focus landed on the spire at the top of the hill.

While the god was distracted, Leo crawled to Thomas. The stone was stuck deep in the boy's abdomen. Muscles twitched at Leo's touch. The chest rose and fell with shallow breaths. Still alive. Barely. Pulling the crystal out now would have the poor boy bleeding to death. Best to keep it in place.

Hand shaking, Leo fiddled for the horn under his coat. Aterus had found them out. The time for deception gave way to battle. He pressed the ivory to his mouth and held the long note to signal the charge. War cries came from Ohr's army as they started their advance.

But what followed, Leo did not expect. And it all happened at once.

One second Leo fretted over Thomas, and within a blink, the tides changed.

A yellow streak of light plummeted to the field like a crashing meteor. The impact rattled Leo. He clung to Thomas, holding him steady. *The blow of one of Jax's cannons?* Leo tossed the thought aside. Even an engineer knew not to fire so close to allies.

Dust and dirt flew from the source of impact. Leo strained his eyes, just making out the new stranger. A sleek, bald head paired with androgynous features. Whatever hope had dimmed within Leo sparked anew. Kole had done it. The plan had succeeded.

The god of earth had joined her kin.

"Seize him, now!" The alarm in the Yellow Soul's voice caught Leo off guard.

Suddenly, as the Souls moved in to claim their foe, Aterus reeled back to Leo and Thomas. He gripped a hand on the ailing boy. Immediately, Thomas' skin ran cold. Leo tried to pry the Soul's fingers off, but he was no match for godly strength. The soul was sucking the last bit of life straight from Thomas' broken body.

It ended too quickly.

"Thomas!" Leo checked the boy's wrist, but the faint pulse had stilled.

A hand clamped around Leo's neck next. He clung to Thomas' body, but his captor pulled him loose and dragged him away.

Aterus lifted him from the floor. "Sorcerer blood will do nicely."

A pressure built in Leo's head from the lack of oxygen. He gasped for air, but it did not come. And that cold sensation. It pricked his heart and spread through his veins. This was it. He'd soon join Thomas. Leo clawed at one of his many pockets for a vial, a weapon — *anything!* — to no avail.

A pillar of water hit Aterus' back, but the strength he'd siphoned from Thomas had empowered the god.

Then.

It all stopped.

The cold left Leo.

The grip on his neck loosened.

Aterus' jaw went slack. Those piercing eyes glazed over. No, not a glaze: a veil of moisture.

Tears.

Aterus placed Leo down on the ground. Tremors shook the god's body, and his skin lost all trace of color. His gaze stuck on Leo but seemed to stare through him.

"Evangeline?" The Gray Soul's voice came soft and tender.

Then, the god with salt-and-pepper hair vanished from the battlefield in a cloud of smoke.

CHAPTER 39

Kole and Vienna stumbled from the spire and fled into the tall, grassy field. A horn blew in the distance. A note of desperation. The war had begun.

Yet when he looked down the slope, no great battle ensued. The army charged, closing in on the Souls, who stood where Kole and Vienna had left them earlier. Something had happened. He felt the tension slithering under his skin.

They tore down the hill. A flutter of wings dove for them from the skies. Kole immediately recognized the silver feathers. Caradin had come for them.

"Obell and Russé have been attacked." The bird sent the thought to Kole's head. *"They need the power of the key."*

"Attacked?"

Vienna glanced between the bird and Kole, concern marking every wrinkle on her face. "What's going on? Kole?"

"Something's wrong with Obell and Russé," he said hastily before turning back to the sparrow. *"Where is Aterus?"*

The bird fluttered in front of Kole's face. *"He has left the battlefield."*

Kole glanced up to the roof of the spire. If Aterus had fled, it meant... it meant Piper had done it. The god was going to his wife's aid. "Piper's still up there." When he spun toward the spire, Vienna restrained him.

"Where are you going? We can't go back."

"Aterus is up there. Piper can't do it alone. I don't care how much god's blood runs in her veins."

"Don't go," she pleaded. "He'll take you, Kole."

Kole looked between the spire and the battlefield, where a huddle had formed around the Souls. They couldn't lose any more strength. Vienna was right. Going back would set Aterus up for victory. But Piper didn't have to be entirely alone.

"Go." Kole commanded Caradin to the spire with a point of his finger. "Get Piper out of there. I'll take care of Russé and Obell."

The sparrow flittered away, dwindling into nothing more than a speck as Caradin soared for the roof.

When Kole and Vienna closed in, the crowd parted, unveiling a troubled scene. Russé and Obell lay on the ground, still as corpses. Leo hovered over their bodies chanting something while Vara, Braxus, and Issira stood by.

"You're back," Shikar said from the edge of the crowd. Her broad smile portrayed her relief.

Leo sat up and ushered them over. Blood covered his clothes, collar to hem. Yet as Kole approached, no sign of ichor stained the scene. Another body lay in the grass a few paces away. Criz and Boogy crouched beside it. Between their hunched forms came a clear view of a still corpse. The eyes held open, like glass marbles forever cast up to the heavens.

Thomas.

His mouth hung agape, as if he'd spent his final seconds in agony. That was where the blood had come from. Certainly dead. Far gone from Leo's, or any healer's help; otherwise, the liberation leader wouldn't have left the boy's side. Not even for a Soul.

The first of many. The intrusive thought burrowed deep in his head. The type of thought that Kole would normally shove away, but denying this truth would sully Thomas' murder. No matter what qualms they harbored against each other, Kole never wanted this.

The rays of the midday sun couldn't hold against the gloom and fear radiating from the army. Tense and thick. Kole forced his feet toward Leo.

Empty and overturned vials lay scattered around the sorcerer along with a bundle of burning herbs and various trinkets, including a metal pendant of the Seven Souls. His spells had left a foul stench in the clearing.

"What happened?" Kole knelt next to Leo, careful to avoid the sprawled-out ingredients. That was when the crystals came into view. A green one had been stabbed into Russé's chest, while Obell had one sticking from his muscular neck. "Why aren't they healing?"

"The crystals," Braxus answered. "They are still alive, but the magic in the stone seems to have blocked their powers. Turned their bodies off."

"We cannot pull them out," Vara said, her dual-colored eyes hard on her kin. "And they won't wake."

"A coma," Vienna said over Kole's shoulder. "Like Evangeline?"

Kole shook his head. "I don't think so."

"My spells are useless." Leo grew quiet and backed away, not bothering to collect his used-up components.

Kole knelt between the unconscious forms and looked at Russé. His eyes lay closed, and the muscles of his face had softened and relaxed as if in sleep. Despite what had been done to his old mentor, the god looked peaceful. A strange feeling came over Kole as he gazed on a helpless Russé. He'd held so much anger for the god over the last month. So much resentment for the lies and manipulation. But the direness of the moment made it vanish.

Kole inspected the crystal in Russé's chest. It looked like the soulstones he'd encountered before. "I think he's trying to imprison them again. Banish them to another plane like before. It must be the first stage because I can still feel them, but they're fading."

"Maybe the key can pull it out," Issira suggested. Blood stained her blue silk sleeves and dappled the fabric of her bodice, as if she'd held her kin in her arms in her own attempt to revive them. "Release him like you did before."

Kole reached to pluck out the stone. His flesh touched the cold edge of the crystal, and a flash of green light engulfed him.

The ground beneath him gave way, and his stomach dropped as if he fell from a great height. The sudden shift took the battlefield away. The murmurs of onlookers faded. Even the body heat from Vienna's hand on his back vanished.

Alone. Bathed in green.

Yet he knew exactly where he was.

"Russé. I'm here," Kole said. He stood and spun, surveying his surroundings. "I've come to release you." Only green light. He was inside the Soul's mind.

"That burden of yours is finished." His old mentor's voice came from every direction. "The last of us is released. You've done what you set out to do. Your journey is at an end."

"End?" Kole found a dark silhouette taking shape. "We are in the middle of a war. Aterus is still free."

The image sharpened, and Kole found himself looking upon a strange creature. Something between tree and human. The body had too many limbs. They stretched out uneven—dendritic. The bottom half walked high on roots like the ramblers, while the many arms spanned out like petals greeting the morning. Vines draped from the arm-like branches, and rich green moss covered every inch. Kole held his ground, reminding himself this all was happening in his head.

It wasn't until Russé spoke again that Kole spotted the face poised at the top of the trunk. "The matter started with the gods, and it will end with us." Though covered in bark rather than skin, the long nose and bridged brow matched the human façade Russé had maintained all these years.

The Green Soul's true form.

"It's you," Kole breathed. Though the eyes had changed. Drooped and round, yet a vibrant green rather than the blue Kole knew.

"There is something I wish to show you." At his voice, the landscape of green light faded. A forest took its place. The trees alone were enough for Kole to know where they stood. Solpate Forest. Home of the ramblers.

Russé had brought them to the base of The Great Red where it all started. The ancient tree had been the god's prison. Where Aterus had locked him away.

Everything seemed so real. Kole swore he could feel the lazy breeze on his face. The scent of decaying leaves and aging blossoms tickled his nose. Home. His heart ached for it.

Just as warmth settled into Kole's heart, he spotted his younger self walking up to the base of the red trunk. Russé had played the memory for Kole before. He watched the ghost version of himself timidly approach the tree. He wanted nothing more than to scream to the child. To tell him to back away. To run and never look back. But the past couldn't be changed. That he knew.

The child laid a hand on the bark. A flash of light claimed the small clearing.

"I took the ritual out of desperation. I knew a life would be forfeit for my return." Russé's voice dropped another octave. "But I took it nonetheless."

As the trunk exploded, Kole's five-year-old self flew back and landed broken on the forest floor.

An old man stumbled out of the hole of the trunk. It took a moment for the newly released god to catch his bearings. Then, he lifted his head, and his eyes trained on the boy. The god raced over.

"When I saw you, I felt the full force of my error. I knew I had to save you, but the only way I knew how would doom my kin."

"What are you talking about?" Kole peeked at Russé in his true form.

Russé extended a branch-like arm to the scene from the past. "You know now that the boy who released me died then and there. His memories are not yours. They never were. And they never will be. My guilt led me to my next mistake."

Kole watched as Russé resurrected the boy in the scene. The act that sapped the color from Kole's hair and eyes.

"I knew nothing of humans and their souls. That was Aterus' expertise. I revived you in the only way I knew how. By planting a new seed. My seed."

"I don't understand."

"It was a mistake, Kole. For all the wisdom a god may have, there is always folly." The scene of the past faded away, and Russé moved before Kole. "I made you into the key by placing a piece of my Soul into you. And what happens to one Soul...."

"Happens to all," Kole finished. He'd heard the saying dozens of times before. Yet now a new truth dawned on him. "You fragmented your kin. It wasn't me or the ritual."

The vines swayed as Russé confirmed. "No, it wasn't. Goren was right. A death was required to release us from our prisons, but I couldn't live with that. In my error, I created more of a problem. I created you. A child with the claws of death dug so deeply into him." A pause. "I doomed you, Kole. And for that, I am sorry."

It took a moment to register. Kole had only ever wanted the truth from Russé. Everything out in the open. Long had the Soul held his secrets, feeding them to Kole little by little when the situation called for it. All of this driven from guilt. Was that what encouraged Russé's tight lip? Guilt for putting a human before the gods? Now that he thought about it, if death was meant to release a Soul—well—it seemed he and Russé had figured out a way to cheat the ritual.

Kole squeezed his fists. "No. You didn't doom me. Goren did. He doomed me to die there in that clearing." A horrible act. Murdering a child. The truth fueled his hatred for his former camp leader. He deserved his fate: death in the fires of the wall. But what angered Kole more was the sliver of understanding in Goren's actions. With everything that had happened since he set foot out of Solpate and into the woes of Ohr, Kole understood one thing clearly now: good and evil shook hands. They lived together in everything. Nothing black or white but rather a mess of color.

Goren had been searching for an end to the Black Wall just as Kole had been for the last few months. That pursuit had driven Goren down a path in which the sacrifice of a child was a necessary evil to spark more hope into the world. He had only wanted what Kole had succeeded in: the release of the gods. A force to stand against Aterus and free Ohr of the darkness the Black Wall cast on the land and its people.

"You brought me back," Kole said in a shaking voice. "You could've left me there, but you chose mercy. Even at the cost of weakening yourself and your kin." He closed the space between him and Russé and reached out to touch the soft moss encasing the bark. "Because of you, others were spared. If we did things Goren's way—the way in his journal—there would be five innocent deaths on our hands. I know fragmenting the gods was a mistake, but it is the only reason this worked."

One of the branches reached down and brushed Kole's face. "I know Souls should never meddle in the business of their creations. But I am glad to have been by your side all these years." A flower bud bloomed under one of Russé's eyes. "Aterus really has created something beautiful."

The mention of the crazed god set a panic in Kole. "We need to stop him. I can bring you back to your body. We can fight him together."

"No. I have hit my limits in that form." Russé pulled away. "There is something else I had in mind." A vine slithered from one of Russé's branches and extended toward Kole. "If you'll have me."

Kole stared at it, then grinned as Russé's intentions dawned on him. He reached for the vine.

"How much you've grown." Russé's voice faded away.

The green light returned. It blinded. It soaked into his skin and zapped every nerve in his body. Kole screamed, not in pain, but in exuberance. A way to release the shock of the pure energy coursing through his veins.

His eyes opened once more to the battlefield. Gasps surrounded him, and the cause caught Kole by surprise, as well. Russé's body had vanished along with any trace of the soulstone. A green hue radiated off Kole's skin. In his head, he felt Russé's presence. Stronger than before. Their connection seamless.

Life burst around him. Beneath his feet, he felt the roots of the grass clinging to the soil as their long blades swayed in the wind. Kole reached a hand to a browning weed. The leaves reached back. He willed Russé's power to his command. It answered freely. One thought, and the wilted plant regained its color. A bud rose from the center and opened a white flower.

Another energy pulsed in the distance. A beacon compared to the blip of the weeds and grasses of the open field. Kole stood. Behind the army sat the horde of ramblers. Resting. Awaiting command. Kole's fingers itched to call them.

"Risil has become whole again." Issira approached him, her kin at her back. It should've been a happy moment, yet Issira's expression read somber. "Within you."

Kole held out his hands. A whole god inside him. Not fragments like before. And, oh, could he feel it. The scars remained, yet his muscles and skin no longer held caution. It mimicked how he felt before his near-death encounter with the Black Wall. No. Not the same. Better. Enhanced.

Kole reached down and pulled the crystal from Obell's neck. The Red Soul awakened: a bit disoriented but on his feet a moment later.

Those fiery eyes made a double take at Kole. "Russé. Where has he gone?"

"Gone?" Kole asked. "What do you mean?"

"Risil has returned," Issira corrected.

Obell cocked his head as he peered into Kole's eyes. Then, recognition. "Brother." Obell bowed slightly in greeting.

"Why are you saying it like that?" Kole glanced between the gods. Their stoic faces told him they understood something more. "What are you talking about? He's not gone. I feel him." Kole looked within and felt the spaces of his mind. That new presence in his head emitted a familiar power. It felt like the energy he drew on when he commanded the ramblers. Shepherd's power. The Green Soul's power. Except the well at his disposal had no limit—beyond his wildest imagination. It filled his body to the brim, threatening to burst if he didn't use it.

"*Russé,*" Kole played the word in his head.

He waited.

No answer.

"*Russé?*"

The more he probed and prodded the presence in his head, the more alien it felt. When he had conversed with Russé previously, there had been a warmth in their bond. A fondness. Though the source of the power held a certain familiarity to Kole; in return, it bore a cold indifference.

"What's going on?"

"Russé is no more, Kole." Only Issira's vibrato could make such words less painful. "It is Risil that is within you."

"I don't know what that means."

But he did. He did.

He just didn't want to face it.

CHAPTER 40

Piper sobbed into the nape of her mother's neck. Her hand slipped from the dagger's hilt, across the slick of blood, and cradled Evangeline's head. The pulse had stopped moments ago. Piper's intuition urged her to run — to flee the scene — but something in her body held her there tighter than an iron vice.

"I'm sorry," she whispered. "I'm so sorry."

Red stained her clothes as she held her mother tight. The moment she let go, it would be over. She'd never lay eyes on her again. Feel her in her arms. Take in her unique scent of lavender and dew that always reminded Piper of sunrise. Now a metallic tang clung to the air. Despite the long years knowing how it had to end, nothing could've prepared her for this agony. Her heart swelled, threatening to burst at the seams.

Lost in her tears, she hardly realized the hair on the back of her neck stood on end until a creak came from the door. She silenced her breathing as another presence entered the room.

"Evangeline?"

Piper slowly raised her head and brought her eyes to the entrance. Aterus stood in the archway, his face contorted in an ugly sadness.

The Soul rushed over.

The quick movement sparked Piper's instincts. Maybe a daughter's fear. Maybe the terror of facing the wrath of a god. She couldn't determine which in that split second, and it didn't matter. Either way, punishment would find her. She slipped from her mother and bolted for the corner, all the while keeping an alert eye on her father.

But he stopped at the bed and draped himself over Evangeline. A guttural cry escaped him. She'd never seen him cry before.

It felt off. Wrong somehow. She'd witnessed Vienna grieve for her brother. In the moment Felix had died, she'd sat by her side and held her back. As her brother turned to ash, a distinct, unnatural scream had rung out from Vienna's lungs. Despite her grave injury, Vienna had kicked and screamed so fiercely, even Piper's demigod strength had trouble keeping her still. Raw desperation. Shock.

This? The scene she watched now? *Fake grief.* That was it. It had to be. The tears. The pained wails. All of it a show — an act. And for what? For Piper? He knew she stood in that corner, observing. Aterus was probably trying to play on her guilt. Trying to make her regret giving Evangeline peace.

Of course. She noticed every movement now. Calculated and measured. The way he sobbed: a wail with two quick breaths between. It seemed patterned. And his mouth agape in that perpetual frown as depicted in those old books her mother had read to her as a child. How could Aterus claim to love her mother after all the torment he'd put her through? He couldn't even conjure up his own sadness at her death.

Anger hardened in Piper. Still, she couldn't bring herself to move from that corner, and she dared not make a sound. *This must be how a mouse feels on the edge of a hungry cat's vision.* The thumping of her heart pounded out of control. She needed to get out while Evangeline held his attention. The open door lay on the opposite side of the room. Farther away than she remembered. The floor seemed to stretch longer with each passing second.

Still Aterus wept.

She thought he'd run through the show by now. Given up on it. Souls knew he'd never cried for anything before. Not even when he lost the loyalty of his own daughter.

Unless....

Unless those tears were real and not conjured to sway Piper's guard. A small piece of her wished for it. Her mind wandered through that fantasy. She couldn't help it. A life where her father had truly loved her mother and doted on his only daughter. Her heart desired that sort of life. One filled with warmth and kindness rather than blood and rage. If there ever existed a time she could live happily and contentedly, it had long passed. Spoiled by greed. Soured by the very god who slumped over her dead mother.

That thought pulled the settling fog from her mind. She focused.

One sidestep. Then another. She slid behind a cushioned chair and braced against the tall back when Aterus' sobs quieted.

She waited, hoping for the small chance that he'd forgotten about her.

With a tender hand, Aterus pushed back the hair that had fallen in Evangeline's face. "I failed you."

The scene stirred a wave of nausea within Piper. Even at the end, he still couldn't see his madness. His selfishness. "You failed her years ago," she hissed. Her nails dug into the soft fabric of the chair. "You know better than anyone the limits on humans. Look what you did to her mind. It's not natural. She needed death—wanted it—but you refused her wishes. That's not love."

"You think because you share my blood you have insight into the nature of gods?" Aterus' fingers trailed across her mother's cheek and down to the dagger protruding from her chest. "You are but a blip in creation. Your existence a mere blink of my eye. You have no idea what is natural. That word alone suggests that there are laws and rules I must abide by."

Finally, those dark eyes left Evangeline and pierced straight through the chair to Piper. No matter how hard she braced, a shiver rattled her bones.

"You are far too human," he said like a curse. "If you had been more of me, you might've understood."

"I'm of my mother," Piper defended. "I did what you could not. I set her free."

Those final words must've dug under his skin because the grief wiped clean from his face. "You call this freedom?" He waved a hand over Evangeline. "Life is freedom."

"Her life was torture." Piper ran on the fumes of waning adrenaline. "Why couldn't you see that? She hated waking up confused. She was afraid of us. It took days for her memory to return—to know I was her daughter. We only had her for a few moments before she left us again."

"I was gifting her time—for her and me. For all of us." His thick brows sank as fury set in. Aterus stood from the bed. "A gift you so easily snuffed out. I shouldn't be surprised. You betrayed this family long before you murdered your mother."

"This isn't a family." Fragments of memories flashed to the forefront of her mind. A vague vision of Aterus' hands covering Piper's as they formed the tower of a sandcastle together. Hikes up the cliff with her mother and father chasing after her. And another, more of a sensation than a true memory; her small body thrown high into the air, a trill of giggles, caught in strong arms, then thrown again. But it had been so long. The moment she tried to latch on to a string of the past, it slipped away like the falling tide. If they had been a family at some point, it had ended long ago. "Families don't conduct cruel experiments on their loved ones. Extending her life... you caused her so much pain. It was grueling to watch her suffer. On and on, all because you couldn't let go."

"There was never a need to let her go. She was safe in my hands."

"In and out of consciousness. Barely remembering who we were. Asleep for decades at a time. You call that safe? She was alive in your hands," Piper corrected. "Don't you dare think that's the same. Death is the way of life."

"Death is a creation of the gods," he roared as he took a step her way. "It is the way of life until I decide it's not." His jaw twitched the way it always did when he tried to reign in his anger.

A small laugh escaped her. "All the while, we played house as the Black Wall took countless lives across Ohr. And you use it as a tool—a weapon—even still. That is what you decided. That mortal sacrifice is required so you can indulge in a human life with a fake wife and daughter." She seethed. "Your cruelty is truly impressive. I bet you twisted her mind to love you. Didn't you?"

"Enough," he bellowed. His voice shook the stone spire.

Piper retreated until her back pressed firmly into the cold wall. Her eyes flicked to the doorway. Aterus stood between her escape. Any gifts her demigod blood granted came up short against him. If he turned violent—if it turned to a struggle of power or strength—her chances were out the window.

The window!

If Aterus guarded the door, she'd have to take what she could. A fall from this height would hurt, but it wouldn't kill her. Keeping her eyes on her father, she inched toward it.

Disdain boiled in his growl. "I had a plan. One that I have been working on since my kin discovered Evangeline. All I needed was time."

He pulled a violet crystal from his pocket. The thing sparkled in the light from the window.

"Imprison your kin again?" Piper scoffed. "What monstrosity will that turn the Black Wall into?"

"Not imprison. Transfer." Aterus turned back to Evangeline and dipped his head to the wound above her brows. "Their pride will never let them ascend or gift me their power. I found a way to take it for myself." He reached back to caress Evangeline's cheek. "All of them put into her would make her whole again. Invincible. Death would never threaten her."

The revelation branded clearly in her head. Still, her mouth quivered, unable to speak it. Everything wrong with Aterus stood out like blaring alarms. To think he'd form and shift anything and everything to please his wishes. An overwhelming disgust gave her voice the courage to speak. "You'd make her a god?"

"It is the ultimate gift."

Piper shook her head. Aterus' answer for everything was always the same. More death. More sacrifice. "A curse. You should've left her alone. Her life was doomed the day she met you. The Souls knew it would end poorly. They were right to separate you." She inched closer to the open window. A bit further and she'd be able to fling herself out.

"I know what you're doing." Aterus' tone changed so dramatically in that instant, Piper thought someone else had said it.

The muscles in Piper's body ached. They struggled against her commands, slow and rigid. He'd done this before: used his power to hold a human. But he'd never used it on her. Never had to. His claim over her fell short, though. A shock to him, it seemed by the surprise in his eyes. She still shuffled along; each movement labored as if dragging a boulder along with her. The window lay within reach. That chill wind hit her face, drying the lingering tears on her skin.

"I will let you go, Piper." Aterus' mouth thinned into a dangerous scowl. "Once I've taken what you've stolen."

Piper urged her body to move. She tried to throw herself at the open window, but her father's unworldly grip only allowed her to lean, which pulled her off balance.

Aterus had crossed the room and caught her body before it hit the floor. Hands strung under each arm, he lifted her up to his eye level. "Your mother would never forgive me if I hurt you. But now she's gone."

Struggling was useless. Nothing she had at her disposal could overpower him. She braced herself as his eyes turned bloodshot. He pushed his consciousness into hers. Like the strike of a mallet on glass, the shield she'd built against him shattered.

The sound of her own scream rattled her eardrums.

Aterus barged his way through her mind. No delicacy or caution. Icy fingers groped and jabbed her mind to the very core until it wrapped around a dark piece and ripped it free. Her body went numb. Her own nerves couldn't register such a scale of pain.

A warm sensation spread through her head as if her very brain hemorrhaged from the wound. That heat moved to the back of her throat, merging with her cry of agony.

Across her tongue. Past her lips. A gray sphere of light emerged and floated toward Aterus. He opened his mouth and consumed the orb, then dropped Piper to the floor.

Her face pressed down on cool stone. Slowly, her nerves revived themselves, and a jarring throb stabbed in her head. Despite the pain, she let out a long sigh. The weight she'd been carrying these last ten years had finally gone. The parasite that was Aterus' fragmented soul had been extracted.

She pushed up to her hands, then fell back down; arms too weak to hold her own weight. If she waited a moment, the power of her demigod blood would soothe the pain and heal her quickly. That meant staying longer in Aterus' presence. Not that she had a choice in the matter. But when her body convulsed—uncontrollable movements—panic roused. She cradled herself in her arms, hoping to still the tremors, but nothing lessened them. Her blood should've started working by now.

Shuffles from Aterus made her draw her eyes up. Her father had stepped back. The air around his body danced with a gray hue. That look in his eyes made her crawl back to the wall.

Hunger.

A grin pressed over his mouth as he inspected the phenomenon radiating from his body. He sucked in a deep breath.

That face. It had changed. Where before she could see hints of a previous life in the soft lines under his eyes and around his mouth, now his skin had smoothed. Less human and more like a sculpture. An etherealness draped over him, head to toe. No longer a father or a husband. He was the Gray Soul, and mania burned in his eyes.

"I won't kill you, Piper. I am not a monster. But I will not save you from the fire. Your fate is your own now."

"Everything will die," she croaked as the Gray Soul lifted his hands. He meant to call on the Black Wall. No matter how many cannons Jax made and had at the ready, it would never be enough for the full force of the wall.

Soft chirps came from above. It took all of Piper's strength to swivel her head and notice the sparrow perched on the windowsill. Silver feathers. Piper grabbed Caradin and hid him in her hands.

"My tether to Ohr has died at your hand." It seemed Aterus hadn't noticed the arrival of his kin. Too distracted reveling in his reclaimed power. "Evangeline is gone. From the ashes I will create a world anew. Better humans. A new life." When Aterus closed his eyes, the air dancing around his body burst out and filled the room.

A hum resonated in Piper. Her gut clenched. Aterus had begun his call for the black flames.

"Go, Caradin. You must stop him. He'll kill us all." Piper thrust her open hands toward Aterus. The sparrow soared out. Mid-flap of its wings, the feathers turned to fur, and the little creature grew ten times its size into a snarling wolf.

Caradin leapt at Aterus, canines bared. The mighty paws struck Aterus straight in the chest and knocked him to the floor. When Aterus slammed down, Piper expected anger. Instead, the Gray Soul's face lit up with excitement.

"You are too late, Brother. It's already done." Aterus grabbed the beast by the neck. Caradin yelped as the god held the wolf as if it were nothing more than a pup, feet dangling a few inches off the floor. In one swift motion, Aterus threw Caradin toward the window, where he landed next to Piper with a whine.

"You're all right," Piper whispered, surprised by the tenderness of her own voice. A bit of red stained the wolf's coat. Piper stared at the blood. Without a thought, she wiped it from the beast and brought it to her lips. The tang sent an immediate jolt through her body. Not enough to restore her full strength, but enough to get on her feet and quell the tremors.

She slid her arms around the wolf, then lugged herself up. The extra weight of the beast made her muscles spasm, but she pressed her back into the wall for support.

One last look at her mother, whose eyes had long lost their light. Then, facing Aterus, Piper leaned back and pushed off her feet, allowing gravity to pull her and Caradin backwards out the window.

Her belly cramped against the weightless feeling of their freefall. As much as she wanted to clench her eyes shut, she forced them to take in the upside-down world that stretched before her.

"Change, Caradin," she pleaded to the barely conscious Soul wrapped in her arms. The fall from the top window had seemed reasonable, but that was before Aterus had severed the Soul fragment from her head. Now the ground came up quickly, and she regretted the decision.

Another squeeze to the wolf's limp form.

"Please, wake up."

So close now. Piper made out the individual blades of grass waiting for her body to smash down on them. If this was the end, she'd face it without fear. She kept her eyes on the impact zone, yet every muscle betrayed her and stiffened with anticipation.

In an instant, a wriggle came from her clutch. Silver fur burst out, growing into a new shape. The wolf had gone. Instead, Piper clung to the broad back of a stag. Vast wings stretched out and caught the wind. A handful of arduous beats sent Piper and Caradin soaring in a new direction.

The grass fell away. Piper collapsed into the neck of the elk as they safely ascended into the sky, back toward the army.

CHAPTER 41

Russé was gone. The details of that remained out of Kole's full scope, but the old man he had known and grown up with was not the entity which now resided within him. Instead, the Souls claimed that Risil and his powers lay in Kole's reach. Yet how did the two differ? He'd thought Russé had merely been a name the Green Soul had claimed to hide his identity from the refugees. The merge with Kole had sparked some sort of change. One that he hoped could be undone again once they split.

The bleat of a stag echoed from above. The beating wings sent a flurry of gusts on the battlefield as Caradin landed with Piper astride.

Vienna raced to the animal's side and caught the demigod before she fell off the mount.

Piper had gone sickly pale. Even the vibrant tone of her fiery hair had dulled to an unvarnished copper. She collapsed into Vienna's arms, lips moving as if mumbling to herself.

Kole rushed past the Souls to her side and helped Vienna steady Piper on her feet. "We should've stayed," he told Vienna. "Look what he's done."

"You know she wouldn't have allowed us to." Vienna cupped the girl's face, trying to calm her.

Despite Kole and Vienna's support, Piper had grown so weak, Caradin had to use his antlers to help prop the demigod up.

When her rolling eyes landed on Kole, a sense of stability came back to her. Piper shrugged off Vienna and gripped Kole by the shoulders. What had come off as gibberish before now struck Kole clearly. "Aterus has summoned the wall."

Kole's innards sank through the earth. The Gray Soul had gone mad. It was the only explanation. "He's going to kill us all."

Piper gave a delirious nod, then her eyes rolled back in her head, and she fainted into his arms. For the first time since Kole had gotten his scars, he had the strength to catch her all on his own. He called out for Leo, who rushed to assist. "She needs out of here. I don't know what he did, but she's weak."

"It is what I thought, then." Issira stepped forward. "I knew her essence was too strong when I met her. Now I can feel the absence."

"What do you mean?" Kole asked.

"Can you not feel it? Her mind has been torn. Aterus has reformed himself."

Kole loosened his grip, allowing Leo to take the demigod. He remembered his talk with Piper on the other side of the Black Wall. She had described a moment ten years ago that coincided with Kole's release of Russé. When the Souls had split and nestled fragments of their spirits inside him, the same had been done to Aterus. Except the Gray Soul's essence hadn't gone into Kole that day. Instead, it latched onto Piper. She had been carrying a piece of her father within her the last decade.

"He took it back," Kole realized. From the state of her, though a demigod, it had nearly killed her. He dreaded what the act would do to him when the time came. "She needs a healer," he urged Leo.

As Leo took her in his arms, Piper awoke again. Through her delirium, something snapped in her. She planted her feet on the ground, refusing to move.

"No." Piper pushed away Leo's arms, but she fell back against him for balance. "I'm staying."

"You can't stand," Leo argued.

As if driven by pure stubbornness, she took two wobbling steps forward. Knees shook, but she stayed up. "The Black Wall comes. I will not be nursed through the last stand."

Kole took a long, hard look at her. Color slowly returned to her nose and lips. Her divine lineage remained. She'd heal in time. He just didn't know how much time they had. Still, if put in that position, he'd make the same call. Her choice. He'd never take that from her. Kole nodded. "Then you stay."

"At least let me fix you up." Leo dug around in his many pockets and brought out a poultice he rubbed on her temples, then ran some bottled vapor under her nose, at which her pupils enlarged with one inhale.

All those things would work on a human. A demigod needed more. Much more. Something only Kole could give now. He took up his knife, made a small cut on his palm, and collected a smear of blood before his skin rapidly reclosed. With Risil's full soul within him, the effect would be potent. Kole passed the blade to Piper. Her hand had steadied from Leo's efforts.

No words passed between them, and yet, recognition flashed in Piper's eyes. Just as Kole sensed the new absence in Piper's head, he guessed she too could perceive his change—his addition. She wiped the blood off with a finger, then brought it to her mouth.

Immediately, color pooled in her cheeks.

While Leo continued fussing over her, Kole turned his attention back to the Souls. "Aterus has summoned the Black Wall. He needs to be stopped before it gets here."

"How long do we have?" Vienna took the question straight from his thoughts.

"I don't know." Kole turned to Piper, hoping she might have more insight, but she shook her head.

A horn sounded at the front of the army. Another responded from somewhere in the back. Jax's cannons pulled along to the outside edges of their forces. Soldiers loaded them up with moonstone. Should the wall make it to the battlefield, the cannons would buy them time. If that happened, though.... *If the wall makes it here, the coastal cities are lost. Zeal is lost. And Solpate....* A grim reality awaited them should that come to pass. So much death. Lingering on the idea only shriveled his confidence. He shut it out.

Kole turned back to the Souls. Obell, Vara, Issira, Braxus, and Caradin all stood in a circle. Kole nodded to Vienna, who stepped back, then he took his place beside the gods. "He's whole again. We are outmatched."

"You have Risil's full powers at your command, child," Braxus reminded. "As long as the Black Wall keeps its distance, we have a chance."

"If the wall is truly on its way, the battle will not last long enough for him to use his Kayetans," said Issira.

True. The sun hung high at noon. Six hours at least until it dipped behind the horizon.

"But if it comes down to it, Kole...." Obell's mighty frame softened as he spoke.

This was the time. From the start Kole always knew how it would end. Only, he thought Russé would be by his side when it came to it. These last few months since he'd left the confines of Solpate had gone too quickly. He thought he'd have more time.

Kole looked over his shoulder at the army preparing for war. So many he loved and cared for stood here in this field. He found Jax off to the north messing with one of her cannons. Streaks of grime marked her forehead where she'd wiped the sweat from her brow. Shikar carried two moonstone trunks on her shoulders. Criz and Boogy. The refugees of his former camp. Azmali. Leo. All the soldiers who had travelled from the cities throughout Ohr to face down Aterus.

He swiveled.

There stood Vienna. Her gaze found his. The fear upon her face softened, and she managed a small smile. He wanted to give her one back, but the image of her burning in black flames tormented him.

"If it comes down to it...." Kole shook the picture from his head, but it lingered, latching on like a hungry leech. He wanted to live more than anything. At least, that was what he had thought up until.... Until. Well, he didn't quite know when things shifted, but it stood as a glaring lie now. He didn't want to live more than anything. He wanted Vienna to live. He wanted her safe. "Take them from me."

The Soul's grew quiet and still in understanding, save for Caradin, who came up to Kole and nudged his wet snout into Kole's stomach. Kole flung his arms around the stag's nose and gave it a great squeeze. He wished to see Russé to give him the same embrace.

"We must restrain Aterus by any means necessary," Issira said. "Only then can we strip away his powers and end his terror."

"What about the Black Wall?" Kole asked. "It'll stop when he's no longer...."

"When we take his godhood, the Black Wall will no longer bend to his will," Issira assured.

"Then let us go to him. I'm tired of waiting for his move," Obell grumbled.

Braxus strode to Kole's side. She gave him a quick smirk, then stroked the stag's neck. "Will you bear me, Brother?"

Caradin knelt in a deep bow, allowing the Yellow Soul an easy hop onto his back. Once mounted, the wings unfurled, and the stag lifted into the air. Kole stepped back, shielding his eyes from the pounding wind.

The two gods flew off around the perimeter of the troops. Braxus' voice bellowed across the field, giving off commands for war. With news of the wall's approach, Jax had the cannons encompass the army. One by one, they lit up. Rays of moonbeams sprouted out in a protective shield.

As the troops gathered themselves to march, Kole rushed to Vienna's side. She welcomed him with open arms. Even on the edge of bloodshed, she made his heart flutter.

"You feel different." Vienna pulled away and touched the skin of his burned hands. "Look."

Kole saw it, too. A slight green aura radiated from him. "It's Russé." No matter what the Souls called the god now, it would always be Russé to him.

"Do you feel...?"

"The same, just stronger. It's still me." Kole took her hand and placed in on his cheek. Though she had touched him there before, it still made him lose all senses.

Vienna took his face in his hands and held him there, eye to eye. Worry flooded those dark pupils. "Don't give up on yourself." She must've heard his conversation with the Souls. "There's more to you than them. We both know it."

"I don't know what's going to happen from here."

"We'll win."

Or die trying. Something in his face must've tipped her off to the intrusive thought, because her brows pulled together.

Her gaze held him for a moment, then she said again, "We'll win. We must." The worry line in her forehead appeared. "No matter what nightmares he brings with him, we will face them head on. Say it, Kole. You need to believe it."

A flood of dread drowned him. His lungs constricted. Whether he believed it or not, this may be the last time he ever saw her face. He took in every freckle, reading them like roads on a map. That road sloped up and over her perfect nose and dusted the skin around her eyes. Emerald green. His favorite color, he decided then and there. The color of summer leaves. The color that reminded him of loss. And hope. But most of all, when he stared into those jeweled eyes, he felt... he felt....

"I love you." The words came easily, like they had been waiting on his lips since the first day he saw her. A brief sense of insecurity plagued his nerves at the thought that she might not return the expression, but he swallowed his pride back. He didn't care. It was his truth. Even if she felt differently, he needed to tell her. "You don't have to—"

Vienna pulled him in. Her lips crashed into his in a fierce kiss. Not like their last one: soft, hesitant, explorative. This came eager and thirsty. He returned her intensity. They both understood the horrors awaiting them. Bloodshed. Death. Either one of them could lay at the end of that sword. Kole trailed his hands up her back and ran his fingers through her hair. Soft as silk. He wanted to stay there forever, locked in her embrace. But he had to breathe.

Kole drew away, panting.

The sides of her mouth twitched as if she were trying to smile. "Kole, I—"

A blaring horn cut her off.

"We have eyes on the Gray Soul!" Jax shouted from the nearest cannon with her spyglass pushed firmly over one eye. "He comes alone."

"What sort of lunatic faces an army alone?" Azmali held her spear at the ready. Unease marked her stance as she shifted side to side.

It only now registered in Kole's head that he'd been kissing Vienna a few paces from an entire army and the Souls. He would've turned bright red if Vienna hadn't already done that. Hand linked in hers, he turned and pulled her toward the gods.

"One that has lost all sense of reason," Vara answered so low, Kole barely caught her words. A step closer to her kin, then, "Piper has done her part well. He will be fierce, but chaotic like a winter blizzard. We should keep our guard up."

Obell clenched his fists, and a massive wave of heat caught Kole's skin.

Caradin landed with a clamor of hooves to Kole's left. From atop the stag, Braxus said, "The army is ready to strike at our command." Her head dipped to Kole. "You have Risil in you, now, child. No more need for mortal caution. Wounds will close. Bones will mend. Do not hide. Do not hold back."

Kole nodded and squeezed Vienna's hand. She reciprocated, giving him a new burst of strength.

Still, it struck Kole as odd. The Gray Soul had truly lost his mind when his wife died. How could anyone think to approach a field of enemies alone? A chill swirled up his spine.

As Aterus neared, it was Issira who stepped forward. She seemed to have taken the lead among the gods in Russé's absence.

"You have no army to command. Risil has become whole. You are outpowered. Surrender. Let us do this swiftly and easily, Brother. No more needless deaths."

Aterus glanced Kole's way with interest, then trailed across his kin. "You think the Kayetans are the only forces I command?" Aterus laughed. "You forget who I am, dear sister."

Another glance at Kole. The gaze their way must've frightened Vienna because she slipped her hand from Kole's and found refuge behind him. "Don't worry, Vienna, he—"

A searing pain came down on Kole's back. He cried out and stumbled forward. The muscles in his back flexed against an object. He gritted his teeth and reached over his shoulder to find the hilt of a dagger. Once he pulled it out with a grunt, the flesh stitched together, closing the wound. It itched with great ferocity, but he was too shocked to pay it mind. That dagger. He'd know it anywhere. Kole turned to his assailant.

"Vienna?"

Her face warped with a twisted smile. The expression seemed wrong on her. Unnatural. As if muscles she'd never used twitched and stretched her mouth into place. "I should've done that a long time ago," she said. What horrified Kole more was the deep voice that came out of her. Distinctly Aterus.

She came at him again. This time weaponless.

Kole caught her by the shoulders. His new strength from Risil made it easy to keep her at bay. Though she bit and clawed at him like some rabid animal, he refused to take up the dagger against her. "Stop it. Vienna, it's me," he urged, but the recognition in her eyes had been wiped clean. Empty.

Piper rushed over and grabbed Vienna. As the demigod dragged Vienna off, one of her flailing arms knocked the weapon from Kole's hand. It fell to the ground. Piper tossed Vienna aside, where she landed still and quiet on the ground. "She's not in control," she warned as she pounced to restrain Vienna.

"Don't hurt her," Kole pleaded. The tone of his voice must've struck a chord in Piper because she halted. Kole spun on his heel to face Aterus. "Release her."

"I don't think so," said Aterus. "I rather enjoy watching the pain on your face."

"You've gone mad," Issira started. "This isn't you."

"How would you know who I am? You never listened. None of you did. You had your chance—your many chances." Aterus held a hand over his heart. "I discovered something that you could never understand. Something intangible. I created a bond—an emotion so deep between living things that it clouds you to your very core."

Love. Aterus meant love. The sides of Kole's mouth weighed down in a scowl. "You have no idea what you're talking about. Love doesn't make you kill thousands. It doesn't make you hurt your own daughter or betray your kin. You were greedy—possessive at best."

Head cocked, Aterus took a step forward. "Greed. Something you know all about, don't you, Kole? You made a deal with me not too long ago. Willing to give the Souls to me so you could have your old body back. To have your precious Niko and Felix returned to you."

"It's different," Kole roared. But he couldn't deny his past. He had done those things—almost sold out the Souls to get what he wanted. In the moment, he'd thought he was sticking up for himself. Finally taking control of things. The distance gave him insight on his mistakes. "I've changed. I've seen reason. And I never wanted revenge."

Silence ensued as Aterus peered over them.

"Call off the wall," Braxus said from atop the stag's back. "Innocents don't need to die for quarrels among gods."

"Pretty words. What innocents do you speak of? What of Evangeline? She is gone. An innocent lost in 'quarrels among gods.'" Aterus sneered. "No deal can be made now. They chose to side against their creator." Aterus pointed an accusing finger at the army. "They are not innocent." He swung that finger toward the Souls. "And the disgust on your faces says it all. You are ashamed of me. What I have become. What you made me into!"

"I know you have lost Evangeline. The wound is fresh," Braxus said. "You are not yourself."

"You have no idea how I feel. And you will never know." Aterus' attention didn't linger on her for long. He swept his head toward Kole. "Except you. You can know. You *will* know. It's only fair, don't you think? I lose my love and you lose yours," Aterus growled. "You wish for me to release her? Then I shall grant you this final gift."

Kole turned to the rustling grass. Vienna had sprung up behind Piper. The movements of her body came awkward, like a sleepwalker stuck in a dream. She scrambled over the dirt, hands searching. But for what? By the time Kole spotted the discarded dagger, it was too late.

Vienna took up the blade.

Kole held at the ready for another strike, but this time Vienna inverted the weapon and sent the sharp edge toward her own stomach.

"No!" Kole screamed.

Piper lurched for the weapon.

Time slowed.

No breath. No sound.

Even his heart stopped beating.

Kole's eyes locked onto the metal point flying ever closer to Vienna's flesh, and Piper was too far away to stop it.

A will so pure sprouted from his heart. All he pictured was another hand on that hilt, stopping its trajectory — stopping it from finding blood. From killing the one thing he still loved in this world.

And it did stop.

The dagger halted with the point no more than a fingertip away from Vienna's leather armor. Try as she might, groaning and straining to push it in, the weapon stayed poised — frozen in the air.

Before he could question how, Kole spotted a brown root at the base of Vienna's fists. It curled around tightly. The source.... Kole followed the long vine back to an abandoned piece of gnarled wood a few paces off in the grass, where he had last seen Russé's body.

Russé's staff. It had answered him. Kole had forgotten the thing was there. It had responded to his terror.

That pause gave Piper enough time to smack the dagger from Vienna's grasp and pull her into a bear hug. Vienna writhed against her, choking and gurgling on screams like a possessed demon.

"How many can you save, Kole?" Aterus taunted.

The earth pounded. Kole glanced at Braxus, thinking she conjured up some kind of quake in retaliation, but the Yellow Soul held a mystified expression that matched his own.

Kole turned to the source. The army. No command had been given, yet the forces had split. A gap appeared between the north and south sides. The weapons that had once been trained on Aterus swiveled to their own comrades. Blank stares. Empty like Vienna had been when Aterus had taken hold of her body.

Impossible. There were too many. No way he could hold every single one of them. Yet even Leo had dropped the ingredients from his hands and stood drained of himself.

Azmali raised her spear and charged the opposite side of the liberation. At her advance, war cries sounded off and Cresthaven's forces launched an attack.

The armies collided with clangs of metal. On impact, blood spilled as spears, swords and hand-cannons found their marks.

"Stop this madness at once!" Issira's cry hit a sour chord.

"A merciful end," said Aterus. "If they're lucky, they'll die before the Black Wall arrives. Now, my brothers and sisters, it is your time to choose." Without another word, Aterus backed away, arm's outstretched in invitation.

The Souls launched after him. All save for Caradin. Braxus urged the stag onward, but Caradin swung his head toward Kole, who hadn't budged. Those dark, marble-like eyes held him, conflicted between following the Souls and staying by Kole's side.

They had been through so much since Kole had released Caradin. The Orange Soul seemed to have a strong protective instinct over him.

"*Go,*" Kole encouraged through their connection.

Caradin stomped in protest.

"Go!" Kole yelled to the beast.

Caradin bleated his objection but heeded the command.

Aterus had become whole again. Only the power of Risil could compete with that. Despite that knowledge, Kole turned his back on the Souls and faced the battling army. He couldn't leave them here like this, mindlessly fighting. Kole had been puppeteered by the gods before. He knew the helplessness the army faced. Though their bodies moved, they retained their minds. Kole couldn't allow them to make mistakes that would haunt them forever.

A flash at his side. Leo's coat billowed in the wind as he bolted for the battle.

"Stop him!" Piper called.

Kole tackled him. They hit the ground hard. Harder for Leo than Kole. Something snapped on impact. When Kole crawled off of him. He noticed Leo's forearm bent in a peculiar way. Broken.

"Save your remorse," Piper said before Kole could utter one. "Get him restrained. Him and Vienna. Shit! She's up."

The alarm in her voice made him swing his head to where he'd last seen Vienna sprawled out in the grass. She sat up, wide-eyed, with her jaw set like she was out for blood. Kole called on the staff once more. While he pinned Leo down with his knee, the root shot out for Vienna. It caught her ankle and brought her crashing down. It pained him to see her take a hit. One that came from him.

"We need to break the connection." If he could figure that out, then he could free the army as well.

With the root now tangled around Vienna's ankles and wrists, Piper lugged her over and set her beside Leo. "Easier said than done."

"There has to be a way."

"There is. Kill the source." Though still paler than normal, Piper seemed to be recovering swiftly. "But I know you and your hero's complex."

"You'd have me leave them like this?"

"No."

The answer caught him off guard. He stared at her.

"But whatever you're going to do, you need to make it quick. We can't keep them restrained for long. They'll hurt themselves just as badly if we leave them like this."

Vienna and Leo struggled against the roots. Already, the flesh at Vienna's wrists started to bleed from the friction. He needed more.

"You're the key, Kole. A shepherd. Keeper of Risil. Use it. It was meant for you."

Kole had no idea what potential power lay at his disposal, but now was the time to test it. He let his consciousness spread over the battlefield and trained his focus on the energy source radiating from the ramblers. In the past, he needed to touch them to command them. To connect and communicate. Reaching out now, he felt that bond deeper than ever from afar.

A single thought from him had his old rambler stampeding toward him. Within seconds, the gargantuan tree had rushed over the field and stood before Kole in all its mighty glory. No matter how many times he laid eyes on the thing, the size seized his breath. A hum came from the tree. Like greeting an old friend.

One of the rambler's legs coiled around Kole's waist. Weightlessness took him as the root carried him up to the trunk. At this height he had eyes on the entire battlefield. The horror clenched his heart. No way he could leave them unprotected. Not Vienna or Leo or any other of his friends.

Kole had the rambler carefully take Vienna and Leo to the canopy, where the branches locked them in separate cage-like enclosures. *They'll be safe there.* Russé's staff unfurled from their limbs and slithered down the bark. He reached for it. The root curled around his arm and snaked down until it found his hand, then stiffened back into its original form. He squeezed the staff and thumbed the grain of the wood. More than comfort came to him. Life. He felt the life within the old, weathered thing.

Kole rolled his shoulders back as he basked in the power at his fingertips. No longer the doe-eyed, naive refugee hiding in the forest. He remembered a time when he feared the ramblers. Now he had complete control. A kinship.

"Are you coming?" Kole called down as he stretched a root toward Piper.

She looked up at him. Something different lay in her expression, though he couldn't pinpoint what. Piper offered her hand to the root, and the tendril swept her up to the trunk alongside Kole. "What's the plan?"

Kole grabbed hold of the bark to keep steady as the tree bounded for the battle. "Contain them." That's what he could do. But he'd need more help for that.

A slow breath calmed him. Focused, he reached his mind for the mass of crystal trees. He tested a command. They stretched high on the tops of their spidery legs at his will like old friends. The forest stomped on, positioning themselves around the army like shepherds herding a flock of sheep. The crystal ramblers took up the army, one person at a time, and protected them within their canopies.

A start. But not the solution.

CHAPTER 42

A roar pulled Kole's attention.

Shikar stood on the edge of the fight, pulling away weapons, but her opponents, garbed in the black-scaled armor of Cresthaven, jumped her. Three hung on her back while two snared her legs, drawing her down.

Kole rushed to her aid.

Before he could reach her, a round of shots rang out. Bark exploded from the trunk just above Kole's head as bullets peppered the rambler. A deep shudder came from the tree's core, one that shook Kole's own body, too. The rambler's distress echoed deep within him. The right side of his abdomen ached as if he'd been kicked. Kole touched the tender spot and winced. Not a bullet, a bruise. The injury marked his bond with the rambler as more than rider and steed. He shared in the pain of his enchanted tree—felt what it felt.

A burst of warmth came beneath his hand. The ache wore away. Risil's powers at play again. *No need for mortal caution.* Kole reminded himself of Braxus' words. Though the powers protected him, the rambler was still vulnerable.

"Are you hit?" Kole looked over Piper, who shook her head. Kole found the source of the assault. Jax had a small squad behind her, hand-cannons poised in their hands, ready for another round.

"Watch out," Piper warned as she turned for the far side of the trunk for cover.

"Jax, stop!" Kole yelled, but her blank eyes told him his words were lost on her. Nothing he said could break them from Aterus' curse.

Before they shot again, Kole ordered the rambler to charge. A dozen roots caught her and her squadron by the arms and shook their weapons away. Disarmed, the rambler carried them up to the canopy, where new branchy cells held them.

Filling up fast. He shared a look with Piper. By her hardened jaw, he knew they shared the same thought.

Jax and Vienna were safe with him, but thousands more still lay in danger. Even with the small forest at his command, they couldn't cage them all.

Still, he had to try. At least until he thought of a better idea to keep his comrades from slaughtering one another.

Kole turned back for Shikar. The rambler flew across the field. Twigs and leaves rained down as Kole's captives fought against their cages. Some struggled so much, their efforts snapped and cracked the branches. The rambler groaned.

"Hang in there," he whispered to the tree.

By the time he reached Shikar, the Yamani lay buried at the bottom of a dog pile. He used the roots to pry them off the stone woman. Two muscular forms stuck under each of Shikar's arms in a headlock.

Criz and Boogy.

Free of the extra weight, Shikar pushed the twins off her. They instantly found their feet and went for each other. Criz held Boogy by the throat. It took both of his stubby hands to cover the massive neck, but Kole could read his raw strength in Boogy's bluing face.

Boogy retaliated with a punch. The force broke his brother's nose. Yet still, Criz squeezed as if unaware of the blood flowing over his mouth and down his chin.

Before Shikar could dive in to separate them, Kole sent a root over. Little space remained in the treetop, so Kole resorted to entangling them in the vines at the base of the trunk.

Shikar sat up, fire behind her yellow gaze as she turned to Kole. They softened. "You still have your head." A comment rather than a question. "What in Souls' name is going on?"

Kole and Piper climbed down to meet the stone woman.

"Humans," Piper said. "He has full control over his creations, which is why you still have your head, too."

Risil's full presence blocked Aterus' curse. Good to know. Otherwise, Kole would've been turned feral like Criz and Boogy.

A wave of new combatants charged the rambler. Kole had the roots drill down into the earth, creating a barrier around Shikar. Despite the grand size of his rambler, the Yamani was too heavy to bear, especially with a dozen already locked in the branches.

Kole took slow steps around the root wall, inspecting the people more closely now that he had a safety net in place. Lips pulled back, baring teeth like threatening wolves. Their eyes had gone dark. No, not dark. The pupils had enlarged into black saucers. The deranged soldiers followed Kole as he passed, climbing over each other to get nearer and shoving their hands through the root barrier attempting to grab him. Wild. Reckless. Thoughtless.

"They aren't in their right minds." Kole moved back to the twins. Matching feral expressions.

Shikar rose to her feet and observed the boys with him. "I caught that. No other reason for these two to go at it."

That was when his heart stuttered. A deep gash marked Criz's side. The unmistakable slice of a sword. Blood oozed from the sinew. White shown from deep inside the cut. Down to the ribcage.

"Boogy," Shikar answered. "He caught him with his sword the moment they turned. That's why I jumped the pair."

Kole reached around for his dagger, but a hand stopped him.

"You have a god running through your blood. In his condition, you'd create a monster." Piper gave his arm a cautionary squeeze then released him. "And I have your blood in my system. There's nothing we can offer."

Kole ground his molars. As much as he hated it, Piper was right. *Always right.* "I'm sorry, Criz. We'll get you straight to Leo when we're through. I promise." It didn't mean he couldn't help now. He unwrapped the fabric from his neck he'd formally used as a hood, then pushed it into the open flesh. Roars of protest erupted from Criz when Kole unbuckled the boy's own belt and looped it around his stomach to keep the wad of cloth in place.

While he finished tightening the leather, something caught Kole's eye. Ensuring the root had the wriggling brothers secure, he stepped in. Both grunted and growled at his approach. He leaned in and studied their faces. Their eyes. Dull and blank like the others he'd seen. A streak of water ran down both their cheeks. Sweat? Kole followed the trail to their eyes. Tears.

"They're still in there. Criz. Boogy. They can see. They can feel. They know what they're doing; they just have no control." Kole pulled back. "To watch yourself beat up your own brother." His innards flipped at the thought. Boogy had possibly sent Criz to his grave with a swing of his sword.

"It's not right," Shikar said low.

Piper came up behind them. "They have a singular purpose in mind."

Kole turned; his hand white-knuckling Russé's staff. "To kill."

"Not just anything or anyone. Look." She gestured to the zoo of soldiers around the gate of roots. "No blood. They are focused on us. And

Jax and her group." The captives in the canopy growled at the army below. "They trained on us only when we came in range. But now?"

"We picked them up on the other side of the army." As the words left Kole's mouth, understanding clicked.

"They don't attack their own faction or whatever division Aterus put in place when he fogged their minds," said Piper. "That line must've gone between Criz and Boogy."

"That's the answer." Kole looked out to the army. "We follow that line and separate them."

A crooked grin grew over Piper's mouth. "It just might work."

Kole called for his rambler to add the twins to the canopy. With them out of the way and safe, the roots returned and hung aloft before him and Piper, waiting to give them a ride to the trunk.

One look at Shikar, then Kole made another call. No way he'd leave her to fend for herself in this mess. One of the crystal trees at the perimeter broke from the line and stomped over, a few soldiers already trapped in the stone embrace of its branches. "It'll keep you safe," Kole said as he trained the crystal rambler to the Yamani.

Those long, gem-like roots dropped around Shikar when she approached. Trepidation had long left the Yamani since their trek across Ohr. She took her place beneath the center of the raised trunk and nodded.

"We'll be the head." Kole braced his arm around the root of his rambler, and it carried him into position. Piper touched down not a moment after. "Separation is priority. Disarming along the way when we can."

He made a final order to the forest of ramblers strewn throughout the battle. Like worker ants, they fell back and circled around the troops toward Kole's location. As long as he created the boundary, he assured himself the rest of the trees could maintain the line.

"Ready?"

The sound of clicking metal answered him as Piper held up a hand-cannon. That was good enough for him.

Kole marched his rambler onward through the front line of battle. Roots at his command, he maneuvered the outmost tendrils as easily as his own hands. At first, he started with two at a time. He spotted a pair of warring soldiers, slithered the rambler's roots to them, then grabbed them by the waist and pulled them apart. They kept swinging their swords through the air. Once Kole placed them down on their respective sides, they endured a quick moment of stillness before switching their attacks to the great tree. By then, Kole had gone too far down the line for them to catch up.

With the first path emptied of troops, it left a clear view of a handful of bodies strewn across the grass. Blood trailed from some, as if they'd tried to crawl back to safety before they'd perished. He hated leaving them there in the middle of the chaos to be trampled and defiled, but his rambler could only do so much. He glanced back.

Shikar's rambler tailed him, and behind it more crystal trees fell in step, forming the line. Though they'd only made it a hundred feet or so, the wall held firm. Kole set them on clean-up duty. As they moved through, the stone trees began grabbing the wounded and dead and placing them on their trunks and in their canopies. Blood stained the white crystal bark as they worked.

A shot rang out next to Kole's ear. He jumped at the sudden noise and so did the tree. A hand on the bark saved him from tumbling off.

Piper held a smoking hand-cannon. She cocked it, preparing for another blast. "They're crawling up," she said.

Kole leaned over for a straight view down. Two soldiers garbed in Cresthaven armor had dodged the walking roots and grabbed hold. Using their crossed feet as anchors, they climbed the roots like ropes.

Piper took another shot. She missed and hit the vine.

Kole winced along with the rambler. "Watch it," Kole warned. He grabbed the top of her weapon and pointed it down. "What are you trying to do, anyway? We're supposed to be protecting them."

"And I'm protecting us," Piper snapped back. "Shall I let them continue their climb? Offer them tea when they come to slit our throats?"

She yanked the weapon from his grasp, then took aim once more.

"Don't kill them," Kole urged. "We're not here to add to the toll."

Teeth clenched her bottom lip. She chewed it, then dipped her weapon slightly. Another blast. The bullet hit the first man's thigh. He fell to the ground. A second to reposition and Piper took out the next with a hit to the arm.

"Compromise," she said under her breath as the man lost his grip and landed beside his comrade.

Wounded? Yes. But not fatally. If they reached a healer in time, they could be saved. That was what he told himself, at least. In the meantime, Kole had the crystal trees add them to their loads when they passed.

Soon, Kole developed enough confidence in his skills to manage more roots. He'd developed a system. One root swung side to side at the front, clearing out the way by knocking down and disorienting the combatants, while dozens more hovered overhead to pluck them up and move them aside. All the while, Piper kept their perimeter. When she ran out of ammo, she climbed up to Jax, still held in the tree, and swiped the bullets she needed.

By now they had reached the last quarter of the battlefield. A glance behind brought a wash of relief. The wall of crystal trees seemed to be working. Their roots held the armies at bay. Surely it wouldn't last forever, and it wouldn't be foolproof. He never expected that. The plan offered him time. That was enough.

"Shikar," Kole called back to the Yamani. The stone woman held a group of refugees at bay with one arm while she dragged a fallen Zeal soldier behind the safety of the roots with the other. "Hold the line as long as you can. If things get out of control, the ramblers will get you out of harm's way."

The stone woman glanced to the ramblers, who pushed back the swelling line of combatants. Shikar alone would hold the wave. The lone Yamani acting in the war and defending the humans their kind harbored an ancestral distaste for. When she drew her gaze back to Kole, he recognized a flash of that same thought behind those yellow eyes. No fear. Instead, she puffed her chest with pride. "Yamani do not retreat."

As strong as she was, if she stood her ground Shikar would fall against this many armed humans. Kole opened his mouth to argue, but Piper stopped him with a tug on his elbow.

"It's her decision," she said sternly. "We must go. Everyone's survival depends on it."

That snapped Kole from his hesitancy. He transferred Vienna, Jax, and the other captives in the canopy of his rambler to the neighboring tree that Shikar worked under. Bringing them along to face Aterus would put them in far greater danger than leaving them in Shikar's capable hands. He held the stone woman's gaze and mouthed to her, "Please."

More than a plea to watch over them. A need.

The Yamani's chiseled jaw softened. She understood. With her nod, they made a silent pact. Nothing less than the absolute resolve in her fiery eyes would give Kole the courage to leave. He'd trust no one else to keep Vienna safe.

Yamani do not retreat. But Shikar would for him.

CHAPTER 43

Under Kole's command, his rambler split from the battle and stampeded east. The sight over the ocean made his innards shrink. Dark flames lay on the horizon. The Black Wall fast approached. Their spot for this war could've been better thought out. Inland. That's where he wished to be at this very moment. The epicenter of the ring where the fires would last reach. They warred far too close to the border. It all came down to a race between flame and gods.

"Kole," Piper said low.

"I see it."

Kole kept his focus on the small forms of the Souls locked in battle a quarter-mile off. The yearning of his heart warred against his mind. One look to his rear might have him reeling back to collect Vienna and carry her far away from here. Away from the encroaching fires at his front and bloodshed at his back. But the wall wouldn't stop so long as Aterus had control. Escape was nothing more than a fantasy.

He pushed his rambler faster, testing its limits. Not an hour had passed since Russé had given himself to Kole. The only way to explore his new power was to dive in without inhibition. He'd surely need every ounce to bring Aterus to his knees.

"This is it. We must hurry." The gravel in Piper's voice matched her hardened expression: brows low, lips curled in a sneer, skin flushed red. "He will fall."

The blaze in her amber eyes told him the blood he'd given her had reached full potency. When Piper had previously faced Aterus atop Vara's floating island, she'd had to hold back. Her and her father's connection—their shared piece of soul—had prevented her from fighting against him, as a direct attack would've crippled her, too. But Aterus had torn his fragment from her mind. Now she could inflict her full potency. That eagerness rolled off her like heat from the sun.

He let the radiating feeling sink into his own skin and soak through his muscles. No matter if she meant it or not, Piper's raw rage embolden Kole. *My fate is my own. The old limits are gone.* He gripped tightly around the rambler's root, and the grand tree stomped harder into the earth.

Braxus' fresh fissures scarred the ground from the gods' battle. It seemed Kole had missed a great deal while he dealt with the army. His rambler easily sidestepped the soil's wounds and made for the center of the scarred land.

Aterus stood at the middle of the fray, calm and cool, while the Souls scattered around him.

The temperature shifted in an instant from a winter's chill to arctic levels. No doubt the work of Vara. Kole swore if he shed a tear, it would freeze before it hit his cheek. But his body didn't shudder. Not one goosebump rose from his skin.

Just like the fissures he'd spotted on his way, the haze clinging to the air marked the aftermath of one of Issira's earlier attacks.

Now, Obell and Caradin charged at Aterus, but he caught them dead in their tracks. One hand ensnared the stag's antler, while the other clasped around Obell's neck. Aterus heaved and flung them aside. They flew backward and landed at the feet of Issira, Vara, and Braxus.

"Take this." Piper pushed a broken branch toward Kole's chest. Kole had been so locked on to the gods, he hadn't noticed the prick-like pain from the rambler when she broke off one of its limbs. "Go on, hold it," she commanded.

"What are you—"

"Obell is near useless out here." Piper brought out a flint and starter and madly scrapped the sparks near the tip of the broken branch. "They can't create, only command."

Russé had told Kole this before. While in their fragmented states, the gods could only influence their creations. Issira pulled the water from the air, clouds, and soil, just as Braxus had an unlimited supply of earth at her feet. But no lava or idle flame burned on the windy cliffs.

One of those rouge sparks landed true on a dry leaf. It ignited in a flash of orange. That was all Obell needed. As if he sensed the very spirit of his creation, he reached out and summoned it. Instead of holding the fire in the palm of his hand the way Issira would with her water, he cast the flicker to the dead grass, and it birthed an inferno around him.

Piper jumped from the rambler's trunk. Though the landing looked hard, she stood unaffected. Her auburn hair shone nearly as brightly as Obell's flames in the dull landscape.

Aterus gave a dark laugh as if amused. "Add your fire. It won't help." He lifted his arms toward Kole atop the trunk. "Not even Risil can withstand me. I have become more than a god. More than all of you." Those open palms curled to fists, and as he did, a chorus of shrills came from the warring army down the field. Aterus drank in a long breath, filling his chest. His eyes darkened, and a gray aura came in whisps over his body.

Kole cocked his head. He'd seen this before. Or something similar. But where? When the veins of Aterus' neck and forehead popped beneath his skin, it all rushed back. *The battle for Socren. Savairo.* It had been months ago, but that moment never left Kole. The warden had massacred his own mages through blood magic and claimed their power in a desperate attempt at victory. It seemed Aterus' protégé had learned that trick from the Gray Soul himself. But Aterus was no mere mortal playing with god's blood. He was the divine. The absolute. The *father* of blood magic. Kole feared the Gray Soul might sacrifice every beating heart on the battlefield if the Souls didn't act fast.

"*He's tapping into our army,*" Kole alerted the gods and Piper through their shared connection. Before they could respond, he pressed his rambler on. Braced against the trunk, he had the rambler lash a dozen roots at Aterus. They came down like whips on the god.

Aterus flinched at each hit, but his skin remained pristine. No blood. No snapping bones. Not even a hint of discoloration. Only dirt streaked where the roots had hit their mark.

After the onslaught, Kole paused. His jaw went slack in horror. The step of a single rambler could crush every bone in a human body. But not Aterus. How many troops had the Gray Soul killed to gain such resistance?

"Useless." Aterus patted the soil from his shirt. "Such power wasted on you. On all of you. It will be better suited in my hands."

A cacophony of thoughts cluttered Kole's mind. His new connection with Russé made communication between him and the Souls seamless and clear, as if the words came directly from their mouths rather than telepathically. The Souls argued.

"*This is our only chance. We need to take back our fragments,*" Obell said.

"*We are not at our end yet,*" Issira argued. "*Kole is a last resort.*"

A swell from Caradin marked his agreement.

"*Together,*" Vara said. "*One final stand.*"

"*Bring the storms with me, Sister.*" Issira reached for Vara's hand. "*Bring the season's fury in my clouds.*"

The moment their hands touched, a heavy cloud unfurled overhead, blocking out the sun. Thunder rumbled. The air invigorated around Kole—buzzed. The sensation tickled his skin.

Aterus lifted his head toward the gloom, eyeing the temperamental sky. "It won't be enough. One boy's death brings you certain victory, and you can't even do that."

"It's not what Russé wanted," Caradin said. Kole had only heard the Orange Soul speak aloud a handful of times before, but his voice came certain and mighty.

Those words, no matter how insignificant to anyone else, touched Kole's heart. Whether he realized it in the past or not, Russé had always had his well-being in mind. Had always been his protector.

"Russé is no more," Aterus snarled with a flex of his jaw. "And you shall follow."

Anger pulsed through Kole. His fingers twitched, and his rambler charged the Gray Soul. Roots battered Aterus. Still the god deflected, standing his ground. His invincibility pushed Kole closer to fury's edge. A viridian hue emanated from his own skin—ever brighter as he opened his mind to the Green Soul within him. He slammed the rambler's massive trunk down onto Aterus, but he dodged with an easy sidestep.

Kole's attack prompted the others to follow suit. Fire swept by Kole on his right and from the left came the beating wings of the stag.

That buzz in the air spiked. A sudden gleam of light blinded Kole. He fell back and smashed into the rough bark of the trunk just as the crack of lightning snapped in his eardrums.

Quiet.

The scent of scorched earth found Kole's nose before the ringing subsided. Three blinks adjusted his eyes back to the scene.

Aterus had fallen to one knee. His head tilted up, a sinister leer on his face, then he rose, unscathed save for the singe of his clothes.

Shots popped off from Piper's hand-cannon. The strike marked the next wave of their onslaught.

When the earth shook, Aterus grabbed hold of one of the rambler's roots as it came down for another strike. He held it firmly, then threw himself onto it and climbed. Not a second later, Braxus' fissure opened where he'd been standing.

Kole ordered his rambler to shake off the stowaway, but the trunk reeled as the soft soil under the roots sank into the fissure. It sent Kole staggering. His foot caught, and he fell from the trunk. Instinctually, he snapped his arms out, flailing for something to hold onto—a vine, anything. At his desire, his staff lengthened into a long tendril and hooked around a knot in the bark. It held firm.

He clung to his makeshift rope as the rambler fell sideways and crashed into the ground. A groan rippled up the trunk. Roots gripped the edges of the fissure, attempting to right itself, but the loose earth fell away like sand. The tree was an overturned turtle.

Hand over hand, Kole pulled himself back up: a feat beyond his capabilities an hour ago. He stood atop the side of the fallen rambler, then peered over the edge.

Still Aterus advanced. The determination in his expression warned Kole that the god climbed for more than safety from the crumbling earth.

Feet steady on the bark, Kole fiddled at his belt, one hand to the worn handle of his slingshot, the other slammed into the pouch, digging for ammunition. Metal jingled. Clumsy fingers snared a few, but when he pulled them out, a handful more spilled forth and bounced down the rambler.

Only a god can kill a god. True divinity coursed through his veins. Kole did not fear pain. Aterus could beat him to a pulp and his body would heal. No. He feared death. And the only entity that could deal that fate crawled up the root.

Kole loaded the slingshot and pulled the band back. His fingers brushed the side of his mouth as he aimed. Released. The silver ball hit the god's finger. No broken skin or bone. Kole guessed that before he shot, but he possessed nothing else that could wound the god.

That was it.

They were going about this all wrong. Aterus could not be killed. Not in a bloody end like Kole had thought. *What did the Souls say? Extract his soul. His spirit.* Maybe their approach was all wrong? Hostility wasn't the way. With Aterus closing in, Kole ran up the side of the fallen trunk toward the canopy to put as much distance between them as possible.

The pop of Piper's hand-cannon echoed behind him. Kole didn't need to look back to know the shots harmlessly bounced off the god.

"We have to trap him," Kole urged. "We can't hold him forever, but maybe long enough." To his surprise, no rebuttals entered his mind.

When Kole reached the first branch of the canopy, he turned. Aterus had made it to the trunk. Before he followed Kole down the length of the prone rambler, Caradin swooped in from behind. The stag's hooves had taken their clawed shape, and those talons wrapped around Aterus' body and pried him from the tree. Caradin only managed a few beats of his wings when the struggling god broke free of the grip mid-air and fell back to the field.

Now was the time. On impact, god or not, he would be vulnerable and disoriented. They only had a small window to act. Seconds, even.

"On landing!" Kole ordered.

With Braxus still mounted on the stag's back, she held her hands out ready to call upon the earth as Caradin heeded Kole's command and veered into a downward spiral.

Though the rambler lay helpless on its side, Kole could still use it. At first, he thought to make a cage, but that would allow Aterus movement. He needed to hold him still. Restraints. A job the roots could do well, yet their strength was tied to the limits of the rambler. This required something more. *An anchor.*

Kole willed the roots into the earth. They drilled to the depths, then turned upward. *"Faster,"* he implored the rambler.

Aterus would soon land, and they needed —

The body hit the ground, rousing a fog of dirt. But Kole didn't need eyes to deploy his next move. He could feel the roots just beneath the surface. They lanced through the land and coiled around every inch of warm flesh. Streaks of fire, water, and a bolt of lightning struck down into the center of the haze. The roots contracted, reinforced by something hard, though Kole could not see it.

Stillness.

Kole spotted Piper below. She cautiously followed the length of the rambler's trunk with her hand-cannon poised at the cloud of dirt. From his vantage, no shadow moved in the dust. He climbed down just as Vara summoned a breeze and swept the haze away.

The scene made Kole pause.

Aterus stood pinned to a vertical spike of stone. The roots Kole had called upon to anchor the god had obtained a rocky coating, making it appear as if the very fingers of Ohr had come to hold Aterus in its fist. A layer of ice encapsulated the body up to the neck and spheres of glowing molten rock weighed heavy around his hands and feet. Caradin stood before Aterus with his antlers pressed hard into the god's chest.

Kole joined Piper at Aterus' front while the rest of the Souls surrounded the impact zone. Braxus slipped from the stag's back and moved into position with her kin.

Guttural roars came from their captive. Aterus swung his head side to side. Try as he might, his restraints held. The slightest hint of exhaustion showed in his face, and he fell quiet. "Piper," he whispered.

Piper laid a hand on Caradin's rump. At her touch, the stag removed his mantle from Aterus and joined his kin in the circle. "This is the end for you."

"You can't do this." The Gray Soul's tone held an awkward sincerity. "Please, Piper," he begged. If Kole had known nothing of Aterus or Piper, the fatherly act might've convinced him.

"The time for you to see reason has passed. You chose this."

His face contorted: an unnatural face for a god. Almost human. "You will erase her forever." A tear slipped from his eye.

Piper took a finger and wiped the tear from his cheek. "I will honor her." She paused, frown deepening. "For the both of us."

With his final plea falling on deaf ears, he jutted his head forward and screamed into her face. The ice cracked at his chest. Issira and Vara reacted fast. They held out their clasped hands. The fracture repaired, and they thickened the frost-like cocoon.

"No time to waste," said Braxus. "You know what to do."

Piper tossed her hand-cannon to the side, then pressed her palm on her father's forehead.

"What is she doing?" Kole asked.

"Allow us free reign to your mind, Kole." Issira set her stormy gaze on him, then nodded. "We will use our powers from within you. It's what Russé wanted."

The circle of gods bowed their heads and clasped hands.

"Piper?" Kole wanted to go to her, but Caradin blocked him with a swing of his head.

"Vessel," the elk said. "She acts as the conduit and vessel."

"For what?"

"The Gray." The large docile eyes of the stag gave Kole an overwhelming sense of solace. "This is her part. You must do yours."

That was when the ground beneath Kole's feet held a faint shake. The wind picked up in a lashing gale. He shielded his face then peeked out. The Black Wall had reached the beach. Its flames licked the clouds as it lurched up the cliffside. The scent of char and dust whirled to Kole's nose. He'd been too wrapped up in the battle to notice it crossing the ocean—getting so close.

Seconds now. That's all they had. He already felt the heat spike in the air. And this time, it wasn't from Obell.

Just as Kole thought it was over, a white beam enveloped the land, halting the flames from descending those last dozen yards. A moonbeam. But how?

He whipped around. Two Yamani had pushed a cannon from the army line and poised the ray directly at the Souls. A swift wash of relief flushed through Kole. The Yamani had joined the battle. In that same second, the moment of hope soured when he realized the stone people hadn't come to Shikar's aid to hold the line between the feral army, but to man the moon cannons lining the outskirts of that bloody battle. Yamani weren't like humans. They had a different maker—a different way of thinking. Obell's way of thinking. Kole couldn't fault them for that.

He shuddered at the timing of it all. If the Yamani hadn't come... if they'd acted a moment later.... *Thoughts for another time.*

He snapped his gaze back to the waiting gods. "Do it!" He shouted to the Souls.

Time ran against them. Whatever plan Piper and the Souls had devised without him—well—that was their prerogative. Kole took a breath, then jabbed Russé's staff into the ground. On his exhale, he fought to relax: a difficult task knowing the deadly fires loomed so close. He cleared his mind like Russé had taught him months ago. Every muscle went soft. Any barriers left in his head fell away. He let the Souls in. All of them.

Kole braced for the mad rush to claim their fragments. Instead, warmth met him. One by one, he felt them float through their doorways, delicate and tender. They expanded their reach over his brain, then sunk down, harnessing their fragments. No ripping. No severing. Only a small pressure. The feeling reminded him of when he'd hang upside down from his knees as a kid and the blood would rush to his head. Odd. But not painful.

The brush of a soft, wet nose pulled Kole's attention. Caradin pranced in place, encouraging Kole to touch his neck. He curled his fingers into the animal's coat. At the same moment, fingers intertwined with his other hand.

He glanced to behold Issira, who had reached for him. The faint glow of cerulean claimed her skin. Kole trailed his eyes around the circle he'd been pulled into. Vara the Violet. Obell the Red. Then Braxus with her golden hue, and beside her, the stag glowed a deep, bitter orange. Kole completed their configuration, filling in as Russé with the color of summer leaves shining from his body. He lifted his gaze. Aterus bore the final piece: a silvery radiance, matching the Seven Souls pendant hanging around Kole's neck.

Except....

That was when something at Piper's side drew his attention. Darkness. Whisps of black spread around her. Yet it wasn't an aura of light like the rest. Instead of reaching out, it seemed to suck inward. More like a void. A hollow space.

The black stone. The one at the center of Kole's pendant.

Kole had once thought that stone represented him. The Key.

He'd been wrong.

An overwhelming sense of sorrow flooded him. For Piper. For the fate she inflicted on herself. His grip on Issira and Caradin weakened, but the two Souls stepped closer to keep him on his feet.

Piper, with her palm pressed against her father's forehead, said, "The Seven cast you out. To keep the balance, I freely act as conduit and vessel."

"No! Stop," Aterus cried. The ice cracked once more, shattering fragments into the air. Kole felt the roots around the god's feet begin to strain.

They had one chance. If Aterus broke free, Kole knew his first target would be the moonstone cannons.

Piper continued, unbothered by her father's struggle. "The Gray Soul will be stripped of title and power and pass to the false daughter."

At the end of her speech, Kole and the gods all glowed with a vibrant brilliance. Something in Kole's head stirred. Russé's energy awoke and reached out to his kin. Beams of light shot out from their chests and set on Piper's hand.

"You will never be rid of me," Aterus yelled. His voice reached an octave so low it vibrated Kole's jaw. "So long as humans walk on Ohr, I will endure. I am in their blood—their nature. I will linger in their shadows and their minds for eternity. They are of me just as much as you, dear *Piper*," he cursed her name. "You cannot deny your nature—your maker."

Aterus' silver light pulled from his feet and gathered up toward his chest. Still, he wailed and thrashed.

"Goodbye, Father," Piper removed her hand from his head. "May you find Mother in the afterlife."

Aterus grew somber at the mention. The gray aura closed in around his head. "Evangeline," he whispered just as the color left him. His mouth hung open, eyes distant and glazed.

Seconds passed. Kole waited, eagerly staring at the lifeless body of Aterus, whose face still held the sunken expression of desperation.

Then, a small light showed itself.

From the back of Aterus' throat came a silver orb. It hovered out of his slack jaw and past his teeth. The colored beams sprouting off Kole and the gods directed the tiny sphere toward the vessel.

Piper opened her mouth, her stance planted and sure, then invited the orb in. That black aura of her skin shone silver, more vivid than polished metal. Once the soul had transferred, the hues around Kole and the others' faded and left.

Save for Piper, who gleamed like a star that had fallen from the sky.

"The Gray Daughter," Caradin said. *"We welcome you."*

"We welcome you," the others greeted in kind.

But Kole stayed silent, staring at Piper. A new god. He didn't quite know what to make of it all—how to feel. If Aterus had truly gone, so had his will. He peered down at the army. The battle had stopped. Most of the soldiers appeared dazed, regaining their bearings. One silhouette broke off from the army and sprinted up the incline. Kole ran to meet her.

Vienna jumped into his arms, nearly tackling him to the ground. He held her tight. The pure relief coursing through his veins made him dizzy. She was safe.

"I'm so sorry," she said. "I didn't—"

"I know." He pulled her at arm's length. By the rigidness in her face, he realized she hadn't raced up here to celebrate their victory but to check he was safe. "It's okay. I'm okay."

Cheering boomed from the army, pulling their attention. Suddenly, the moonbeams shut off. A prick of fear encompassed him before he noticed that the brutal winds had stopped. The shaking earth had calmed.

"Kole, look," Vienna said, breathless, then spun him around.

The Black Wall retreated over the cliff and toward the distant ocean. Steam rose from the brine as the ebony flames passed. A whirl of wind brought a curtain of ash through the air. The scent of scorched earth gripped the cliff, but the land appeared whole.

A victory indeed. They'd sent away the flames. No longer would they threaten the lands of Ohr. They were safe from becoming the crumbled ruins he'd seen on his quest for Vara.

Rattles and clangs. The army had thrown down their weapons, some falling to their knees while others embraced their comrades—Human and Yamani alike. Kole should be adding his voice to that victory cry. Celebrating. They'd done it, after all. Actually done it. But his voice never came. His head wouldn't allow it, for he knew what they didn't.

Safe, yes. For *now*. But the dark fires endured miles off the coast. Retreated but not destroyed. So long as Kole held the Souls' fragments within him the flames would remain. Only one thing could extinguish the fiery disease on Ohr. He knew what had to be done, he just wasn't ready.

Epilogue –
Nine Months Later

Kole sat on the lowest bough of his rambler, feet dangling and swinging in the open air. Blue waters crawled up the sands, caressing the roots in its white froth before dragging back. The bubbles in the tide tickled the tree: a sensation that came to Kole as a faint tingle on the bottoms of his soles despite his boot-clad feet.

Spring had come and gone. Along with summer. Though his rambler retained its lush emerald canopy, the sweltering temperatures had waned these past few weeks. Autumn's change stirred the air.

One year ago, he'd set out from his home in Socren in search of the gods. He rubbed the burn scars on his arm. *Nearly to the day.*

Kole eyed the horizon. The Black Wall stood miles offshore, where it had retreated to after the battle. If Piper had taken her father's Soul any later, they'd be living a very different reality. The wall hadn't moved since that day. And wouldn't ever again. Kole had long stared at the dark flames. The terror it sent through him in the past had subsided. Maybe because he knew it couldn't inch closer — couldn't touch him again. Or maybe staring at it each day had desensitized him. Either way, he was glad to be rid of the fear. And soon the wall, too.

Despite the deathly flames raging over the cliffs the day of Aterus' fall, grass and wildflowers sprouted on schedule with spring's grace bringing color back to the bare land. As quickly as the flames had ravaged the earth, the earth had reclaimed its vibrancy. It gave hope for the rest of Ohr's recovery. People, plants, animals, they still had no clue the full spectrum of damage the shrinking wall had taken. But that was an answer to seek after today.

"I wish you could see it like this," Kole said. The god lingered ever-present in his head. No matter how hard he tried to speak with Russé —

or Risil, as the Souls now referred to him — he never acknowledged Kole. Comatose. That was his best guess. Gone but not dead. Just... recovering. Still, Kole found it cathartic to talk to him in the fleeting quiet moments when he was alone. That and thumbing the staff the god had left behind. It never left his side. Even now, it lay across his lap. He swirled his finger down the grain.

He'd thought a peaceful morning might tame his nerves. A naïve hope. Not even Vienna could lift the gloom clinging to him. He turned the staff over in his hands. The intrusive thought he'd been fending off for hours crept back to the surface. *This could be my last day.* He scolded himself and banished it back to the depths. Thinking like that would do nothing. He needed to hope — no, more than that — he needed to *believe* it true. And to trust in Piper.

She'd been increasingly elusive these last few months. So much so, he'd only seen her in passing once since midsummer. She wouldn't talk to him. Always holed away in her tent. He'd gotten so nosey, he'd resorted to spying overnight. A full week with his eyes set on the tent and only Issira had come and gone. They were up to something.

Even from two hundred feet up, Kole felt the grass smush under the stride of a graceful gait. A smile pressed on his mouth. He'd gotten use to his new ability. And something about her presence, the way she stepped, gave herself away.

Kole turned the rambler from the waves and had it begin the steep climb up the cliff. They made it to the top as Vienna neared the edge. Her beauty made him brace against the trunk.

A gown of silver hugged tightly around her arms and down her waist before flowing loosely to her feet, where it pooled. The fabric rippled with every shift of her body like a liquid mirror. Her hair pulled back from her face and off her neck in an elaborate style of intertwining braids that reminded Kole of the woven baskets the Solpate refugees used to make from deveined rambler leaves. A grand style, indeed. Nothing less would do for the ascension. Though Kole harbored a secret fondness for when she held a sheen of sweat, frazzled hair, and flushed cheeks as it called back memories of the day they first met. And their first kiss. The whisp of a thought made his cheeks hot.

"You're not dressed." Vienna patted the viridian jacket draped over her arm.

"I was coming back for it. I still have plenty of time."

A string of horns bellowed from deep within the coast.

"Do you?" She sighed. "I swear, you're just as bad as Felix."

"I'll take that as a compliment." Kole grinned. Though he meant to tease, a swell of pride washed through him at the comparison.

"Can I at least catch a ride for saving your butt?"

At Kole's will, the rambler reached for Vienna.

Vienna made a face at the incoming, sand-riddled tendril, then held a finger toward it and warned, "Watch the dress."

The root used the grass to wipe off the clinging sand from the beach before coiling around the fabric. She braced against Kole's shoulder as she landed on the bough beside him, then unfurled the jacket with a shake. Hands on the collar, she held it open for him.

After resting his staff against the trunk, Kole pushed his hands through the tailored sleeves. Vienna helped shrug it properly onto his back. He inspected the arms. Gold and black embroidery decorated the cuffs: a design of leaves and flora. The same pattern lined the hems. The garment lay open, falling sharply to his knees. Subtle darts brought the structure in at his waist. That along with the boxy shoulders gave him a muscular, broad-shouldered shape he clearly lacked.

Vienna's hand brushed at his hairline. "Sand." She tsked, but amusement held in her bright eyes. "Let's go. The guest of honor can't be late."

Kole grabbed his staff as the rambler crawled down the slope of the cliffs. To the south spanned the enormous coastal city of Rush. He'd spent plenty of time there with Leo and the recovery team. They did everything from aiding the injured to building shelters. Mostly, Kole used his ramblers for transporting large supplies of materials to and from the city. During the last battle, the Black Wall had ravaged small towns and villages in its wake as it shrank. The outside rim of Ohr held no life for nearly fifty miles, it seemed from Leo's informants. But some of the people had been spared thanks to Jax.

Apparently, Zeal's engineer had sent thirty moonstone cannons along with a technician to dwellings scattered around the border. She had anticipated Aterus would weaponize the wall and sent out evacuation letters to every hamlet Zeal had record of. They were to flee inland or to the nearest major city. When Aterus summoned the black flames, thousands were saved because of beams granting them safety. Lives spared but not all. And certainly not their homes.

Kole hadn't allowed himself to wonder too much of the death toll. Of the raiders in Zeal that had been too stubborn to follow Tena out of the city. What was even left of Zeal? No one had gone that far west-- or north — yet to check the full scope of the mess. At least fifty miles all around the original known border had been scarred. The Yamani had reported their city had been leveled, though their underground system remained intact. Half of Hawthorne had been razed, but Azmali welcomed their survivors into her city. Cresthaven and Rush served as the central points of Ohr since the flames had rebounded after Aterus'... death? Release? Kole had his questions about that as well. But there was one thing they knew for certain. Help was needed across the land.

That was where the ramblers came in. After testing his limits over the trees, he'd discovered he could send them cross-country on errands. It led to many supply trips to the central cities of Cresthaven, Hawthorne, and even as far as Grayfall, where the homeless of the annihilated cities could gather materials to start rebuilding.

The heat of a hand touched Kole's upper back. Vienna idly rubbed the spot between his shoulder blades with her thumb. She'd taken to this after she woke from the feral spell cast on her in the battle. She and the whole army had regained themselves after Aterus' demise. Although the enchantment had washed away, it hadn't spared any of them the mental torment of their fratricide. Vienna included. Kole could always tell when those thoughts crept up in her mind because she'd rub the place where she had stabbed him. Just like now. She had made countless apologies, no matter how many times Kole reassured her they were unnecessary. He'd been under the Souls' control before. Their will was absolute. But a deep, swelling ache clamped down on his heart knowing he could never free her mind from the burden. Or from any of his comrades.

Kole slipped his hand around her waist and pulled her close. The sides of their bodies melded together like moss on bark. He played with the slick fabric at her hip while she rested her head on his shoulder. It only took a moment for her hand to cease the nervous impulse and cross from his back to his shoulder. Only then, when she had fully relaxed, could he, too. He'd never get enough of this. Of her.

Dozens of boats speckled the bay, some small old fishing vessels, or cargo transports, but they all acted as ferries today. Hundreds upon hundreds had arrived in Rush. The influx began a week ago and never let up. An invitation from the gods themselves surely drew a crowd. It never dawned on Kole just how many people Ohr still held until they crested over the final hill overlooking the ceremony site.

Vienna gasped along with him.

The crowd spanned the hills as far as Kole's eyes registered. Chatter buzzed in the air. *All of Ohr has come to see the Souls.*

The center of the ceremony proved easy to spot by the color change. All those who fought in the battle stood near the center garbed in matching silver outfits like Vienna's.

As they approached the crowd, the people parted for the rambler. Or tried to. Their path, which would've made an ample aisle for a sapling, barely managed to clear wide enough for one of Solpate's last standing grand ramblers. It may have been a feat previously, but Kole knew every root of his tree like his own fingers. He slinked them down between the patrons without harm. Faces tilted back, plastered in wonder as the house-sized trunk floated above them.

No frilly platform or stage. The Souls had simply cleared a small ridge for their use. It was strange seeing Piper among them. Though she'd taken her father's role, she still just looked like Piper to him. Little had changed outside of her avoidance. Even now as he approached, her eyes stared straight ahead. Not like she could write off an entire rambler. Piper knew what she was doing. He only wished he knew why.

Two roots lowered Kole and Vienna to the grass. Issira stepped forward and welcomed them both with a bow of her head. Vienna gave his hand a squeeze before pulling away to join the front line of the audience.

Criz and Boogy stood at Leo's side. They'd stepped up since Thomas' death. Both had lost the youthful spark in their eyes since that dreaded day. Boogy more so. It seemed every time he looked at his brother, he became a little more solemn. He relived attacking his brother. The haze over Boogy's eyes gave it away. That same sort of distant gaze washed over Vienna when she'd rub Kole's back. Except Kole had recovered from his injury and Criz had not—not entirely.

Criz had been bedridden for a month before Leo cleared him to walk. Even then, it had been difficult. Despite Leo's best efforts, Criz was maimed and scarred for life. He took to mentoring under Leo rather than his usual strength-based tasks with his brother. The bulky physique had faded: the thinning neck being the most drastic change. The twins would never be mistaken for each other again.

"Kole," Issira's warm voice called him back to his surroundings.

He blinked and realized he'd been staring. A swift turn and he hustled over to the Souls.

The gods shifted to open a spot in the middle for him, but Kole continued past and squeezed in at Piper's side. A gray velvet cloak draped over her shoulders. The hood sat atop her auburn hair: the contrasting colors reminiscent of smoke and flame. Her chin dipped ever so slightly his way but maintained her stone expression.

The hillsides hushed when Issira stepped forward to commence the ceremony.

"Welcome, people of Ohr, to the last day of gods," she began.

Kole side-eyed Piper and whispered, "You've been avoiding me."

"I haven't been—" she caught herself. "I've been busy," Piper said through the side of her mouth. "We really shouldn't do this now."

"Shall we do it once you've ascended then?" Kole couldn't hold back the bitterness seeping into his tone. "Or after the soul fragments have been ripped out of me, where I may or may not survive?"

She turned her head to him, mouth open ready to speak.

"We will commence the first step." Issira turned to Kole with open arms. Her silken bell sleeves grazed the earth. "Let us bring forth Risil."

Kole left Piper's side and stood before Issira.

"The staff, please." She held a palm to him.

His hand instinctually tightened around the soft wood. The curves seemed to be made for his hand. It pained him to give it up, but he relented.

A small stream of water swirled up from the ground and took the staff gently from his grip. With a wave of Braxus' hand, a hole appeared in the ground. The water lowered the bottom tip of the wood into the ground as if it were planting a sapling. Once secured, the ground pulled in snugly around the base, and the water soaked into the freshly turned soil.

The Souls all stared at him in kindness. Even Obell's persistent hard mouth had softened.

The stag stepped forward. He nuzzled his nose into Kole's chest. Kole drew his fingers across the god's cheek.

"Risil has granted his soul to you. And you have accepted." It amazed Kole how far the Orange Soul had come since encountering him as a feral beast in the marsh. The god had only been able to communicate through emotions then; now he had the eloquence of Issira. "With that offer, he has given himself freely to a worthy successor. Just as we have accepted the Gray Daughter, we will welcome the Green Son if you so choose."

Kole flinched away from the stag. "What?"

The elk cocked his head. "Godhood, Kole. You would become our brother."

"You want me to... to take Russé's place?" Utter shock froze Kole's mind.

"Not take his place. Merge with him. Become one. Forever bound to Risil and in turn, to us. It is his gift to you for the burdens you have faced through your journey." Caradin pawed a hoof at the ground. "Pain will never touch you again. Nor sadness or fear."

Kole scanned the Souls once more, but he only saw Piper. Emotionless, yet something under the surface homed in on him. A forlorn hope. He wished to know what she was thinking. When he opened his mind to read her surface thoughts, he encountered silence. Utter nothingness. She concentrated hard to keep something from him.

Caradin must've sensed Kole's anxiety, because the stag stretched out his nose and nudged his arm. "It is a choice, Kole, not a summons."

The staff caught his attention. He walked up to it and grazed his fingers over the swirling grain. The power within it called to him. Like the refugee horn calling him home at dusk before the ramblers awoke. But was it Kole it called to? Or was it Russé who lay dormant inside him?

A god. He could become the Green Soul. He could ascend. No more suffering. No more scars. The painful memories of Niko's and Felix's deaths would no longer torment him. He'd never have to go back to those limitations with which the Black Wall had shackled him. True peace. All within his grasp.

And yet....

A sense of terror came at the mere thought of accepting. A god could do many things. Blessings. Miracles. Terrible atrocities. Each one of the Souls, no matter how good intending they were, had danced on the edges of morality. Some had crossed that boundary irrevocably. Even Russé. A god's mistake proved greater than any Kole had ever committed. One wrong step, even for good reason, would tear Kole apart. Or worse. Guide him down a path that mimicked Aterus'. A more horrid fate than burn scars.

His hand dropped from his staff.

He'd witnessed the impact of the gods firsthand. Understood them better than any mortal would ever hope. Because of that, he couldn't bear to turn into one himself. He wasn't like Piper. He didn't have her strength. And it terrified him what he might do.

Kole turned his back on the staff and faced the crowd. When his eyes met Vienna's, everyone else seemed to disappear. His heart leapt through his chest. True happiness. Undeniable.

She smiled at him.

In that moment, he knew he never wished to part from her side again. No offer from the gods could tempt him. Nothing could sate the pull from his heart to hers.

"No," Kole said. The single word broke a dam of emotions. They bombarded him all at once. Sadness. Regret. Relief. He sensed flickers of them all and more, but they were too blended to distinguish which reigned stronger.

Caradin joined his side and rested his head upon Kole's shoulder. "Why do you cry?" His voice soothed Kole.

Only now did his flesh register the warm trails on his cheeks. "I will miss you." It was all he could say. And it was true. He would miss his dear friend.

"And I, you." If a stag could smile, Caradin managed it. Kole spotted his reflection in those soft, large eyes. They swallowed him whole. "Let us take away this burden."

Kole followed the stag back to the staff, where the other Souls had gathered around. The same sort of circle they'd formed to extract Aterus during the last battle. The memory sent a shudder through his bones, and yet this was the easy part. They still had one more ritual left for him after this—the one that made his heart pump ice at the mere thought: returning all the fragmented Souls that kept him alive. *Just get through this first.*

He flicked his eyes to Piper. Stoic as ever. Yet something had ever so subtly shifted beneath the surface. Less cold. She took up his hand as the others did. Kole placed his other on Caradin's neck, completing the ring.

Their light within bloomed across their bodies. Kole took on that same green hue. It stayed like that for a moment, all standing there around the propped-up piece of wood.

The pull came. A tug within him. Not his heart or his head, but all of him, everywhere at once. The force sent him shuffling forward. Piper tightened her grip on him. His insides stretched, though a glimpse down showed him nothing had changed.

Save for the glow. It had dimmed around his hands and feet as if draining away. The light pooled in his chest and drifted up. Soon the only green left swam in his head. A tickle in his throat. He opened his mouth.

A green sphere floated out. It bobbed in the air toward the staff. When it came close, the green aura touched down on the wood and soaked into the grain. The staff ignited in a blinding radiance.

The Souls dropped hands and stepped back. Kole followed suit.

He knew it was gone from him. Completely. He knew because of the grass around him. He no longer sensed it. The weeds and flowers had cut off from his mind. The worst part? His rambler. Though he glanced at its roots, none moved at his will. A friend turned into a stranger.

Groans and creaks of wood filled the quiet hill and rushed out over the whispering crowd. The staff grew and enlarged, reforming into a shape Kole had seen once before in his head. Half rambler, half human. Russé's true form. The aura waned, allowing Kole a clear view of the face in the bark. There in the wood. Russé's unmistakable eyes.

"Russé." Kole couldn't help his feet. They carried him straight to the Green Soul. He wrapped his arms around the trunk. No matter the form he took, Kole was glad to have him back. For some reason he'd begun to think his old mentor was lost forever after he transferred to Kole's body. A silly thought.

"Russé?" The deep voice held a speck of confusion. "Hmm. Is that your name, little one?"

Kole froze. His arms fell to his sides, and he withdrew.

"His name is Kole, Risil," Issira pointed out. "He has been your keeper these past months while you were recovering."

"He released you and the others from Aterus' hold," Piper offered.

"Ah." The Green Soul held a vine out to Piper. "I thought I sensed a new spirit. You are the daughter. I can see it in you."

Piper dipped her head.

Then he turned back to Kole and bowed. The branches lowered, looking more like spikes of a crown than tree limbs. "My kin and I owe you great thanks, indeed, Kole."

The same voice. The same inflections and everything. Even the eyes, down to the deep creases in the bark that Kole had known as crow's feet in the old man's skin. Only... the recognition was missing. Kole noticed that glisten in the god's eyes when he looked on his kin, even Piper, but when they cast his way... when they landed on Kole... nothing. It was as if they'd never met.

"Russé?" Kole fumbled for the staff that had comforted him since the war. Gone now. His hands settled for the hem of his new jacket. "You don't remember, do you? You don't remember anything."

"Kole." Not even Issira's sing-song voice, as soothing as it came, could untangle the matted knot in his stomach.

Russé is gone. Is this what they meant by gone? Wiped of his memories? But he couldn't forget everything. Not after what they'd been through. "The shepherd trials. I was your apprentice." Kole tried to jog his memory. "You taught me to tame the trees. You pulled me from the Black Wall—brought me back from the edge of death. We traveled Ohr together in search of your kin."

The god's vines recoiled as if sensing Kole's pain, but he stayed silent. "I'm sorry, dear boy."

They had called him Risil all this time while Kole had refused to use that name. Now he understood why. All those memories had been wiped. Russé had been the persona the Green Soul had developed while living among the refugees. If the god had truly been reset, then the last eleven years had been wiped along with it.

Eleven years. Practically Kole's whole existence. He couldn't recollect a single moment when there was no Russé. But that same period to a god... a speck of dust in time. So easily wiped away.

His lungs refused to breathe. Though he stared straight into the eyes of the god who had been his companion since he was five, all he could see was death. Another loss. His heart gaped like he'd been freshly stabbed. The only thing that could close it was having Russé back. If only for a moment.

Worse, he knew this day would come. The time when Russé would ascend and leave him behind. But he never thought he'd have to go through with it without saying goodbye. If only he'd known then on the battlefield when Russé offered himself.... If Kole had known the full effects merging had meant.

A vine came up under Kole's chin.

"I do not doubt your memories, Kole," said Risil. "I know they are real. I see it in your mind and in the minds of my kin. I see our past. What Russé was to you and what you were to him. A bond that cannot be denied. I do not know it for myself, but I see it."

Kole swallowed back his pain. The hole in his chest remained wide, but the ache eased at Risil's words.

"The time has come." Issira stepped forward with her booming voice. "We must reclaim our fragments and become whole. Only then will the Black Wall extinguish and Ohr can be at peace."

Fate came down to this. He'd convinced himself he was more than just a medley of the Souls. So far, he'd been proven right. Risil had been extracted, and he still felt whole, alive, himself. Would that feeling hold after the last five were taken? Kole braced for Issira's approach, but she stopped a few strides from him, and her stormy eyes trailed off to the right.

Piper planted herself before Kole. "Are you ready?"

"*You're* doing it?"

"And why not me?"

"Do you know how?"

One side of her mouth twitched as if she held back a smile. "You'll find I'm better equipped than anyone."

"I don't understand. What do you mean?"

"I've been working on something. Me and Issira. Experimenting. Look, I know you have this notion that you have your own spirit inside you. I don't doubt that, but just in case, I have a fallback."

"What sort of fallback?"

"Me."

His mouth opened, then closed.

"I have the full spirit of the Gray Soul in me now. But that doesn't change that I was human. I still have that part of me. I am gifting it to you."

"You can... ensure I live?"

Piper nodded.

"Is that why you've been holed up in your tent all these months? Why didn't you tell me? I've been out of my mind all this time."

"I had a hunch from the beginning that it was a possibility. I just needed to know for sure. I didn't want to get your hopes up. That's why I didn't tell you. Empty promises aren't my thing. Only, it's never been done before. And I needed to be sure."

"You're sure now."

That smile emerged. "As sure as I was about you and Vienna."

She meant to tease him, but it didn't bother him anymore.

"It will work as long as you are open to receiving it."

"I'll still be...." Kole looked over his shoulder at Vienna, whose brows had pinched together with concern. "...Me?"

"It's less of my soul and more of my human life force. My essence." His silence must've told her he needed more assurance. "Yes, it will be you, Kole. Completely."

Kole nodded. "Then of course I'll take it."

When she moved a hand toward his face, ready to begin, he stopped her.

"Wait. Can I ask why?"

The question must've caught her off guard because her mouth opened like a stunned animal. "Well, I have no use for it anymore."

"Now. You don't have a use for it now," Kole corrected. "But you said you knew from the beginning."

Piper only gazed at him.

When he'd first met her, she'd shown a bitterness toward him, yet deep beneath that, he'd sensed a conflicting warmth. She had hidden her true nature and cause from Kole and even Leo for a long stint—playing both sides. All the while she'd been acting on her own agenda no matter anyone's interference.

"Since I knew what you were," Piper finally said. "And I knew I needed to be a god if I had any chance of doing it."

And that only confirmed Kole's theory. His eyes narrowed on her. "You never wanted to be a Soul."

"No," she confessed. The hard line of her mouth portrayed a sense of regret. "No, I didn't."

"But then why—" He understood. The signs were there. She'd set this up all along. "You did it for me. But you barely knew me then—didn't at all, actually."

"I knew you were robbed of a life by the gods. Just as I was. You deserve more than sacrifice, Kole. And I've lived my life. Lived longer than any being should. I am half human, but death would not meet me on its own. I am half god, but ascension was not an option. Not in my former state. My options were to fade away into the wall or live on alone and watch anyone I chose to attach to die. A waste in my hands. I wanted something good to come of this burden, and who better to give it to than someone who had been dealt the same torments?"

He moved to speak, but she started again, "And I didn't tell you all these months because you needed to make the decision on your own. I knew they'd offer this choice after what happened to Russé in the battle. God or human. My offer might've put weight to one side. It had to be your choice, Kole. That's important." Her eyes trailed to the crowd at his back, then returned to him. "Some will call you a fool for turning away such power. *They* are the fools. It's easy to take something like this. To be handed immortality and the gifts of the divine. The difficulty—the thing that marks those who are meant for greatness—is refusing it when it appears to you. It's an odd thing, really. You denying godhood makes you the most likely, in my eyes at least, to wield it well. Because you recognize the weight of it all. The devastating responsibility that ultimate power is tied to. You know it because you've seen it firsthand as I have."

It was true. No other than the two of them had peeked behind the veil of the nature of the Souls. Not even Leo with all his wisdom, or Vienna, despite traveling with them for months.

Still, one thing stood out to Kole about Piper's path. "Now you're living a fate that you did not want."

Her lips pulled thin. "I knew my fate the moment I met you. Maybe even long before that when I grew old enough to understand Aterus' madness. Wanting it or not doesn't matter. I am the only one fit to claim the Gray Soul's title. It is my duty just as it was to see you through to the end of this. My only hope is that my time living as human will keep me from the corruption that claimed my father."

"You'll do great... Gray Daughter." The title felt funny on his tongue. He'd need to get used to that.

"Ready?"

He nodded.

"We have to do it all at once." Piper signaled the Souls to gather around. "Stay relaxed and keep your mind open."

Kole sent one last look to Vienna, then readied himself with a deep breath.

The blue silk of Issira's dress rippled as she addressed the crowd. "The boy from the forest. The key to our freedom. Kole has traveled the land in search of us. Faced down the violent volcano. Walked through the black fires and back again. Raised an entire forest. He has found death and sacrificed his body on his journey." She grew quieter and angled her melancholy chin his way. "It took his childhood."

Kole tightened his jaw. Before this all started, he remembered envying Niko for how mature he looked with the cover of stubble across his jaw. How his own puffy cheeks had made him look so young. The scars he donned took away the childlike look, but his search for the Souls had taken his youth. All those years wasted wanting to be older, and now he yearned to go back.

"Without him," Issira continued, "this day would be no more than a distant dream. Without Kole, Ohr would have fallen further into the nightmare. We thank you for your duty."

Caradin tucked one of his hooves and lowered his body into a bow. The tips of his antlers touched the floor. The rest of the Souls followed suit. Even Piper, who stood before him. Then something else caught the side of Kole's vision. He turned. Like a wave pulling back from the beach, the people knelt. Off to the side, he spotted Shikar and the Yamani down on one knee.

The lump in his throat threatened to choke him. They cared not of his scars or his age, but of what he'd done. A part of him still felt like an imposter. They saw the end. Heard tales of the journey. But would they bow if they knew his darkest secrets? His regrets? That he'd once forsaken the Souls and joined with Aterus. That he wanted to quit for fear of death claiming him in the end.

"Of course they would," Piper said as she rose. The conflict must've shown plainly on his face. "You let your past define you. You need to recognize all the good you've done. Not even the gods are perfect."

She gave him no time to think. Piper placed her hands on either side of his head and tipped his forehead to hers. The moment their skin touched, a shiver ran over his body. Her mind was already inside him. The alienness made him want to brace, but that'd only cast up a barrier.

He closed his eyes. A hum filled his ears. Voices. The gods called to their fragments. His heartbeat drummed in his head as his mind swelled against his skull. Kole ground his teeth. It was all he could do to fight off his instincts to shield himself. He had to let them in—had to give himself up.

Vertigo hit him. His head spun despite the solid feel of earth under his boots. One by one, the pieces dislodged. First Obell. His hunger swiped back the fragment quickly and cleanly. The empty void left behind spurred an overwhelming sense of loss. Kole felt as if he was once again drifting in the warped gravity around Vara's old prison; turning and floating away with no tether to haul him back.

Then, like a downpour replenishing a dried lake, Piper came crashing into him. She filled Obell's cavity, and Braxus', who left next. Her energy kept his mind from drifting into delirium. He latched onto it—focused—until the last of the gods left with their pieces.

Then Piper pulled away.

His head quieted as it settled into its new normal. Yet the silence felt strong and thunderous. He stood utterly on his own. *The way it always should've been.* A faint pang of loneliness came along with that thought.

Kole stood frozen in those first moments, waiting for something to happen. Maybe Piper's essence would reject its new host. Maybe it would change him. Make him ill. To his solace, his lungs went on breathing and his heart continued its lively beat. "Thank you."

A hint of a smile marked Piper's lips. "No one is more worthy."

Kole rolled his shoulders. The tightness in his skin had returned. An inevitability. Without Risil's power, his body reverted to the old restrictions of his scars. The boundless energy had left along with it. That absence left a heavy fatigue. He felt... human. A change he'd need to get used to again. Disconnection meant he had his mind to himself. It also meant his powers were gone. No healing or invulnerability lay at his fingertips.

Piper joined the line of Souls. Though they all still looked the same in their human façades, save for Risil and Caradin, the air rolling off them felt different. Thicker.

He retreated to the onlooking crowd by Vienna's side. She reached for him and pulled him close to watch the ascension side by side.

"How do you feel?" she asked, worry shading her eyes.

The question made him pause. Kole's part had ended. Relief filled every muscle and limb. He shrugged. "Normal. Just normal."

Vienna squeezed him tight.

The Seven spoke in unison. "The age of gods is over. Upon our ascension, mortals shall guide and mold Ohr to their vision. Choose your paths without interference. Live without fear of eternal fire consuming your lands, for the Black Wall will leave with us."

The crowd cheered. An exuberance pulsed through the gathering as if a bolt of electricity connected them all.

Kole took each Soul in as they tilted their heads to the sky. Columns of colored light shone from their feet up past the clouds. Up they drifted. Away from Ohr and their creations. The awe bubbling in Kole must've stretched over the valley as well, because all went quiet. Only the light whisper of the wind sounded over the cliffs. Piper and Caradin were the only two who cast their gazes downward as they left.

He let the tears come freely and as they faded from view. Two more friends gone.

Kole stared long after they had vanished.

A cheer roared from the east. Kole turned his head to the ocean—to the cause. The Black Wall.

Kole gazed at the flickering shadows off the coast. The pyre faltered. Shrank.

"It's fading," Vienna's voice came breathless in his ear.

Kole dropped to his knees. Long had he dreamed of this moment. He'd done it. They had all done it. They'd vanquished the Black Wall. He should be happy—ecstatic. When he thought of this moment, he'd imagined himself jumping up and down, cheering their victory like the people did below. Yet, a great cavity twisted in his chest. While watching the fire die, all he could think of was Felix and Niko. Some things had righted. Others would always be out of reach.

"If only they could see this."

Vienna crouched by his side and laid a hand on his shoulder. "They can. I know it. And they would be so proud of you."

The dark flames desperately clung to the open air, but its fuel had gone. The very ocean itself seemed to swell up to vanquish it once and for all. A large wave devoured it whole. Though Kole only witnessed this small patch, he knew the ring suffocating Ohr's lands shared the same demise. He could feel it in his body, rising from the ground through his feet. It was as if the earth had exhaled all its woes.

The Black Wall was no more.

Over the next couple weeks, many sought out Kole to pay their respects. Although grateful for their thanks, the show of it all left a sourness in his mouth. They'd been calling him "the boy marked by the gods" and in turn, treating him as a god. Kole had to put a stop to it before it could spiral into something more, so he'd spoken with Leo. The liberation leader had given him a task. One that lay far off from the city. Any city. And any living thing, for that matter.

Night had fallen. Kole leaned up against the trunk of the rambler — a nightly habit he'd developed since the ascension — and watched the stars appear as the sky darkened. The great tree had rooted shortly after the Black Wall vanished. All traces of the Souls were leaving Ohr, little by little. A sad thing. Even Kole had caught himself trying to reach out to Caradin. Those words never left the barrier of his skull, for nothing was out there to speak to.

A rustle came over the hill as Kole shifted against the rough bark. Vienna crested the incline, with a horse and wagon in tow. "Everything is packed." A chirp came from the sky. The tawny hawk spiraled down to Vienna's stretched arm. "He's lent us Fiona."

Kole shoved off from the ground and went over to stroke the bird's head. "She'll come in handy." The hawk leaned into his hand. "What about the map?"

Vienna nudged her chin to the wagon, where two long scrolls, almost as tall as him, sat propped up in the far corner. What surprised him more was the person sitting across from them.

"One of the old lands, and a blank one for the new." Jax patted a hand on each map as she spoke. Her pearly teeth shone in the darkness.

"What are you doing here?"

Jax tapped the satchel at her side. "Seeing as you two aren't cartographers, the war council thought it best for me to come along."

"No offense or anything, but aren't you an engineer?"

She folded her arms across her chest. "I draw models well enough. Leo gave me a crash course in the equipment as well." A shrug, then a coy, "Dabbled a bit in portraits when I was younger. Think I'm pretty decent."

Kole smiled at her pouting lip. He waved a hand. "It's not that, Jax. I only thought we were reporting findings, not charting the land."

"Surveying the damage to Ohr is one thing," said Jax. "Seems the council has decided it's best to have it all charted down to the very blade of grass. North and west for us. Shikar is handling the southern region. Souls know—" she stopped herself. "Er, well, we all know the Yamani won't be welcoming visitors anytime soon."

"Two-in-one mission." Vienna absentmindedly stroked the horse's neck. "Honestly, a mission like this is extensive for just the two of us. Leo will likely dispatch a second team once we send Fiona back with our initial findings." Her head tilted to the side and her stare narrowed in on him. "Leo only allowed us to go ahead because he knows you're itching to get out of the city."

Kole sighed. "There's too many people. I'm not used to it."

"The boy marked by the gods?" Jax relaxed against the back of the wooden cart. "Yeah, I'd be looking for a way out, too."

"There's more than that." Vienna side-eyed Jax, then left the horse's side to stand before him. "Kole. I know it. Leo knows it, too. Why do you think he invited Jax? If you'd just tell us what—"

"When I was out there looking for Vara... I saw.... Well, I'm not sure."

Jax and Vienna fell quiet, their eyes set strong on him.

The image of the fleeing silhouette pounced to the front of his head. The footprints leading to the fissure. Caradin catching a scent....

"We can help you figure it out."

"I don't think you'd believe me." Kole grabbed his head envisioning the footprints—that unmistakable human silhouette. "I don't even know if I believe me."

At that, her eyes softened. "I just watched gods ascend. There's nothing I won't consider."

Kole studied her face. Open. Honest. Every guard had been pulled down. His gaze swept to Jax, who had leaned forward with her nail gripping the wagon in anticipation. "I think I saw someone. A person— human—on the other side of the wall. Piper said it was a product of Vara. Of her prison. Something in the air made me see things. Maybe it was nothing. But Caradin saw it, too. More than that, he tracked his scent. Caradin said the person smelled like me. That's why I think it was a human. And then there were footprints that led...." The more he said, the more farfetched it sounded. In his head it seemed plausible but something about saying it aloud made him pause.

"That led where?" Jax whispered from her seat.

"Into a fissure. Straight down as far as I could see into the darkness."

Vienna remained silent. The light in her eyes flickered as if entangled in a thought.

"I know what it sounds—" A hand on his arm made him stop.

"Vara's powers were the seasons." Vienna gave a gentle squeeze to his elbow. "That's what we know. But what do seasons have to do with the shifting gravity and slowed time you talked of back there?"

"That's what I'm saying. There's no link," Kole confirmed.

"Maybe there is...." Vienna turned her chin back to Jax, and they shared a knowing look.

Kole flicked his eyes between the two of them. "What do you mean?"

"Jax?" Vienna said. "Time. Gravity. Seasons... change?"

A groan came from the wagon as Jax shifted back and looked up to the velvet sheen of night with her bottom lip sucked in. Her thinking face. Kole had seen it several times before when she had worked to tweak her moonstone canons to tunnel him through the Black Wall. "It's certainly possible."

"What's possible?"

Vienna paced before him. "We know the Souls had specific powers. Those are the ones that we could see, feel, touch, but some powers are invisible. Like Vara's."

"Okay, I follow." Kole splayed out his fingers and counted them out. "Russé and plants, Obell's power over fire, Issira manipulated water—"

"Those are the things we could *see*," Jax clarified. "Vienna's talking about the opposite."

"Like...." Vienna held out her arms as if searching for the words. "Russé communicating with the trees! *That*, no one could see. The only reason we knew of that power was because he shared his skills with the shepherds—with you."

"Invisible powers." Kole chewed his lip. It would explain the time situation behind the wall. No one could see time. "The Souls had more powers than what we knew about."

"Exactly. We only thought Vara as the god of the seasons because we can see the change from one to the next. Feel it."

"But what does that have to do with the figure I saw? They were behind the flames. No one can survive that." A lie. He had. "Not without a god," he added.

Vienna halted mid-step, then smiled. "Not without a god."

"Not without a god," Jax repeated while nodding.

"I don't follow."

"It's Vara, Kole. The chance that you saw this... person near her prison. Well, it may not be chance at all. It could be the perfect recipe for a survivor."

Jax perked up. "Or survivors. It's been centuries since that land was taken. Unless whoever you saw is immortal, they'll have to be more."

"Yamani?" Vienna laid out her guess.

It smells like you. Replaying Caradin's words in his head sent ice up his spine. "Not a Yamani. It's human." Those bare footprints were human. "It smelled like me. Like the Souls, he said." He wished to talk to the stag once more—ask one question: how did it smell like the souls? Because it was a mix of Vara in the air? Perhaps the god smelled flesh that had been touched by the black flames. Or had it truly smelled of... divine blood? Someone like Kole.

Jax stood and planted her fists on her hips. "Well, there's only one way to find out, I say!"

He had to be certain of what he'd seen., especially with the god factor in all of it. With the Souls gone, the task fell to him. But not alone. He was glad to have Vienna and Jax on his side. They believed him.

Even though the wall had been banished, he held a healthy dose of caution. They knew little about the crumbled lands save for what he saw. He wished he was better equipped. Felix's old slingshot only offered so much.

"We'll need to be on our guard." When his eyes refocused on Vienna and Jax, their jaws hung open in awe. They stared at something behind him.

A light touch came to his ankle. Familiar notes of bitter earth hung in the air.

Kole gasped. He turned on his heel and peered up at his rambler. The trunk sat firm atop the soil, but a root had slipped free and curled around his boot.

"How is this possible?" Jax asked,

"I thought the Souls took their powers along with them," Vienna added.

"So did I." Kole traced his fingers over the root. His heart ached for his old connection to the rambler. He'd watched them all root after the ascension—thought he'd come to terms with the knowledge they'd never walk again. That the shepherds were no more. Maybe it had sensed Kole's fear. A lingering reflex. *But what if...?*

He had to try. One last time.

Kole knelt, wrapped his fingers around the unearthed root, and focused his thoughts to picture the morning sun draping its golden silk over the land—awakening all it touched.

A stir came from the trunk. Then the low groan of bending wood. The horse at the head of the wagon whinnied. He was once afraid of the ramblers. Their size and sheer strength were deadly to anyone who misunderstood them. Perfect nightmare fuel for a child. But now as he witnessed the roots pulling from the ground and standing tall on its many legs, it felt like he greeted an old friend. He had developed more than an appreciation. The rambler had captured a soft spot in his heart.

"It still answers to you?" Vienna had come up beside him to wipe off a chunk of dirt from a nearby root.

"I tried before in those first few days after the Souls left. It never...." He forgot his words, and instead focused inward, testing his connection with the tree. A root wrapped around his waist and carried him up. The wind on his face sent a bubbling thrill throughout his body. His smile hurt his cheeks as the rambler set him down on the base of the trunk. Two vines poised before his hands, ready to be steered. He gripped them: worn and familiar like the handshake of an old friend.

A pressure touched the far side of his mind. A brush of consciousness not his own. Warmth filled his core as tears brimmed Kole's eyes. He knew that presence. And he knew it would not last for long. It would never come again.

A goodbye.

Russé.

The Green Soul sent no words, just that intense serene feeling radiating across his every nerve.

Then it faded little by little. And oh how he longed to latch onto it and pull Russé back through. Back to him.

But he was gone. Totally. Completely.

Save for the final gift he bestowed upon his apprentice: the powers of the shepherd returned to him.

"Send the horse away, Vienna," Kole called down. "We'll be going by rambler."

Once all the supplies had been safely tucked away in the thick green canopy, Vienna patted the horse's rump, and it trotted back toward Rush.

Vienna and Jax sat on either side of him. The engineer, being her first time on a rambler, braced against the trunk with a vice grip, while Vienna dangled her feet over the edge.

"Where to first? I imagine we can cover twice the ground now."

"To Solpate. I'd like to see the forest again. Make a proper site for Niko." Kole knew just where to put the memorial. Under the ruby of Solpate, where Russé had sat for centuries. And he'd like to test just how much power Russé had granted him.

"He deserves nothing less," Vienna said low as she smiled up at him.

"Then after, we'll circle around west and visit Felix along the way." The mystery in the West called to him. An itch that refused to leave him until he knew for certain what he'd seen — what Caradin had claimed smelled like him — had truly been an illusion of Vara's former prison. Or if it would lead to a great discovery no one inside the ring of fire had ever imagined possible. But that could wait a little longer. His friends needed rest. Proper rest.

"I'd like that." Vienna rested her head on his shoulder, eyes to the sky at Fiona lazily soaring overhead.

Kole urged the rambler forward. Its spiderlike legs trotted northwest toward the distant range of the Poleer Mountains. They headed toward Solpate — to the start of it all. He headed home.

THE END

ACKNOWLEDGEMENTS

Thank you to my readers. I hope you enjoyed Kole's journey as much as I did. His story is about discovering, accepting, and loving yourself no matter what changes may come into your life. As a writer, I'm supposed to be good with words, but there really isn't a way to describe just how thankful I am for your support throughout this series. For the reviews, for the messages, for visiting me at signings, for letting Kole's story reach more people through word of mouth. Thank you.

A big thanks to my writing group buddies, who helped me forge this series from book one. To my mother and dad, who continuously encourage me to follow my dreams no matter how impossible they may seem. I never would've started writing to begin with if it hadn't been for your early support. And to my husband: without your encouragement, I never would've found the courage to put myself out there. All it takes is one yes.

I give all the thanks in the world to the amazing editor and friend, Darren Todd. You continue to help me grow in this profession and challenge my story by asking all the questions I never thought to answer, and for laughing with me when my brain has me write ridiculous things.

And finally, to David Lane (aka Lane Diamond), who is responsible for this story in your hands. I will forever be grateful for the chance you've given me and for welcoming me into the Evolved Publishing family.

ABOUT THE AUTHOR

Parris lives in Mesa, Arizona with her husband and two golden retrievers. She discovered her love for reading when a middle-school reading assignment led her to the fantasy section of the library. This passion sparked stories of her own imagination, yet she never put pen to paper until after college. When she's not consumed in her writing, she enjoys Olympic weightlifting, playing Dungeons & Dragons, and coaching color guard.

For more, please visit Parris online at:
Website: www.ParrisSheetsAuthor.com
Facebook: @AuthorParrisSheets
Twitter: @Parris_Sheets

MORE FROM EVOLVED PUBLISHING

We offer great books across multiple genres, featuring high-quality editing (which we believe is second-to-none) and fantastic covers.

As a hybrid small press, your support as loyal readers is so important to us, and we have strived, with tireless dedication and sheer determination, to deliver on the promise of our motto:
QUALITY IS PRIORITY #1!

Please check out all of our great books,
which you can find at this link:
www.EvolvedPub.com/Catalog/

Thank you!